D1346294

The
Wedding
Dress
Sewing
Circle

BY JENNIFER RYAN

The Wedding Dress Sewing Circle

The Kitchen Front

The Spies of Shilling Lane

The Chilbury Ladies' Choir

JENNIFER RYAN

The Wedding Dress Sewing Circle

MACMILLAN

First published 2022 by Ballantine Books, an imprint of Random House
a division of Penguin Random House LLC, New York

First published in the UK in paperback 2022 by Macmillan

This edition first published 2022 by Macmillan
an imprint of Pan Macmillan
The Smithson, 6 Briset Street, London EC1M 5NR
EU representative: Macmillan Publishers Ireland Ltd, 1st Floor,
The Liffey Trust Centre, 117–126 Sheriff Street Upper,
Dublin 1, D01 YC43
Associated companies throughout the world
www.panmacmillan.com

ISBN 978-1-5290-9432-9

1 3 5 7 9 8 6 4 2

Book design by Dana Leigh Blanchette

A CIP catalogue record for this book is available from the British Library.

Printed and bound by CPI Group (UK) Ltd, Croydon, CR0 4YY

Visit **www.panmacmillan.com** to read more about all our books
and to buy them. You will also find features, author interviews and
news of any author events, and you can sign up for e-newsletters
so that you're always first to hear about our new releases.

Everyone needs a circle of friends to give support and courage, and I would like to dedicate this book to my writing group: Barb Boehm Miller, Julia Rocchi, Emmy Nicklin, and Christina Keller, with warmest thanks.

The
Wedding
Dress
Sewing
Circle

Clothes Rations, Britain 1942

40 coupons per person per year

Women's skirt suit or long coat – 18 points

Dress – 11 points for wool, 7 if not wool

Skirt – 7 points

Blouse or jumper – 5 points

Women's underwear or apron – 3 points each

Stockings, if available – 2 points per pair

Shoes – 7 points

Men's suit or coat – 20 points

Trousers – 8 points

Shirt – 5 points

Men's underwear – 4 points each

Men's socks – 2 points per pair

A yard of fabric – 2–3 points

Brides are expected to wear their best dress or skirt suit for their wedding, unless they are in the military, in which case they are to wear their uniform.

SOURCE: MINISTRY OF TRADE MATERIALS

GRACE CARLISLE

The Vicarage, Aldhurst Village, England
January 1942

'I found it!' the Reverend Ben Carlisle's voice called from the attic. Grace felt her breath catch as she dashed across the vicarage landing to see him come down, a long, flat box held ceremoniously in his arms, a bittersweet smile on his face.

'Where was it?' she breathed.

'It was hidden in a corner behind some boxes of books.' Her father's black trousers and shirt were flecked with dust, the edge of his white vicar's collar smeared with dirt, but he still looked good for almost fifty, Grace thought, with his tall frame and his dark hair silvering at the sides.

'Bring it into my bedroom,' Grace said as she raced ahead of him, tidying the small bed in the corner, smoothing down the quilt her mother had made for her. 'I can't believe you found it after all these years.'

He put the box onto the bed. 'She always hoped you'd wear her wedding dress.'

Even ten years after her death, his eyes still betrayed his grief. Grace worried about him, sitting alone in his study, distancing himself from not just his parish but the world. Already battling shell shock from the last war, her father had been brought so low in his grief after her mother's death that Grace had had to take on much of his parish work, organizing weddings and funerals, baking loaves at harvest, and setting up the nativity for Christmas. She'd also taken on his parish visits, looking after the sick or bereaved, helping the poor, fitting them around her job with Mrs Bisgood at the village shop. The villagers were sympathetic about his seclusion, but Grace fretted over what would happen to the parish once she left for her marital home.

'Open it, then,' he urged.

As she pulled off the box lid, the gleam of ivory satin shone brightly from beneath. 'Oh, it's beautiful!'

'Take it out,' her father said. 'Let's have a look at it.'

As Grace pulled the length of shining fabric from the box, a cloud of dust and particles cascaded into the air, a flurry of soft wings bursting out as a dozen moths swept around her bedroom in the shaft of late afternoon sunlight.

She let out a gasp, her gaze shifting from the whirlwind back to the dress, beholding the fitted bodice decorated with glistening pearls. 'Oh goodness, it must be pure satin.'

While he budged open the window in the eaves to let the moths out, her father said, 'I hope they haven't eaten the whole thing.'

Grace brought the dress up to hold against her tall, willowy form, walking over to see herself in the mirror.

She was speechless.

The dress was truly magnificent. A length of ivory satin swept to the floor, decorated with intricate embroidery of trailing, entwined roses, carefully stitched with tiny pearl beads, giving it the shimmering, polished look of a top couturier's design. The part above the satin bodice was covered with lace, allowing the breast bones and shoulders to be delicately visible beneath. The long sleeves too were lace, showing the colour and contours of the skin beneath.

'But do I live up to it?' Grace's hand went to her thin, lank hair. With all her parish work, she never had time to set it properly, not that she could ever get it to hold a curl. 'I hope Lawrence will like it.'

At twenty-four, she'd almost given up hope of marriage, especially since she had such a small circle of friends and rarely left the village. She was plain, her slight, boyish frame only emphasized by her taller than average height, and she had a habit of hunching her back, of trying to make herself smaller, less conspicuous. She'd always felt that no one would ever want someone like her, and so, with every passing year, she'd ploughed ever more of her energy into her work in the parish.

Until the former curate, Lawrence Fairgrave, proposed.

'He'll think you look mesmerizing; that's what I thought when I saw your mother wearing it.' Her father stood back, watching her. 'I never did find out how your mother came to have such a lovely gown. I suppose I was too busy in those first days of married life, and then it was packed away in the attic and I forgot all about it.'

'How wonderful to be married in the same dress as her! It'll be as if she's here with me every step up the aisle.' Grace brought the fabric to her face, smelling it for her mother's perfume, any semblance of her soft warmth. It was there, even if Grace only imagined it.

In the delight of the moment, neither of them mentioned the obvious.

The moths had eaten through large swathes of the delicate lace across the shoulders, leaving it hanging from the seams. One of the sleeves was held together only by threads, and parts of the bodice were puckered with holes, as was the back of the long skirt.

'It's not in perfect shape, but I'm sure you can mend it.' A trace of doubt couldn't be hidden behind her father's optimism. 'All it'll take is some new lace and a bit of time and skill.'

Grace sighed. 'Three things I haven't got.'

'Why don't you take it to the Sewing Circle, see if they can help?'

'They're busy with a second-hand clothes sale to raise money for the village hall. It's in desperate need of repairs now that it's a nursery school, a training room for the Home Guard, and a meeting place for every other village group.'

Determined to salvage his daughter's excitement, her father inspected one of the sleeves. 'I'm sure they'll find a way to patch it up.' His eyes shined at Grace. 'You need to stop letting your doubts get in the way. Go on, try it on. Let's see how it looks. I'll pop downstairs and put the kettle on while you change.'

Within a few minutes, Grace had taken off her old brown skirt and fawn cardigan and slid the dress over her head, wriggling it down over her slip.

This was her only chance of having the white wedding she'd always wanted. Nazi U-boats patrolling British coasts had brought imports to an absolute minimum, and fabric was one of the first items to go. The population had been issued with a sparse number of clothing coupons to buy essentials, and now the government stipulated new bridal gowns could only be made from thin butter muslin, if you could find or afford it – which few could.

Now, as she looked at herself in the mirror, she felt something inside her shift.

'Mum,' she whispered, putting an uncertain hand out to the mirror.

Instead of lanky Grace, the woman reflected back at her was truly beautiful, the image of her own mother. She felt herself stand more upright, and her face – usually wearing the caring expression expected of a vicar's daughter – took on a new energy, as if she were someone special after all.

But then a strange chill came over her, and it was gone. The mirror only showed tall and willowy Grace, tired and pale, wearing a once-beautiful gown that now hung from her, tattered and faded like a sepia photograph.

'Oh, Grace! You look lovely!' Her father came in with the tea, and together they looked at her reflection.

'Did you see that?'

'See what, my dear?'

'For a moment, it was as if Mum were here, looking back at me.'

He smiled sadly. 'I would love to tell you that you look just like her, but I'm afraid you take after me, tall and dark-haired. And your eyes are even larger and darker than mine. But you're no less beautiful than she was.'

She reached up and scooped her hair onto her head, feeling a shiver of cold as she exposed her long neck. 'Maybe if I put my hair up, I'll look more like her.'

'She would have been heartbroken to miss your wedding, you know.' He picked up the family photograph from the table beside her bed. It showed the three of them huddled beneath the wisteria in the garden. In the centre, her mother was laughing, her face warm and heart shaped, her fair curls tumbling down to her shoulders. Beside her in his vicar's cassock, her father looked healthier and happier than he did now – how Grace wished she still saw him smile like that. Grace must have been around fourteen when the photograph was taken, her tomboy self in a pair of long shorts and a shirt baggily tucked in. Her hand was on her forehead, blocking the sunshine from her eyes, and she grinned as if all the world belonged to her. Sometimes she wished she saw herself smile more often too.

'It's still hard to understand how your mother went from

being such a healthy woman to bedridden and then, well . . .'
His words petered out.

'Tuberculosis is like that. We can only be grateful that we
had her for as long as we did.' She swallowed back her own
grief, putting an arm around her father. 'At least we still have
each other. It's good that I'll still be living here at home with
you for the time being, until Lawrence gets his own parish after
the war.'

As soon as war was declared, Lawrence had dutifully signed
up as a Royal Navy chaplain, and shortly thereafter he was sent
to Portsmouth to help with the injured and dying coming off
hospital ships.

A frown came over her father's face. 'It must be harrowing
work down in the naval base.'

'From his letters, it sounds rather overwhelming. I wish I were
there to help him.'

'You're such a great help to everyone, Grace.' He looked back
at the picture. 'I sometimes forget you used to be so adventurous
before your mother died. We'd have to send out search parties
for you, only to find you halfway up a tree or swimming in the
lake at Aldhurst Manor with Hugh Westcott.'

Her mind drifted off to those summer days, how much fun
she used to have with Hugh, playing pirates, creating makeshift
boats that invariably sank in the lake. 'I miss those days. It's a
shame it all came to an end, him vanishing off to boarding school
and then Oxford.' Her face fell. 'And then Mum died. Everything changed so quickly.'

'Do you know, I haven't seen Hugh at all since he moved back
to Aldhurst Manor. With his father's death, I'd have thought
he'd want to discuss the running of the parish. He has to take up
the mantle his father left behind.'

Grace found some clips to pin up her hair, one lock resist-
antly tumbling down the side of her face. 'I haven't seen him

either. I heard that he prefers to stay in London. He's high up in the War Office apparently.' Grace couldn't help but feel that her old friend, now an important politician, would think she'd grown up to be very plain.

As if reading her thoughts, her father smiled as he looked at her in the mirror. 'I can't believe how lovely you look in that dress. You have a natural beauty, Grace.'

She looked at her thin hair doubtfully, but then stirred herself with a playful nudge at him. 'You're only saying that because I look like you.' She laughed, but it ebbed quickly. 'In any case, it's what's on the inside that counts. That's what Lawrence says. He wants to marry me because I'm me – a good vicar's daughter who will make a good vicar's wife.' Her heart filled with relief threaded with a vague apprehension that the rest of her life could look much the same as it did now.

'Only a few months until the big day.' Her father took her arm, as if about to lead her down the aisle, and they looked at the vision reflected back in the mirror.

'I can hardly believe it,' she murmured, but as her eyes drifted over to the shreds of lace, the holes, and the frays, she felt her spirits fall. 'I only hope I can find a way to mend this dress. If I can't, I don't know what I'll do. Lottie's offered me her blue dress for the day, but it's a little too big and not really my colour.'

Her father smiled gently. 'Whatever you wear, you'll look lovely.'

But the more she looked at herself in her mother's worn, white dress, the more she knew that this was the dress she was meant to wear; she'd simply have to find a way to mend it.

CRESSIDA WESTCOTT

Chelsea, London

January 1942

It was one of those crisp winter mornings, and Cressida West-cott, noted couturier, paused to relish the bright sunshine before stepping into her Chelsea design house. The grand, double-fronted building on the King's Road had been home to her prestigious brand these past twenty years, and every time she walked through the doors, she felt a surge of pride. This was her business, her empire, her life that she'd built, in spite of the odds being stacked against her as a woman. She'd put her all into building it, making her name synonymous with exceptional evening gowns in the minds of London's aristocracy.

'Good morning.' She greeted each of her shop assistants by name and briskly walked through an array of gowns in every colour, from peacock blue and garnet red to soft ambers and pale pinks. While styles were tempered by the new government rules to save fabric, colour was not. New blended or synthetic fabrics were becoming more common, even in haute couture, and rayon, viscose, and the new nylon from America all shone with exuberance, tempting the upper classes to have their own garments specially created.

Behind the shop, dressing rooms and a client lounge gave way to carpeted stairs that led up to the offices, then up again to the cutting rooms and machine workshops on the floors above. The place ran like clockwork.

'Any news this morning?' she asked her personal assistant as she went into her office, taking off her fedora and picking up the latest copy of *Vogue* that had been placed on her desk.

'We have an advertisement on page twenty.' Her assistant bustled in with a cup of coffee, taking note of Cressida's perfectly fitted pale grey trousers. They were considered a little risqué, but a properly tailored pair of wide slacks put her at the forefront of women's fashion – and on a par with the men who dominated the profession. Besides, the look went so well with her sharply bobbed bronze hair.

There was no doubt about it, at forty-six, Cressida Westcott was at the very top of her game, in spite of the war.

She flipped through to page twenty, where a tall model wore a beautifully cut maroon jacket and skirt, a coordinating fascinator atop her dark blonde hair. 'We need more of this kind of advertisement. Too many of my regulars have fled London because of the bombs. We need to attract every last duchess, dame, and lady left in town.'

'Absolutely.' Her assistant dutifully took a note before running through her appointments. 'It's mostly client meetings today. And remember, you have luncheon with Miss Muriel Holden-Smythe at the Champton at one.'

A smile crept over Cressida's face. A journalist at *Vogue* magazine, Muriel had begun as a useful contact and grown into a friend of sorts over the years. Even though Cressida thought friendship was overrated, she couldn't deny a certain spark of excitement at the prospect of a fine luncheon discussing industry gossip.

Thus it was that after a busy morning of client meetings, Cressida collected her hat and coat and set off for the Champton. As soon as she spotted Muriel, sitting in the prime position in the celebrated French restaurant, she cocked her fedora to a dashing angle and made her entrance.

'Cressida!' Muriel stood to kiss her on both cheeks, taking in her outfit. 'Such devilish shoes! And I adore the slacks.' Muriel herself was wearing a red-and-orange-swirled viscose dress.

'But that dress, Muriel! It's divine!'

'It's one of Hartnell's. I call it "Wildebeest at Sunset". I can't decide if it's daringly vibrant or garishly brassy.' Muriel laughed and glanced around at the other tables for anyone she knew as they took their seats. This was a place in which to be seen – exactly why she'd booked their lunch there.

'Fabulous!' Cressida exclaimed. 'But I think perhaps a little too outré for my clientele – well, the ones that are left, what with all the bombs.' She sighed. 'I simply don't know what to do, my dear. Half of my clients have moved to the countryside, and the rest have no use for gowns, especially now it's fashionable for women to wear uniforms all the time. I can't very well start designing those, now, can I?'

'I heard that more and more fashion designers are following their prey to the counties,' Muriel said lightly. 'Did you know that Digby Morton's taking a touring fashion show to Bristol?'

'Yes, and Hartnell told me he's considering a move to Oxford, but I can't imagine how he'll get on. He's always called it a frightful backwater.'

Muriel lit a cigarette. 'Hartnell's couturier to the queen; he can go wherever he likes and do superbly well. He told me he's had enough of the bombs here in London, going down into a shelter every night, dealing with the danger and the chaos.'

'You can hardly blame him. Although, I hear the odds of actually being hit are terribly low. I'll take my chances, at least for now.' Cressida frowned. 'I only wish my clients were as valiant.'

'I can't help thinking that perhaps you too should be branching out into the counties?' Muriel elegantly tapped her cigarette on a silver ashtray.

'Really?' Cressida chuckled. 'Me? I wouldn't last five minutes outside London. I don't think I've even set foot in the countryside since I left for Paris when I was twenty.' She grimaced. 'I'm not sure I could spend even five minutes outside of Chelsea these days. Life has been so simple since I moved into a place just down the road from my design house. It's absolutely perfect, why would I leave?'

Muriel sat back, her eyes scrutinizing Cressida. 'I had you pegged as a businesswoman who would do anything for her clients. Don't tell me that the same Cressida who works all hours prefers her Chelsea comforts to a little time in the sticks for the sake of her clients?'

'We're still doing well enough here in London. Lady Marley and the Duchess of Kent still have a plethora of charity galas. In any case, with less stock in the shops because of the bombs and the shortages, more people are coming to couturiers. Did you hear that Selfridges has reduced its fashion space down to a single floor so that it doesn't look so frightfully sparse? The garments in the windows are hideous.'

A waitress came, and they perused the rather meagre menu, both ordering soup and then haddock, knowing it would be an indeterminate white fish in a makeshift sauce. The rationing was testing chefs in the same way it was testing designers, who were now forced to use less fabric, more synthetic materials, and absolutely no metal fastenings or elastic – it was all needed for the war.

'Did you hear about Digby Morton's new idea?' Muriel asked once the waitress had gone. 'He and a few other top designers have come up with the idea of redesigning the government's

Utility Clothes so that people actually want to wear them. He's calling the organization IncSoc, which stands for the Incorporated Society of London Fashion Designers.'

'Now that's a good idea! When the government started forcing clothes factories to mass-produce standardized clothes, I knew it would be a disaster. Who wants to have a government-issue wardrobe? It's no wonder they're so unpopular.'

Muriel lit another cigarette. 'That's why IncSoc is such a wonderful idea – a way the haute-couture industry can really do its bit for the war. Instead of the bland, uniform-like Utility Clothes the factories are designing, we can give the clothes flair and style – make people proud to wear them.'

'But how are they going to convince the government they'll do a better job?'

'There's to be a contest of sorts. All of London's top designers will hand in their best utility designs, and the top thirty-two will be chosen for a big fashion show to display them to the Board of Trade. I know you'll come up with something fabulous for it, darling. Do say you'll join.'

'I'll think about it,' Cressida said, taking note. She loved a contest, and there was something tantalizing about designing chic Utility Clothes – it was an oxymoron, surely? Each garment had strict stipulations, from the amount of cloth allowed to the number of pleats and buttons. No embellishments were permitted, so you had to make it stand out using colour and technique. It was the ultimate challenge.

'Oh, do come on board,' Muriel begged. 'If the doyens of London's fashion world get involved, the press will love it. It'll raise the profile and get the nation behind the war. And just think about the excitement of a grand fashion show. You wouldn't want to be left out, would you?'

'It does sound intriguing. I'll have to ask Morton about it when I see him.'

The waitress arrived with their soup, a thin, white affair, described noncommittally as 'vichyssoise.' They looked at it plaintively, their eyes meeting as one and then the other began to laugh.

'What passes for food these days!' Cressida exclaimed as she took a tentative sip.

But Muriel was already asking, 'Now, Cressida, tell me about your lovely new house. Have you finished decorating?'

Cressida laughed. 'I haven't even begun, my dear. You can't get wallpaper or paint for love or money – and before you ask, I tried the black market and even they're running short. It'll have to remain Edwardian gothic for now. But it's the perfect location, just around the corner from my fashion house.'

Muriel eyed her knowingly. 'Perfect if you're as obsessed with work as you are, darling. I've heard rumours that since you moved, you're there even more hours. It can't be good for you. All work and no play make Cressida—'

'But I enjoy it, Muriel,' she cut in. 'It's my passion. In any case, what else would I do with my time?'

'What about friends, family, perhaps the occasional beau? You should enjoy your success, revel in it. Why don't you make friends and live it up as much as you can? That's what everyone else is doing with all these blasted bombs.'

But Cressida only shrugged. 'I have plenty of fun in my own way, and more friends than I need.'

'Have you?'

'Well, there's you, and then there's Morton and Hartnell, Audrey and Cecil – although he's obviously on the next tier down.'

'I can't help but notice your "friends" tend to overlap with your work; the first two are couturiers, Audrey is the editor of *Vogue,* and Cecil Beaton is the top fashion photographer in the country. Do you ever see people who aren't in the fashion world?'

'Oh Muriel, what on earth would I have in common with anyone else?'

'Nothing, I suppose,' Muriel let out a peel of laughter, and Cressida joined in a little too emphatically.

Cressida knew she worked too much, but that was how she'd succeeded. Her design house was the reason she had money and prestige – it was the means by which she could live the way she wanted. Yes, should she begin to look through the cracks, there were moments when she could do with more company, but there was always work to take her mind off it. Though sometimes, in the dead of night, she would feel that loneliness acutely, threading into her veins with a cold stealth. But she would never admit that to Muriel.

'Oh, and there was something else I meant to ask you about, darling.' Muriel broke into her thoughts. 'I was reading *The Times* the other day, and there was mention of the death of one Eustace Westcott a few months ago. Wasn't he a relation of yours?'

Cressida stiffened. 'A much-older brother – my only sibling and absolutely vile, if you must know. He disowned me when I left home at the end of the last war. I'm sure I've told you about it.'

'Remind me?'

'My fiancé was one of the two million killed in the war, and Eustace put me down as one of the' – she put on a gruff, disdainful voice – '"unfortunate spinsters destined to be an embarrassment to their families and society at large". He'd never liked Jack anyway, which didn't help. Eustace was my guardian after our parents died, and when I didn't marry, he insisted that the only way to salvage my reputation was for me to stay at home to be a companion for his poor wife and a nursemaid to his children.'

Muriel grinned. 'And instead, you fled to Paris with a few other debutantes and joined the bohemians. I remember now.' She let out a squawk of a laugh. 'Those were the days to be in Paris. I bet you had a ball, all the soirées and artists. I shouldn't be surprised if there's a nude of you hanging in some prestigious gallery.'

'Now *that* would be telling.' Cressida's eyes lit up with delight. 'Do you know that's how I began to design, in those days modelling in Paris? I was perfect for the flapper look, and somewhere down the line I stopped simply putting on what they told me to wear and started having ideas of my own.'

'You've always been opinionated, darling. It's one of the reasons I adore you.'

'You adore me, dearest Muriel, because you can get all the best gossip out of me.'

The waitress came to take their bowls, the soup having been consumed more from a dread of the main course than any particular liking of the flavour.

'So, tell me. Despite the estrangement, did you go to your brother's funeral?' Muriel continued. 'I gather it was held in St Paul's Cathedral.'

'I confess I did slip into the back, just to make sure he was truly gone. Eustace never forgave me for my success, for doing what I loved in spite of his forbidding it. I think he was resentful of me. He'd always had a passion for grand architecture, but he'd had to push that to the side to be lord of the manor. It made him so frightfully staunch about family duty, and if it ruined his life, it should ruin everyone else's.'

'And where is your country pile? In Kent, isn't it?'

'In a village by the name of Aldhurst. It's not far from Canterbury.'

'Did you see any of the family at the funeral? The newspaper mentioned two children.'

'That's right, he had a son and a daughter, my nephew and niece. Hugh would be about twenty-five now. I recall that he's doing something for the War Office. He's inherited the manor, and I'm sure little will change in its running.'

'Hugh Westcott, the name sounds familiar.' Muriel's face screwed up in thought. 'Isn't he the one courting that socialite, Astrid Fortescue? I'm sure I saw a photograph of the couple in some dreadful society magazine. And his sister is Violet Westcott, isn't it? A blonde beauty of about twenty-one – more charm than brains, if the rumours are to be believed.'

Cressida grimaced. 'It sounds as if I'm lucky I escaped when I did. I imagine even an evening with them would be deadly.'

'Were you left anything, part of the estate perhaps?'

'Eustace would never have left me a thing, not that I have any interest in ever going back there again. It was beautiful when I was a child, covered with climbing roses and splendid gardens, but Eustace ruined it for me after our parents passed away.' She heaved a sigh. 'In any case, I loathe leaving London for anything. There's nowhere else I'd rather be, Blitz or no Blitz.' She looked at her dramatic trousers and bright red high-heeled shoes, a smirk on her lips as her eyes met Muriel's. 'In any case, I simply wouldn't make sense anywhere else.'

VIOLET WESTCOTT

Aldhurst Manor, Aldhurst

January 1942

A bright shaft of sunshine beamed into the cold, austere dining room at Aldhurst Manor as Violet Westcott toyed with her bread omelette. The butler had just brought in the latest copy of *Vogue*, and it already lay open beside her. Shaking back her golden curls, she wondered if she were simply too delicate for the maroon skirt suit on page twenty. How irksome it was that patriotism had made uniform-style clothes all the rage. Was a feminine gown really too much to ask?

'Fashion is out of fashion,' she read with annoyance.

The shortages caused by the Nazis' shipping blockade meant that it was out of style to be flamboyant, and all her society friends were showing off their uniforms from various dull military jobs.

Contrary to her expectations of excitement, drama, and romance, the war was not going well for Violet. 'Wardrobe Planning' was the new euphemism for putting up with what you had, and government leaflets, posters, and magazines were instructing you to 'Make Do and Mend.' Everything was rationed, everyone was too busy, and now her father had died, leaving her to fend for herself when it came to arranging her future.

And her future was rapidly becoming a pressing matter. Lord Ombersley had been all but ready to propose when he was shot down over Malta. Who was she going to marry now? Why did all the eligible young nobles insist on being pilots, for heaven's sake? There were hardly any aristocrats left!

Vogue offered her a brief respite, and her eyes drifted back down, resting on the designer's name, Cressida Westcott. Violet had been secretly following her career, aware that it was her disobedient, estranged aunt. Her father had forbidden Cressida's name to even be mentioned in his presence, but Violet had always held a secret dream of meeting her, socializing among her set, trying on her gowns, and gadding about to society clubs, arm in arm with the top female couturier in London.

'Good morning.' Her brother Hugh looked as serious as ever in his Westminster suit as he took his place at the head of the table, telling the aged butler, 'Just toast this morning. I have to catch the early train. Oh, and I'll be staying in London for the week.'

There was a maturity about him these days, as if he thought he was the only responsible one. Violet often felt that he treated her like a child, not least because she didn't have any patience for the war, which was patently ridiculous. Who did have any patience for it, with women expected to roll up their sleeves to take on war work and get all gung-ho about jam making and taking in evacuees?

'Hugh,' she began, but trailed off. The two were not close and had grown more distant still since their father's death a few months ago. Four years his junior, Violet hadn't had much to do with him before he was sent to boarding school. And now he was far too busy and important to bother with her; she knew he thought her too frivolous for words.

'Yes?' His tone was businesslike.

A ball of frustration formed in her chest, and the words came spilling out, emotional and confused. 'You can't just run off to London for a week and leave me here to run things by myself. The place is chaos without Father, and how am I to find the right sort of husband without him here to help make introductions? I'm going to end up a spinster at the rate eligible young men are dying!'

Hugh's voice softened. 'I know things have changed with him gone, but you'll get used to it soon.'

'But don't you take your estate duties seriously? Don't you care? The manor needs upkeep, attention. If you keep letting it slide, the family name will slide as well, and then no good aristocrat will want me!'

'I do care, Violet. But my work in the War Office is more important than minor household responsibilities. In any case, I'm not ignoring the estate. There's a list of things that our father left on his desk, and I'm dealing with those for now. After the war, I'm sure I'll be here more often.'

'Why don't you come back to live here *now*? Where is your sense of duty?'

He was beginning to lose patience with her, his face contorting into a scowl. 'Oh, have no fear, Violet. Our father drummed a sense of duty into me just as much as he did you. You might have a fondness for this place, but I most certainly do not.' His eyes strayed out of the window down to the lake, and he added thoughtfully, 'Except perhaps for the grounds.' He looked back at her frankly. 'You know that I was never on good terms with our father, but I know my duties to the place, despite my aversion to it. I will see to his list as soon as I can.'

The butler returned with the post, handing a number of letters to Hugh, one of which was an invitation card.

After reading it, his eyes flickered up to Violet's. 'Lord Flynn has invited us to a reception at Darley Grange at the weekend, if you'd care for it? Maybe that will cheer you up.'

'Has he?' Her spirits lifted at this special attention. 'What's the occasion?'

He reread the invitation. 'Darley Grange has been requisitioned by the army as a new Allied HQ, and the reception is being held to welcome the Americans. There'll be plenty of officers and higher ranks.' Then he added, 'You never know, you might meet your future husband there. Lord Flynn is considered quite a catch, I believe.'

Violet had met him and his mother at a London gala a few years ago. 'If my memory serves me right, he is quite charming, although he has a round face, like a chubby little hamster. And he doesn't have proper blue blood, does he? His father got the peerage as an industrialist.' She heaved a long, dramatic sigh. 'But with Lord Ombersley gone and the others going down like flies, I might have to lower my sights. The Duke of Davenport is an option, I suppose, but he's so dreadfully dull and more than a little odd, if truth be told.' She huffed, opening her hands with exasperation. 'Look what this war has reduced me to!'

Ignoring her remarks, he passed her one of the letters. 'This one's for you.'

It was typed, official looking.

'What's this?' she said, cautiously taking it.

'I'm not sure, but it has the hallmarks of a conscription letter.'

Fear shot through her, quickly followed by indignation. 'I thought they weren't forcing us women to do war work!' She tore the envelope and pulled out the typed letter. As she read the first few lines, her face fell.

Ever the bore, Hugh started getting preachy. 'Surely you knew it was only a matter of time, especially after they asked all women under forty to register last year. We need more factory workers, more Land Girls, and more military drivers, cleaners, and cooks. Conscripting women is the only answer.'

'It's telling me to go to the Conscription Office in Canterbury next week.' She began to panic, scanning the letter. 'I couldn't possibly do factory work, Hugh. I'm simply not built for it. My job is to find a husband, to give birth to sons who will govern this country. *That's* my war work! You have to get me out of it, Hugh.' Her voice was rising. 'Father could always pull strings. You'll have to do the same.'

'But this is conscription, Violet. It would be difficult to get around, even if I were inclined to help you dodge it, which I'm not. You need to play your part just like everyone else.'

'How could you be so heartless, Hugh! You simply have to help me!'

He shook his head, vexed with her hysteria. 'You can't shirk your responsibility, though I suppose I could try to get you an easy job somewhere close to home. It would be better than a factory job, at least. The new Allied HQ at Darley Grange will need drivers, and most of the women in that pool come from the upper-class women's unit, the FANYs – they're the ones who already know how to drive – so at least you'd be with your own kind.'

'Well, that doesn't sound too bad. They might even let me live at home if I tell them it's a billet.' Violet brightened, her mind whirring with plans. 'And if I'm stationed at Darley Grange, I can spend more time with Lord Flynn.'

'You might have to do a few weeks of training, but don't worry, I'm sure it won't be too taxing.'

'I *can* do taxing, you know, Hugh. I simply choose *not* to.' She sniffed, suddenly miffed at the notion that he didn't think she was clever enough.

But Hugh was already getting to his feet to leave. 'Let's hope you're right. It'd be embarrassing for the family if the military gave up on you.'

'Oh, come on now, Hugh. I'm not that useless. I'm head of

the village Sewing Circle, and it's doing awfully well.' She neglected to add that she was a figurehead rather than an active
member. It was Mrs Bisgood who *actually* ran the group – the
woman ran the whole village, for heaven's sake.

'Then maybe you should actually attend a meeting for a
change?' He turned to her from the door, giving her a smile. 'I'll
be home on Friday evening and look forward to hearing about it
then.'

And with a perfunctory 'good-bye,' he was gone.

'But Hugh . . .' Violet's voice petered out. First the conscription, and now having to mend clothes with the motley assort-
ment of women in the hall.

As she sat back in the dining chair, she couldn't help feeling
that it was all terrifically unfair.

Ridiculous war!

GRACE

Grace stood on the platform of Aldhurst station, a chilly afternoon wind peeling strands of her hair out of its bun. The hum of the rail line heralded the arrival of the train, and as the steam cleared on the platform, she saw a door open, and there he was, his naval uniform punctuated with his white chaplain's collar, Lawrence, the man soon to become her husband.

The jacket made him look broader than usual; she supposed that's what her friend Lottie meant when she said that uniforms made men look more handsome and heroic. Yet he looked older than he had the last time she saw him, more exhausted, probably due to his long hours with the injured and dying soldiers. His dark hair had receded a little farther from his forehead, reminding her that he was ten years her elder. She'd always thought that it was practical, having an older husband, someone she could rely upon, who would be steady.

With a slight hesitation, she hurried forward to greet him, clasping her coat together, a tentative smile on her face. 'Hello, Lawrence.'

He took off his hat, bending his head down to give her a kiss on the cheek. 'How lovely to see you.'

Suddenly shy, she flustered with a button coming loose on her coat. 'It's so wonderful that you could come.' She walked along-side him as they made their way through the station to the lane, words spilling out anxiously. 'It's been so busy here, with more bereaved parishioners. I thought perhaps we could visit Mrs Hanley on our way home, if that's all right?'

'Of course.' He smiled down at her. 'You're so very good to the villagers. I hope you won't find it difficult to leave after we're married. Every parish needs help, and with you by my side, we'll be moving up to larger parishes and more. My name was even put forward for a position as a deacon.'

'Oh, a deacon! How wonderful. I hope we won't have to go too far from Aldhurst, though.'

'It's a tremendous honour,' he said with pride. 'They might send us to the north, or even abroad. There's no better way to serve God, is there?'

She felt her breath falter. 'I suppose not.'

As they reached Mrs Hanley's house, she quickly explained, 'Her husband is a prisoner of war in Singapore, and she has to look after their three young children while pregnant with their fourth. Let's hope we find the children in a calm, quiet mood.'

They weren't.

The two older Hanley boys chased a large ginger cat around the small sitting room while a younger girl screamed as if the world were coming to an end.

'I'm sorry for all the trouble, Grace,' the dishevelled woman said. 'I've been trying to put on dinner, but they won't settle down. Oh, is this your husband-to-be?' Mrs Hanley said, seeing Lawrence. 'Come in! We're a bit of a mess, I'm afraid.'

Grace slid past her, shooed the cat outside, picked up the screaming girl, and cleared a space to sit down on the sofa, draw-ing the other children near with a rhyme.

'We're here to help you, Mrs Hanley.' Lawrence followed her into the kitchen. 'The Bible says that we have to persevere.'

And as Grace quickly coerced the children to listen quietly to a story, she heard Lawrence quoting inspiring passages from Deuteronomy to Mrs Hanley. Not quite as practical as helping with the cooking, but she supposed it was something.

After another half an hour, Mrs Hanley seemed much relieved to finally have dinner on the table and thanked them heartily as they left. 'I'm very grateful, as always.'

As they made their way back down the lane, Lawrence said, 'You deserve a medal for taming those children, Grace.'

She smiled up at him. 'I don't mind it at all. I love children. Perhaps we'll have some of our own one day. I've always dreamed about a nice house, a few little ones playing in a pretty garden, a lovely parish community with plenty of village festivals and events.'

'It sounds like your life here in Aldhurst.'

'I suppose that's what I want, really – my mother seemed to have everything she needed to be happy, before her illness at least.'

'I know how hard it's been for you since her death, with your father's grief and his shell shock coming back. Does he still have nightmares?'

'They still come, but not so very often. It's the guilt that's the worst. He can't seem to dispel the idea that he could have done more to save his friend Jack – although in the middle of a muddy field in the Somme being bombed to pieces, I'm not sure what he could have done. My father himself was so badly wounded, he was almost left for dead. Somehow Mum could make everything all right for him, quiet the nightmares, but when she died it all came flooding back.' She pulled his arm tighter.

Lawrence patted her hand. 'You lost so much when she died.

It was truly God's design that I was chosen as the curate to come to help you both.'

She looked at their hands, folded inside each other's. 'All I want is to rebuild the family that I lost.' She turned to him, and as she felt tears sting her eyes, she muttered, 'Th-thank you, Lawrence, for asking me to marry you, for making my dream come true.'

'Now, now, Grace. Don't cry. In any case, I should be the one thanking you.' He flushed with embarrassment at her emotions. 'You're so good for agreeing to marry me. I don't know any other woman so well suited to the life of a busy vicar.'

'I can't believe our wedding is only a few months away. Have you thought about a place for our honeymoon?' she asked nervously.

He looked at the ground. 'I meant to talk to you about that, Grace. I'm afraid I can only get a twenty-four-hour leave. They can't spare me for any longer.'

'Oh, that's all right,' she said quickly, trying to ignore the flicker of relief that passed through her. She wasn't sure why, but she was more anxious than excited for her honeymoon – probably just wedding nerves.

'I thought I would book us into a small hotel in Canterbury,' Lawrence continued. 'Somewhere in the old town, close to the cathedral museum, which I always enjoy.' He reached for her hand. 'I thought you would like that too.'

'How well you know me, my dear Lawrence.'

As they rounded the corner into the village, the sound of a lone plane came from Aldhurst Hill and they both turned, squinting into the sky.

'Is it one of ours?' Lawrence patted his pockets to find his glasses.

Watching the sky in trepidation, Grace laughed in relief as she recognized a little fighter plane nipping primly through the clouds, the underside of its elliptical wings emblazoned with roundels. 'It's only a Spitfire, thank heavens. Strange to see one before dark.'

'It must be part of a training exercise.'

'Or perhaps it's being delivered,' she mused. 'I read an article about women pilots ferrying planes all over the country, freeing the men for the fighting.'

'It's a shame what this war has led us to, women flying fighter planes. Women shouldn't be working at all, least of all in war machines.' Lawrence looked at her and smiled. 'I'm glad you're not going to have to do anything untoward like that.'

But Grace was watching the trail of white dissipating in the sky. 'It must be wonderful to fly, don't you think? Zooming around the sky, in and out of the clouds like a bird, completely free.'

He laughed gently. 'I would have thought you'd prefer your two feet firmly on the ground.'

Taking her arm, he resumed their walk to the vicarage, pausing only for Grace to pick a few stems of laburnum spilling onto the lane from a front garden. 'It'll brighten up the church for Sunday. It's what Mum used to do at this time of year.'

And as he smiled at her, she felt a wave of warmth, a closeness to her mother. Lawrence was here, he loved her, and he would give her the family she'd always wanted.

CRESSIDA

A crash of shattering glass woke Cressida with a start. Stunned, she cowered in horror beneath the bedcovers for a brief moment before frantically pushing them off. Explosions sounded inside and out, the dark house rumbling as though it were about to collapse beneath her.

'Why didn't they sound the air raid sirens?' she gasped, frantically shuffling her feet into her court shoes to tread over the glass-crusted floor to the window. Peeling back the blackout curtain, she peered into the smoke-rent air. A fierce gold-red fire billowed from farther up the street, casting a murky orange glow into the dark, and the acrid smell of cordite spilled through the cracked windowpane with a gush of sooty air.

First one, then two, and suddenly a band of Nazi planes was thundering low across the dark amber sky, their bellies swollen with bombs, heading straight towards her precious home.

Frozen in fear, she felt a cry clamp dry in her throat.

Everything seemed to go silent as she watched six or seven dark fingers of bombs spilling carelessly into the night sky, descending fast, twisting in the air and diving towards the row of terraced houses below.

Her breath stopped.

Were they going to hit her street? A bomb or two could ground several houses at once; a fire could ravage them all, stealing down the row with growing speed and ferocity.

She darted down the stairs, grabbing her handbag and coat as the colossal sound of the explosions began. Heaving booms jerked the house furiously, followed by a drill of smaller blasts – incendiaries breaking into a thousand explosive sparks.

She had to get out.

Tugging at the front door, she hauled it open and ran out, not even pausing to close it as the force of another explosion propelled her down the road. She fled, wrenching her coat around her against the debris and the mayhem, tears coursing down her face from the fumes, the explosions, and the raw, unabating fear.

For a brief moment, she looked over her shoulder, and that's when she saw it.

Great coils of fire snaked out of her house, busting through the windows, the roof already a massive furnace sending flames twisting up into the heavens. 'My house!' she cried. 'My house!'

Sprinting down the road towards her, a woman sobbed as she clung to her baby in one arm, her other hand connected to a chain of two young children, struggling to keep up.

'Come on!' she yelled at them. '*Come on!*'

Behind them an older man was pulling his wife, running, like Cressida, in their bedclothes, down to the end of the street. Debris surged up behind them, igniting the woman's dressing gown, which she quickly discarded, too frightened to stop or put out the fire. A black-and-white dog raced back and forth, barking incessantly, desperate to find its owner. The roar of the inferno soon overpowered the sound of the vanishing planes, the too-late wail of the air raid siren, and the heavy pounding of the anti-aircraft guns coming from the local park.

Pushed on by the force of more explosions, Cressida joined

the throng, rushing as fast as she could to the end of the street, her sobs catching in her throat, fright and panic overwhelming her.

At the junction she stopped, her chest wheezing with soot and exhaustion – heaven only knew how long it had been since she'd last sprinted so hard. Her whole body wanted to crumble with fatigue.

The street was a morass of smoke and blasts, the fires spreading fast from building to building, and she looked frantically down to the corner where her fashion house stood, hoping to see its reassuring heft.

But in its place was a tremendous ball of orange-gold fire, tall and volatile, covering the entire row of shops as it fed hungrily off the timber and furniture and fabric.

'My design house!' she cried, not even covering her face as sobs poured out of her. 'My work!' She tried to run towards it, unable to believe that every shred of material, every design and desk and machine was being ravaged by the flames, but the heat and smoke forced her back.

She felt like screaming. Hadn't she paid the price for her space on the earth through her long hours, her sleepless nights? Hadn't she given enough?

A sudden wrench of defeat tore into her.

In that moment, the entire wretched war, the danger, the rations, the loss, and the misery all thundered down onto her. She couldn't ignore it any longer. She couldn't show Mr Hitler she was keeping calm and carrying on, as the newspapers and radio urged.

Crumpling onto the pavement, she began to cry with uncontrollable grief. This war was going to take everything from her, just as the last one had taken her one true love. The only saving grace was that she herself had not been engulfed in flames –

although for a moment, she wondered if that was much of a grace at all.

Life began to take on a dreamlike vagueness in the hazy heat of the fire, at once shimmering and impossible to grasp, and yet unbearably crisp, as if it had happened before, a déjà vu that she was destined to replay in her mind again and again.

'Are you all right, madam?'

She looked up to see a man in black, a round tin helmet on his head with the letters ARP.

Air Raid Precautions, she recollected in a daze.

He took her arm and helped her up off the ground, walking her to the main road. 'Why don't you go to the ARP Centre up by the Tube station. You'll be able to get a nice cup of tea there, collect yourself.'

Others were being told the same, and numbly, she trailed along with them, urged by a yearning for the familiar comfort of hot tea. Sometimes she'd walked this way to take coffee in a café before work.

And just like that, it occurred to her that she wouldn't be going to work in the morning.

Her life was going to change completely, and a stab of anguish stopped her in her tracks: What was she going to do?

It was easy to see the ARP Centre. People were spilling out into the street, and although the blackout curtains stopped light coming from the building, the thin beams from the handheld torches of those outside is ued an eerie cascade of moving lights, like fireflies circulating in the night.

Inside, she was handed a cup of lukewarm tea. When she asked if they had anything stronger, someone pulled out a flask and poured a finger of Scotch into it. Although tea and whisky weren't perhaps the ideal cocktail, she could only feel grateful.

It's the small kindnesses that make devastation bearable.

As the whisky started to bring her back to life, Cressida spotted some of her neighbours, a well-to-do couple wearing those ghastly all-in-one siren suits.

'This is it, then,' she muttered to the woman. 'We're homeless.'

'Well, we're going to stay with my sister in Hampstead. The Dorchester's been full since the Blitz began, and all the other decent hotels too.' The woman clutched her handbag, one of the designer ones with a circular bulge in the base to conceal her gas mask. Cressida thought of the gas mask she'd never worn, having ignored the government instructions for the sake of vanity. She frowned as she saw it in her mind's eye, discarded in the cupboard under the stairs, which now didn't exist.

The woman's husband didn't look at all happy with the idea of staying with her sister in Hampstead, but standing in a siren suit in the early hours makes even the worst relatives seem bearable.

A young, nasal ARP woman bustled up and asked if Cressida had anywhere to go, any family or friends with a spare room.

Without a moment's thought, she replied, 'No.'

It wasn't strictly true, but there was no one with whom she felt she could stay. Muriel and her other fashion associates weren't the type of friends she felt she could land on, and she couldn't bear to think of begging her niece and nephew for hospitality; it was the only thing that could possibly make her situation any worse. She didn't know her brother's son and daughter at all, but in all likelihood, they would be as vile as he was.

The ARP woman went on. 'Well, you can think about that tomorrow. For tonight, you can stay in the Emergency Homeless Shelter in the school hall.' She pointed to the old school opposite, whose pupils had been evacuated to Wiltshire when the war began.

For a moment, Cressida stood deliberating, watching as ambulances whizzed past to pick up the injured, closely followed by trucks of men to lift heavy debris and find the dead. It seemed impossible that this was happening to her.

Eventually, she muttered, 'Well, I suppose needs must,' and crossed the road to the old school.

Outside the main door, a wiry ARP man directed her into the makeshift dormitory in a school classroom, and Cressida followed the others inside.

It was even worse than Cressida had been expecting. Not unlike an underground shelter, the floor was covered in blankets in various states of disrepair. Many displayed the telltale contours of people trying to sleep underneath, while others lay empty, awaiting the expected occupants.

She joined the queue to register with an older ARP woman with a clipboard.

'I say, are there any more blankets?' an upper-class woman asked no one in particular.

'You can't get blankets for love or money these days,' a balding man in the line said. 'The army gets first dibs on everything.'

Someone called out, 'Don't fault the army. Our young men, fighting on the front line, they're the ones who need the blankets.'

The balding man bickered back, 'It's worse than the front line here, with the bombs.' He went into a spasm of coughing. 'My wife's been in hospital for over two months.'

A murmur of commiseration went round. The government wasn't saying how many had been killed or injured in the bombings, but everyone knew of someone.

When she reached the front of the line, Cressida asked the ARP woman, 'What am I supposed to do tomorrow? My house has gone. I have no clothes, no toiletries, nothing.'

'I'm afraid you'll have to borrow what you can until you can buy some more. There'll be a few boxes of used clothes in the morning for everyone to have something for the day, and you can get a new ration book and more clothing coupons at a local community office. There's plenty of jumble sales around, and a lot of the women's groups have started clothing exchanges in each neighbourhood.'

'But to stock a whole house, a whole life, from scratch?' The notion seemed impossible. Even though she'd heard of so many others homeless before her, she could barely think of where to start. All that furniture, her clothes, and then the little necessities. And then there was her design house. 'It's everything I worked for – everything I had.'

But the woman was busy writing Cressida's name and her now former address onto her list, briefly looking up to say, 'You're lucky to still have your life.'

A tremor ran down her spine. How close to the truth that was, and she had the eerie recollection of cowering beneath her bedclothes, telling herself it would all go away.

How close she had been to oblivion.

She felt the world shift, unstable and erratic, before quickly telling herself to focus on the immediate problems, think of the practicalities. 'But where will I go, after tonight? How can I buy a new house without an old house to sell? What about my business?'

'You can apply to the government for a part payment for your lost property, but it'll take a while, maybe until the end of the war.' The woman gave her a sorry smile. 'You can stay with relatives, or there are a few hotels on the outskirts of town that might still have rooms.'

'But . . .' Cressida began, not really sure what else she could ask.

'For tonight, you'll be over there.' She pointed with a pen to an empty blanket at the end of a row of sleeping bodies, although it was hard to see how anyone could sleep with all the commotion.

Something inside her seemed to shrivel, but she took a deep breath and trod carefully down to her place. On peeling back the tattered, dark grey blanket, she hoped to find a sheet or at least another blanket underneath, to no avail. With a heavy sigh, she lay down on the scuffed wooden floorboards, pulling the blanket over her body, holding her handbag as tightly as she had held her teddy as a child. Now it was her only, and thereby her most precious, possession.

Her eyelids closed, and she suddenly found herself incredibly tired, her body like a dead weight, her limbs immovable.

Yet sleep evaded her. She continued to turn the events of the night over in her mind, hoping to somehow find a solution to her problems she hadn't previously considered. But no matter how much she tried to stop listening, her ears were trained on an incredibly dull debate between two elderly sisters about what a third sister was going to have to say on the matter of their sudden homelessness. Meanwhile, the overhead light, although dimmed by a green paisley headscarf hanging around the shade, gleamed through her eyelids, a glaring reminder that all was very definitely not as it should be.

Which was why, when the first light of dawn began to be seen around the edges of the blacked-out windows, she decided that the best course of action was to find a warm café.

With a whisk of the blanket, she got to her feet, picked up her handbag, and made for the door. On the way, she let the elderly sisters know that the third sister would probably be happiest if they tried to get some sleep.

Outside, the smell of smoke and cordite lingered in the frosty air. From habit, curiosity, or just sheer longing, she found herself trudging back to her old road.

The blaze had been put out, and a black, smouldering smoke

lingered around the street. Great mounds of rubble lay cold and still, like the dead.

Nobody was there, only a few shadows of looters sifting through the burnt debris for valuables. Fortunately, Cressida had most of her jewellery locked in a bank, a safeguard she had thought ridiculous at the time, but for which she now felt unbearably grateful. Only an ornate ladies' wristwatch and a silver necklace with a locket had been on a bedside table, now, she imagined, lost to whichever scavenger had found them first.

Otherwise, the street was deserted – if, indeed, one could still call it a street. The heavy teams had found and removed any dead bodies, everything else would be dust and ashes by now. She wondered if her neighbours had got out in time: the family in number four, the old lady in nineteen.

Suddenly, the black-and-white dog from the night before appeared, still running for his life. In his mouth something pale caught the dim light, and she realized with a heave in her stomach that it was a child's cloth doll, limp and bloody.

She slumped down and retched, bile searing acid through her throat and mouth, her stomach heaving long after it had emptied, desperately trying to empty more, to remove every essence of this scene. And as she bent her head and sobbed, loudly and incredulously, it felt as if the world – and her inside it – had simply gone insane.

Eventually, pale gold threads of sunlight pulled her out of her misery and she dried her eyes. As if in a trance, she peered at the heap that formed the only remnants of her home, her life.

'What does it amount to?' she asked softly into the wind. 'What do *I* amount to?'

She had never felt so desolate, with nowhere and no one to turn to for help. For the first time, her loneliness loomed large and threatening, and there was nothing to distract her from it. Her work, her design house . . . gone.

And now she'd have to find a way to start all over again. She had never thought it could happen to her, no matter how many buildings she'd seen burned to the ground since the Blitz began.

But now she was just another homeless survivor. There must be thousands – hundreds of thousands – in London alone.

Deep inside, something seemed to collapse – her standards, her pride, her control? With few other choices, perhaps now was the time to mend her relationship with her remaining family. She worried that her brother had poisoned his children against her, but with him gone, things might be different.

The chill of night was transcending into the new brightness of day, and slowly, she made her way to the station.

Whatever she felt about her brother, the countryside, and even Aldhurst Manor itself, there was nowhere else she could turn.

It appeared that the entirety of the US Army had arrived in the forecourt of Waterloo Station at this ungodly hour in the morning. As she stepped over kit bags and studiously ignored wolf whistles, Cressida couldn't help thinking that the world had turned upside down.

'Wanna cigarette?' a GI asked with a cheeky grin.

'No, thank you,' she replied, her mind on the gruesome task in hand.

As much as she didn't want to make this telephone call, she knew she had little choice. She had to simply grit her teeth and get on with it, and it was with a determined huff that she lifted the receiver in the telephone box.

'I need to get hold of Aldhurst Manor in Kent, please,' she told the operator, fumbling in her handbag for some coins and pressing them into the machine.

'That's Aldhurst 467. I'll put you through,' the young woman said.

Cressida felt the hairs on the back of her neck tingle as the telephone began to ring.

After a few rings, it was answered by a sharp-sounding man. 'Aldhurst Manor. How may I help you?'

'I would like to speak to Mr Westcott.'

'This is Mr Westcott speaking. With whom do I have the pleasure?' The voice was cold and rather pompous.

Just like Eustace, she thought with irritation.

Why had she thought this a good idea?

She battled the urge to hang up the receiver.

'This is Cressida Westcott. I believe I'm your aunt.' Just the word made her feel old and plain, the kind of woman Eustace would have had her become.

'Oh, yes, of course.' His voice was clipped, not precisely hostile, but not warm either. 'How may I be of help?'

'I'll just get to the point. My house has been bombed, and I am in need of a place to stay for a short duration. I thought I'd ask you because you have plenty of spare bedrooms and I'll be able to stay out of your way.'

There was a pause.

'I know it's quite early in the morning to spring this on you. And of course, if it's inconvenient, I'm sure I could find somewhere else.' It hadn't crossed her mind that he might turn her away. It would be considered incredibly bad form, as well as unpatriotic, perhaps not ideal for a man in the War Office.

'No, no, of course you must come. I wouldn't have it any other way,' he said somewhat blandly. 'You are welcome to stay for as long as you'd like.'

'Thank you.' She tried to keep the peeved tone from her voice. 'I am catching the seven-forty-seven train, so I'll be with you soon. Don't worry about sending a car around, I can walk from the station.'

'Don't you have luggage?'

She looked at her handbag and replied, 'No,' in a pointed way.

There was a silence, both wondering if there was anything else to be said. In the end, Hugh said, 'Well, I wish you a good journey. Good-bye.'

After another thanks and good-bye, she hung up the receiver, dispirited.

Well, she thought as she stalked to platform four and stepped onto the train, *as soon as I get there, I'll telephone an estate agent to find me a new place in London as quickly as they can.*

The train pulled out of the station on time for once, and Cressida slouched back in her seat, gazing out of the window as her beloved grey, smoky London dissipated into the green blur of the countryside. The buzz of city life, the arena of everything new, the anonymity; how on earth was Cressida going to survive without it?

The city was a place where she could retain her independence and privacy. A place where no one asked questions, no one made judgments about single women living on their own.

And now she was returning to the place where everyone knew exactly who she was. The manor was bound to bring back unpleasant memories, even without the villagers' noses in her business.

Her thoughts turned to Jack, her fiancé, Aldhurst reminding her irrevocably of the last time she'd seen him. A month before his twentieth birthday, he had been killed on the Somme. No matter how much she had begged him not to go, he wouldn't be stopped. He had been on the front only nine months before he was dead.

She quickly turned her thoughts to other things, clutching the handles of her handbag tighter. Beneath her camel cashmere overcoat, she still wore only her mauve silk nightdress, and she could only thank heaven she'd had the foresight to put on her tan-coloured court shoes. There was little for which to be grateful, but they were her favourites, Italian, and therefore impossible to replace now that Italy had joined the wrong side. A chic pair of shoes was a silly comfort, but sometimes it's small things that make all the difference.

Aldhurst station looked smaller and more antiquated than Cressida remembered, and she quickly bustled through so that she wouldn't get trapped by the old station master – still the same man after all these years. She wondered if any of the other locals were still around.

Outside the station, she stepped into the village lane, looking down towards the church beside the village green. The pub was still going, but beside it, the dress boutique had closed, the clothes rations and fabric shortages taking their toll. A few doors down, the village shop was already open for the day. What was the name of the woman who ran it? Mrs Bisgood, that's right. Cressida had campaigned with her to have the war memorial erected on the green after the last war.

She crossed the road to look at it. More weathered than it had been at the unveiling, the Aldhurst War Memorial still held pride of place. She looked through the list of names for the one that meant so much to her, Jack Brompton. It had always brought a lump to her throat, but now, so many years later, she felt only a numbness, a sense of how everything could have been so different, a flickering movie of the life she could have had with him flitting behind her eyes.

Kissing her fingertips, she reached forward and gently traced them over his name. 'I'll always love you, my darling Jack.' But suddenly the granite felt cold beneath her fingers as she realized that she was now older. If he were somehow there in spirit, would she be a stranger to him?

Beside the green, the grey-spired church nestled behind the graveyard, and a lone young woman, thin and pale, stood in front of a grave, reminding Cressida all too clearly of her own loss all those years ago, the intensity of grief. But quickly, she forced it to the back of her mind, pressing determinedly on to the big house.

Just a short walk from the village, Aldhurst Manor was reached via a narrow lane weaving through the fields, and as Cressida approached, she felt the grisliness of the last time she'd been there, those horrific final scenes with Eustace before she'd left for Paris.

She'd vowed never to return.

And yet, here she was, this time with nothing, not even a hat in her hand. It was just as Eustace had predicted.

'But however much like his father my nephew is,' she murmured, 'I'm older, wiser, and I have far more clout.'

As the driveway turned and the house came into view, she caught her breath.

Had she forgotten the magnificence of the place in her time away?

The cream-coloured Georgian manor house ran over a hundred feet wide. Three stories high, the windows ranged from the tall, elegant casements of the drawing rooms on the ground floor to the classical ones of the bedrooms, and above them, partially in the roof, the small square windows of the servants' quarters. Formal stone steps rose resplendently up to the grand front door, great pillars standing guard on either side. She remembered how they had been softened by climbing roses when she was a girl – the pink was as pale and delicate as her favourite summer dress. Eustace had let them die away, of course.

A grey-haired butler opened the door and showed her in.

'It's all right. I know the way.' Cressida stepped inside, mar-velling at the extraordinary déjà vu sensation of being some-where so utterly familiar and yet so distant in her memory.

The colossal galleried hallway with its regal double staircase was still overlaid with the same oak floorboards, now a little more scuffed and worn. Looking up, she gazed at the massive murals coating the upper walls all the way up to the domed ceil-ing far above them. Scenes of ancient warfare and power merged into the pale heavenly skies of angels and gods.

'Thank goodness he didn't get rid of those,' she murmured. Her brother had never been a lover of art.

The great drawing room too looked the same as it had when she had last been there twenty years ago. Memories of endless evenings sitting on that stiff brocade sofa flooded into her mind. How she'd perched, upright, listening to first her father and then her brother expound at length on the duty of the Westcotts and her obligations to the precious family name.

A portrait of Eustace, easily the largest in the room, hung above the mantel among shooting memorabilia. He wore hunt-ing pink, of course, and the sneer on his face bespoke a man who was master over everything he surveyed.

At that moment, the sound of someone entering came from the other side of the room, and she shuddered as she saw, stand-ing in the doorway, a man who was the image of Eustace him-self.

It was only as he came into the light that she realized that this severe-looking man was taller than her brother, leaner. Despite the differences, there was no mistaking that it was his son, Hugh. In his mid-twenties, he was pensive and watchful. Although handsome in a way, there was something in the depth of his brow and the slant of his eyebrows that formed a natural scowl.

She tried to recall the quiet boy she had known before she left, cowed by his strict father and stunned by the loss of his

mother soon after his sister was born. But in this shrewd, polished gentleman, there was no trace of any vulnerability whatsoever.

With a perfunctory smile, Hugh put forward his hand. 'You
must be my aunt.'

Cressida shook hands with him. 'I am indeed, but please
don't use the word *aunt*. It makes me sound so frightfully old.'
She laughed. 'Call me Cressida.' She glanced around, noting the
fraying curtains, the sagging armchairs. 'It's very generous of
you to let me stay at such short notice. Thank you.'

'We have rooms available, so it's no trouble,' he said. 'And
Violet, my sister, will be pleased to have some company.'

'Happy to be of service,' Cressida said with an ironic smile,
thinking how ridiculous her life had become that she was to act
companion to an insipid debutante.

Registering her scrutiny of the surroundings, he enquired
politely, 'It must be strange to be back after so long.'

'Yes, although it's certainly easy to recognize the old place. It
looks almost the same as it did the last time I was here.'

He looked around, frowning. 'I suppose it does. I'm too busy
with my work in the War Office to spend time on the estate,
apart from a few items my father left needing my attention. But
I expect to be married quite soon, so I'll have some help putting
this place back in order.'

'Oh, to Astrid Fortescue, isn't that right? I thought I heard a
rumour along those lines. Wasn't her father one of Eustace's
friends?'

'Indeed,' he said coldly. 'We have been promised to each other
since we were young, and it seems incumbent upon me to play
my hand.' By the scowl on his face, he did not have the joys of
marriage forefront in his mind. 'She will have plans for the
manor, I have no doubt.'

'Quite so,' Cressida said, thinking that Hugh was his father's image not just in his looks, but also in his loyalty to the family name. Cressida didn't give marriage a lot of thought these days, but when one of her assistants flew into a passion about some dreadful chap, at least love was in the offing. Hugh looked positively stoical about the prospect of marriage, as if it were a business deal.

'Let me take you to your room.' Opening the door into the hall, he gestured for her to go first. 'Violet thought we should put you in the Chinese room, overlooking the gardens.'

'How lovely.' She wondered if it too remained unchanged. 'I will need to make a few telephone calls if I may? I have to hire an estate agent to find me a new property, and there are some pressing business matters to which I must attend.'

'Of course, you must use my office. Violet speaks often about your clothing designs. Will you have to give it up?'

'Heavens, no. But I suppose I'll take a break until I find a new location. My design house was destroyed, and there's a lot to sort out; what to do with my staff and the orders that have already been placed.'

'I believe most people in your situation place an advertisement in *The Times* to let their clients know. You may give the telephone number here should anyone need to contact you. I have to go back to London today, so my office is free for you to use as you please.'

He led her, as he would a stranger, up the staircase, and she felt oddly as if it should be her leading him – it was her childhood home before it was his, after all.

'Ah yes,' she said as she walked into the familiar guest room. 'The teal and ivory wallpaper.' Now faded, the room at least had a fine aspect over the lake. 'This room hasn't changed at all.'

He heaved the sigh of a man with much on his plate. 'It hasn't. I'm working my way through a few other issues left unresolved by my father's death. Top of the list is to reclaim the village hall to store the family art and portraits. They're currently in the cellars, and the damp is ruining them. It's a large collection and my father was in the process of relocating it to the village hall when he died.'

A frown formed on Cressida's face. 'Doesn't the hall belong to the village? I don't recall the family ever having possession of it.'

As if reading from the legal papers, he said, 'It was built by the manor as a school for the labourers' families. Since then, it's been absorbed into the community, but officially it belongs to the Westcotts.' Pointedly, he looked at his watch. 'I'm afraid I have to leave for my train, but Violet will show you around.'

Nodding her thanks, Cressida watched as he closed the door behind him, and then she sank down onto the bed. Although not as domineering as her brother, Hugh Westcott was dismissive and traditional, polite to the point of pompousness.

A shiver went through her. The place was taking her back to a time when she wasn't in control of her life, a time when she had been made to feel like a useless, unwanted young woman, and deep inside her, she felt her tightly drawn twines of control slowly break apart.

VIOLET

The arrival of her aunt had sent Violet into a tailspin. What should she wear? How should she do her hair? Would Cressida be in favour of mascara, or would she consider it too tacky for words?

As soon as Hugh had explained that Cressida Westcott would be staying, two salient points came to Violet's mind. Firstly, how she could brag to her society friends, use the connection to meet more fashion-minded people, with a vision of sojourning to the Ritz to meet the queen's couturier coming to mind. But it was the second reason that blazed largest inside her: how many new garments she could now obtain. The rations had been such a bore, and now she had access to her own new source of clothes.

After a quiet knock on the Chinese room door, Violet opened it to see an exceedingly chic woman in her forties turning to her from the window. The woman's sharply bobbed copper-brown hair was cut to precision, her steely blue eyes and high cheekbones were almost feline, and her full lips were pursed inscrutably as she too appraised her niece. 'You must be Violet.'

'Yes, and you must be *the* Cressida Westcott.' Suddenly Violet felt incredibly countryish in her box-pleat skirt, desperately wishing she'd worn something more modish. 'Welcome to

Aldhurst!' She sprung forward to help Cressida with her coat. 'Shall I take this for you?'

'No, I have to . . .' Cressida began, and then she started to laugh. 'Do you know that underneath this coat, all I'm wearing is the flimsy bit of silk I call a nightdress.' As Violet nervously joined in, Cressida's laugh became more raucous, as if she too could hardly believe it. 'Thank goodness I thought to put on a coat and shoes when the air raid began last night.'

'Don't you have any other clothes at all?' Violet looked her up and down, incredulous.

'Nothing except what I'm wearing.'

'Well, I don't want to be presumptuous, but would you like to borrow something from me? I expect we're a similar size, although you're a little taller. It would do for the time being.'

For a fraction of a moment, Cressida seemed to pause, uncertain, her eyes travelling to the box-pleat skirt, but then she smiled and said, 'That would be very kind,' and allowed herself to be led to Violet's bedroom.

Eyeing the blue décor, Cressida sighed. 'This used to be my mother's boudoir. It's like being plunged back into one's childhood without warning.'

But Violet was already in her dressing room. 'What kind of thing would you like? A skirt and jacket or a dress?' She pulled out her most avant-garde dresses, praying she wouldn't lose face to her new aunt within the first hour of meeting her.

'Why, they're lovely,' her aunt declared, but then she waved them aside and walked into the dressing room herself, briskly going through the rails as if in her own home. 'This will be perfect, and this cream blouse.'

It wasn't until she'd taken them out that Violet saw what they were.

'Trousers?' she gasped. 'Only yesterday, I read in *Vogue* that you should wear trousers only for the garden or war work.'

Violet had bought them on a whim, and had never worn them herself.

'Sometimes *Vogue* can be so frightfully conventional,' Cressida said before closing the dressing room door to change.

When she came out, she looked the opposite of conventional – and she certainly didn't look as if she were about to do the gardening. The chestnut brown wide-legged trousers were far more elegant on her than they were on Violet, the billowing silk blouse adding a sense of drama. On her feet were her beautiful tan-coloured court shoes.

'Goodness, you look terrific!'

Cressida's manner was warm, but also crisp and no-nonsense. 'Thank you. Now, would you mind lending me a few other items? If you have time, that is?'

'Well, yes, of course.' What else did Violet have to do, after all?

Cressida was evidently asking the same question in her mind as she surveyed the bedroom, the makeup, the hairbrushes, and the abundance of clothes, most of which had been stockpiled at the beginning of the war in case of rationing.

On a table was Violet's box Brownie, a few of her photographs beside it, and Cressida stalked over to look at them. There was a still of one of the housemaids walking away from the camera down a picture-lined corridor, a tray high on her hand. Then there was one of the lake, smooth and serene, a deer wide-eyed on the island, watching the camera as if looking into life from the outside.

'These are very good. Did someone teach you photography?'

'No, I read a few books about it. It's rather fun, documenting the manor. There's a room in the cellars that I use for developing. It's not as easy as it looks, but the war has given me more free time than usual.'

'You have an eye for composition. That's very useful.'

'Did you study photography?' asked Violet.

'We designers need to take photographs of various garments, so I've become proficient.' She picked up the Brownie. 'This is a very decent camera.'

'My father bought it for me.' She joined Cressida at the table. 'He always insisted on buying the best. Hugh says he spoiled me, but he would say that, wouldn't he?'

'Why's that?'

'Well, I may as well tell you. Hugh and our father didn't see eye to eye. Hugh was never quite what Father wanted – he disliked hunting and shooting – and when Hugh was old enough, he decided that our father wasn't what he wanted either.' She made a small laugh.

'Why is that funny?'

'It's just that despite Hugh's supposed objections, he's still being the dutiful son, doing what our father wanted him to do. It must have been beaten into him so much that it took hold. He's keeping up the family name, what with Eton and then Oxford; he hunts, he shoots, he attends all those dull club dinners in London; and now it looks like he's actually going to marry Astrid Fortescue too. The match was made when they were infants, and Hugh is proceeding, no questions asked.'

'Are they to marry soon?'

Violet tossed back her long curls. 'That's anyone's guess. My brother is infuriatingly difficult to read. Word has it that her family is putting pressure on him to announce the engagement.'

'How dutiful of him to follow through on a betrothal in this day and age,' Cressida said. 'He does seem to be his father's son.'

'Well, not in all ways. He loathes being down here in the manor, always using work as an excuse to escape back to London. But the estate needs to be looked after, and he simply seems to lack any desire to get involved. He's the lord of the manor now. He needs to take it seriously.'

Cressida raised an eyebrow. 'Perhaps he didn't have a good childhood here, so he doesn't like coming back.'

'You could be right. Our father certainly didn't spoil *him!*' She began to tidy away the clothes on her bed. 'I say, why don't you come shopping with me tomorrow? There are some boutiques in Canterbury that are quite good.'

The look on Cressida's face said it all. 'I suppose I shall have to.'

'Although you could always ask your own designers to whip up some outfits for you?'

It was the wrong thing to say.

'My design house was bombed. There are no designers, and therefore, no outfits.' Cressida stalked to the dressing table, poking around the makeup disappointedly.

Sensing the longed-for new gowns drifting away from her, Violet urged, 'But surely you'll find a way to keep going?'

Cressida helped herself to the mascara, taking a seat on the stool. 'There's nothing I can do until I have a new building.'

'But you simply can't stop designing. Your work is so beautiful.' Violet felt her heart sink. 'Can't you carry on working here until you go back to London? We have plenty of spare rooms.'

'No, it's not worthwhile. In any case, I'm hoping the business will be back up and running in a month or two, as soon as I find new premises.' There was a grit to her voice, her mouth set in a hard, ruthless line. 'I can't think what I'm going to do with myself in the meantime.'

A maid brought in some coffee and scones, and Violet gestured for Cressida to join her at a small, round table. 'You must be famished.'

But Cressida was more interested in the coffee, pouring herself a cup as she took a seat. 'Now, why don't you tell me more about yourself? How has this war been for you?'

At last, someone who wants to listen! Violet felt the flood-gates of her heart open.

'It's simply too awful. They want me to do war work, but I'm not built for that kind of thing. I need to find a good husband – an aristocrat, preferably – but now all of the best men are too far away or being imprisoned or killed. I'll have to do something or I'll be left a spinster—' She broke off, but not before registering Cressida's shudder. 'I'm sorry, I didn't mean it to sound that way.'

But then the most curious thing happened. Her aunt began to laugh, tossing her head back as if it were the most ludicrous thing in the world. 'Do you really think it's so very bad, to be a spinster?'

'Well, it's not the same for you. You have such talent, you've built so much. But my father always said . . .' Her words petered out as Cressida began to laugh again.

'Your father? Your father wanted to have me cooped up here like an unpaid servant.'

'But he was adamant that I should marry a title, a duke or a lord. I can't let down the family name. You of all people must understand that.'

'You can't be serious?'

But Violet wasn't listening. 'Poor Lord Ombersley was killed, and now I'm going to have to make do with Lord Flynn.' She sighed, explaining, 'He's new money, not a proper peer, and he has a somewhat round face, but he'll have to do. At least he lives nearby in Darley Grange, which is handy, don't you think?'

'I suppose so,' Cressida said without conviction.

'And he invited me to a reception next weekend. It's just a small event, a speech and a few drinks, something about wel-coming the Americans. But it'll get the ball rolling. I'm sure I'll have it sewn up in no time.' She shook back her hair to demon-strate the power of her good looks.

Then Cressida ruined the effect by saying, 'I always think there's more to romance than the way you look. Beauty is such a random asset, after all. It's just a superficial illusion that presents the holder with a mask behind which they can hide.'

Frowning hotly, Violet looked back into the mirror. 'I'd have thought a fashion designer like you would think more highly of beauty.'

'Oh, I think highly of it all right, I simply view it for what it is: a physical appearance that has absolutely nothing to do with what's inside.' She raised an eyebrow. 'The same could be said for lords and dukes. You need to look underneath before you marry, Violet. See who it is beneath the veneer of a title before chaining yourself to the man behind it. Your father wanted me to wed one of his wealthy hunting cronies so that he could plough the money back into Aldhurst estate. The man was twenty years older than me, with horridly traditional ideas about women. Do you think I would have been better off with him, just because he was titled?' She laughed. 'Never marry for anything less than love, Violet. You'll only do yourself a disservice.'

'Well, who knows, perhaps I'll learn to love Lord Flynn,' Violet said, suddenly vexed. Her aunt didn't seem to understand the urgency of the situation. 'In any case, it's not as if I have any skills to support myself. You were lucky you knew how to make clothes.'

'Do you think I had a clue about sewing when I left this house? I was a model first, and then I began to style my own fashion shoots. It was only then that I learned how to design clothes.' She made a large, frustrated sigh, her mind returning to the bombs. 'And now my design studios are gone. I don't know how I'm going to get through the next few months.'

'Why don't you come with me to the Sewing Circle meeting tomorrow evening? I need to show my face from time to time, as the figurehead. You could meet some of the villagers.'

Cressida didn't look up. 'No, thank you.'

'But it's for the war effort, and they're a jolly friendly crowd. Mrs Bisgood runs it – well, she does when I'm not there,' she quickly added. 'And then there's old Mrs Todd, the Kettlewells, and Grace Carlisle, and . . .'

Cressida cut in. 'Grace *Carlisle*? Any relation of Ben Carlisle?'

'That's right. He's the parish vicar, and Grace is his daughter. Do you know him?'

'Yes, well, I knew him when I was young. Do you know him and Grace well?'

Violet shrugged. 'I don't really mix with the villagers. I heard he wasn't quite right after he came back from the last war – apparently a good friend was killed right next to him – and then he seemed to simply collapse after his wife died.'

'Ben's wife died? I heard that he'd married, but not that he was a widower. When did it happen?'

'About ten years ago? Tuberculosis, I think. He's had a difficult time, but at least he has Grace. She's very dedicated to the parish. You know, the do-gooder type.'

Cressida seemed to think this through, and then she said, 'Perhaps I will join you for the Sewing Circle after all.'

GRACE

The night was clear and chilly, hurrying Grace along as she trotted to the village hall. It had already been a long evening of parish visits, and she could hardly wait to get into the cosy hall for the Sewing Circle.

'Grace! Wait for me!' Lottie Kettlewell's ebullient voice came from the lane, and Grace turned to see her friend waving an arm in the air, a bright grin on her face. Even for an evening with the Sewing Circle, Lottie wore high heels and a modish mackintosh, belted tightly to emphasize her curves.

'Hurry up! We're late,' Grace called back. 'The parish visits kept me longer than usual.'

'You're too busy for your own good, Grace.' Lottie caught up and inspected her friend. 'And you look like you could do with a good night's sleep. I hope you remember we're all supposed to stay smart to keep spirits up, "Beauty is Duty" and all that. Did you try that lipstick I gave you? Red is patriotic, to keep the nation cheery. I heard it on the wireless. Or if you want to save some money, you can use beetroot juice for lipstick and boot polish for mascara.' Three years younger, Lottie was outgoing and carefree. Grace sometimes wondered how they could be such close friends when they were so different, but they'd been neighbours all their lives and the good-heartedness of both kept them together.

'I'm not sure lipstick's quite the thing for my parish calls.' Grace laughed gently. 'In any case, I'm sure the bishop wouldn't approve. Lawrence wants to become a deacon, and I wouldn't want to hinder his chances.'

'A deacon? That sounds very grand. And you, Grace, will be the best deacon's wife there is.' She laughed, taking Grace's arm and hurrying her along. 'I hope that's not why he proposed, because you're such a good parish worker?'

Playfully, Grace slapped her arm. 'Oh, Lottie, that's ridiculous! There's far more to it than that!' But then she added more ponderously, 'Although I'm sure our shared love for the church is part of the attraction between us.'

'How utterly unromantic you are, Grace.' Lottie sighed. 'I want to be loved for my beauty, my wit, and my – well, for simply being me.'

'Whereas I like to be helpful. It makes me feel wanted.'

'I don't mind giving a hand in the church at the weekend, but honestly, Grace, don't you find it draining? You certainly look like you could take a morning off to give your hair a wash – Mum gives a good cut if you're interested. And surely you can find something nicer than that old skirt and cardigan. Some of the girls in my factory are swapping evening dresses every week, just to have something different to wear. I got a lovely dark-blue velvet one last week, we call it "Mary's Midnight Mantrap".' She clapped her hand in front of her mouth with glee.

Grace looked at the ground. 'But it's only me and Mrs Bisgood working at the shop, and we could hardly swap clothes. She's far larger than me.'

'I could lend you some, or you could try the cheap Utility Clothes, although I have no idea why the government thinks anyone's going to wear those drab low-cost clothes. No one wants to look like everyone else. Clothes are about showing off what you've got, making yourself stand out.' She smoothed the mackintosh over her curves to emphasize her point.

'But I don't like to stand out. In any case, other people's needs are greater than my own. Lawrence says modesty is one of the greatest virtues.'

Lottie rolled her eyes and said in that impulsive way of hers, 'I hope you're not marrying Lawrence just because he asked you?'

'That's easy for you to say, Lottie. With your looks and personality, you could have any man you want.' She paused and then added, 'I'm lucky anyone wants me at all.'

But Lottie wasn't listening. She was humming 'Follow the Yellow Brick Road' as she linked arms with Grace and made a little shuffle-hop-skip up the lane. 'So do you think you'll be able to mend your mother's old wedding dress? You could always buy a new outfit, you know. You must have plenty of clothes coupons to spare.' She eyed Grace's old brown coat.

'I gave all my coupons to Mrs Hanley. She needs them for her little ones.'

'I can't believe you, Grace. We get only forty points to last the whole year, and you're giving them away,' Lottie said with feeling. 'It's almost impossible as it is, with a dress at eleven points and stockings at two – if you can find any in the shops.' She patted her dark curls. 'And you never know when you might meet a handsome stranger and need a new dress.'

'And have you met a handsome stranger, by any chance?'

With a charming smirk, Lottie whispered, 'I might have done. But not a word to anyone.'

'Why, is it anyone I know?'

'Let's wait and see, shall we?' She winked. 'Who knows, perhaps both of us will be heading to the altar in the not-so-distant future.'

The two women smothered their laughter as they pushed open the double doors into the bright warmth of the village hall.

The large, dusty room was the venue for all village activities, from voluntary groups to village dances and the weekly news-reel with a film – often a musical, as they were Mrs Bisgood's favourites. Many of Grace's best memories had taken place in this building – school plays, Christmas parties – and it was soon to be the venue of her own wedding reception too.

Most of the Sewing Circle ladies were already there, seated on fold-up chairs around a long table, pausing their chatter to welcome Grace and Lottie, and pouring thin tea from a large metal teapot into the hall's stock of chipped cups.

Mrs Bisgood was busy cutting pieces of grey material at the front, her red gingham apron too small for her generous frame. A tall, bulky woman, she had the look of a large, friendly bird, her imposing nose evened out by a large smiling mouth. She'd had a difficult life, widowed young during the last war and forced to work long hours in the village shop to provide for herself. Although she loved children, her husband's death had effectively closed any hopes of having offspring of her own. Instead, she had played aunt to the village children, watching as they grew, taking care of any strays, tucking them under her abundant wing, and chivvying them into shape.

'But Fred Astaire always dances with Ginger Rogers.' Her voice boomed to Lottie's mother, who sat darning a sock. 'He can't dance with anyone else. It wouldn't be right.'

'That's what the magazine said.' Mrs Kettlewell shrugged timidly. 'He's doing a movie with Rita Hayworth.'

Martha, at fifteen the youngest of the Kettlewell family, spoke up to set everyone straight. 'But it's not the first time he's danced with another woman, is it? What about Judy Garland in *Easter Parade*?'

'And *Gone with the Wind*,' old Mrs Todd added without

looking up from her knitting. 'He was marvellous in that, sweeping around the stage in a tornado.'

'That was Clark Gable,' Martha said, peeved with everyone's lack of precision. 'Fred Astaire wasn't in that at all, and there weren't any tornados either. They were in *The Wizard of Oz*.'

'But Judy Garland was in that, wasn't she?' Mrs Todd didn't look up but there was a victorious little smile on her lips, as if she'd won a point on that score. Approaching eighty and widowed these past ten years, Mrs Todd wore her tawny wool coat inside to battle off 'the chills'. On her head was a green felt hat complete with feathers collected from a local hen, and around her neck was coiled a multicoloured scarf of irregular proportions. As usual, she was ignoring any sewing project, knitting yet another colourful scarf out of remnants of wool.

Grace slid into the chair beside Lottie, the jaunty dark-haired girl fiddling with the waistband of her new trousers. 'They say trousers make life a lot easier, what with all that traipsing in and out of shelters, but they're biting into my stomach something rotten.'

On the other side of the table, Martha leaned across, as if her older sister were simply too idiotic for words. 'I read in *Vogue* that you have to be under forty and under 140 pounds to wear slacks, and I'm not sure you fit into the latter category, Lottie.'

Regardless that she was the youngest of the large brood, Martha had taken charge of the Kettlewell family, having reached the conclusion that she was the only one with any sense. Since she was a capable leader, albeit a slightly bossy one, they had let her get on with it. Mrs Kettlewell had even confessed to Grace that she was grateful to Martha for taking over the family, as there were too many children for her to handle on her own. 'Everything's so much more organized. Meals are on time, everyone present and correct. It's made life so much easier.'

'Well, Grace?' Mrs Bisgood beamed at her excitedly. 'Did you bring it?'

'Bring what?' Mrs Todd looked up from her knitting.

Grace took out the box, unable to bite back a hopeful grin. 'We found my mother's wedding gown, only it's half-eaten by moths.' She eased off the lid. 'I'm not sure we'll be able to save it, but I wondered if anyone has any good ideas? If you help me to mend it, I could lend it to anyone who would like to borrow it. After all, it's such a shame that the war's put a stop to white weddings.'

The ladies clamoured around to take a closer look.

'Aha,' Mrs Bisgood cried as Grace spread the fragmented dress onto the table. 'What we have here is,' she grappled to find the right word, 'a sewing emergency! That's what we like, isn't it, ladies?'

A kerfuffle ensued, and Mrs Kettlewell was jostled to the front, where she took out her spectacles and looked critically over the broken fabric. 'Well, I don't know how easy this is going to be. I'm not sure we have the skills to mend it, and with extra satin impossible to get, let alone the coupons and the price. It would take a lot of work, and with all of us so busy, I'm not sure we can.'

Mrs Bisgood folded her arms in thought. 'The biggest problem is that this lace part is almost completely destroyed, and there are holes all over the rest of the gown too. It's such a shame. The embroidery is magnificent. What a pity!'

They all looked consolingly at Grace.

'If we'd had it earlier,' Mrs Kettlewell said, taking off her spectacles, 'perhaps we could have formulated a plan. Or there might have been a chance we could find a strip of parachute silk to patch it up.'

They glanced at Lottie, who worked in the parachute factory in Canterbury, but she said, 'We only get to take the flawed panels in rotation, and I gave my last one to a friend to make a negligee for her honeymoon.' She sighed. 'But I'm always looking out for parachutes coming down over Aldhurst. Some Land Girls in Chartham found a dead German pilot last year, and they used his parachute to make French knickers and then sold them on the black market at four shillings a pop.'

In her usual matter-of-fact way, young Martha said, 'You know you're supposed to hand in any parachute silk to the police. It's illegal to keep it.'

But the remark went unanswered as everyone was looking at Grace, whose face had fallen.

'Chin up, dear,' Mrs Bisgood said. 'There's something else we have up our sleeves, don't we, ladies? We've all been saving up our clothing coupons for you so that you can buy a lovely new outfit for your big day.'

Grace's hands flew to her face in surprise. 'Oh, that's too much – far too generous.'

'Oh, come on, Grace,' Lottie said. 'It's not every day you get married. And you'll be able to wear the outfit for years to come, unlike a wedding dress.' Under her breath, she added, 'And it's high time you had something decent to wear.'

Everyone grinned, except for Martha, who had been doing the sums and murmured cautiously, 'Well, I'm not sure if there'll be enough for a whole outfit, but you'll be able to buy a skirt, maybe a blouse too. Hats aren't rationed, but it might be hard to find one . . .'

As Grace gazed at the dress, weighing her options, there was a sudden commotion at the door, and there, exquisite in a sable coat, was their figurehead and patron, Miss Violet Westcott, sauntering in as if she attended every week.

Grace sighed, and Martha murmured under her breath, 'That's all we need.'

'Hello, everyone!' Violet called, her high heels clipping across the wooden floor.

'Violet, we weren't expecting you,' Mrs Bisgood said, a new politeness to her voice.

'I came to introduce you to my aunt. She'll be staying with us for a while. Her London house was flattened by bombs.' Violet smiled as if elated by this turn of events.

They all turned to the door to see possibly the most chic woman ever to set foot in Aldhurst. Wearing a man's grey pin-striped suit with high-heeled shoes, her red-brown hair cut crisply to the level of her chin, Cressida Westcott gazed over them, a smile quivering on her painted lips.

Grace drew her breath, straightening her fawn cardigan and hiding the safety pin holding it together. How odd they must look to this picture of elegance: an old woman knitting a rem-nant scarf, a frazzled mum with a girl in school uniform, Lottie in her tight-fitting blouse, and larger-than-life Mrs Bisgood, who bustled forward to greet the newcomer.

'Miss Westcott! How wonderful to see you back! Do you re-member me?' She stuck out a big hand. 'Mrs Bisgood.'

'Of course I remember you!' Cressida took the proffered hand, looking around at the others. 'But you must call me Cres-sida – everyone does.'

A murmur rippled through the women.

'*Cressida Westcott?* The clothes designer?' Lottie Kettlewell whispered, though evidently not quietly enough, as the woman gave her a small nod.

'Violet told me about the stellar work you ladies do, and I hope you don't mind if I join you. I'm keen to help the war effort, and it would be marvellous to meet some other dress-makers while I'm here.' Her voice was low and professional, her eyes flickering to the ivory dress on the table.

As Mrs Bisgood introduced the Sewing Circle members, Cressida seemed to study Grace when she came to her name, making the young woman fluster with her cardigan again. And she wasn't the only one trying to make an impression; Martha tugged at the hem of the school skirt that she'd had for too many years, and Mrs Todd tilted her green felt hat to what she no doubt considered a nifty angle.

'It must have been dreadful for you to be bombed.' Mrs Bisgood pulled up a chair for her, gesturing for Martha to make her a cup of tea. 'But at least you're safe and sound now. We'll do the best we can to make you feel at home here.'

'How long will you be in Aldhurst?' Martha asked as she passed over a cup of tea.

'It depends how long it takes to find another place in London. A month or two, perhaps longer.' But Cressida was unable to keep her eyes off the gown on the table. 'What are you working on today?'

Mrs Bisgood seized the opportunity. 'Well, since you ask, I wonder if you could help us with a conundrum. We don't have any idea how we can mend this dress for Grace's wedding without new material.'

Blushing at the unexpected warmth of Cressida's gaze, Grace handed over the dress for inspection. Could this brilliant designer salvage the gown?

After a few minutes looking over the holes and pulling up the fragments of material, Cressida said, 'Goodness, this is quite a dress. I would say that it was made in Paris a few decades ago.' She turned the bodice over, looking at the rose-patterned embroidery, and then at the inside seam. 'Aha,' she declared. 'Just as I thought. It's a LaRoche.'

'What's that?' Grace inched forward to see the stitched label.

'LaRoche is a prestigious couturier in Paris. It was made

before the last war, I'd say.' She looked up. 'And it must have cost a pretty penny too.'

'It belonged to my mother,' Grace said nervously. 'I expect she borrowed it from someone else. She would never have been able to afford the cost, nor would my father. He's a vicar, you see.'

Cressida's eyes appraised her, shifting from her fawn cardigan to the old skirt and sensible lace-up shoes. But then she smiled. 'I wonder who the first owner could have been. It must have been created for a very grand wedding indeed.'

'Do you think we can save it?' Grace asked.

'Why don't we take it apart? Then we can see how much good fabric is left. If you quickly unpick the waistband, we can divide it into two, and then we can begin to separate the rest of the pieces.'

They cleared the tables while Grace sat with a small pair of scissors, taking out the stitches at the waist and giving the bodice over to Mrs Kettlewell while she continued with the skirt, handing out parts to the others as she went. Before long, the women were all sitting around the tables carefully unpicking.

Mrs Bisgood enthusiastically told Violet and Cressida, 'Thank you so much for helping us. Grace has generously offered to share the dress with anyone who'd like to borrow it, once it's finished, of course.'

Completely oblivious to how offensive it might sound, Violet declared, 'Who would want to borrow a wedding gown? I shall be ordering a new one, have no doubt about that.'

Other than a few surreptitious glances, no one chose to comment on this remark, and the women began to chat among themselves, Cressida turning to Grace. 'You must be excited about your wedding.'

Hot under her cardigan, Grace could barely bring herself to speak to the elegant couturier. 'Y-yes, it's not far off now.'

'How lovely to wear your mother's own wedding gown,' she said in a kind way that made Grace feel more at ease. 'I heard that she passed away.'

'That's right, it was almost ten years ago now. How did you know?'

'Violet told me. I was acquainted with your father when I was young. I asked after him when she mentioned that he's the vicar here.'

Grace looked up. 'Were you friends?'

'Your father was, well, a friend of a friend.' She smiled at the memory. 'He always seemed rather clever, interested in animals and science.' Her brow creased in thought. 'I confess I was rather taken aback to hear he'd gone into the church. Not that it's a bad choice, only I thought he would become a veterinarian or something similar.'

Grace was surprised and, truth be told, curious. 'He's certainly bookish, and he's always outside, birdwatching and so forth, but a veterinarian?' As she spoke, she realized how little she knew him. He'd become so lost it was easy to forget that he was probably a different kind of man before the war. 'He changed a lot through his time in the trenches.'

Everyone knew what that meant, even though it was rarely discussed. Physical disorders were deemed heartbreaking and honourable; emotional ones made people uncomfortable.

'That must have been a difficult time.' Cressida gave her an understanding nod. 'And to lose your mother too. I can see why you'd like to wear her dress.'

'It will be like she's there, not to mention how perfect it would be to wear a white dress.'

'Yes, it's part of the theatre of a wedding, the drama, isn't it?' Cressida mused.

But Grace shook her head. 'For me it's more about the tradition. I don't think it would feel like a proper wedding if I didn't wear white. Even the act of sitting here, unpicking my mother's dress, makes me feel closer to her, part of something bigger and older, a lineage of women through the ages, all experiencing the same as we prepare our white bridal gowns.'

With a raise of an eyebrow, Cressida said, 'Actually, it's not a long-held tradition. Brides have only been wearing long white gowns since Queen Victoria donned one in 1840. Before that, women wore any colour they wanted. There's a lovely portrait in the manor of a bride in the most brilliant blue. It's from around 1790, I think. She looks very young and utterly petrified.' Cressida laughed.

'I think I know the picture. It's in the corridor behind the dining room, isn't it?' said Grace.

'That's right.' Surprised, Cressida asked, 'Do you know the manor well?'

'Hugh and I were friends when we were children, until he went to boarding school.'

'How extraordinary,' Cressida said. 'You seem so utterly different.'

Grace shrugged. 'People change as they grow up, don't they? But as children, we both loved to adventure around the country-side, building dams, climbing trees, that kind of thing. And now, I suppose, we stay with our own kind. It's the way things are supposed to be, isn't it?'

'In my experience, the way things are supposed to be isn't necessarily the best way. Sometimes you need to step outside the way your life has been mapped out, find your own path, your own place in the world.'

'I don't like stepping out of my world,' Grace said timidly. 'Even the more well-to-do parish events I have to attend with my father fill me with nerves. Next week we have to go to an officers' reception at Darley Grange to welcome the Americans to the parish, and I can't tell you how much I'm dreading it.'

'Oh, I believe Violet's going to that,' Cressida said, adding more thoughtfully, 'Perhaps I'll go along with her.'

Silence fell between them until Cressida held up one of the tattered lace sleeves. 'I have no idea what to do about these. It's impossible to get hold of lace these days.'

'Perhaps I can find a strip of a different kind of white or ivory material,' Grace said. 'It doesn't need to match the satin, just coordinate with it. Depending on the width of the strip, we should be able to get half-sleeves out of it.'

'What a wonderful idea! You must have a knack for design!'

With an embarrassed laugh, Grace muttered, 'I've had a lot of practice, remaking and mending old clothes.' She gestured to her brown skirt. 'I made this out of one of my father's old jackets. It's tricky, imagining something in three dimensions and then having to unravel it in your mind into a series of flat pieces that can be sewn together, but I like the puzzle of it.'

Cressida's eyes gleamed. 'There are methods for doing that, you know. You could learn how to do it properly.'

A flicker of curiosity sparked inside Grace. 'It must be such a marvellous thing to do, to make beautiful gowns like you do.'

'I learned the skills as an apprentice. You should think about it.'

But Grace's face fell back to her work. 'I-I could never do it, though. My work is here in Aldhurst and in Lawrence's new parish once the war's over.'

Cressida mulled this over, and then looked brightly around at Grace. 'Well, why don't you bring the wedding dress over to the manor on Friday evening? We can see what we can do with all these parts, and I'll give you some tips I've learned about redesigning garments if we have time.'

'Goodness, thank you.' Grace bit her lip with nervous uncertainty. 'Are you sure?'

'Of course, I'm sure. It will give me something useful to do. Come at eight o'clock.'

As usual, the Sewing Circle meeting went on a little late, and it wasn't until half past ten that Grace bade Mrs Bisgood goodnight at the door and set off through the graveyard to the vicarage.

As she walked, she began to think about Cressida and the appointment on Friday. Nerves mingled tentatively with excitement. How strange it would be to go back to Aldhurst Manor again. She hadn't been there in years, not since Hugh had vanished off to school. She prayed she wouldn't bump into him. Of course, university would have changed him, made him more upper class, more educated. There were rumours around the village that he was pompous and haughty these days, not unlike his father. Would he even deign to speak to her?

And she was only too aware that time had changed her as well. Her mother's death had made her grow up fast. Her father had needed a housekeeper, a parish worker to help in the church, and a nurse to sit up with him after his nightmares. She had taken on all of these roles, without thought or rancour.

As she walked, memories of her childhood came back to her. So much of it had been spent in and around the sprawling manor. Her friendship with Hugh had been all-encompassing, beginning when she was so young that she could barely remember a time he wasn't there. They were always together, exploring the countryside and the manor grounds or the island in the lake.

The island.

With a flush, she remembered that last time they'd swum, how he'd leaned forward as they stood in the shallows, their wet bodies connecting, his lips touching hers, gently at first, but then more fervently as they entwined their arms around each other . . .

Then she recalled the bellows of Hugh's father, 'What's that dreadful vicarage girl doing here again? Get her out!'

And that was the last time she'd ever seen Hugh.

CRESSIDA

Over the next few days, Cressida found herself looking forward to helping Grace with her wedding dress. Now that she had the time, the gown presented a good challenge. Besides, Grace was the daughter of an old friend, and Cressida was only too happy to help.

Also, it had occurred to her that making a new friend might help counter the chilliness she felt in the manor. No matter how she tried to dispel it, the place brought back memories she preferred to forget. Hugh had been cold and distant, and although Violet was more affable, Cressida had been in her trade long enough to know when someone simply saw an opportunity in befriending her.

A vague flicker of guilt needled her: Perhaps she should have kept in touch with her niece and nephew after she left for Paris. In only a few days, it had become clear how much their father had coerced them into becoming traditional and duty bound, Hugh by brute force, Violet with praise and gifts. He had viewed their own wants and needs as superfluous, and after their mother had died, there'd been no one left to stand up for them.

As she came into the drawing room to greet Grace, she found the young woman standing as still as a statue before the fireplace, the wedding dress over one arm. Her clothes were colourless from wear, her shoulders thin and hunched, and her long neck was angled forward as she gazed up at the glowering portrait of Eustace Westcott.

And in that split second, Cressida realized why she'd taken such a shine to Grace. Beneath the slouching shoulders and the drab hair was a beauty, she was certain of it. And perhaps Cressida could do more than just bring the dress to life – she could bring Grace to life as well. The girl had potential; she just needed confidence. And Cressida had confidence galore.

'How lovely to see you.' Cressida strode forward. 'I can see from your expression that you've met my late brother, Eustace.'

Startled, Grace looked over nervously. 'I remember him well, even though I haven't been to the manor for such a long time. I thought the place might have changed, but it all seems so, well, familiar.' She took in Cressida's sophisticated coffee-coloured dress, new from Canterbury, and the emerald silk scarf tied around her neck in the Parisian style.

'I felt the same way when I arrived. I'm not sure I can pinpoint a single thing that's changed in the last twenty years,' Cressida said. 'I know you mentioned that you and Hugh were friends, but I didn't realize you'd spent so much time here.'

'We were mostly in the grounds. Hugh's father didn't like it when I came into the manor.' She looked over to the stag's head on the far wall. 'I remember when Eustace made Hugh shoot that stag. Hugh loathed him for it.'

'Eustace came from an era when a boy's first stag was a momentous occasion, as was blooding at the first fox hunt.' Cressida looked at the wedding dress on the young woman's arm. 'Did you do some more work on it?'

'I stayed up the last few nights and managed to stitch the main parts together. You were right. The fabric from the back panel covered the holes in the bodice. I wasn't sure how to do the sleeves or the upper bodice, although I have some ideas. I wondered if I could get your opinion on them?'

'Of course, that's why I asked you to bring it tonight. Besides, I certainly have time on my hands to help.' She let out an aggrieved sigh. 'I might be here in Aldhurst longer than I expected. My search for a new property in London is not going well. The whole situation is ghastly.'

'That's how war is,' Grace said simply. 'So many people's lives ruined.'

And Cressida suddenly felt dreadful for all those people worse off than herself, those who'd been injured or lost someone dear. 'How horrific it all is,' she said quietly.

Grace stepped towards her, pulling the dress up from her arm. 'Shall I show it to you here?'

'Why don't we go upstairs? There are a few empty bedrooms beside mine, and we can lay it out properly.' She gestured for her to lead the way out to the hallway.

But as they reached the door, it flew open, and there was Hugh.

Not in the best of humours, he had evidently just returned from London. He was pristine in his single-breasted suit, dutifully obeying the new clothing rules.

He glowered from one to the other, seemingly annoyed that Cressida had invited a guest into the manor so late in the evening. But then he stopped as he recognized Grace.

His scowl deepening, he looked her up and down, taking in the old clothes, the woollen stockings, the sensible brown lace-up shoes – no doubt leftovers from a jumble sale. Her hair was coming down, and she hastily tried to pin a loose strand back into her bun, his glare boring into her.

'Grace?' he said quizzically, as if he could hardly believe that this woman was the girl he once knew.

'Hello, Hugh.' She tried to keep her chin up, her voice firm, but her shoulders caved with embarrassment at the undisguised look of revulsion on his face.

Then his eyes caught sight of the wedding dress. 'Are you getting married?'

'Yes, in a few months' time.' She swallowed, the sound echoing around the room.

'What surprising news!' he said without enthusiasm. 'And who is the lucky groom?'

'The Reverend Lawrence Fairgrave. He was a curate here before the war.'

'A churchman?' He seemed to work the idea around his mind. Then he shrugged. 'I suppose it stands to reason.'

Cressida looked at Hugh. 'I didn't realize that you two knew each other,' she pretended.

'When we were young, we sometimes crossed paths.' His eyes flickered dismissively past hers, and he looked at his watch, as if the women were too menial for him.

Poor Grace was standing quite still, holding on to her dress, desperately trying to hold up her world, and a burst of annoyance built up inside Cressida. 'Well, tonight, Grace is here as my guest,' she said sharply. 'I've offered to help her with her wedding dress.'

Hugh hardly seemed to register this. His eyes had gone back to Grace, a look of disdain on his face. 'Well, then. I shan't keep you,' he said, and without waiting for a reply, he turned and strode back out to the hallway.

They listened to his footsteps as he marched down to his office at the back of the house, and Cressida felt a wave of anger that Hugh hadn't been more polite. It reminded her of how Eustace would have been, his high-handed dismissal of women, especially those without titles or money to their names. Was he too embedded in his own importance that he had forgotten how to be civil to an old friend?

'He barely recognized me,' Grace murmured, almost to herself. The look of dejection on her face – running through her entire body – was enough to make Cressida absolutely livid with him.

'He's as rude as his father – worse, even!' she huffed. 'I'm sorry he behaved so poorly.'

'I-I'm sure he didn't mean it,' Grace stammered. 'I've changed a lot since we were friends. He was probably a little shocked, that's all.'

But Cressida was fired up. 'I think we need to teach him a lesson. He'll find out that he can't treat people like that. What do you think, Grace?'

'Well, I'm not really . . .'

'Absolutely. Now come on, let's see what we can do.'

As they went up the staircase and onto the galleried landing, Cressida continued, 'Don't let him upset you, Grace. If it's any consolation, I don't think he's especially nice to anyone.'

She turned into the bedroom beside her own.

'Let's use this room.' She smiled as she led Grace inside. 'Hugh said that I could use it, so I created a makeshift design room to run up a few clothes for myself.' The bed had been removed, and in its place was a table with chairs. A treadle sewing machine bought in Canterbury stood in the corner.

'Are you sure you have time to help me? You must be busy, and now you have your own clothes to make too.'

'Don't be silly, Grace. I offered, didn't I? Don't ever hesitate to accept help, and for that matter, don't hesitate to speak out when people are vile to you, like Hugh – and stand up straight.' She gently tapped between Grace's shoulders. 'I have faith in you, Grace. Now I need you to have faith in yourself too. You're a clever, beautiful young woman. Stand up and be proud of that, and don't let anyone make you feel otherwise.'

Grace's hand went to her hair, tucking in the loose strand

nervously. 'But I'm *not* beautiful. In any case, I don't like to stand out. It's not for me to think I'm more special than others.'

'Oh, Grace! No one achieved anything without setting modesty and selflessness to one side. Do at least try to make the most of yourself.'

'Lawrence says that modesty is the truest virtue,' Grace said uneasily.

'Is he your fiancé?' Cressida huffed. 'I sometimes think that men tell women that just to keep us in our place. Now, tell me, Grace. What is your own opinion about modesty?'

'Well, I agree with Lawrence. It's in the Bible, and it's his job to interpret it. Who am I to say otherwise?'

'Oh, do try to form your own opinions, Grace. All it takes is belief in yourself. You have to think about what *you* want. It's not a sin to make the most of your skills and abilities, to let them shine.' Cressida watched her as she took a deep breath. 'And on that note, why don't you try on the wedding gown and we can see how lovely you look.'

Leaving Grace on her own, she trotted briskly into her own bedroom, opening the wardrobe to look through her new garments. Three dresses and a pair of trousers formed the beginnings of her new wardrobe. Taking one of the dresses from the hanger, she bore it back into the sewing room.

But as she opened the door, Cressida stopped in her tracks.

There in front of her was the most stunning bride she had ever seen.

'My dear, you have quite taken my breath away!'

Grace was a natural model; that was now indisputable. On her, the dress was transformed into a luxurious ivory silk sheath that skimmed her body to the floor, as timeless and elegant as an old master's painting. Although the embroidery still needed work and the sleeves mending, the dress hung from her exquisitely. Beneath the dress, her pale skin shone, her chest rising and falling with her amazement as she looked at herself in the mirror.

'It's the gown,' she murmured. 'It makes me feel different. It's like I'm someone else, someone stronger, braver.'

'Clothes do that sometimes. They have the power to make you into someone else. They can make anything seem possible. Look at your reflection, Grace, and realize that you can be anyone you want to be.'

'All I can see in the mirror is my mother. Perhaps an essence of her is being passed through the dress to me.'

Cressida began to tweak the material, walking around her, checking the seams. 'What was she like, your mother?' she asked as she worked.

'She was kind, adventurous, spirited. She was always outside, walking the hills, gathering mushrooms or nuts from the wood or fishing – she loved to fish. I can still smell the mackerels on the campfire.' Her laugh faded. 'She was too full of life to die. That was what was so crushing about her death. It was impossible to believe that someone so vibrant could somehow stop being alive.'

'Death is so very hard to understand.' Cressida thought of the poor girl, her small life looking after her father and his parish at such a young age. 'It must have been hard for you without her here.'

'That's why I'm so glad to be getting married. I'll have a family just like the one I lost, with a father who is a vicar and a mother who is fun and kind. We'll have a little girl, a bit like me, and maybe a boy too.' Her eyes shifted wistfully, shining with oncoming tears.

Not well versed in dealing with this type of situation, Cressida reluctantly put an arm around her shoulder. But as she felt the girl shudder with sobs, a sadness crept into her own memories, her own lack of a warm, loving family. Cressida had worked hard to ignore it, even bragging to her friends that she'd never needed anything as base as relatives. But now, back in the place where she had felt that cold neglect, and with the girl crying in her arms, the chill of loneliness crept inside.

'Oh, I'm sorry.' Grace tried to control her tears. 'It's just that I was beginning to feel that marriage was never going to happen for me, that I would never have my own children. I'm too busy to meet people outside the parish, and I'd never thought about Lawrence like that – he's quite a bit older than me, you see. I was so surprised when he asked me to marry him.' She sniffed loudly. 'I can still hardly believe it.'

'Well, you deserve to be happy. And hopefully we'll be able to send you off in good white wedding style.' Cressida smoothed down the satin. 'Why don't you slip the dress off, and we'll see what we can do about the sleeves.'

Carefully, Grace changed out of it, and together they spread it over the table.

'Now, what would you suggest, my dear?' Cressida asked.

Reaching into her bag, Grace pulled out a strip of white gauze. 'I found this net curtain in the jumble sale box. Perhaps we can fashion it into a transparent layer to go above the bodice and to cover the shoulders and arms, tapering to the elbows.'

'Show me.'

With dexterity, Grace quickly positioned the curtain across to form two sleeves. 'And in the front, here,' she indicated the centre of the bodice, 'we could have a V-neck in the gauze, which I think would add more shape.'

'That's a splendid idea.' Cressida looked over the result. 'You're better at this than half my assistants. You must have done a lot of remodelling before.'

'It's the second-hand clothes sales we do with the Sewing Circle. Everyone needs clothes these days, with so few in the shops and clothes rationing, and the wartime Utility Clothes the government makes are so dull and unflattering, no wonder no one wants them. We raise more money if the donated clothes are mended, using the good parts to patch up the bad parts, or by seeing the useful fabric in the garment and recutting it into something new, a skirt out of a pair of men's trousers or an apron out of an old dress.'

'Well, that's a wonderful way to learn. When I get back to London, I'll try to pass that on to my assistants.' Cressida went to fetch more pins. 'And you work in the village shop, don't you?'

She nodded. 'It's convenient for my parish visits, being here in the village, and it's nice to be close to Dad too. A month ago, I received a conscription letter telling me that I had to do war work, and I was worried I'd have to work away from home. But when I went to the conscription office in Canterbury, they told me that since I'm about to be married, I won't need to do it. Married women don't have to do war work, which I hadn't realized. It's such a relief to know I won't be sent away.'

'Did you know that clothes manufacturing is considered a reserved occupation? Design assistants can't be conscripted, even if they're unmarried. You see, our work is too valuable, either designing and making uniforms and Utility Clothes or helping with exports,' Cressida said proudly. 'Haute couture is booming, and our exports are helping to fund the war. The world has been looking to London for fashion ever since the fall of Paris, and we're still selling our wares across the world, especially to America. Some of our top male couturiers were ordered home from the front to get back to designing clothes. Every penny from our craft is needed.'

After the curtain was trimmed and pinned, they sat down to begin to carefully stitch it to the top of the bodice, chatting as they went.

'I know you're desperate to regain a family of your own,

Grace, but surely it's not *everything*. I've spent my life running away from mine, and I'm fine,' Cressida said with a laugh.

But Grace didn't join in. 'Perhaps it's because I had a wonderful family and then I lost it, while it seems you never got on with yours. In a good family, you're loved simply for being you, and whatever happens, wherever you go, you will always know that you're loved. It doesn't matter how successful you are, how beautiful, or how rich. The only thing that matters is that you're you and that you belong, and that's what I've missed.'

'That's a delightful notion, my dear, but I can hardly begin to imagine it. My parents were reserved and distant, and there were always so many rules, so many ways I was expected to live my life. I suppose it might be a positive thing in one's life should the family be loving.'

The girl heaved a long sigh. 'Did you ever think about having a family of your own?'

'Children? Well, I should think they're quite nice in their own way, but I haven't thought about them a great deal. I'm sure I would have had some of my own had my fiancé not been killed.'

'I'm sorry to hear about your fiancé.' Grace looked over kindly. 'What was he like, if you don't mind me asking?'

Although Cressida rarely spoke about Jack, she was amazed how quickly a vision of him came crisply into her mind's eye: the photograph of him in his uniform. 'He wasn't especially tall, nor all that handsome, but he was such a lively, generous man. A lover of literature – comedies were his favourite – he would amuse us with witty quotations, Noël Coward or P. G. Wodehouse, making everyone laugh. His hair was slightly auburn, and his eyes a hazel green, and his face always seemed to be covered in a smile.' She found herself smiling with him, his brightness warming her inside. 'But it wasn't meant to be. How were we supposed to know that war was on the horizon when we met?' She focused her eyes on the dress. 'Eustace didn't approve of him, probably because his family wasn't wealthy enough to be of service to him. But we secretly became engaged anyway. Oh, I loved him more than anything. He was so utterly dashing, and yet there was a kindness about him, his attention always on me as if nothing else in the world mattered.'

'Wasn't it difficult to keep seeing each other back in those days, without a chaperone?'

'Yes, it was a different world then. We would meet at events and parties, and then I found a way to escape from the manor after dark to meet him in the woods.'

'Weren't you scared of being caught?'

Cressida laughed. 'Where's that sense of adventure you had as a child, Grace? Life isn't about doing what you're told. It's about bravery and pluck. It's about not putting up with anything less than perfect.'

There was a moment of silence, and then Grace quietly said, 'But what if second best is the only option? What if the alternative is nothing at all?'

'There are always more options. You just have to venture out and find them.'

Grace studied her sewing, her needle rhythmically pulling thread through the delicate fabric as if she were in a daze, and then after a few minutes, she surprised Cressida by asking, 'Why didn't you marry your fiancé before he left for the front?'

'In those days you needed a parent or guardian's consent to marry if you were under the age of twenty-one, and my brother wouldn't give it. And then the groom-to-be inconveniently met with a grenade at the Battle of the Somme.' It was the sardonic version she always told, but perhaps because she was here in Aldhurst, or maybe because of Grace, Cressida could hear the strained tone in her own voice.

Grace stopped sewing, looking up at her, but Cressida determinedly kept her attention on her work. 'That must have been devastating.'

'It was,' Cressida said, unable to stop herself. 'Eustace had heard the news through the grapevine and called me into his office to lord it over me, watch me try to keep my countenance. He declared that the Westcotts had been relieved of a catastrophic marriage and that I was now free to marry someone of his choosing.'

'How cruel! Is that when you left?'

'No, I waited a few miserable years for the war to end, by which time it had become abundantly clear that there weren't many men of my generation left, and that I would never marry anyone – and especially not someone of Eustace's choosing. He then became adamant that it was my duty to remain at home to help look after his heir and be a companion for his wife, but I refused. I was determined to show him what an unmarried woman could make of her life.' A feeling of pride in what she had achieved welled up inside her, only to deflate as fast. 'Only now, those foul Nazis have left me with nothing to show for my life.'

'I'm sure you'll build it up again once you find a new place.'

Suddenly impatient and annoyed with the pity this remark elicited, Cressida briskly went back to her work. 'I'm sure it will be settled very soon,' she lied, to herself as much as to Grace.

The evening passed quickly, and it wasn't until after ten that they began to pack the dress away. Before Grace left, Cressida remembered the gown she had set aside for her and hurried to fetch it, intrigued to see its effect on the girl.

'What do you think of this?' Cressida asked, holding it up.

'It's gorgeous! Is it another of your new dresses?'

'It is, but I'd like you to wear it for the reception at Darley Grange. I'm sure it will look sensational on you, my dear. Since you said these functions make you nervous, I thought it might help.'

Grace's mouth opened with astonishment, and she reached forward and felt the soft fabric between her fingertips. 'It's very lovely, but I couldn't possibly borrow something like this. I'm sure it won't look as good on me as it would on you.'

'Pluck, Grace. Always find your pluck.'

Grace put on an uncertain smile. 'All right then, if you're sure.'

'Absolutely. In fact, I insist.' Delighted, Cressida stood back. 'Now, why don't you come here before the reception, and we can do your hair and put on a little makeup. We'll make you the belle of the ball.' Although Cressida genuinely wanted to help the girl, she was also intent on putting Hugh in his place after he'd been so dismissive of her. What better way to kill two birds with one stone?

As Grace shyly draped it over her arm and made her way downstairs, Cressida shivered with anticipation. She could hardly wait to see the look on everyone's faces when they saw the quiet vicar's daughter transformed into a beautiful model.

As they walked to the door, Grace patted her wedding dress. 'How can I thank you, Cressida! The Sewing Circle will be amazed when I bring it in to show them.'

Remembering Hugh's plans, Cressida's face fell. 'Is the Sewing Circle still meeting though? I thought the village hall was to be closed? That was what I understood from Hugh.'

As she spoke, Grace's eyes narrowed in dismay. 'Hugh is closing the hall?'

'Didn't you know? Something to do with storing the family portraits, I believe. I assumed it had all been arranged?'

But Grace was barely listening. 'The village hall, repossessed? He can't do that!'

'Apparently, he can,' Cressida said. 'He said it belongs to the estate, although now that I see how much it's used, it strikes me as a rather uncharitable decision.'

'It is indeed! How dare he throw us out! What about all our groups? It'll be as if he's closing down the entire village community.' She glared at Cressida furiously. 'I simply can't believe he would do this.'

Calmly, Cressida took her arm and began to lead her down to the front door. 'Why don't you discuss it with your father and decide what to do. You can speak to Hugh about it the next time you see him, find out if there's another solution?'

But it was as if Grace were in a different world as she headed out into the night, frowning back at Cressida. 'How could he do such a thing?'

'He is his father's son,' Cressida said.

'But he used to be so generous, so kind-spirited.' Her face fell, distraught. 'There's not a single trace of the boy I knew.'

And as Grace strode out with a hasty 'Goodnight,' Cressida couldn't help wondering what their friendship had been like – how these two people could ever have been allies.

VIOLET

A mile outside the village, Darley Grange was a Victorian country house around half the size of Aldhurst Manor, with slightly smaller, less formal rooms. The former owner was a fan of the Arts and Crafts movement, and as Violet, Hugh, and Cressida were shown into the wood-panelled reception hall, Violet couldn't help thinking that it wouldn't be a bad place to call home.

'I wonder where Lord Flynn is,' she muttered to Cressida, peering into the ornate drawing room for him.

A crowd of men in dress uniform stood in groups, the khaki British jackets amid the deeper, greener US ones, all emblazoned with medals, stripes, and polished gold buttons. Among them mingled the amber, turquoise, and sky-blue gowns of the officers' wives, none of them too young or too pretty, Violet noted with satisfaction. She never did like to share the spotlight.

Impeccable in a dinner jacket, there in the centre was Lord Flynn himself. With his dark suit and his light brown hair oiled back, he looked sophisticated in spite of his round face, and Violet made a small nod of resolve. It was fortunate that she didn't have tendencies for one specific kind of man, tall or handsome, as some women did.

No, all she needed was a title.

'Yes, he'll do nicely,' she mused to Cressida. 'And conveniently, Hugh's managed to get me a job here in Darley Grange as a driver in the upper-class FANYs – they're the First Aid Nursing Yeomanry formed in the last war. They don't do nursing anymore, only ferrying important people around and being scintillating company for officers. All I have to do is get through initial training, but how difficult will that be? After all, I already know how to drive. And then I can get back to the real work of having Flynn fall at my feet.'

But Cressida seemed hardly to hear. Her head was turned towards the door, and Violet followed her gaze.

'Good heavens! Is that *Grace*?' Violet took a step forward disbelievingly. 'She certainly brushes up surprisingly well.'

Far from the dull, slouching girl Violet was used to seeing around the churchyard, the woman she beheld was a beauty. Not pretty like Violet, Grace was more the type that looked wistfully out of casement windows or sat in rowing boats looking beautifully forlorn. The dusky pink bias-cut evening dress brought out her height and slenderness, and she wore a little makeup, her hair swept up the back of her head to reveal her elegant neck and shoulders.

'I had a feeling she'd do very well with a good dress and a little makeup,' Cressida said. 'Thank goodness she didn't ruin her hair as she walked home to collect her father.'

'Well done,' Violet muttered, trying not to sound distraught. Violet had chosen to wear a classical lilac ballgown she'd bought before the war, which looked almost childish beside Grace's new elegance.

A murmur of hushed conversation rippled through the crowd as Grace stepped carefully into the room, the ladies asking who she was, the men speculating if she was married, and the locals wondering how plain old Grace had managed to transform into a goddess. Violet could see even Hugh looking astonished, his eyes softening as he slowly took her in.

It wasn't long before someone rapped a spoon against a whisky glass, and Lord Flynn stepped to the fireplace to say a few words of welcome, after which the crowd began to disperse, most of them heading to the drinks table.

Violet watched as Lord Flynn went to join his mother, the dowager Lady Flynn, who was talking to a few of the officers.

She took a deep breath. A great deal of her future depended on tonight. Shaking her long curls behind her shoulders, she held her head up high and approached them.

'Lady Flynn, how splendid to see you again.'

The older lady's frail smile didn't reach her eyes. 'We all try to do what we can for the war, don't we?' It was said in a way that suggested that Violet was fortunate to be honoured by her presence, not vice versa.

'And Lord Flynn, thank you for your invitation.' Violet shook Flynn's hand, and as his eyes smiled into hers, she felt as if a special connection had formed between them.

He must have liked what he saw, as he said, 'Delighted you could make it.'

'Is that you, Flynn?' Quite ruining the moment, a loud American voice came from behind her, making her jump forward in surprise.

It was a large man in American uniform who stepped over, uncouthly ignoring her – even nudging her slightly out of the way.

'McCauley, I didn't know you were coming!' Flynn declared, shaking hands effusively, Violet quite forgotten to him.

'Wouldn't miss it for the world.' McCauley, in a typically American display, proceeded to go into a long-winded monologue about how dismal the food was at these local receptions because of the rations, ignoring the fact that he was making

these complaints to his host. 'Not to mention the British cuisine'
– apparently a joke – and how he was pleased to see such a 'swell'
crowd. 'And to get such fine-looking gals in the middle of nowhere and in the middle of a war, now that's quite a feat,' he
said as he looked across the room.

She followed his gaze to see none other than Lottie Kettlewell,
trussed up in a risqué royal blue dress, far too much of her on
display as she laughed, surrounded by a captive male audience.
Quite the spectacle, Violet thought, wondering why the likes of
Lottie had been invited.

Violet glanced sideways at Lord Flynn, as if to share a private
joke: Trust the new American to like something as brassy as Lottie. But to Violet's annoyance, Flynn too was watching Lottie,
his eyes fixed on her with unmistakable interest.

Had he been taken in by the shapely girl as well?

Violet turned back to the group, desperately thinking of
something to say to bring Flynn's attention back to her, only to
find the brash American watching her, amused, as if he had read
the situation perfectly.

With a little sniff, she shook her hair out in an elaborate
preening gesture that would bring Flynn's focus back to her.

But it wasn't until McCauley said, 'Why don't you introduce
us?' that Flynn dragged his eyes away from Lottie.

'Oh, do beg my pardon.' Flynn blushed affably. 'Lieutenant
McCauley is one of the new American officers based with us in
Darley Grange. McCauley, I think you know my mother, Lady
Flynn, and this is . . .' He gestured to Violet, as if he'd forgotten
her name.

Violet felt the swift heat of embarrassment.

'Violet Westcott,' she said herself, trying to keep the huff
from her voice.

Clearly entertained by the whole scene, the American put a
large hand forward and shook hers incredibly brusquely as if

she were a man, not a gently born lady. 'Pleased to meet you, Miss Westcott.'

As soon as she could, Violet released his grip, turning her attention back to Flynn's mother. 'What a lovely idea, to hold a reception to cheer us all up.' Violet prided herself in spirited conversation. 'Don't you agree, Lord Flynn?'

'Oh, quite!' he replied with polite enthusiasm.

'Absolutely,' Lady Flynn agreed. 'I think we all need a break from talk about the war, especially with Darley Grange requisitioned.' Then she added in a low voice to Violet, 'It was bad enough when we were overrun by army officers, but now we have Americans too. They've turned the old dining hall into some kind of battle headquarters, maps everywhere.'

'I hope we're not too much of a bother,' McCauley said with a grin. 'We're all officers, so at least we're house-trained.' He laughed, although it wasn't clear if Lady Flynn realized this was a joke, as she simply grimaced.

Sensing unease, Flynn peeled his eyes off Lottie, where they had once again strayed, and rejoined the conversation. 'It's lovely to see beautiful girls in gowns rather than uniforms for a change.' He turned to McCauley. 'What about you, McCauley? Is there a pretty girl back in Connecticut?'

There was a swagger about McCauley as he raised a cocky eyebrow. 'There might be more than one.'

Violet smothered a scoff, trying and failing to imagine him catching anyone's eye. McCauley was not a looker by any means. Large in height and with a somewhat muscular build, he had nondescript brown hair and his nose was slightly wonky from a former break. His eyes slanted down at the edges, giving him the look of a sad dog. He was certainly no Cary Grant.

'I imagine your American weddings are very grand affairs compared to ours these days,' she said politely, hoping to bring marriage to Lord Flynn's mind.

'My cousin's wedding was bigger than one of your royal ones,' McCauley joked. 'My uncle is still complaining of the bill.'

Flynn laughed along. 'Isn't that how all women want it.'

'We're such frivolous creatures, aren't we? Everything has to be just so,' Violet said, thinking of her own wedding plans, how she had every detail worked out. Now all she needed was a groom.

'Absolutely,' Flynn muttered, but his gaze had slipped back to Lottie. He was transfixed by her in precisely the way he should be with Violet.

With another preen of her hair, she turned to give him her special coquettish look through her eyelashes, opening her mouth to enquire about his health.

But he had gone, and when she spun around, there he was, stepping forward to speak to Lottie. Violet watched in dismay as, enthralled, he pulled the local girl to the side for a more private tête-à-tête.

Annoyance seeped through her. She'd heard friends complain that the war was breaking down social barriers, but this was ridiculous. Flynn might not have true blue blood, but all the same, it was obscene that he should sideline Miss Violet Westcott of Aldhurst Manor for the likes of Lottie Kettlewell of 14 Church Lane.

Deserted, she felt a blur of humiliation.

'I wouldn't worry, I'm sure that a pretty girl like you has plenty of other men lining up.' It was McCauley, probably enjoying the spectacle of her embarrassment.

'Obviously,' she snapped, wishing he would leave her alone.

He picked up her hand. 'You could always talk to me?' There was an oafish grin on his face, mocking her.

Snatching her hand back, she looked peevishly around the room for someone to come to her rescue. 'If you think I'm the kind of woman who accepts offers for the sake of pity, you are very much mistaken, Lieutenant McCauley.'

With that, she strode off in search of someone who would make her look less like a wallflower.

But Flynn was now talking to Lottie, and Cressida was with Grace, who was looking far too elegant for Violet's comfort. And where was Hugh? After a few moments, she spotted him. He was standing on the other side of the room with his arms folded, and he had that dreadful scowl on his face. But his eyes told a different story as they looked across the room. And as she saw what they beheld, she couldn't help but feel a sense of all social conventions somehow falling apart.

Because the person he watched with such intensity was none other than Grace.

GRACE

As she gazed around the crowded reception, Grace was uncertain of what to do with herself. She felt out of place and kept wondering if her father would notice if she slipped away.

'Why aren't you mingling, Grace?' It was Cressida, handing her a glass of punch.

'Well, I'm not terribly good at things like this.' She sipped a little punch, which was pleasingly sweet. And then, thinking of Lawrence and her father, she added, 'I'm far more at home in a church or with the parishioners.'

'Oh, come on, Grace. It's just a reception. In any case, you look disarmingly beautiful in that dress, especially when you hold your shoulders back. I'm sure any young man here would simply love to talk to you.' Cressida smiled encouragingly. 'You have far more poise and conviviality than you think.'

Grace stood a little taller, part of her quietly heartened by the compliment. 'I wish I had your ability to talk to people, Cressida. It's as if you belong in any room you enter. All I'm used to is giving Make Do and Mend classes in the school.' She gave a small laugh, thinking about it. 'And they never go down all that well. The government's posters with Mrs Sew and Sew have put everyone off; she's too bossy and a bit of a know-it-all.'

'You should come with me to some of my events. My clients often invite me to charity galas, and a few of them aren't too far from here. Lady Marley and some of my other customers live around Canterbury.'

'Why don't you design for them here in Aldhurst? It might suit them better now that you're closer. I imagine half the gentry in Canterbury would love to have a gown made by Cressida Westcott.'

'No one outside of London has the money nor the clothing coupons these days.'

'Well, what about reworking old gowns, like we're doing with my wedding dress? The posters and leaflets are always talking about "New Clothes from Old". The fabric doesn't need to be new, just the design.'

But Cressida shook her head. 'By the time it gets off the ground, I'll be back in London. In any case, I wouldn't want to remain in the countryside a single second longer than need be.' Then she quickly added, 'That doesn't include you, though. You and your gorgeous wedding dress have been keeping me sane.' Before Grace could answer, she saw her father approaching, smart in a suit with his white collar.

A look of recognition dawned on his face as he saw who she was with. 'Cressida Westcott? Is it really you?' A gleam shone in his eyes. 'Grace told me you were here in Aldhurst. I gather you've become terribly successful. Very well done indeed. I'm sure it would have annoyed your brother something rotten.'

They both laughed, Cressida saying, 'I imagined him trembling with rage every time he read about me in the newspapers.'

Grace was transfixed. Her father was usually such a measured, introverted man. She was surprised to see him laughing so readily. 'I didn't know you two were such good friends.'

Cressida turned to Grace. 'Ben was a dear friend of my fiancé, Jack Brompton, so we spent a lot of time together.'

Startled, Grace swallowed hard as she recognized Jack's name. She'd heard it time and time again, shouted out in her father's nightmares. 'Jack was your fiancé?'

Cressida's eyes met her father's. 'His death was hard on me, as I'm sure it was for you, Ben. I learned to focus on my work, but Jack always remains in my heart.'

Her father's pale grey eyes pierced hers. 'We all need something to keep us going. I have my books and my hill walks: philosophy and nature.' He smiled, and his eyes shone. 'Jack would have been proud of you and your success.'

'I like to think I've shown the world what women can do in this day and age, albeit temporarily paused.'

'I was sorry to hear about the bombs. It must be very disconcerting to lose your home.' His voice was gentle, kind.

'It was an unspeakable night, with all the chaos and danger. I was incredibly grateful for the ARP wardens. They were astonishing, risking their own lives just being on the streets to help the rest of us.'

'We have an Air Raid Precautions team here in Aldhurst,' Grace said. 'There's only a dozen of us, but you should join! Not that much ever happens around here, but we have to man the telephone and turn on the air raid siren. Otherwise, it's making sure people keep the blackout rules – we don't want the Luftwaffe to spot our little village. Why don't you join us? Mrs Bisgood runs it, and Dad is a warden too.'

'We'd be delighted to have you come along.' He looked at Cressida in his intense way. 'Isn't it funny how you've been gone so long, and yet now that I see you, it feels as if it could have been only a month or two.'

'To me it feels like a lifetime ago.' Cressida put on her professional smile, but Grace could see that her usual façade had dropped.

And as they began to catch up, Grace pulled away, trying to mingle, as Cressida had instructed.

A maid came around with a tray of drinks, and Grace took another, feeling a jolt of headiness as she sipped the sweet concoction. Alcohol wasn't something her father had at home, and she wasn't used to the effects. But as she took another gulp, her nerves seemed to dissolve, and soon she found herself talking to some of the officers, sensing their admiration. It was the dress, it made her feel different, more assured, as if she could step inside any high-society event and slip in seamlessly, as if she truly belonged.

On the other side of the room, Grace saw Violet looking over, evidently in a fractious mood.

And Violet wasn't the only one watching her. Beside the door was Hugh, a look on his face that was difficult to read.

Just as the officers began to peel apart, he walked towards her, taking her arm and deftly turning her away from them.

'May I speak to you a moment?' he said with polite precision. The dismissive look from their previous meeting had quite vanished, and she watched as his eyes betrayed something akin to admiration.

Why would I want his approval? she smarted to herself, suddenly irritated by his presumption that *she* would want to talk to *him*. And besides, she was livid with him! What about the village hall? How dare he try to close it down with no regard for the villagers? It was just another example of how much he'd become like his father.

As he led her to one side, she remembered what Cressida had told her about speaking up for herself, and putting on a reserved smile, she became determined not to let him get the better of her.

'I wanted to apologize for rushing away when I bumped into

you in the drawing room,' he began. 'It had been a busy day, and I feel that I wasn't as polite as I could have been.'

Although it was an apology, there was a haughtiness about it, as if he expected her to fall at his feet, delighted that he should pay her so much attention.

But this only served to provoke her all the more.

'Evidently civility isn't one of your strong points.' There was a sudden waspishness in her voice. 'Especially where the villagers are concerned.'

'I don't think I understand what you're getting at,' he said carefully, sensing the change in her mood.

'Don't you think it would have been polite to ask the villagers before repossessing their hall? Or perhaps you could deign to let them keep the one useful thing the manor has ever given them.'

He stiffened, frowning. 'My father had already settled the plans to repossess it before he passed away. I'm simply following through. There weren't many details, but the legal documents state clearly that it belongs to the manor to be used as necessary, and my father deemed it necessary to use it to store the family portraits. They're valuable works of art.'

'And portraits of dead aristocrats are more important than the needs of living people?'

He made an impatient sigh. 'I can't imagine the hall was being used that often, otherwise my father wouldn't have seen fit to take it back. I'm sure there are other places the villagers can use instead. It will only be until the end of the war.' He took a step closer to her. 'Let's not bicker about this, Grace. Everyone has to give up things because of the war. We all have to knuckle down.'

'Why is it that knuckling down applies only to villagers?' She knew she was working herself up, but she couldn't stop herself. 'There aren't any other places for us to meet. The hall is where we come together to help the war effort. The Home Guard on a

Monday, the Sewing Circle on a Tuesday, and so forth. A few women have started a daytime nursery to enable mothers to do war work, and at the weekends, Mrs Bisgood shows news reels and films for anyone too busy to get to the cinema in Canterbury.' She shook her head in disbelief. 'Do you have any idea what goes on in the village that you are supposed to be leading?'

Silenced for a moment, he took a step back. 'I confess that I didn't know that the hall was so busy. I assumed my father had properly weighed the pros and cons. His notes suggest that it had already been discussed and agreed.'

'And yet no such discussion has taken place.'

There was a pause, and he glanced uneasily around the room. 'Perhaps my father was a little out of touch with village life.'

'Perhaps your father didn't care about being *in touch* with village life,' she retorted. 'But I always thought you had more compassion than that, Hugh. Isn't the great lord of the manor supposed to be the person *helping* the community, not hurting it?'

His jaw clenched. 'My work in the War Office is incredibly demanding. I barely have time enough to spend here, let alone tend to hapless villagers.'

'We're only asking for the village hall to remain available to use, that's all. I don't see how that requires much *tending*, especially as we're the ones raising money to repair the place.' She couldn't keep the disdain from her voice. 'It's not as if we ask much from the manor.' And with a growing hurt, she snapped, 'You're not as considerate as I thought, Hugh.'

Suddenly furious with her, he said, 'I don't have time for this. Whatever happened to you, Grace? You used to be so' – he reached for the right word – 'so free-spirited.'

'Free-spirited?' she repeated slowly, the crushing blow making her glower back at him. 'I was a child, Hugh. And then my life collapsed around me. My mother died, my father was distraught, and you, my best friend, disappeared without a backward glance. Of course I'm different. I had to grow up. And for all your talk of your important work, it doesn't seem as if you ever did.'

His scowl came back, heavy and angered, and abruptly he stepped back. 'You must excuse me,' he said curtly, turning away from her, and with a terse 'Good-bye,' he strode swiftly towards the door and was gone.

VIOLET

Predictably, the morning was overcast as Violet stood on Aldhurst station platform, a solitary suitcase beside her. 'I can't believe that Hugh can't pull some strings to get me out of this ridiculous training,' she moaned to Cressida. 'I'm simply not built for it.'

'You'll be absolutely fine, my dear.' Cressida had insisted on escorting her, probably to make sure she didn't make a dash for home. 'A spot of discipline and a few skills won't do you any harm at all. You never know, you might find you do rather well. I know there's a capable mind beneath all those blonde curls, however much you like to pretend otherwise.'

As if reminded of it, Violet shook her precious hair, hoping that it would afford her a little special treatment – she'd found that her good looks often did that, especially with men. 'I just don't see the point when I won't have to apply any of it. I always loathed classes. My governesses all gave up on me.' She gave her tinkling laugh.

Cressida shook her head. 'Do you think I got to where I am today by blocking my ears so that I never learned a thing?'

'All they're going to teach us is how to march, how to mend

engines, and how to do what you're jolly well told.' Violet sniffed ruefully.

'And all those things are useful in their own ways. Mechanics and driving will help you become more independent, which is always a benefit. Marching and doing what you're jolly well told is good for getting on with people, realizing your place in the world, how playing the game can get you ahead.' Cressida's eyes met hers with emphasis. 'Do at least try, Violet. Promise me that.'

The train's whistle echoed around the hills, and as it pulled into the station, Violet looked at Cressida. Through the last weeks, they'd nurtured a friendship of sorts. It was nice to have her aunt around – yet another reason why she didn't want to leave. She made an exasperated huff. 'Oh all right. I promise to try if it makes you happy.'

Cressida helped her up into the carriage. 'Always do your best, Violet. You have absolutely nothing to lose and plenty to gain.'

'I'll try,' she replied, more from a sudden sadness of having to leave her than in any real way. Trying was beneath her, she'd always thought. 'Cheerio,' she murmured, not feeling cheery at all.

And as the train pulled away and gathered speed, she couldn't help thinking how much she'd missed having a woman like Cressida in her life, how different her life would have been if she'd had a mother, or even a friendly aunt.

The train journey to Waterloo was not a happy one, but all too soon she was being shuffled off the train and down to the great station forecourt. As she stood looking at the board for the ten twenty to Camberley, her small suitcase in one hand, the train ticket in the other, she heard a raucous voice beside her.

'You must be going on military training like us!'

Violet turned to see a gaudy young woman. She was wearing the most hideous red hat that clashed horridly with her close auburn curls clustering around her chin. She grinned, showing a smear of lipstick on her large front teeth, and added in her distinctly lower-class voice, 'I'm Lena. It looks like we're all heading the same way, so we may as well make friends now. This is Becky. I just spotted her too. It's the small suitcase we all had to bring. It gives us away.'

Becky gave a weak smile. Her eyes were puffy from tears, and she looked positively drab beside Lena.

'Look, it's on platform four,' Lena suddenly squealed, pointing at the train board. 'Let's make sure we all get seats together.'

'I was hoping to buy a newspaper,' Violet lied. 'I'll meet you there.' She went to slip away, but Lena was there, sliding her arm through Violet's, pulling her along to the platform.

'We can't lose each other, or we'll never find each other again.' She let out a grating laugh. 'In any case, who needs newspapers when we can have a good old chat? We can get to know each other before the horror begins.'

That laugh was going to get on Violet's nerves.

Lena took them down the platform together, finding what she described as 'the best carriage', and forcing them inside.

Thankfully, amid the guard's whistles and some shouts from the platform, the train soon shunted forward. This provoked more squeals from Lena, and Violet tried to block out her voice, focusing instead on the damaged London buildings as the train chugged dismally through the broken city.

For the life of her, Violet couldn't understand why Lena wouldn't stop talking. Her lower-class accent and manners were an utter embarrassment, but she simply chattered on and on regardless.

Not to mention her choice of conversation.

'I told Billy I wasn't that kind of a girl,' she said. 'But, of course, he soon found out that I was.' A cackle of laughter erupted from her.

'Well, at least you've seen a bit of the world, Lena.' Becky was clothed head-to-toe in third- or possibly even fourth-hand clothes. 'I've never been away from home before. What about you, Violet?'

She had been hoping they would stop trying to converse with her. Hugh had given her the impression that she was joining an aristocratic group of girls. These two were the absolute opposite.

How had her life come to this?

The rail tickets had arrived the previous week, along with a few forms and a letter telling her she was to do six weeks of training at Camberley, just southwest of London. No matter how much she begged them, she couldn't get out of it. Thankfully, Hugh had arranged for her to live at home afterwards, seconded as a driver at Darley Grange, and so she had little choice but to get on with it.

Much to her confusion, she was told only to bring one small suitcase containing two pairs of pyjamas. No other personal clothes or possessions were allowed. She had to flick through the pages several times to be certain she hadn't missed a more complete list. But there was nothing. Since pyjamas were not a thing she was in the habit of using, she had to go to London to buy a few pairs at Harrods, using her increasingly precious clothing coupons – now that she was to be given a uniform, she would get only fourteen coupons a year, supposedly for handkerchiefs. Her uniform was to be worn on all occasions, dances and weddings included. How much more dismal could it be!

On top of that, Lord Flynn was evidently besotted with Lottie Kettlewell, for heaven's sake. How absurd the world was becoming! People were choosing their partners not along class lines but however they liked. Everything was turning upside down.

'But what will society look like once the world's turned right-side up again? No one's thinking about that, are they?'

During a long, tearful discussion with Cressida, she had admitted that she'd never had real affection for Lord Flynn. Rather, it was all part of a practical plan to marry the last remaining lord in the area.

But instead of admiring Violet for her pragmatism, Cressida had made her promise to think about what she truly wanted. 'Making do simply isn't good enough when it comes to marriage, Violet. Swallow your pride and follow your heart.'

Well, that approach might be all right for commoners, but not for Violet. Without sentimentality or believing themselves in love, commoners would have nothing to get them through the hard times in marriage. For an upper-class woman like herself, a title and an estate would be crucial to make any marriage bearable.

And what does Cressida know about marriage or tradition anyway? she thought defiantly. Cressida had never married, and she'd turned her back on the family too. Violet would never do such a thing. She knew that any power she had originated from the Westcott prestige. With a grimace, her thoughts turned to the Duke of Davenport. Would it be worth putting up with the oddness of the man for the sake of his title?

As the train drew into Camberley station, she hoped that a FANY official would be there, whisking Violet away to her elite unit. But as she saw a single, lonely army private holding up a sign, ATS NEW RECRUITS, this appeared not to be the case.

Nevertheless, she sped up her walking to get to him before the others. 'I think there must be a mistake. You see, I'm here to join the FANYs.'

He nodded. 'That's right. FANYs too.'

'But I was told—'

He interrupted her. 'The motor mechanics in the FANYs were

merged into the ATS not long ago. If they sent you the train ticket for Camberley, this is the place you're meant to be.'

Her heart plunged. Was she to be grouped with women from lower classes? The humiliation of it!

'This is us,' the clanging vowels of Lena rang out from behind her. 'Watcha, soldier. Hope you're ready for a bit of Lena!' She addressed the army man thus, wiggling her body in a most embarrassing manner, and he quickly barked at them to follow him to the truck.

A handful of other women joined them, and Violet sized them up, taking in the lack of properly tailored clothing – one woman was even wearing overalls.

'It's a bit scary, isn't it?' Becky from the carriage had caught up with her. Her voice was that of a country bumpkin, an impression only intensified by her posture.

Violet attempted to speed up, but the silly girl kept bustling after her, like an ugly duckling who wouldn't get the message.

Outside the station was an army truck onto which they were expected to clamber, regardless of their footwear. They took seats on the benches on either side, and as the truck started its journey, Lena began to sing 'My Old Man', raising her hands for everyone to join in. Extraordinarily, everyone in the truck apart from Violet seemed to know the chorus, yet no one knew any of the verses, so they just sang the chorus again and again until Lena forced everyone to move on to 'Down at the Old Bull and Bush', to which the whole row began to sway, Violet included as she was wedged in the middle. Never had she felt so out of place in her entire life.

Once inside the barracks, the truck pulled up beside a large army building, and they were told to register and then report for medicals.

'Medicals?' Violet winced. Hugh was going to get a stern letter as soon as she had the time.

The first line was to have her heart and lungs tested. A medic pressed a stethoscope beneath her blouse and listened intently to her chest and back, and then passed her along to the next line, where she had to undress behind a curtain.

'Surely we can do war work without having to undergo this kind of indignity,' she muttered.

Becky shrugged, but it was Lena who replied, her raucous laugh ringing above the chatter. 'I lost the old indignity years ago.'

Next, a nurse gave them each three injections, one in each arm and the other, to Violet's consternation, in her right buttock.

Sore and irritable, she was also starving. Her last meal had been breakfast. Even a cup of tea would have provided some form of sustenance.

'We'll break for a late lunch,' the short, bossy female sergeant announced, 'after FFI.'

Violet felt it was time to give the woman some harsh words and stormed up to her. 'What's FFI?'

'Freedom from Infection,' the sergeant said, the slightest hint of a smirk on her face. 'You'll be checked for head lice, nits, and other parasites.'

Violet was affronted. 'There are no parasites on me, I can assure you,' she said crossly, although considering some of the miserableness of her colleagues' beginnings, she couldn't vouch for everyone. 'I insist on being served lunch now. I haven't had anything to eat for hours. It's inhumane.'

The sergeant let out a laugh, then began mimicking her accent. 'Like I said,' she said in a hoity-toity way, 'lunch will be served after you have had your FFI.'

Hands on indignant hips, Violet glared at her. 'I will not tolerate this treatment any longer and insist that I be allowed to leave. I will even be so generous as to not ask for my train fare to be reimbursed.'

The sergeant puffed herself up and marched up to her, an angry growl coming from her.

'You'll be court-martialled if you defy orders.'

'I don't even understand what that means. In any case, I've changed my mind. I don't want to join anymore. I've decided to take some other kind of war work.'

The woman smirked. 'You signed the papers; you can't get out now.'

Violet's mind flitted back to the forms that arrived in the post and the ones she'd signed on arrival earlier that day. She hadn't thought a great deal about them, or even read them for that matter.

As she fought back tears of frustration, she silently raged at Hugh. He had insisted this would all be so terrifically easy.

How she was going to throttle him!

The sergeant's arm shot out, pointing to the place Violet had left in the row. 'Back to your position for the FFI check.'

A cloud of self-pity washed over her, and she firmly resisted the urge to scream – she wouldn't give the vile sergeant the sat-isfaction. Head held high, she went back to the line, looking defiantly down to the end to see what she had coming.

Nothing could have prepared her for the mortification of the nit search, which involved another complete strip. Who knew there were so many parts of the body where lice could thrive!

But as one or two other women saw their protests come to nothing, Violet realized there was nothing to do but subject her-self to the embarrassment of it all, trying desperately to remem-ber the easy driving work she would be given at the end of the ordeal.

As she watched, one or two women were picked out and told to go and stand at the side, and it soon became clear that these were the infested ones. Violet looked at the motley group, mostly women from lowly backgrounds, judging by their clothes.

How horrific to be so publicly called out!

Before long, she watched as Becky endured the inspection, resulting in her making the sorry walk of shame to the motley group.

'Next,' the sergeant bellowed, looking at Violet.

The woman was enjoying this, Violet had no doubt. Just because she was resentful of Violet's breeding, she was going to make her suffer.

As the sergeant went through her hair, Violet hummed the national anthem loudly inside her head to blot out the reality. It took an inordinately long time.

'Aren't you finished yet?' Violet muttered, desperate for the ordeal to be over.

But the sergeant was smirking at her. 'You'll have to go in the infected group.'

'What?' Violet felt more puzzled than irritated as she was pulled out of the line and marched to the huddled group. 'There must be some mistake. I don't have head lice, or anything else for that matter.'

'We found one in your hair, and one is enough.'

'But how? I live in a manor!'

The sergeant sputtered in her gravelly voice, 'I don't care. Get over there.'

The lice group welcomed her into their sorry midst, some evidently feeling that her upper-class appearance increased their rather dismal standing. If a posh lady can get lice, it can't be that embarrassing.

But humiliation gripped her. Never in her life had she been singled out for anything other than glory and success. Hardly bearing to glance at the group of cleared women watching on, she heard the now-familiar cackle of Lena. How could she be reduced to this?

The inspection over, the sergeant told the others it was time for their lunch, and they were quick marched out, delighted and relieved.

'Right, you lot.' She turned to the dozen nit-ridden women. 'We're off to the disinfection room.'

Grimly, Violet marched behind Becky, watching the stupid girl scratch her head.

Did one of her lice somehow make its way into my lovely clean hair? she thought, growling under her breath. She should have sat beside Lena on the train.

What exactly the process of disinfection comprised became horrifically plain when they stepped into a smallish room. Three chairs stood in the middle, and on a table beside each lay fine-tooth combs, jars of black ointment, and, alarmingly, a large pair of scissors.

Violet began to back out of the room. 'You can't cut my hair,' she gasped. 'You simply can't!'

The sergeant wasn't even trying to hide her enjoyment now. 'You upper-class girls get no preferential treatment here.'

With that, she grabbed Violet and roughly shoved her into one of the chairs, while another sergeant pinned her down.

'Please! I beg of you,' was all that Violet could cry as the sound of the scissors rang sharply through the room. The other girls let out a collective gasp and cowered back against the far wall.

It was over in minutes.

'There you are, nice and tidy.' The sergeant sifted a comb through what felt like a bottlebrush cut.

Fat tears slid pointlessly down Violet's cheeks.

Who was she without her beautiful mane?

How would she marry a lord now?

'Is there a mirror?' she asked, her voice quaking in shock.

But the sergeant snapped, 'What do you think this is, West-cott? One of your beauty salons?'

She was unceremoniously removed from the chair and shoved in the direction of the others. There she slid down the wall into the corner, and not even caring if her skirt got dirty on the floor, she began to cry.

When they were finally all sheared and combed, they were shown to the canteen, where a ladle of thin stew was sloshed beside a spoonful of runny mashed potato. Silently, Violet went to sit beside the others. With all their shorn heads together, they must look like convicts.

Never had she felt so low.

Becky passed her a metal tray. 'You can see how you look on the back of that,' she said miserably.

Unsure whether she wanted to look or wait for the shock of the whole encounter to subside, Violet finally pulled it up.

Gazing back at her through the shimmery silver was a street urchin or something equally as grimy. Her neck looked long and skinny and the head on top rounder than usual, the uneven tufts making her look like a fluffy dandelion. She tried flattening them down, but they relentlessly bobbed back up.

The tray clanged as she put it back onto the table.

'You'd better eat up,' Becky said. 'We're behind everyone else now, and they won't wait for us.'

Violet could hardly bear to look at the stupid girl whose stupid hair had given her stupid head lice. Instead, she picked up her thin, tinny fork and brought a mouthful of stew to her lips, barely bothering to taste it, let alone complain.

After all, she had no idea when they would get dinner – if at all.

As Becky predicted, they were promptly ordered to their next venue, the kit and uniform department. 'It'll be the first time I've ever had a set of brand-new clothes,' Becky said, a quiet pride in her voice. 'I can't wait to show off my new uniform when I get to go home.'

Dismally, Violet felt the opposite.

At the uniform centre, a series of female soldiers looked each woman up and down to approximate a size before handing them various khaki woollen items: a boxy jacket, a shirt, an A-line skirt, a tie and cap, brown woollen stockings with suspenders to hold them up, a bra, and three pairs of enormous bloomers.

'No one should have to wear things like this,' Violet whispered furiously, looking horrified at the baggy short-style underpants, which were pulled in by elastic at the waist and at the bottom of each leg, just above the knee.

'My cousin's been in the ATS since the war began, and she says they call them "passion killers",' Lena said with a chuckle.

Violet didn't join in. 'I can't imagine any passion happening at all with a hairstyle like this.'

'Ah, you look lovely, duck,' Lena replied. 'You're lucky you've got a pretty face. It'll be fine once we tidy it up a bit.'

They were ordered to put on their uniforms. All the clothes that they'd come in were to be folded and placed into a package with their home address, to be sent back, no longer needed.

Frowning, Violet took a last whiff of the French perfume on her cream blouse as she packed away her beautifully tailored clothes, her last vestiges of home.

The rumours about the bulky, unflattering uniform were all too true. The large front pockets below the thick belt made one's hips and behind look enormous, and the skirt was unfashionably long, leaving one's legs below looking as though they belonged to a child.

As the sergeant approached to get them in order, Violet decided it was time to address a question that had been on her mind.

'I was told I was to be a FANY. Aren't we to have a more slimlined uniform?'

The sergeant smiled kindly, but then, as she drew close, she boomed, 'No,' loud enough to make Violet wince. But then the sergeant softened, a sarcastic smile on her face. 'Oh yes. I forgot: You are allowed to wear the special flash on your hat, if you so choose.'

Since the notion of a flash did nothing to quell Violet's mood, she quietly decided to leave it for another day.

After all, she thought. *I won't be here for long. One way or another I'll find a way out of this bedlam.*

Next, they were given two bedsheets and led to their wooden dormitory huts, sleeping thirty women apiece. Each sparse bed frame was topped with a stack of three mattress 'biscuits' that were to be laid in a line over the springs. There were three rough grey blankets with every bed, and a hard bolster to use as a pillow.

Too exhausted to feel anything except relief at the sight of a bed, Violet set to work making it. Never having done this before in her life, she had to glance at Lena's beside her to make sure she was on the right track.

When Violet finally collapsed into it, after a quick supper of sausage-meat pie, she barely cared that the bed was as hard as nails and that the bolster pillow did nothing but bolster her gloom. But what bothered her the most was her hair, not improved by the sergeant bossing her about, enjoying her downfall. It was as if the woman had no respect for Violet's upper-class status.

How was she to get through this if no one respected who she was?

At least she was out of sight of her society friends now that her hair was cut shorter than a boy's. Although not exactly a bright side, training would give her somewhere to hide until she felt sufficiently composed to face the world.

As she lay uncomfortably in bed, she wondered what her father would say if he could see her now.

And it was with this dismal thought that she began to lose control of her emotions. At first, tears formed in the corners of her eyes, and then, a more full-hearted sob shuddered through her as she embraced the complete, vile horror of the day, how the next day wasn't going to be any better.

She'd never truly been away from home before, away from where she made sense. How she longed to be back in her soft, large bed in Aldhurst Manor, a maid bringing her up a glass of hot milk before bed, the sound of Hugh working late in his office, and more recently, Cressida in her rooms across the landing. She even missed the villagers; she'd take their company over the sergeant's any day.

How lovely her life had been – how little she had appreciated all that she had. She thought of the letter she'd write to Hugh once she had a chance. She had quite a few choice words for him.

But then she imagined him receiving it. 'How typical,' he would say. 'Nothing is ever good enough for precious Violet.'

And she realized how right he was. She was never satisfied, always finding fault. A new wave of tears engulfed her.

Suddenly, she felt something on her shoulder, and then a warm, friendly arm was put around her. Someone had come to comfort her, and judging by the rise of new sobs, that someone was also crying.

Turning, she saw that it was Becky. The girl she had branded as idiotic, lower class, and stupid had broken the rules to get out of bed to comfort her.

'I hate it here,' Becky said with a sob.

'I miss my home,' Violet said with a snivel. 'I miss my bed. I miss my hair.'

Then another sob was heard, and they felt another pair of arms around them, as Lena joined the circle, sobbing, 'I'm just glad it isn't only me. I miss my mum.'

'I wish I'd never signed up, not that I really had a choice,' Becky said, sniffing.

More of them joined, and soon there was a little huddle of young women, a varied collection of rich and poor, upper class and lower, each of them crying and comforting each other as best as they could.

CRESSIDA

As Cressida walked briskly into the village in the cold dark of night, she felt an unexpected lift of pride. Tonight she was going to her first Air Raid Precautions meeting. She would be able to repay her gratitude to the organization that had helped her in her darkest hour.

Yesterday she'd spoken to Mrs Bisgood about joining the ARP, before their conversation turned to the matter of the village hall. Hugh had rescinded his claim, and even organized a box of crockery to be sent from the manor.

'How thoughtful,' Cressida said, wondering what had come over him.

She'd mentioned it to Grace when she came over to work on the wedding dress, but the young woman had only muttered, 'Perhaps he has a conscience after all.'

While Cressida walked, her mind flitted from Grace to the letter she had received from Muriel Holden-Smythe that morning.

My dear Cressida,
  London society is still reeling from the shock of
your departure, darling. Why not do some designs from

*Aldhurst? Surely, it's better than nothing? And what
about the IncSoc Utility Clothes Contest? The fashion
world is all abuzz with the big fashion show, and we
all know it wouldn't be the same without you. Do say
you'll submit some designs.*

With best wishes,

Muriel

Cressida smiled to herself, thinking about writing a reply:
'Dearest Muriel, I have no intention of doing any fashion design
here.' But that wasn't strictly true. Grace's wedding dress was
coming along nicely. It had reawakened a passion she had for
tailoring, and it was so very satisfying, mending the embroidery
while chatting to the quiet girl. Perhaps she'd been spoiled, having too many assistants and her choice of fabrics for too long.
Or maybe she'd simply forgotten her love for designing a single
article from scratch.

What's more, she'd completely forgotten about the IncSoc
Utility Clothes Contest. Perhaps she'd write to Morton, find out
more. It was simply too challenging to ignore.

The Aldhurst ARP office was located above the village shop,
and Cressida trod cautiously up the narrow staircase and opened
the door into the small, low-ceilinged space.

Dimly lit and smelling of old boxes and mothballs, the office
could be called cramped if one was feeling kind. Three rows
of fold-up chairs were set facing a desk covered with books,
ledgers, and a large wireless radio, with notices taped or pinned
to the wall behind.

A sea of faces turned to see who it was.

'I hope I'm not late,' she said, sliding into a chair beside Ben
Carlisle at the back.

'It's wonderful to see you here, Cressida,' Mrs Bisgood
boomed from the front. Dressed in an ARP black trouser suit

and tin hat, she looked rather formidable. 'You'll get the gist as we go along.'

Ben leaned over. 'Well done for making it.'

She grinned. 'I couldn't wait. This is my chance to pay the ARP back for their help when my house was bombed.' Cressida shivered at the memory of the raging fire, the injuries, and that dreadful black-and-white dog darting frantically around, the bloodstained doll in his mouth. It kept replaying in her mind at random times, especially in the dead of night.

Around them were the others: Mrs Kettlewell and Lottie, Lottie's older brother Archie with several other men in Home Guard uniform, and Grace, who volunteered for everything it seemed. All the women and some of the men were knitting, the new national pastime, and Cressida diligently took her needles and wool out of her bag.

Even though it was deemed patriotic to knit wherever you happened to be, Cressida had felt herself above knitting. But that was before she'd joined the Aldhurst Sewing Circle. Upon hearing that Cressida 'didn't knit', Mrs Bisgood handed her some needles and a ball of government wool to start knitting hats and socks for the troops. The wool was dispersed by the government to sewing groups around the country, the quantity of wool depending on the amount of finished clothes sent back to them.

'If everyone uses any spare time they have to knit, we won't need sock factories. After all, what else are you doing with your hands when you're on the bus or listening to the radio?'

Under Mrs Todd's tuition, Cressida had mastered a number of stitches, and as she added her first pair of army socks to the Sewing Circle's box for the troops, she realized how easy it was, and how self-important she'd been to think herself above it.

Wool for personal use was still available in some shops, but you had to use clothing coupons for it, much like sewing fabric.

Most people, like Mrs Kettlewell beside her, unravelled old woollens to make something new.

'Before I begin, I want to look at the ARP duty calendar.' Mrs Bisgood took down a handwritten list stuck to the office wall. 'Because we now have Cressida, we'll each be on overnight duty once a week, with two people manning the office, touring the village, and then waiting for telephone calls warning of aircraft.' She gestured to the upright telephone on the desk, beside which was a narrow cot with a few grey blankets. 'You can take it in turns to get some sleep, provided there aren't any active air raids. Since our village is a small one, our air raid siren is a hand-crank one, always kept beside the door.' She pointed to a large fanlike contraption with a turning handle on the side. 'Cressida, you're on duty with me tonight so that I can show you the ropes, but after that you'll be with someone different every week.'

As Mrs Bisgood began to prepare for a first-aid session, Cressida turned to Ben. 'Is there a lot of walking?' She eyed her high heels, gloomily accepting that she'd have to buy some of those ghastly flat lace-ups.

'You have to go around the village telling people to "Put that light out!"' he said with a sigh. 'That's the part of the job I dislike. It makes you so very unpopular, especially if you have to give someone a blackout fine.'

'Have you had to do that?'

He confided, 'I might have let a few people off. Mainly it's children or older folks, the bereaved not paying enough attention.' He looked at his hands, reminding her that he too had lost a loved one.

'It's a hard, frightening time for a lot of people,' she said softly, wanting to put a hand on his arm, as she might have when they were young. But how do you traverse a friendship when it has been dormant for decades?

Mrs Bisgood began the first-aid training, demonstrating how to deal with severe burns on Grace's arm, and Cressida leaned towards Ben and asked, 'Have you ever had to perform any of these tasks?'

'Aldhurst hasn't had any direct hits, but we've been lucky. Kent is on the flight path to London, and a lot of villages nearby have had their fair share of deaths and injuries. A whole terrace was knocked out in Chilbury, two dead and one injured. That's when Grace convinced me to become a warden. We all have to do our bit, look after the community.'

'I never thought to join when I was in London,' she said. 'It's far more anonymous there, so you don't have anyone telling you to help.' She smiled, adding, 'No one's looking over your shoulder in London. That's why I prefer it.'

But Ben only replied, 'If no one's looking over your shoulder, no one's there to catch you when you fall.'

'What if you make sure you don't fall?'

'You could try to stop bad things from happening, I suppose, but what kind of a life would that be, never taking chances, never letting yourself go?'

She opened her mouth for another quick riposte but found herself unable to think of one. Only a stark memory of the echoing loneliness she'd felt in the city came to mind, the price she'd paid for her success.

It wasn't long before the meeting ended, and the group rose to disperse, most of them going home or off to the pub for a quick pint. Ben wished Cressida good luck, and then joined Grace to head back to the vicarage.

As soon as they were alone, Mrs Bisgood looked Cressida up and down, not unlike a keen Girl Guide leader accommodating a poorly prepared Brownie. 'I'm not sure your outfit is quite the thing for blackout checks.' Tuts spilled unstoppably from her mouth. 'Let me have a look.'

Within moments, she pulled a large cardboard box from a cupboard, and bending from the waist down, she plunged her head and shoulders into it, coming up for breath a minute later. 'Here's some overalls for you to pop on.'

With a combination of revulsion and amusement, Cressida pulled on the blue monstrosity. 'You're just trying to torment me, aren't you?'

'Magnificent! Now you're ready for anything,' Mrs Bisgood declared at the sight. 'Didn't you know that overalls are all the rage now they're deemed work clothes and you can buy them without clothing coupons? I heard that Harrods has them in every colour.'

'Surely you have to draw the line somewhere. You'll be wearing a button-up siren suit next.' Cressida laughed.

As they stepped outside, Cressida couldn't help thinking that it wasn't the best of nights for a village walk. Particles of drizzle were held captive in the air, sparkling in the beam of her torch as she dimly lit the lane ahead.

'Thank you for getting involved with our little village, Cressida,' Mrs Bisgood began. 'It's good to have someone from the manor on board. Your help is very welcome in the Sewing Circle too. It adds a little prestige to the group. It must be nice to have that sort of success.'

'It's the fruit of a lot of hard work, long hours, and calculated risks.' Cressida made a sigh. 'If I'm honest, being here – cut off from the London fashion world – has made me realize that I've had time for little else. Work was all I ever did. My reading was fashion magazines. My shopping entailed seeing what the competition had to offer. My friends were people who worked in the industry. This break – and the gruesome bombing that caused it – has made me stand back, reevaluate, shall we say.'

'Then why are you so desperate to hurry back to London? You're already becoming part of our community, with the

Sewing Circle and now the ARP, helping Grace with her dress. Why don't you stay a bit longer?'

Cressida chuckled at the older woman's forthrightness. 'I agree that it's been more fun than I'd imagined. My family isn't that dreadful after all, and the Sewing Circle and ARP have been warm and welcoming. It's funny, I never thought about helping the community, but now that I'm here, lending a hand, I can see how good it is for the spirit. Grace took me to help at her Make Do and Mend class in Chartham yesterday, and it was terrific to see so many women eager to get through the war looking good. Did you know that now there's a shortage of laundry soap, women are rubbing warm bran into wool skirts and using ground rice to clean delicates?' She chuckled. 'And home-dyeing has become all the rage to make a coat feel new or cover a stain, although it's a bit of a risk, don't you think?'

Mrs Bisgood laughed. 'It sounds like you've become a local already. You must stay for longer.'

A breeze caught Cressida's neck, and she pulled her coat closer. 'Oh, this is all just a marvellous holiday. I have to go back to London as soon as I have a place to live.'

'Surely you're a big enough name that you can take a break, can't you?'

Cressida shook her head. 'I need to work. I find it comforting. People always wanted to pity me, for being a spinster or losing my fiancé, and I could hardly bear it. My designs are the one thing that put a stop to that pity.'

Surprisingly, Mrs Bisgood agreed. 'I know what you mean. After I was widowed, I threw myself into the community to make me more than a pitiful widow. But I've found that friendship always sees you through. If you have friends, what more do you need?'

'I haven't had a lot of time for friendship, but I suppose I can see your point,' Cressida said, thinking how different their lives had been, one hard and lonely, yet full of luxury and sophistication, while the other was basic but busy with warmth and humour.

On they went, their footsteps echoing in the lane, and as they passed the church and graveyard, the two women stopped, gazing into the dark, misty silence.

'My ancestors are buried here,' Mrs Bisgood said proudly.

'Mine are too,' Cressida replied.

'Funny how you're a lady and I'm a shopkeeper, but we both end up in the same place.'

'Oh yes,' Cressida said. 'We all end up in the ARP sooner or later.'

They both began to chuckle, and Mrs Bisgood nudged Cressida playfully. 'You're not so bad, are you? I have to confess, some of your family haven't been so good to us villagers. But you're one of us at heart, aren't you?'

'I suppose I am,' Cressida said. 'Isn't it strange how a birthright or the death of a loved one can pivot the axis of a life. One small change and it all goes down a different path.'

'Sometimes I think about that too,' Mrs Bisgood said thoughtfully. 'There are so many different people we could have been, so many lives we might have led.' Her eyes glinted at Cressida's. 'That's why I keep my eyes open; I don't want to miss a single one of those pathways, heading off into something fun.'

It was eleven by the time they returned to the office. Mrs Bisgood made them tea with a small kettle in the back and began to show her how the paperwork was organized. It was a long, arduous task, and by half-past midnight, Cressida was yawning.

'I'll take the bed first,' Mrs Bisgood said. 'Take it from me, it's easier to stay up late than to be woken up at three.'

Without more ado, she strode to the little bed, took off her shoes, and lay down, pulling a blanket over her. Within minutes, a soft snore came from the large mound on the bed, leaving Cressida to her own thoughts.

She tried not to doze as she listened to the BBC World Service on the wireless. Crackling voices from exiled governments in London were sending news to their citizens in occupied Europe: Poland, Czechoslovakia, Denmark, Belgium, France. And through the dislocated voices, Cressida couldn't help but think how lucky they were to still have their freedom. How much worse it could all be.

GRACE

The Sunday afternoon sunshine beamed through the blue-and-gold stained-glass window above the altar as Grace and Lottie arrived at the church with dusters and some freshly picked daffodils.

'Lord Flynn proposed to you?' Grace said to Lottie, confused. 'But you hardly know him.'

'Well, actually it's been going on longer than you think,' Lottie said coyly.

'Ah, is he your mystery man?'

Lottie laughed. 'He is indeed. It's been quite a few months now. You know how small this village is – especially with gossips like Mrs Todd and Martha.' She giggled. 'We wanted to find out if it was right first, just us and no one else.'

She turned the large sapphire one way then the other, the gemstone catching the light, sprinkling the apse with a gilded blue glimmer.

'It's beautiful,' Grace murmured. 'How did he propose?'

'It was only yesterday evening. After a fine dinner at Darley Grange, he walked me home down the quiet, empty lane, and, well, we began to kiss, there underneath the big oak tree down Church Lane. He was getting a little carried away, so I pulled back a little and said as a joke, "You'll have to marry me if you want to go any further," and he just grinned and pulled out a small velvet box with the ring inside.'

'That's wonderful, Lottie!' Grace could hardly believe her friend was plunging into everything so fast. 'When will the wedding be?'

'As soon as he gets leave for the honeymoon. It won't be until after yours, I expect. I can't wait!' She began dusting the altar, a spring in her step. 'But you must be getting excited too, Grace. Only a few weeks to go!'

Grace felt her heart beating faster. 'Sometimes it feels as if it's coming too quickly. There's still so much to do. I have the dress to finish, the decorations for the village hall, the food to organize. The rations and shortages have made everything so much more difficult. And then there's the problem of getting our families here, what with fuel rations and the trains being so sporadic. It's all rather overwhelming.' A surge of anxiety welled up inside her.

'Don't worry so much. Everyone knows there's a war going on. No one expects a banquet or a full contingency of relatives – you're probably better off without some of them, if your family's anything like mine.' Lottie laughed gently. 'Do you know, I don't think you ever told me how Lawrence proposed to you, Grace.'

'Oh, there really isn't much to tell. It was last summer, when he came to visit. We weren't even courting, but he came over to see how Dad was getting on, as he often does. It was after dinner, when my father had gone back to his study. I was clearing the plates, and he said that dinner had been wonderful and began asking me if I ever planned on leaving the vicarage. I told him that I hoped to be married one day, and it was as if the idea occurred to him right there and then. Then he simply came out with it, "Would you like to marry me?"'

'That's frightfully unromantic of him,' Lottie said. 'Did he have a ring?'

'No, but he went out and bought one the very next day. It's only a simple one, with jewellery being so hard to get these days, but I don't mind.' She showed Lottie the modest silver band. 'As Lawrence says, it's easier for a camel to go through the eye of a needle than—'

'A rich man and so forth,' Lottie concluded with a dull huff. 'Oh, come on, Grace. Even you must enjoy a little spoiling every so often. It isn't every day you get engaged.' She sighed dramatically. 'Just think. It won't be long before I'll be Lady Lottie Flynn and you'll be Mrs Grace Fairgrave.'

A breath caught in Grace's throat, but she quickly turned it into a lilting laugh. 'Mrs Grace Fairgrave, how odd it's going to be!'

'You're not nervous, are you?'

Grace cast her an uncertain glance. 'Of course I am, aren't you? Getting married is a serious step, a big commitment.'

But Lottie only replied, 'Not me, I can't wait to get married! I'd run off and do it tomorrow if I could. Like I've always said, you know when it's right – and it's certainly right for me and Flynn!' Lottie looked ebullient at the thought, then as she saw her friend's face, she asked more hesitantly, 'Don't you feel that way about Lawrence?'

Grace studied the daffodils she was arranging as she thought about her answer. 'It's not quite like that for me. I think there are lots of different kinds of love, and my love for Lawrence is a quieter, steadier love. He's a good man, and he makes me feel as though I'll always be valued, and that's enough for me. I've never been one for great bursts of emotion, so I'm not sure why getting married should be any different.'

But Lottie was dwelling on her own nuptials. 'I can't wait for the honeymoon. Flynn says he knows a lovely little inn on the

Dorset coast. We'll cosy up together in their best room and have dinner brought to us in bed.' She slapped her hand in front of her mouth and giggled. 'You're probably doing the same, I bet?'

'Lawrence can only get one night off, and we're going to stay in a hotel in Canterbury. The cathedral has a museum he likes to visit.' She stopped at the sight of Lottie's horrified face.

'Oh, come on, Grace. Surely, you'll be keen for more than a museum.' Lottie laughed. 'The way Flynn looks at me simply makes my body melt. And when he starts to kiss, well, I'm finding it hard to tell him to stop.' She giggled, giving Grace a playful nudge. 'Is it the same with Lawrence?'

'Y-yes,' she stammered uncertainly. 'Although we're being very good about saving all that until after the wedding.'

'But you must have had a jolly good kiss.'

'W-well,' Grace stammered, unsure if it wasn't horribly disloyal to confess it out loud. 'Actually, we haven't. It's not long to wait, so why ruin it all beforehand?'

Lottie pulled her over to the front pew and sat her down. 'It's not often that I feel the need to tell you anything, Grace, as you're usually the sensible one, but I really must insist that you drop your high morals this once and let the man give you a good, hearty kiss. You'll never know if you're right for each other until you do, no matter what you say about his quiet, steady love. There's such a thing as being *too* quiet, you know.'

Inside, Grace quelled a new wave of panic. What on earth would Lottie think if she knew the truth, that it was Lawrence who was holding back? She'd tried to put it out of her mind, but there it was, larger than life, leaving her wondering if he was interested in her in that way. If anyone ever would be.

Lottie eyed her quizzically. 'Grace, are you all right?'

But Grace hastily gathered the cleaning rags together to leave. 'Of course I am. Now stop asking me silly questions. I have a lot of parish calls to make this afternoon.'

'Who is it today?' Lottie trailed behind as Grace walked to the door.

'Mr Farlow dislocated his hip, poor thing, and there's a long list of others. We'll have to have this conversation later.' Grace scooped up her basket from the back pew and headed outside.

At the door, Lottie bid her a bewildered good-bye, leaving Grace to hurry down the track to the glen, walking rapidly to diffuse her frustration. There was nothing to question, after all. Her marriage was going to be absolutely fine. It simply had to be.

Mr Farlow lived in a remote cottage on the Aldhurst estate, and she increased her pace, focusing on her errands to blot out Lottie and her questions. As she pulled together her old brown coat, she thought about the difficulties in getting clothes for her honeymoon. The government's Wool Control meant that most of it went into uniforms, and Grace sighed that perhaps joining up had its perks. Maybe she would get some slacks, she thought, remembering how good they looked on Cressida. The war had made them popular, not least because they overcame the near impossibility of getting stockings. Fuel rations had made cycling de rigueur, and war work had made trousers all the more practical – part of the new Functional Fashion all the newspapers talked about. She could keep them hidden from Lawrence, at least until the end of the war.

It wasn't until she was going past the fields, bright spring saplings pushing up through the brown earth, that she saw a figure in the distance cutting onto the path ahead from the wood, and she faltered.

It was Hugh.

What was he doing here? It was on the outer reaches of the estate's land. No one from the manor had set foot in the area for years.

Wondering if she could avoid him, she looked for a break in the path. But it was too late. He had seen her.

Her quarrel with him at the Darley Grange reception had been embarrassing and clumsy – the result of too much punch. That said, she absolutely stood by her views that his repossession of the village hall was profoundly misplaced. And even though he'd retracted it and donated some crockery, Grace was still mistrustful.

Today he looked casual, wearing a country jacket instead of his usual London suit, his hands in his pockets. As he saw her, he paused, as if deliberating, but then his pace quickened and he came towards her.

'Grace, what are you doing in this neck of the woods?' His eyes went to the basket on her arm, her brown coat, and the pilling maroon beret on her head.

She gazed past him, as if in a hurry. 'I'm visiting parishioners. My first port of call is Mr Farlow.'

With a glance in the direction she was heading, he frowned. 'Does Mr Farlow live on estate property?'

How ignorant he was! 'Don't you know your own employees? He was injured falling from the roof of one of *your* barns,' she snapped. 'His cottage is on the track beside the stream.'

At least he had the decency to look abashed. 'I haven't spent enough time here, getting to know everyone. I can see that now.' He leaned forward to take her basket. 'Let me come with you. Perhaps you can introduce us?'

She took a step to the side so that he couldn't take the basket. 'I'm perfectly fine by myself.'

'Look, Grace,' he pushed his hair back, his hand lingering on the nape of his neck, 'I'm sorry about the village hall. I didn't mean to importune the villagers. I was wrong to step in without confirming that it was all agreed. You were right to point out my mistake.'

'I'm glad to hear that. Your people in the government think you're so important, but it's villagers like us who are holding the country together in this war, the little groups sewing and knitting, looking after other people's children, learning to defend a village if need be. We're the ones the government should be supporting.'

He made a closed-lipped nod in recognition. 'I agree. I should have been more thoughtful.' Then he looked at the ground. 'Grace, we used to be such good friends. Is there a chance we can be so again? I don't like this animosity between us.'

She shrugged, the memory of his disdainful face as he saw her in the drawing room difficult to push aside. 'We live in opposite worlds, Hugh. You're part of the institution at the top, and I'm the parish worker at the bottom. You give orders, while I help those who have been hurt by those orders.' She looked ahead, down the path to Mr Farlow's cottage. 'I'm not sure we have anything in common anymore.'

'But surely, as a statesman I'm doing precisely the same as you, helping the people, only I'm defending them from invasion, ensuring husbands and sons are looked after properly in prisoner-of-war camps, putting in place procedures to keep everyone fed and clothed. It's in a different setting, but aren't we both working to the same ends?' He took a step forward. 'I was wrong before. I never realized how much my father neglected to consider the people he was supposed to be looking after. I didn't have a good example to follow when I took his place.'

'Your father put us all down, demolished any respect for those who live in the manor.'

He slowly shook his head. 'I knew he could be pompous and selfish, but I didn't realize he was so very' – he paused, trying to find the right word – 'callous.'

'Perhaps if you feel able to become a proper lord, you can try to make up for it, Hugh. You can start off by treating the villagers as people, not just as a source of revenue for your estate.'

The colour had drained from his face, and he stood for a moment, thinking.

'I'd better get on,' she said. 'I have a lot to do. My Sunday afternoon parish calls have been growing with the war, someone new every week dealt a difficult card.' Her voice had softened, and she realized that she felt sorry for him – he really had no example to follow at all. 'It might not be the right time to say this, Hugh, but now that your father's gone, it's your turn. You can shrug off his influence, decide to take a different path. The village would thank you for it.'

He paused in thought, and then said, 'Perhaps you could let me come with you today, Grace? I'd really like to see Mr Farlow, help if I can.'

With a shrug, she said, 'All right. He is your employee, after all.'

She continued down to the riverbank, and he joined her, keeping her pace.

'Who else do you have on your list today?' he asked.

'Two older couples with lost sons, a young widow, and an elderly father, now all on his own since his daughter was killed in the Blitz.' She patted the basket. 'I have a small package of scones for each of them.'

'That's a lot. Do you have time to visit them all?'

'No one else will do it if I don't,' she replied. 'I don't like to think of anyone grieving on their own.'

She felt his eyes on her but resolutely looked ahead.

'I'm beginning to wonder if it's you who's on your own.' His voice was gentle, careful.

'Don't be ridiculous. I'm surrounded by people: my father, the parishioners, the Sewing Circle, the ARP—'

'But it's always *you* helping *them*, Grace. There's a self-sacrifice about you these days, as if everyone else comes before you. Supporting others is a wonderful virtue, but sometimes you need help too. Everyone does.'

'I had to learn to put myself last,' she snapped back at him.

'My father collapsed after my mother died, and I learned that if I didn't hold everything together – my father, my village, my world – then no one else would.'

'Can't you ask someone else to help?'

She felt her pace quicken. 'Who has time? It's too much to ask. In any case, I'm fine. Unlike other individuals, I enjoy helping people. It's what I've been brought up to do, and I'll continue to do that, even after I'm married.'

'I can't believe how much you've changed since we were children,' he said. 'You were such a tomboy when you were young, a hoyden even.' He looked up at Aldhurst Hill in the distance. 'Don't you remember how we built a wigwam out of tree branches and stayed up late watching for badgers? You were always kind to everyone, but you had no interest in the parish. You wanted adventure, something more out of life.'

'I was a child then. It was my mother helping with the parish. Now it's my turn.' She marched ahead, hurrying.

They had reached a rundown stone cottage beside the stream, the long grasses around the building making it look desolate and neglected. Beside the old door were the woody remnants of bushes. Hugh's hand went up to one. 'Cressida told me that there used to be rose bushes all over the estate. My great-grandfather had them planted in the manor's heyday, I believe, because they were his wife's favourites. An act of love.' There was a softness to his voice, but then it changed. 'It seems that my father let them all go to ruin.' He glanced at the dilapidated building. The roses weren't the only thing he had let fall into disrepair.

Grace knocked on the battered wooden door. 'Mr Farlow, are you there?'

A voice from inside called, 'Is that you, Grace?'

By anyone's reckoning, the man who appeared at the door looked far too old to be mending a roof, if indeed he should be working at all. Small and bent, he leaned on an old walking stick. His face beamed at the sight of Grace, and he put a hand on her arm. 'Will you come in for tea? I saved my chocolate from the rations to give you.'

As Grace stepped forward, his eyes focused on Hugh.

'Oh, you brought a friend.' Then he leaned over and chuckled, 'Is this your young man?'

'No, no.' She felt the blood rush to her face. 'This is Hugh – Mr Hugh Westcott – from the manor.'

Hugh put a hand forward. 'I think we met at the large gathering of staff after my father's death,' he said, a cheery nod overriding the discomforting reality that neither worker nor employer recalled each other.

She could tell that the old man was unsettled by Hugh's presence, his smile weakening as he showed them inside.

'What a cosy place.' Hugh had the manners not to react to the simplicity of the hovel, the smell of unwashed clothes, the dirt on the floor. Only a few small, square windows let in a dull light, and a small but lively fire in the hearth filled the room with a flickering, amber glow.

'Why don't you help Mr Farlow put the kettle on, Hugh?' Grace said. 'It's the pot on the right.'

Turning to Mr Farlow, Hugh said, 'Little does she know that I have to make my own tea when I'm in London, and I make a very good pot too.'

'We'll see about that,' Mr Farlow said in a way that showed he wasn't kowtowing to him, lord of the manor or not. He was of an age not to care what people thought, after all. But then he added pointedly, 'Your father wouldn't have even drunk a cup of tea with the likes of me, let alone made one.'

While not rude precisely, it was antagonistic. But Hugh only nodded, getting on with the tea, saying as cheerily as he could, 'Well I'm not my father, and I must say I'm very pleased to meet you properly.'

Mr Farlow's mouth moved hurriedly as he built up to speak. 'My brother died working this land, and do you know what your father said?'

There was a tenseness in Hugh's form. 'No.'

'Nothing.' The old man took a step towards Hugh, his finger outstretched in bitterness. 'He never cared a jot about us folk working the land for him. When the money started running low – which it always did with him in charge – he'd come up with ways to get more out of us. And then he'd tell us to be grateful, grateful to him for letting us work for nothing.'

'I'm sorry that he wasn't as good an employer as he could have been,' Hugh said gently. 'In fact, I've been learning more about how unfeeling he could be.' He exchanged a look with Grace. 'And on that note, if you don't mind my saying, Mr Farlow, you shouldn't be mending a roof at your age.'

'I like to work. It keeps me busy, and I need the money, now I'm on my own.'

Hugh took a seat beside him, pulled the chair closer. 'But there must be less dangerous tasks? Let me speak to the estate manager and see if we can find something more suitable.'

The water began to boil, and he went to take the kettle off the small cooker.

Grace pulled a bag of scones from her basket. 'I always say that a good estate should be a working community, not a business.'

'That's a good way of putting it,' Hugh said.

During tea, emotions calmed, and by the time they left, Mr Farlow at least nodded good-bye to Hugh. 'I'll give you the benefit of the doubt, Mr Hugh. If you stick with Grace, you'll find out how things work around here.'

The other visits went far more smoothly, people bustling around with excitement that the lord of the manor had come for tea, although it became clear from others that their feelings

about the Westcott family were not at all warm. Elsie Carter
said plainly that the Westcotts had neglected their duty as village attendants, and Mr Porter said that if a certain ditty
written in the men's lavatory of the village pub had any truth
in it, Eustace Westcott should stick his precious checkbook up
a certain part of his anatomy.

Dusk was setting in as they left the last house, walking slowly
to the crossroads beside the church, where they would part ways.
Above the oak tree in the graveyard a rippled mackerel sky
glowed a gleaming golden pink against the valley, and Grace
battled to find a good way to end what was probably a difficult,
uncomfortable afternoon for Hugh.

'You bore up well,' she said at last.

Gently, he laughed. 'It's not easy, discovering that you're the
bane of the village – or at least your father was.' He sighed. 'But
I'm glad I know. At least now I can see what I have to do. It's a
great responsibility, and I want to tend to it well.'

'I've found that often it's the little things that count the most.
Sometimes all they need to know is that someone's thinking
about them, caring. Letting us keep the hall is a good start.'

He glanced down the lane, pondering, then looked back at
her. 'Thank you, Grace, for taking me today. I learned a great
deal more than I would have thought.'

'I'm glad we bumped into each other,' she said. 'It was good
that you came.'

'I hope we're friends again, Grace.' He put a hand out to
shake hers, and she took it.

'All right, friends it is.'

Yet his smile was thoughtful. 'I don't know about you, but I
could do with a good friend at the moment.'

'You probably have plenty of friends in London. I heard that
you have a young lady there too.'

There was a change in his posture, a twist away from her as

he looked over the valley. 'A friend is different from that though, don't you think?'

'In what way?'

The colour of the sunset reflected on his profile. 'A friend doesn't have anything to gain or lose. Friendships contain no promises.' He let out a small sigh, then glanced in the direction of the manor. 'I should be getting back. Thank you again, Grace.'

'Cheerio,' she said with a smile, and then as she reached the vicarage door, she paused to watch him heading down the lane away from her. Just before he went out of sight, he turned back, lifting his hand to wave, and the action was so natural, so spirited, that all she could see was the boy she had known, disappearing away from her, just out of reach.

VIOLET

Violet's hair had grown approximately half an inch, and with the help of a pair of first-aid scissors, Lena had managed to 'tidy it up' into a neat kind of shingle cut, parted at the side.

'I'd say you can get away with calling it a Liberty Cut, Vee. That's the patriotic one all the officers talk about, short up the back and not afraid to show the ears.' Lena chuckled. 'At least we're allowed a little plain makeup, and your hair's a good colour too, the blonde makes it look a bit more glamorous. I've put a drop of oil on it to stop it sticking out so much, but it's still looking a bit tufty, I'm afraid, Vee.'

'Oh, blast it all!' Violet said with a huff. 'It's all because of that beastly sergeant. I'll get my own back on her once we're out in civvy street.'

Lena nudged her playfully. 'You'd be better off staying out of trouble. Look what they've done to poor Becky.'

The girl had been found wanting, first on the marching ground, then on cleaning duty in the latrines, and finally on her night off, when she was discovered in the gentlemen's toilets of the Bull's Head in the arms of a quartermaster. Rather than send her to detention, the sergeant had her do extra work, which entailed acting as her personal servant: cleaning, ironing, and making beds as necessary.

Violet, meanwhile, had been continually pulled out of ranks for minor misdemeanours.

'They all pick on me,' Violet complained. 'Just because I come from a better class. It isn't fair.'

But Lena cackled with laughter. 'It's completely fair. Look at you, with your fancy manor and your friends in high places. The rest of us have to do the best we can, struggling to stay alive, while you're swanning around acting all la-di-da.' She grinned. 'Well, now you're a private, the same as the rest of us. For once in your life, we're just the same, you and me.'

'It's you and *I*, Lena,' Violet corrected with an exasperated sigh.

A few weeks into her incarceration and Violet had been shocked at how fast she'd adapted, although she doubted she could ever get used to the upheaval in the social order. After long nights spent polishing the officers' boots, peeling potatoes, and cleaning the hallway with a toothbrush, she'd been exhausted enough to submit to her situation and behave herself. At least no one she knew was there to see her humiliation at having to answer to the lower classes. As soon as training was over, she could forget about it once and for all.

At the end of the first three weeks, the young cadets had been separated into groups to train for their specific jobs. Violet was pleased to see that Lena was also picked for the transport corps, while poor Becky had been put into the cleaning regiment.

'It's the worst job going,' she'd moaned. 'Fancy doing your bit for the war by scrubbing toilets.'

After drill every morning, the transport group went to a classroom to learn about engines, and then they were taken to various garages to open up the hoods of military vehicles, trucks, and motorcycles. They needed to make repairs themselves, on the road, as part of their job. After lunch, they were taken out in each of the vehicles, and although Violet had been borrowing her father's Bentley since she was fifteen, the rules of military driving were frustratingly rigorous.

No passing, no tailgating, and definitely no speeding, unless one was driving an ambulance or fire vehicle – Violet wanted to know how to get one of *those* assignments.

At the end of their training, they had to take a series of tests and exams in order to pass into active duty, and no one was keener than Violet to be finished.

'Why don't you bat your eyelashes at the male examiner?' Lena teased. 'Didn't I hear you brag that every man can be won over?'

Violet huffed. 'It doesn't work with this ridiculous haircut. In any case, everyone here sees me as a joke. I'm the target for all their pent-up proletariat grievances.'

Lena was an odd choice of friend, blending supportiveness interspersed with vaguely insulting home truths, all delivered with an inappropriate air of entertainment. Violet knew she should be miffed, but she couldn't help being rather amused too. It had also begun to dawn on her that her high status in life was not, as her father had told her, because of her superior family blood, but simply a fluke of birth.

In essence, she was much the same as everyone else. After all, what was special about her now? Uniforms were a social leveller, and now that she looked the same as the likes of Becky, she had no choice but to pull up her woollen socks and get on with it. In any case, out of the spotlight and away from the expectations of society and class, it didn't matter so much what she said or did. And if she wanted to make friends with a brash London cockney, why shouldn't she?

Lena laughed. 'You're secretly a bit of a dab hand at this

mechanical stuff, aren't you, Vee?' She jabbed a finger at her. 'Who would have pegged you as a brainbox, eh?'

'Oh, you're such a joker! I've never been able to do anything remotely clever.'

'Bet you never even tried.' Then Lena's eyes narrowed. 'I hope you're not one of those ladies who pretends to be stupid because they think that's what men like.'

'Of course not!' Violet protested. But a puzzled frown came over her face. 'But sometimes it's just easier to act frivolous – the path of least resistance, and all that. In any case, if it weren't for this war, I'd be living my normal life and I wouldn't have any need to do anything clever, would I? All I would need to know is where to seat everyone at a banquet, how to mix a good Sidecar, and when to use the right sort of gloves. I don't need to be good at engines for that.'

'Do you ever wonder why men like stupid women?' Lena nudged her jokingly.

'Because we entertain them?' she said, remembering the good old days, practising her witty remarks, finding lighthearted trivia to make men laugh. Hadn't Lord Ombersley's pet name for her been his 'little ninny'? She frowned at the thought but then remembered what her father had told her. 'Men need us to take their minds off their work and all the important, awful things that are happening in the world. They like to think that we women are above all that, beautiful creatures who aren't tainted with life's drudgery and horrors.'

Lena shook her head. 'Oh, Vee. That's not why at all. It's because if we're told we're stupid, we won't question anything.' She gave a little laugh. 'Or complain. We'd do as we're told. For someone who hates all the orders you get around here, I'm surprised you'd be happy to take them from a husband.'

The bell rang, as it perpetually seemed to do, and their conversation was left there, hanging in the air.

Yet the remark remained with Violet. Had she been trained to act stupid, her father's old-fashioned ways instilled into her as he pointed out what other society women were doing and how she should copy them? She had taken delight in showing off how charmingly uneducated she was, congratulating herself at her proficiency in doing so. But now she thought about it, that seemed not only pointless but rather perilous as well. And she wondered if perhaps she herself had started to believe she was a 'little ninny' too.

The notion that she was actually far cleverer than she'd let on seemed to take hold and spur her on as she stepped into the garage for the practical element of her final exam.

The beefy male training officer stood, his hands on his hips, beside a large truck. He'd spent every lesson ridiculing her, and as he saw her, a chuckle came out of the corner of his mouth. 'If it isn't lady muck, afraid to get her hands dirty.'

Instead of backing down or arguing back, she held herself taller, snapping to attention. 'Sir.'

He gestured to the vehicle. 'Right, first off, we'll have a look at this truck engine, shall we? It has a problem, and you need to find out what it is.' A smirk covered his face, and she knew it wasn't going to be anything easy.

He was using this test – like he'd used the entire course – to show her who was boss.

The first thing she did was climb into the cabin and start the engine. It didn't even turn, which indicated that there was a problem with the ignition, if not more. Then she lifted the bonnet and made the preliminary checks. Still nothing.

Trying another tack, she went into the back of the truck and found the starting handle. She brought it to the front of the engine, inserted it into the hole below the radiator, and then began the hefty job of turning it. It was stiff, but undeterred, she continued, until the engine began to shudder.

She had it. He'd given her a trick problem, and she'd spotted it.

The officer had his arms folded, foot tapping. 'Well, mend it then! You're running out of time, Private Westcott.'

Within minutes, she had the ignition fuses out, testing and replacing them until she had the engine starting like clockwork.

She smirked as he belligerently made a note on his clipboard.

'Send in the next candidate,' was his only remark as she strutted out, a grin on her face.

Thus it was that Violet passed through training with excellent scores, among the top in engineering and mechanics.

'How very different from what I was expecting,' she mused as the train pulled into Aldhurst station the following evening. Kit bag over her shoulder, she straightened her uniform before alighting from the train, and there was a swing to her step as she headed through the darkening village towards home. The weeks she'd been away felt like a few hours and a thousand years all at once – so much had changed. Now she was to have a few days' leave before reporting for duty, which for her was at Darley Grange, a mile's walk from home. Provided she wasn't needed on site, she was allowed to live at home – at least Hugh had got something right.

But just when she longed for someone to admire her uniform, Violet felt rather miffed that the village was deserted. The shop was already closed, the vicarage looked dark, and while there was often a little activity outside the pub, tonight it was empty.

'Perhaps everyone's in the village hall,' she muttered, deciding to poke her head in to see. It was a Tuesday, and some of the Sewing Circle might be there early.

At the door, she paused, listening hard. But all she heard was some shuffling noises and a few incoherent voices.

'Hello?' She opened the door slightly and spied inside.

'Violet?' A jumble of voices echoed around the hall.

First Lottie Kettlewell, followed by Grace and Cressida, dashed over to greet her.

'And in uniform!' Cressida said. 'Let's have a look at you!'

And Violet was pulled into the room for them all to see. 'You look . . . smart, efficient . . . different . . .'

'And what's happened to your hair?' Mrs Todd squawked, trying to look underneath her cap.

Without more ado, Violet simply took off her hat, running her hand through the short crop and smoothing it down. 'No more curls.'

'Goodness!' Mrs Bisgood declared. 'You look, well, not at all like you used to look, if you don't mind me saying.'

'That uniform and the hair, it's like a disguise, isn't it?' Mrs Todd said with a laugh. 'Do you turn back into the usual Violet once you take it off?'

'Not at all! But it does make you feel part of the great force, especially when you first go out into that parade ground, every-one looking the same, an army of women.' Violet laughed, but she felt it falling a little flat.

After six jaunty weeks with the ATS girls, Violet was sur-prised by the restraint of the Sewing Circle. Then as she saw Martha exchanging a smirk with Mrs Todd, she realized how she'd always kept her distance from them, how she'd gone to meetings only when she wanted the ladies to do something for her.

'I learned a thing or two while I was away,' she said in a softer, more congenial tone. 'And I realized that perhaps I wasn't al-ways the best leader for the Sewing Circle.'

'Actually, you've never really been our leader at all,' Martha said, crossing her arms. 'It's always been Mrs Bisgood.'

'I know. I just wanted to say that I'd like to be a proper mem-ber of the group now.' She smiled hopefully. 'But not as a figure-head this time. I'm happy to be a normal, everyday helper. Sewing may not be my strong point, but I'm willing to learn and do what I can.'

The others looked at each other in surprise, which Violet had to admit was perhaps well deserved, and she took the proffered seat beside Mrs Bisgood.

'Well, let's start by showing you how to mend this skirt for the jumble sale.'

Calmly following instructions, Violet began to sew, moving on to a pair of boy's shorts and then a pinafore dress.

As they worked, Lottie and Mrs Todd entertained everyone with gossip and funny tales from the grapevine, and it struck Violet how she'd missed out on so much. Her father had always told her how menial the villagers were, that it was her place to be above them, but now she wondered if he'd been wrong. After all, if you're presiding over a village, you need to get to know it in order to help, don't you?

Afterwards, Cressida walked home with her, amazed by her transition. 'My goodness, army life has put a real spirit into you, I must say. What happened?'

She felt a blush coming to her face. 'Well, it was rather more fun than I was expecting, if you ignore the marching and hair cutting and so forth. And as it happens, I turned out to be rather good at mechanics, and I did frightfully well in the clerical duties too.' She grinned, taking Cressida's arm. 'I've decided that I really ought to do the same with my life, organize it better. How incredibly vapid I've been, sitting at home, moaning about my father's death and the inconveniences of war, when I should have been putting plans into action, making things happen instead of waiting for my father or Hugh to help.'

Quizzically, Cressida enquired, 'And what plans do you have in mind?'

Violet grinned as her eyes met Cressida's. 'For now at least, I plan to be a jolly good army driver.'

CRESSIDA

Whatever Cressida had expected her life in Aldhurst to be, she hadn't anticipated it to be quite so busy. There was a lot to catch up on with the ARP, and far from being a dull little group, the Sewing Circle was a dynamic force, especially when it came to raising money for the war effort. There were plenty of extra meetings and two special Saturday gatherings, the first to sort out the jumble sale and the second to hold it.

'This must have been the largest sale in Kent,' Lottie insisted as they folded tables and swept the floor afterwards. 'And the way the crowd went straight for the school uniforms, you'd have thought they were gold dust.'

'You try wearing a skirt two sizes too small,' Martha said pointedly.

They'd kept the sale going into the evening to cater to the new need to work on Saturdays, and outside it was already dark, the bright lights inside the hall blacked out with curtains. Mrs Bisgood's record player was pounding out 'Anything Goes' as they swayed and sang along while they cleared up, Mrs Todd muddling through the words.

Mrs Bisgood eyed the homemade scones she'd been saving for after the clean-up as she put away the remaining clothes.

'Only a few very tattered clothes weren't sold. Everyone's become so good at doing up old clothes that anything will do –
they can be patched or dressed up to make anything you like.'
She took a smell of a man's shirt. 'Although some of them are a
bit whiffy now that laundry soap is so hard to get. It doesn't
help that we're only supposed to have a five-inch bath twice a
week to save fuel.'

'Have you tried the new deodorant?' Lottie said. 'It's not
easy to get, but we all need it in the factory, being so close to
each other. Some of the girls say it's bad for you, but I can't see
how. It's not always easy to find in the shops, but you can dab
a bit of bicarbonate of soda under your arms instead if need
be.'

'Sounds a bit newfangled to me.' Mrs Todd had donned her
purchase from the sale: a bright red cape with two holes for her
hands. 'Oh, I do love a jumble sale. It's a chance to find something a bit different. It's like stepping into someone else's shoes,
isn't it?'

'And I found a new coat.' Lottie held up an aging fur.

'Filled with insects,' Martha yelled, tugging it away in horror.

However much Cressida wanted to stay and enjoy the
clearing-up party, it was time for her to leave. Tonight she had
ARP duty, this time with Ben, and after ebullient cheerios from
the group, she took her leave.

A bright full moon spilled a milky light over the village roof-
tops, the spring bringing some warmer weather, and Cressida
filled her lungs with the fresh evening air as she watched Ben
walk over from the vicarage.

'Well done with the jumble sale,' he grinned. 'I gather it was
the best that Kent has ever known.'

She laughed. 'You've been talking to Lottie, haven't you?'

They made their way past the clutch of cottages on Church
Lane. There was something peaceful about keeping watch over

the village, as if they were tucking everyone up in bed for the evening.

'The evenings are so beautiful here,' she said, as the hubbub of her sewing friends in the hall faded into the distance. 'Everyone in London is paranoid when there's a full moon. A bombers' moon, they call it, the visibility helping the Nazis see where to bomb.'

It was good to be partnered with Ben Carlisle, his tall, measured form beside her as they walked, his gentle wit and deeper understanding of the world perfect for a great discussion, from art and books to rivers and birds. Since the first ARP meeting, they'd rekindled their friendship. Ben had invited her to the vicarage a few times, and he'd stop for a chat whenever they bumped into each other in the village.

But until now, the conversation had been light, not touching the topics they both knew stirred the other during the night: the terrors of the last war, the Blitz, and Jack.

'There was a full moon on the night my house was bombed.' She drew a deep breath, unsure whether to go on.

'It must have been dreadful. I can't imagine how frightening it must have been.' There was something in the kindness in his voice, in their friendship going back so many years – she knew that it made her drop her guard.

'It was terrifying, to be honest. Sometimes I have bad dreams: There was this dog . . .' Her voice trailed off.

'Carry on,' Ben said. 'I certainly know what nightmares can be like.'

But she chose not to, not wanting to burden him, or perhaps herself, on such a beautiful spring evening. Specks of pollen and dandelion fluff were held captive in the evening air. Two deer paused in the lane in front of them, their eyes glistening in the moonlight as warily they watched: friend or foe? Ben pulled Cressida to a halt, and for a moment, the two pairs watched each other, and Cressida felt a sudden connection with them. After all, weren't they all simply creatures, trying to stay alive?

But then one of the deer looked at the other, and as they sprang together into the woods, Cressida realized there was more to their lives than just staying alive; they were staying together.

'It's a good night for nature-watching,' Ben said as they resumed their walk. 'We might even see a hedgehog or a badger.'

'It's a lovely season to be here. Something about the smell of spring takes me back to my childhood, the sweet honeysuckle, the heady lavender,' she said. 'You can't get this in London. From my old balcony, all I could see was the back of the neighbour's house. Our wildlife might be a pigeon or the occasional fox.'

'You must miss your life in London, your smart Chelsea house.' He took her arm in his, as if trying to console her, and a pang of grief shot through her, as if this one kind gesture had somehow unlatched a mass of hurt.

'It's all frightfully inconvenient.' She tried to laugh it off, but a lump caught in her throat, and she found herself saying, 'I lost everything I have in one night. But the strange thing was that it made me realize how little like a home it truly was. It was a place where I could escape from the world, prepare myself for the next day. But it was never somewhere I enjoyed. The place,' she paused, 'it lacked joy for me. I can see that now.'

'And now you're back in Aldhurst Manor. How odd it must be to return to the place where you grew up.'

'I confess, it wouldn't have been my first choice. I thought it would remind me of the past too much. But my niece and nephew are welcoming, and the village is far more bustling and friendly than I remember.'

He smiled. 'It's always been busy. Do you remember when we were young, the dances and the fairs. The hunt balls were splendid affairs, the magic of those evenings, the swirl of the gowns around the vast ballroom floor. Even then, you were always well-dressed, I recall, the most beautiful girl everywhere you went. Jack felt like the luckiest man on earth to have you.'

'I was lucky to have him. He made me feel alive, with our precious stolen moments, far away from the stifling manor. How fun and giddy everything was when we were together. He made everything reel with the sheer euphoria of life.'

'Jack was like that, full of spirit and laughter – glad to be alive.'

'You two were partners in crime in those days, dressed in your tailcoats, joking and laughing, always together.'

'Even at the end.' Ben's voice became taut, quiet. 'We both went to war together, fell together, and for some reason, I'm the one who lived to tell the tale. I couldn't save him.'

'Who could have known what it would be like? No one could possibly have imagined it. I know you would have done anything you could have to save him, but you can't save everyone, vicar or not.'

She pulled his arm in closer, and slowly as they walked, they began to unfold their pasts. And the more they talked, the more she remembered, her memories blending with his as they prompted each other, laughing and smiling, trying to hold back their tears.

'I hope I'm not stirring up too many memories,' he said.

'I've spent too many years trying to avoid them – avoid Aldhurst completely. It almost felt like I had too many feelings, and if I let them out they'd get tangled chaotically inside me, and I just needed to push them to the back of my brain in order to keep going.'

'I know that feeling all too well,' he said softly. 'What you need to do is divide what is important from the jumble, then let everything else fall gently back into place.'

Through the silence, she began to feel a rare peacefulness come over her, as still as the quiet, moonlit night.

They walked in silence up the lane, becoming aware of a faint hum in the distance that began to rise to a thrum.

'It's a plane,' Ben said quietly.

They stopped in the middle of the road, the hedgerows and fields around them seeming to pause too, as if nature itself were aware of the threat.

The noise gathered impetus, increasing in range and ferocity, stirring the air around them. Ben retreated beneath a tree beside the lane, pulling her back to shelter with him. From there, they watched the horizon, the church spire and Aldhurst Hill silhouetted in the moonlight.

'It's coming from London,' Cressida whispered. 'Does that mean it's ours or theirs?'

'It might be one of theirs, homeward bound after bombing London. Sometimes they shed any extra bombs they have over Kent, lightening the load to get over the Channel. We need to keep watch.'

Cressida whispered, 'Should we sound the siren?'

'It's too late. It'll be over us before we've even reached the office.'

The noise rose to a deafening roar, and then it appeared.

A single grey-black bomber thrust through the sky, the engine vibrating the air around them.

'It's theirs.' Ben raised his voice as the engine echoed loudly through the night. 'A Heinkel, by the look of it.'

Together they stood as it came closer, the throb building, and then, through the darkness they watched as its dark underbelly opened, the silhouette of bombs coming down over Aldhurst Hill, and then more coming closer towards the village.

'Quick, get down!' Ben shouted.

And without a pause, he pulled her down to the ground, partially covering her body with his own, leaning on his hands so as not to crush her, his face so close that she could feel the heat of his breath. It was a chivalrous move she'd heard about, people shielding others, how it could mean the difference between life and death for the person underneath.

The tremendous blow of one explosion and then another shook the ground beneath them, each one closer to the village. Cressida felt a surge of panic. Memories of her house being bombed, that dreadful feeling of the earth giving way – her life on a knife edge – sliced through her as sharp and frightening as a cold blade, a scream coming out of her.

'Cressida?' It was Ben's voice, soft but urgent. He pulled away from her. 'Cressida? Are you all right?'

'Ben?' Mumbling his name, her eyes flickered open, bringing her back to earth, remembering where she was. The explosions had stopped, the roar of the plane falling away as it banked, heading out towards the sea.

And then there was silence.

As the dust settled, Ben carefully clambered to his feet, reaching down to help her up. She could feel that he too was shaking.

'It was in the next field, too close for comfort.' His voice juddered as he tried to control his fear, and she remembered his shell shock – what it must feel like if you've been bombed in a trench day after day and then left for dead.

Cressida looked at the full moon, still spreading its milky light over the village, impervious to the brutal human conflict below.

What was it all for?

A shudder of fear went through her, and she felt something inside her break. It was as if all the bravado was gone, all the upright practicality upon which she prided herself had fallen away, replaced by a hollow acceptance that the world wasn't made up of rationality and structure. It was horrific and brutal, so fierce that it could destroy even the quietest of corners.

Ben took her arm. 'We should go back to the office. We need to make calls, alert the proper authorities.'

Wordlessly, they walked back, and Cressida sat fraught on the small bed, while Ben telephoned the Canterbury office.

Then he pulled a bottle from under the eaves. 'Mrs Bisgood keeps something in the cupboard for these kinds of situations.' It was brandy, and he poured a little into two cups. 'I think we both could do with a little, couldn't we?' He sat down beside her. 'You're trembling.'

'I can't seem to stop. It reminded me of the night my house was bombed.'

Slowly, he put a warm arm around her shoulder. 'I think we're friends enough for you to tell me what happened, about your bad dreams, if you'd like.'

A sharp gulp of air had stuck in her throat, guttural and close, and slowly, for the first time, she began to talk about that night. 'My street – my neighbours – were bombed, dead within minutes, burned in their beds, crushed by collapsing roofs, buried alive. Someone's mother, someone's child, someone's baby—' She broke off. 'And then there was that black-and-white dog, a bloody doll in his mouth. I could think only of the child, the poor child . . .' She swallowed hard. 'I could have been gone too. It was sheer luck that someone else's house was bombed first, giving me time to escape. I should have done more to help everyone else.' A tremor went through her, a strange flair of electricity that she had been holding inside. 'That's why I joined the ARP, so that next time I would be able to help. It haunts me every night.'

For a long time, they sat talking, huddled against the world together, the clock on the desk slowly ticking, until Ben slowly pulled away. 'Are you all right?' She nodded, and he got to his feet. 'I need to start the paperwork, and you should get some sleep. Why don't you take the bed for a few hours, and then we can swap over?'

He busied himself, cleaning the cups and putting them back in the small cupboard while she slipped off her shoes and lay down on the bed, pulling the blanket over herself.

'Goodnight,' she said as lightly as she could, but it wasn't until he sat down at the desk and switched the table lamp to its very lowest setting that she felt the cold reality of death stealing into her veins. Quietly, she began to sob for all the fear, for all that she'd lost, for Jack, for her family, for her life.

'Cressida, are you all right?' She felt a warm hand on her shoulder.

Hastily, she wiped her eyes. 'Yes, well, maybe not as all right as I thought I was.'

And then, as softly as he could, he lay down beside her and put his arms around her. It was a gesture of friendship, of unity, and the panic inside her rose and then fell as she felt the disconcerting comfort of another person beside her. It had been such a long time, and a crushing need seemed to uncurl inside her, like a deep hunger desperate for some kind of human contact.

And slowly, she turned and put her arms around him too, returning the favour, the warmth and humanity that he was giving her now shared between them, quietly soothing them as the hours slipped by till dawn.

GRACE

The following Sunday, before making her usual parish visits, Grace was busy in the village hall, the Hanley children chasing each other around the stage. The upper shelf in the large store cupboard had collapsed, breaking and cracking the brackets that held it in place. But as she stood on the wobbly ladder inside the cluttered room, her mind was elsewhere.

Lawrence was arriving on the late afternoon train, and she had to get ready for him, prepare a good dinner, make sure the spare bedroom was tidy. It was the last time she would see him before their wedding, and there was still so much to discuss, so many things up in the air, unsettled.

'Hello,' Hugh called as he entered the hall. 'Grace?'

Ever since the first visit with Mr Farlow, he often helped with her parish work on a Sunday afternoon. Initially, she'd invited him along to open his eyes to his responsibilities, visiting his estate workers so that he could get to know them better. Yet now she found that she simply enjoyed his company.

'Let's get him!' Within moments, the three small Hanley children went charging towards Hugh.

'Hello,' he said, crouching down. 'And who do I have the pleasure of meeting?'

As the children squabbled for his attention, Grace called over from the store cupboard, 'I'm looking after them for the afternoon.'

He shook hands with each of them. 'I hope you're going to behave well for me, because I'm lord of the manor,' he said grandly, and they seemed rather taken aback until the girl giggled and the boys joined in.

'Did you manage to find some spare brackets?' Grace asked.

He raised a bag in his hand. 'There were some spares in the cellars. Let's see if they fit, shall we? Do we have something to keep the children happy? Ah,' he spotted something on the stage. 'What about these boxes of jumble?' He slid one down onto the floor.

Quickly descending from the ladder, Grace hurried over. 'Now you three, would you be my helpers and put these into piles? The clothes go here, the books can go here, and everything else can go here.'

With shrieks and giggles, they dove in, a boy pulling out a shirt made from old flour bags, which were becoming all the more common. The girl found a pair of wooden-soled women's shoes, which had a hinge at the ball of the foot to allow easier walking. Now that leather or rubber soles were impossible to get, clogs were becoming more common. These days, clothes were being made from anything available, old curtains to blackout material and even the cambric used to make architects' drawings. Grace had heard of someone bleaching silk from a funeral parlour, which became 'a very elegant lilac evening gown.'

Sliding an old man's flat cap onto her head to make them laugh, Grace went back to the cupboard, where Hugh was already up the wobbly ladder looking at the shelf.

She pulled up a chair to stand at the other end, and together they detached the broken shelf from the brackets.

'I don't suppose there's a spare plank of wood we could use as a shelf?' he said. 'It doesn't have to fit exactly, but it has to be long enough to reach both of the brackets.' There was a lightness to his voice, an eager camaraderie, reminding her of how he'd been when they were building rafts or dams as children.

She felt it too. Part of her was slipping seamlessly into the carefree girl she'd been, up for adventure. She tugged at the old man's flat cap on her head in mock subservience. 'I'll see if we have some in the vicarage shed.' She glanced in the direction of squeals as the youngsters began trying on the clothes. 'Could you keep an eye on the children?'

Hugh laughed. 'They're having fun. Leave them here. I'm sure we'll be fine together.'

With a hasty 'Be good' to the children, Grace dashed off to the vicarage to find a plank.

When she came back through the double doors, she couldn't help but laugh. There was Hugh with the girl on his shoulders, the boys pointing and shouting, as he stood wearing one of Mrs Todd's multicoloured scarves and a purple ladies' hat.

'Try on another one!' one of the boys yelled, jumping up and down with excitement.

But Hugh's eyes were on the plank. 'I'm afraid you're going to have to try them on by yourselves while Grace and I put up this lovely new shelf.'

He helped her take the plank to the store cupboard.

'It should do the trick.' Hugh pulled over the chair and trod up onto it. 'Could you go up the stepladder at the other end?'

Together they brought the shelf up and lifted it into position, taking it in turns with the screwdriver to attach it to the brackets.

When he'd finished, Hugh stepped back down from the chair. 'Probably not the most precise shelf in the world, but still, it will live to hold large quantities of jumble once more.'

He went to hold the bottom of the ladder for Grace to come down, and as it wobbled, he automatically put his hands on her hips to steady her. The feeling made her start, an unfamiliar heat surging through her.

'Sorry, I don't want you to fall,' he said politely, guiding her down the last few steps.

As she reached the bottom, she turned, and they stood in front of each other, close in the small space, and as the shrieks of the children blurred into the background, Grace could smell the strangely familiar scent of him, feel the warmth from his body so close to hers.

Lightly, he touched the old cap she still wore, pushing it up a little to see her face. 'This hat suits you.' His voice was soft and warm. 'The tomboy is still in there after all.'

'You know, when you first returned to the manor,' she said, 'I thought that you'd grown up to be like your father, but now I can see that the old you is still there too.'

They were standing so close that a new kind of sensation flooded through her – or was it an old sensation, one that had been buried inside for so many years?

'We should put these things away,' she said, although she didn't move.

For a moment, everything seemed to pause, only the beat of her heart and the blood pulsating through her body, as the memory of that last summer day flashed through her mind, his arms around her, lips on hers.

Then suddenly, the sound of the door came from the hall, footsteps entering, the children's laughter falling silent.

The pair jumped apart, and Grace rushed out.

'Lawrence!' she gasped, glued to the spot for an awful moment before springing over to him. 'You're early!'

There he stood, upright in his crisp clerical uniform. 'I made it in time to catch the one o'clock train.' His eyes moved to

Hugh, who had come out of the store cupboard behind her. 'Won't you introduce me to your friend, Grace? I don't think we've met.' He stepped forward, a polite smile on his face.

Had he seen anything? Not that anything had happened – nothing at all.

She studied his poise, his stance, yet all she saw was his usual clerical gravitas.

Quickly calming herself, Grace introduced them. 'Lawrence, this is Mr Hugh Westcott. He lives in Aldhurst Manor. And you're already acquainted with the Hanley youngsters.'

'Pleased to meet you,' Hugh said, curious as he shook Lawrence's hand.

'May peace be with you,' Lawrence said with his usual solemnity, only reminding her that she'd never mentioned Hugh to Lawrence, nor his recent help with the parish work.

And she hadn't said anything about Lawrence to Hugh either, except for his profession.

A bemused look came onto Lawrence's face as he turned back to Grace. 'What's this you have on your head?' Frowning, he took the old cap off in a swift, deft movement.

'Oh, I forgot. I put it on to amuse the children.' Blushing, she took it from him and put it back into the jumble box. The children had fallen silent, eyeing Lawrence with wariness.

And as she turned to look at her husband-to-be, she suddenly saw what the children saw, and probably what Hugh saw too. Lawrence was very much a man of God, wrapped up in his own world. She was going to be his appendage, the vicar's wife. The lighter, happier Grace she was just rediscovering was about to be thrust back into the shadows, just like the old hoyden's cap tossed back into the jumble box. She was to become his companion and helper. His work would be hers. She would become the pleasant and hardworking woman behind the scenes, a worker bee without a life of her own.

Why was it that only a month ago she would have revelled in this honour, but now the idea made her feel somehow wrong – as if it were all meant for another woman, another Grace, someone who didn't exist anymore.

And she could see the same thoughts going through Hugh's mind as his eyes went from her to the staunch clergyman, who was patting his pockets to find his glasses.

Embarrassed, Grace smiled, slipping a hand onto Lawrence's arm. 'We've been mending the shelf in the store cupboard. Hugh has been helping.' She tried to keep her tone light, and while Hugh's gaze lingered, Lawrence adopted his usual compassionate nod, making her wonder if he ever stepped out of his role, if he were ever anything other than a clergyman. She'd always assumed there was more to the private man inside, felt she'd seen glimpses of it. But had she invented it, filled the gaps in her knowledge of him with her own imaginings?

Suddenly, all she wanted was to get Lawrence away, to stop Hugh from spending too much time with him. It was as if she could read Hugh's thoughts: *Do you really have much in common with this man? Are you sure you want to marry him? Could he really make you happy?*

'You're probably gasping for a cup of tea, Lawrence.' A wavering smile hid her discomfort as she drew him to the door, but instead he began to put the jumble on the floor back into the box, ignoring the fact that it was in piles.

'Let's put this away first,' he said in his serious way. 'Cleanliness is next to godliness.' He picked up the hat Hugh had been wearing. 'Such a shame that the war has forced women to go hatless. The government even persuaded the archbishop to declare that it was no longer necessary to wear a hat in church, and stockings too, would you believe it? Decency and decorum gone down the drain to save a little fabric.'

'But they need the fabric for the war, Lawrence darling,' Grace quickly appeased him. 'And it's much less bother for us women, especially with hats so difficult to get. It's almost fashionable to not wear one these days, patriotic even. "Fashion is out of fashion," as the newspapers tell us.'

'Well, I can't wait for it to all go back to normal.'

Hugh had stepped forward to help them put the jumble back into the boxes. 'A naval cleric must be a difficult job, with all the tragedies abroad.'

Lawrence looked up. 'It's what I was put on this earth to do, although I must say that the war has been a tremendous loss for so many, either with their lives, their families, or with injuries and homelessness.'

'Hugh works in the War Office,' Grace said, hoping the conversation was not going to be a long one.

Lawrence shook his head. 'That's a difficult job too, but we're the ones dealing with the casualties. Delivering last rites twenty times a day weighs heavily on the soul.'

'We try our best,' Hugh said. 'There will always be losses, but we aim to keep them to a minimum. I'm constantly aware that these are real men out there, real individuals bravely putting their lives on the line.' He paused, and Grace thought how stressful his job must be, the responsibility for all those men. Behind the adventurous boy, Hugh had always been sensitive – that was probably why they'd got on so well. It must crush him to think that his decisions could lead to people dying.

As they finished clearing away the jumble, Hugh turned to Grace. 'We should be getting these children home. I can go on my own if you let me know where they belong.'

'Thank you, but Lawrence and I can take them back. You go ahead to Mr Farlow's. I baked a pie for him.' She handed him her basket. 'And there's a bit of ham to cheer him up.'

He nodded. 'I'm sure he'll like that.' And after he made his good-byes, Hugh left, the door swinging closed behind him.

'Why are you looking after these children, Grace?' Lawrence asked now that the company had left, watching in horror as the boys began to race chaotically around them. 'Your dedication to the villagers is to be commended, Grace, but this isn't part of your role.'

'Don't you recognize the Hanleys? I offered to take them for the afternoon to give their mother a break.' She urged the children to put on their coats and head through the doors, the girl slipping a small hand into hers. 'Come on,' she said to Lawrence with a smile. 'We'll take them home, and then I'll put on dinner.'

As they walked, she readied herself for his questions about Hugh, their burgeoning friendship, what they were doing in the store cupboard together, but Lawrence's mind was on his duties in Portsmouth. 'Some of the men have had such a horrific time that they've begun to doubt,' he murmured dolefully. 'It has become my role to lift their eyes back to heaven.'

Mrs Hanley was not thrilled to have her offspring returned early, but Lawrence was becoming impatient, and it wasn't long before it was just the two of them, strolling back to the vicarage. She took Lawrence's arm in hers, but somehow it only made her feel more tense. The first few hours of their meetings were always difficult, but didn't everyone with a sweetheart or husband away agree that it wasn't always easy, getting to know each other again, finding that spark?

'I have a loin of pork to roast for dinner.' She'd been delighted to get it, expecting to make the evening a real celebration. But now it seemed to fall a little flat, although she couldn't pinpoint quite why. The reason seemed on the cusp of her fingertips, a barely visible shape hovering in the background of her mind.

'How marvellous.' Lawrence seemed appeased, his pace lifting as he turned to her. 'But how did you get it with all the rations?'

'I joined a pig club with the Kettlewells, and my reward is a joint of pork every few months, ration free.'

'How wonderful.' His arm seemed to grip hers closer, a step towards normality, whatever normality was.

Returning his gesture, she said, 'I'm glad you came early. Once we're home and the joint is on, you can help me choose the readings for our wedding.' The word, which usually made her glow inside, felt scratchy and hot. Wedding nerves, she told herself, quickly adding aloud, 'What we need is a lovely evening making plans.'

'You do need to remember, Grace, that you don't have to make it into a big or complicated event. You have such a busy, hard life with so much parish work to do. I don't want you to be overrun.'

She opened the vicarage door and hurried through to the kitchen. 'It's all right, Lawrence. Dad's a lot better, and I have more help now.' Sitting him down at the kitchen table, she sped around making tea. 'Hugh and Mrs Todd have been sharing out the parish visits, and Lottie and Archie have taken over the up-keep of the church and graveyard. All sorts of people have stepped forward to do what they can. It seems rather silly now to think I was struggling to do it by myself for so long. All I had to do was ask.'

Lawrence sat back, watching her. 'From your letters, I ex-pected you to be a little the worse for wear with the palaver with the wedding dress and so forth, but you look rather well. Have you done something different to your hair?' He leaned around to look.

'Oh, nothing much. It just took a few extra minutes to curl it and pin it back. Cressida taught me.' As she regarded his quiet profile, she acknowledged that had she known Lawrence would come early she might not have done it.

Judging by Lawrence's letters, she could tell that he wasn't overly keen on Grace's new friendship with Cressida. Phrases like, 'I'm surprised you have time with all your parish work,' and 'Sewing is a useful skill, but you already know the basics,' cropped up often.

So he began pensively, 'I know you say that you're learning more about sewing and so forth, but fashion design and new hairstyles are so trivial for a woman of your calibre.' He cleared his throat. 'What's more, I'm not at all sure it's suitable for your role as a vicar's wife – not to mention if I become a deacon.'

'But Cressida's joining the IncSoc Utility Contest – it's an important war initiative that will boost home-front spirit. She said that I can help,' she began, but he held up a hand to stop her.

'But your expertise in the parish is far more valuable. I simply don't like to see you wasting your time.'

Confusion swept over her. How was it wasting her time if it was useful and she enjoyed it?

'But doesn't it matter what I want?' she said in a small voice.

He turned to her, horrified. 'Surely you want to dedicate your life to helping others. That is why we're so very well suited.' He looked earnestly into her eyes. 'You're not like all the other girls, worrying about clothes and your appearance. You're not selfish or silly or vain. You're a good woman, Grace, the one everyone can rely on.'

These last words echoed through her mind. She'd spent the last month realizing that the mantle of responsibility had been throttling her. How much lighter her life had felt after she had some extra help. Her hand went instinctively to her throat, where she felt duty tighten its grip once again.

He went to get up. 'Are you all right, Grace? I hope nothing's upset you?'

Taking a deep breath, she sank into a chair. 'Sometimes I wonder if I'm selfless enough to be your wife.'

And without hesitation, he picked up her hand. 'You're the

very best of women, Grace, one who will always be respected and loved because of your good deeds and humble care for others.'

Under her breath, she murmured, 'But is that who I am? Sometimes I remember a time when I was so different.'

'You're worrying far too much about it. Perhaps you do have too much on your hands, with the wedding coming up.' He shuffled his chair closer to hers, as he would a grieving parishioner who needed comfort. 'You need to put your faith in God. Rest assured that all will be as it should be.'

The words calmed her, as they always did, and she slipped her hand into his, feeling the world rebalance itself. Yes, of course Lawrence was a good, wise, and dutiful man. She would be honoured to be his wife, helping him in his mission, supporting wherever she could.

And just as her mother would have done so happily twenty years before her, she got up and prepared a Sunday roast, there in the vicarage kitchen for her new love, her new family, her new future.

VIOLET

Once host to garden parties and croquet, Darley Grange was now home to military vehicles and uniformed men, officers, and some women too. As Violet marched briskly up to the door on her first day reporting for duty, she couldn't help but admire the beautiful Victorian mansion in the morning sunshine.

Perhaps army life wasn't going to be that bad, after all.

Inside the galleried main hall, Violet approached a large reception desk, where a tall ATS woman saluted, other staff bustling around tables and cabinets behind her.

'Oh, here you are, Private Westcott.' She looked down at her list. 'You've been assigned to the Americans until their support staff arrives. You're to go to Room 34.' The woman had clipped tones, but then she leaned forward and added in a low voice, 'Don't let the Americans take advantage. They're NSITs.'

Violet stifled a laugh, grateful for a little friendliness. NSIT was the code society girls used for 'not safe in taxis', meaning that a man was prone to making unwanted advances on the back seat.

'Thanks, I'll look out for that,' she said, and although the woman spoke with a perfectly good middle-class accent, Violet

toned down her upper-class voice. She'd realized through training that her la-di-da vowels often made people hostile.

It was strange walking down the carpeted halls and corridors
of a great house, only to find oneself following handwritten
labels on doors. A room that might once have been a library or
billiards room was now OPS ROOM 2, and the old drawing room
she was directed to was named ROOM 34, US ARMY RECEPTION.

Behind a desk sat a woman in the far more flattering US
women's army uniform. She saluted and gave Violet a perfunctory smile. 'Do you have your papers?' Violet handed them
across the desk, and the woman looked down her list before instructing her, 'You're to wait outside, Private Westcott.' Salut-
ing, Violet went out to the hallway, where she sat down in a small
row of chairs.

It seemed to take eternity for someone to collect her, and just
as she was beginning to feel forgotten, she heard an American
man's voice behind her.

'Cheer up, sunshine.'

She jumped a mile in the air, turning to see the infuriating
American officer from the Darley reception. 'McCauley?'

He smirked. 'Lieutenant McCauley, if you please.' He looked
her up and down. 'Well, well, well, you're looking very different
today.'

Smarting, she smoothed down her boxy jacket. She wasn't
going to let this comedian look down on her.

'As a matter of fact, I'm doing my bit for the war,' she said
haughtily, as if to prove a point. 'It'll be a bit of a lark,' she
added, although it came out pompously, nothing like a lark.

He leaned forward, trying to look at the spikes of hair poking
out at the edges of her cap. 'Hey, did they give you a buzz cut?
Take off your hat, let me look.' He smiled at her, laughter in his
eyes. 'I dare you.'

'No!' she snapped, pulling it down. 'If you must know, my new hairstyle is easy to keep and looks perfect with the uniform. Femininity is passé with the war, didn't you know?' She tried to keep her voice brisk and spirited.

'Well, I think you make a very good chap, with your uniform and short hair. You remind me of my young cousin Fred,' he said, a laugh in his voice.

'I don't have time for your nonsense today, Lieutenant McCauley. I have an important meeting. Good-bye.' With this, she got up to return to Room 34, determined to press the woman to hurry things up.

Inside the office, the stern woman looked at her wristwatch. 'Haven't you been collected yet?'

'No—' Violet stopped abruptly, her head spinning. The only person who had come to the waiting area was . . .

Her heart dropped like a stone weight.

Meanwhile, the woman was checking her list. 'I have Lieutenant McCauley down here.' She looked back up at her. 'You're his driver.'

Violet glanced at the open door. He was probably out in the corridor listening, enjoying his little moment of fun.

How humiliating.

But she was an army private now, and she knew she had to put on a good face. With a few little chats with the right people, she'd be able move to another position later.

When she returned to the waiting area, Lieutenant McCauley was sitting in her chair, one ankle nonchalantly on his knee, his hands behind his head, as if he were king of the world.

'Ah, Fred. I see you're back,' he said.

'It's Private Westcott,' she snapped. 'And I believe I am to report to you, Lieutenant McCauley.'

'That's right.' He got up and came to stand in front of her.

'But I would like to remind you that as a subordinate, you're supposed to call me "sir". And a salute would be nice too.'

'Yes, sir.' Her hand snapped up to salute him as professionally as she could, her eyes glaring through him into the middle distance. She wasn't going to let him see how much this bothered her.

'Right then,' he said, leading her back to the corridor. 'The staff in my section will show you the ropes.'

He chatted all the way, pointing to various rooms and explaining the drill, not expecting any responses. Soon they were at a central reception area, and much to Violet's relief, it was manned by a fair-haired ATS woman.

'Private Harding, this is Private Westcott.'

The fair-haired woman saluted from the desk, a smile on her face. 'Glad to have you on board, Private Westcott. Call me Sally. Come in, and I'll show you around.'

Lieutenant McCauley turned to Violet. 'Well, that will be all for now, Fred. I'll meet you outside at two for a jaunt to London. You'll have the details on your itinerary.' His mouth twisted into a half-smile, and he stalked back into the corridor.

'Did he just call you Fred?' Sally muttered as she showed her into the long office.

'Unfortunately, I've had the pleasure of meeting Lieutenant McCauley before.' She grimaced, and Sally stifled a giggle.

Sally introduced her to the other drivers and showed her to her desk before taking her out to the garages, which were formed from a long stable building. Inside were rows of black saloon cars, some rather old.

'They're waiting for the American ones to arrive, so we're using British ones for now, which are a medley of whatever's available.'

Violet's car was a sleek black Austin 12, the interior nicely upholstered in leather.

'You've got one of the better ones,' Sally said. 'It's a bit long – especially on the country lanes – but you'll get the hang of it quickly enough.' Sally had a crisp Welsh accent and a buoyant enthusiasm. 'It's rather fun, driving around the place. The officers are all very friendly. Most of them chat to you on the way, and you can have a bit of a laugh.'

'Do you ever get women officers to drive around?'

She looked bemused, then chuckled. 'Women officers are only in charge of women soldiers, nothing as important as the men. But you posh girls are always getting promoted. Why don't you take an officer's course? You could become one yourself.'

Violet looked at the car, thinking about the unpleasant task of driving around the brash lieutenant. 'Perhaps that's not such a bad idea.' A promotion would be a sure way of getting away from him.

The morning went by quickly, and at two o'clock precisely, she stood spick and span beside her saloon car at the front of the building, awaiting Lieutenant McCauley.

Five minutes behind schedule, the front door swung open, and out came the man himself, his gait wide and easy, as if he were strolling in from one of those frightful cowboy movies. 'Ah, Private Westcott. Still here, I see.'

She saluted, and then opened the rear door for him, as she had been trained. 'Where else would I be, sir?' She was determined to stay professional.

He got in, and she closed the door and curtly got in herself, starting up the engine and driving the car down to the lane.

It wasn't until they were into the journey that he asked, 'Don't you have any conversation, Fred?'

Carefully ignoring what was apparently her new nickname, she replied, 'My role is to drive, not make idle chitchat, sir.'

He fell into silence for a few minutes, and just when she thought he'd given up, he asked, 'So how do you like army life?

You didn't strike me as the kind of girl who would enjoy marching around parade grounds or learning how to drive and fix a car.'

'Actually, I could already drive before I joined the army, and as a matter of fact, I came top in my mechanics training,' she couldn't help but add.

'Well, well, well, Fred. You're quite the chameleon, aren't you?'

Despite her best efforts, she betrayed herself with a short huff. 'Since you seem to think you're an expert on me, why bother asking questions?'

'All right,' he mused. 'If that's what you want, let me tell you all about you, Fred.'

The cheek of the man!

He took a deep breath and began dramatically, 'You were born in the majestic Aldhurst Manor, and after a childhood of pampering and flouncing around in pretty dresses, you were put out to auction as a wife to the highest bidder, probably through the usual route as a debutante. You shone around your rivals. Yet although you were taught to read the classics and speak Italian by your dreary governess – who you occasionally and hilariously pranked – you never really learned anything. Oh, unless you went to a good boarding school, but I doubt that.' He stopped. 'Well, how am I doing so far?'

Some of what he said was right, of course, but she wasn't going to tell him that. 'Tell me what happened after I was a debutante, then?'

'You evidently failed to secure a husband, although it's hard to understand why. Perhaps you aimed too high and there was too much competition for the top bachelors, the lords, dukes, and princes. After all, you don't even have a title, and I've heard that's what you need over here, isn't it?'

She scowled. He'd annoyed her so much that she'd forgotten

her plan to stay calm and professional. 'Is that what you think of me, some kind of fortune hunter? As a matter of fact, I haven't had it nearly as easy as you seem to think I have. My mother died when I was young, my father a few months ago, and I was as good as engaged to Lord Ombersley when he was shot down over Malta.'

That'll show him! she thought primly.

'How very sad,' Lieutenant McCauley said at last, his voice serious and subdued. 'I'm sorry. I didn't realize you'd had so much loss in your life.'

Their eyes met in the rearview mirror. 'You see, you don't really know me, Lieutenant McCauley. I'm not a pampered princess at all.'

She pulled the car into a petrol station and took care that he saw her efficiently filling in the ration forms, checking the oil, wiping the windscreen to perfection.

By the time they were on their way again, she was surprised that his mind was still on the same topic.

'Perhaps it explains why you are the way that you are, Fred. I mean, your father probably spoiled you because you had no mom, and now your father's gone too, the burden of spoiling you falls to your husband-to-be, whoever that poor soul will be. And until then . . . Hold on a minute: Don't you have an older brother?'

She glared at him furiously. 'Who gave you the authority to analyse my life? First of all, you can't blame my father for spoiling me. Secondly, any husband-to-be has absolutely nothing to do with you, thank you very much. And thirdly, yes, I have a brother, not that it's any of your business.'

For a moment, she sat silently watching the road ahead. Then she asked, 'Pray tell, what kind of life have you had that gives you the right to scrutinize me?'

He shrugged, unperturbed. 'Well, if it makes you feel any

better, although I know they love me, my parents were both too busy to pay much attention to me.'

'I'm sorry,' she said, disconcerted by his openness. Then, after a moment, she asked, 'Why was that?'

'My dad's a big businessman too busy for kids, and my mom's a society hostess. I'm the youngest of five children, and no one had an ounce of time for me. My next-older brother was in a coma for a long time after a car accident when I was twelve, and after that I had to grow up pretty fast.'

'That must have been hard. Is he all right, your brother?' Violet felt a little sorry for him.

'He's all right, I guess.' He made a laugh, but it was strained. 'But he hasn't been the same since. My father gave him a job, and everything seemed to be going fine, but then he married this society woman who's been having affairs.'

'Does he know?'

'I can never tell if he's too busy to notice or just finds it easier to ignore it.' His brow creased in thought. 'Sometimes I wonder if he loves her so much that he just wants to give her anything that makes her happy, and if this is the way she finds happiness, so be it.' He looked at Violet again in the mirror. 'Maybe that's what's going to happen to you, Fred. Some guy will treat you like a goddess, and you'll be able to do or have whatever you want.' His eyes narrowed. 'But would you really want a life like that?'

Was she expecting her future husband to spoil her? Of course she was! Wasn't that one of the traits she was looking for? She'd always imagined that would make her happy.

But what if it didn't?

'Maybe you should try going for what you really want, Fred. That's what I do,' he said lightly. 'Cut the act and get on with real life.'

'I don't know where you get all your ideas, Lieutenant,' she said, laughing it off. 'But I do know that you need to find someone else to pester. You have no idea what my life is about, and I'll thank you for keeping your ill-informed ideas to yourself.'

From then on, Violet studiously ignored the man as much as she could. When she returned that afternoon, she found her superior and requested a change of position, only to be told to stop complaining.

'We can't move people around willy-nilly, Westcott,' the starchy corporal told her. 'In any case, the Americans will have their own drivers soon, so it won't be for long.'

CRESSIDA

A utility dress or skirt suit must be made
within the following guidelines

It must use a piece of fabric no more than 2 yards
long.

It may have no more than 2 pockets and 5 buttons,
and no metal fastenings.

There may be no more than 6 seams in the skirt.

A maximum of 2 box pleats or 4 knife pleats may be
used.

In total, there must be no more than 160 inches
of stitching.

No superfluous decoration is allowed.

It should be simple and inexpensive to make,
practical and agreeable to wear, and made of a good
quality material that will last (see list of approved
materials).

SOURCE: MINISTRY OF TRADE MATERIALS

Extra mirrors now filled one side of Cressida's new design room, and as she walked around her model, she inspected her first stab at the utility skirt suit, modelled by Grace.

It was one of Cressida's entries into the IncSoc Utility Contest. Every fashion designer in the group had agreed to send in four designs: a dress, a skirt, a blouse, and a coat. The best thirty-two would be chosen for the grand fashion show, and Cressida was determined to show off her finest creations.

'It's ideal.' Cressida looked over the navy-blue number. 'A woman could wear it to an office, to the shops, to a tea party, to church, or as a skirt to do the housework. The single pleat down the front saves fabric, and it uses only buttons – the only fastening we're allowed.'

Grace was looking quietly delighted to be asked to act as a model. She'd popped over to work on the wedding dress and was all too ready to set down her tools and try on a few items so that Cressida 'could see how they hung'. Determined to stand straight and still, she instinctively knew how to move, how to show each garment to its best.

'I like the gathering at the top of the shoulders,' Grace said. 'It builds the shoulders up, making it look like a chic kind of uniform.'

'It's part of the Look-Alive Look that *Vogue*'s been talking about: fit, trim, and ready to work,' Cressida said thoughtfully. 'The skirts are knee-length, the sleeves can be rolled up if need be, and open-necked blouses are easier for work. And all of it needs to be interchangeable, a jacket that goes with a skirt or trousers or can go over a dress.'

Cressida adjusted her new pieces: Flashes of cerise fabric were used on the collar and as a trim for the jacket pockets, contrasting elegantly with the navy of the main garment.

'The colour is a terrific way to add drama without using extra material,' Grace said. 'Why don't we put a strip of cerise beneath the pleat in the skirt? Every time the wearer walks, it'll show a wonderful flash of colour, a kaleidoscope effect.'

'What a fabulous idea!' Cressida narrowed her eyes on the skirt to pinpoint where it could go. 'The government wants people to wear more bright colours so that they can be seen during the black-out. Women can change these highlights after a year or two, create a new look with, say, yellow or turquoise.' She fetched her pins. 'And everyone loves a splash of colour. Ever since Deborah Kerr modelled that sensational raspberry-coloured coat at the IncSoc press launch, everyone wants to brighten up their wardrobes.'

'It made a beautiful image, and on the front page of every newspaper too,' Grace said. 'The fashion show is bound to be a hit.'

Cressida nodded thoughtfully as she began to pin the hem. 'It was a clever move to engage the very top designers; the press can't leave it alone. The entire proposal is revolutionizing haute couture in this country, that's for sure.'

'Do you really think so?'

'It's making us all strip back design to good lines and excel-lent cuts. Design becomes all about quality when you have to curtail so many of the extraneous elements. It has to be simpler, more classical, but with clever details to make it modern.' She bustled about, a spring in her step.

'It must be quite a challenge with all the restrictions.'

Cressida grinned. 'That's why I'm doing it. It's like a compli-cated and creative puzzle. I couldn't possibly stand back and watch the others try their best without putting my own ideas forward.' She glanced at Grace sideways, adding, 'That and the fact that I need to show Hartnell I can still get a garment or two into the fashion show. I couldn't have all the men taking the glory, could I?'

'Bravo!' Grace said. 'And it's a great way to show the Nazis too. I heard that fashion in Germany is nonexistent. Didn't they have a fashion industry before the war?'

'They did, but it was run largely by Jewish families and they began to leave a few years before the war. That's why the Nazis don't like fashion. They think it's frivolous and foreign, against their "Gretchen" values, you know, all dirndl skirts and no makeup. A woman is honoured for motherhood, so corsets are out too, and trousers are now banned for women in occupied France unless they're on a bicycle.' She grimaced. 'After the Germans occupied France, the Nazis wanted to move the entire Parisian haute couture industry to Berlin, make Germany the centre of fashion. Thankfully, the French managed to persuade them out of it.'

'Goodness, that would be flagrantly stealing part of their culture!'

'That's what the Nazis do. They seize what they want and make it seem like it was theirs all along. They've turned Paris into a tourist park for well-behaved Nazi officers, although from what I hear, they're not terribly well-behaved once they get there.'

They fell into silence, thinking about the war as Cressida continued working around the garment.

As she was turned this way and that, Grace's eyes strayed over to a series of evening gowns hanging from a rail, emerald green, purple, and magenta. 'Are you doing some client redesigns after all? Those gowns are made with far too much good satin to be recently made. They must be relics of better days.'

'I gave in.' Cressida tossed her head to hide her smile. 'Lady Marley telephoned me so many times, and in the end she had her chauffeur run them over with strict instructions to leave them here, regardless how much I tried to foist them back onto her.'

'They look quite a challenge too,' Grace said.

'Not really. There's so much fabric in them, I could probably make two garments out of each – perhaps I will do just that! It'll make it more fun to see if I can. She can have a simple, straight-skirted evening dress, and then I can form a jacket from the extra skirting.'

'It must be wonderful to be able to do that, to have so much experience and knowledge.'

Cressida stood back. 'Grace, you have to do me a favour and stop being in awe of me. I'm just a normal person like you or anyone else, I've simply found something I love and focused all my skills and energies on it. You, my dear, could do exactly the same if you wished. Treat me as a friend. That would do us both a good service.'

Grace opened her mouth to object, but then she saw the look on Cressida's face and grinned. 'All right, then. Friends it is.'

Cressida worked in silence for a minute or two, and then stood back. 'Well, Grace, that'll be all for now, thank you. I must confess, you make an exquisite model. If you weren't to be married soon, I'd suggest a change in profession.'

Predictably, Grace had a never-ending stream of reasons why that wouldn't be possible, and yet Cressida could see the girl giving a swirl of delight at the compliment. Perhaps she could change her mind yet.

Cressida turned to hide her smile. How much more fun she was having in Aldhurst than she'd thought.

Evenings were stretching longer with the spring, and Cressida had been pressed by Ben to join him after work that day on a walk up to the top of Aldhurst Hill.

'Bring good shoes,' he'd said.

The idea of it sounded exhausting, but by the time she reached the top, the sunset spreading a red-gold light over the land, a lightheaded exhilaration mingled with an awe of the world stretched out before her. Her breath was quick from the final climb, blood pumping through her veins, and everyday life suddenly felt juxtaposed to this greater exuberance of being alive.

'Breathtaking' was all that she said, basking in the complete silence surrounding them. A sense of peace came over her, as sharp and bright as the sunshine warming her skin.

Ever since the night in the ARP office, she'd seen more of Ben. At first, she was unsure of him; she'd let her guard down, let him see her at her weakest. Yet he had taken it in his stride. There was something solid and yet soft about Ben, a strength mixed with a deeper kind of understanding. When you spoke to him of worries or grief, instead of your words striking a brick wall and ricocheting back at you, they sank into him, as if he had absorbed them into himself, understanding everything completely.

He stood beside her, his eyes bathed in the golden sunlight. 'Sometimes I come up here because it makes me feel close to those I've lost, dear Elizabeth and Jack. I used to walk up here with them both. It's as if every step I take on the path, every view that we once shared, brings me closer to them.'

'I find it easier not to think about it too much. It makes me wretched when I remember Jack.'

'But that's the only way to truly come to terms with death. With every time we think or talk about him, we chip at the hard granite of sadness, and through the cracks we begin to see how much light he brought to the world.'

She knew he was right; by pushing away her grief, she'd somehow only been preserving it. How many people – how much love – she'd passed by to spare herself the agony of thinking of him. Instead she'd buried her feelings in her work. A sudden sorrow came over her for all the lost time in her life, for all the joy that was there if only she'd stopped to let it inside.

She moved closer beside Ben, letting the warmth of him seep into her core. This man, this intelligent, sensitive being, had seen beyond her fame and chic exterior to the wronged, determined spirit hidden inside. He knew her better than anyone had for decades. When she shared her feelings and fears, it was as if he collected all the elements of her and put them into the right order, allowing her to make sense of herself.

A sudden shiver of fear made her pull away. *What was she doing, becoming so close to him?* But as she watched him turn to smile at her, his eyes squinting in the sunshine, she couldn't help but smile back.

'I thought we could descend down the steeper path,' he said, getting up beside her. 'It's a little rockier, but you have the view of the vale all the way down.'

The path was certainly steeper, but the view was as mesmerizing as promised. So engrossed were they, that it was only when they'd reached the wood that they realized they were being followed.

'Do you hear that?' Ben stopped, and with a finger to his lips, he slowly crept forward. As he crouched down and put out a hand, something emerged from the shrubbery.

It was a dog.

Instantly, Cressida began to back away. The dog wasn't black and white, more of a mottled brown colour, but in her mind's eye, she saw him racing, sprinting dementedly back and forth, the bloody doll in his mouth.

Ben pulled on her arm, bringing her forward. 'There aren't any bombs,' he said gently. 'And this little fellow is just a poor victim like you and me. It's become difficult enough getting meat to feed a family, let alone a pet. It's not the owner's fault. Sometimes people have no choice.'

Slowly, the dog edged forward, and sniffed Ben's hand. 'I

think he'd run away if we tried to catch him. I'll come back later with some food for him, and maybe he'll become more friendly.'

They peeled away, the bushes and trees giving way to the fields beside the stream, and soon they were in the paddock behind the church, clambering up the stile and over the old stone wall into the churchyard.

And it was only then that they heard an almost imperceptible *yap,* a movement on the wall behind them.

There was the dog, trotting over to Ben expectantly.

'He must have followed us,' Cressida said. 'I think he likes you.'

Ben gave his head a rub. 'I'll see if we can find his owner.'

'What will happen if no one claims him?' Cressida asked.

He grinned. 'We'll have to keep him.'

She bent down and gave his ear a rub. 'Don't worry, Morris. Ben will take good care of you.'

'Morris? Is that his new name?'

'There was a dog in the stables when I was a girl, and I called him Morris. Sometimes he was my only friend. I think that's partially why the black-and-white dog upset me so much. I could only think of the poor child, what could have become of her – and what had become of me, the girl I had been.' She stood back to appraise the dog. 'I think the name suits him.'

'I never imagined you as a dog lover, Cressida.'

'I haven't had time for pets – actually, there seem to be a lot of things I haven't had time for, like walking up hills or making new friends.'

'Or cooking a makeshift supper with a hungry clergyman?' he suggested.

She laughed. 'I am no chef, Reverend, so you'll have to do the cooking. But I'll be very happy to keep you company.'

The rest of the evening was spent preparing and eating Lord Woolton Pie, followed by a fireside chat.

And as she walked home much later that evening, she couldn't help smiling, musing to herself that she had spent far too long burying herself in her work.

'When was it that I forgot,' she murmured to herself, 'that life is for living?'

GRACE

A few weeks after Lawrence's visit, Grace stood at the vicarage door, looking out into the morning deluge as a clap of thunder echoed around the hills. It was no use; she couldn't find her umbrella and she absolutely had to get to work. Unfolding a newspaper, she held it rather uselessly over her head and dashed out into the driving rain.

With less than a week until her wedding, Grace was busier than ever, desperate to combat her wedding nerves. After work, she was to go to the manor for the fitting with Cressida, and her dress felt heavy in her bag, a reminder of what was to come.

As she darted through the graveyard, the newspaper she was holding over her head sagged down over her eyes with the downpour, and she hastened into a sprint, dodging puddles as she went.

Naturally, she wasn't thinking that someone might be coming in the opposite direction.

Nor that she might bump into him.

'Grace! Slow down!' Two arms came around her to stop her from tripping, and there in front of her was Hugh, an umbrella in one hand, a package under his arm.

They looked at each other, bewildered, and then she

laughed nervously, stepping away, pushing her wet hair back from her face. 'Goodness, I should have been looking where I was going!'

'Don't worry, no harm done.' He offered her the handle of his umbrella. 'Would you like to borrow it? That newspaper isn't doing awfully well.'

The sodden newspaper tore apart, and she laughed, stepping into the shelter of his umbrella, realizing only too late how close it brought them.

Laughing along with her, he put his hand up to remove a disintegrating piece of sodden newspaper from her shoulder, his fingers gently pushing back the hair on her neck. 'It's a coincidence I bumped into you, Grace. I have something for you.' He gestured towards the package.

Intrigued, she looked over her shoulder for the nearest shelter. 'Let's go into the church, out of this downpour.'

And as he watched her, a mischievous look came over his face. 'All right, I'll race you there.'

It instantly took her back to their childhood, and before she knew what she was doing, she hastily called out, 'Go!' and took off, her long legs running down the path, zigzagging around the puddles.

'Not so fast!' he called, trying to pass her down the narrow path. But she blocked his way, and he had to take a detour, culminating in a dead tie as they both arrived at the church door, Hugh sliding quickly ahead, causing Grace to collide into him.

'I knew I'd win,' he laughed.

'It was a tie, you rascal,' she replied, but as she steadied herself against him, she suddenly sensed his body so close to hers.

Hurriedly, she peeled herself away, the rain dripping off them both, their breath heavy with laughter and their hearts beating fast, their eyes meeting in a glow of exhilaration.

'I haven't run like that in years.' He suddenly looked so

youthful, with his hair wet and the rainwater dripping off him, the delighted grin on his face.

'London has taken all the fun out of you,' she joked, and without thinking, she put a hand up to brush a stray leaf from his chest, abruptly feeling him tense with a nervous energy.

And suddenly she knew that if he leaned forward and took her in his arms, she wouldn't be able to stop herself. The more he reminded her of his old self, the more her old feelings were reawakened, this time stronger, more pressing.

Swallowing, she pulled back, her heart hammering, wondering if he felt it too, as he quickly looked away, turning to pull open the door.

'After you, madam.' He made a mock bow for her to enter.

Inside, the church was cool and dark, still and echoey in its emptiness. Trying to ease her nerves, she switched on the dim gold light, the thrumming rain on the roof and windows making her feel like they were enveloped, isolated in a little safe haven all to themselves.

He slid his package onto one of the pews at the back of the nave. 'I was going through the attic rooms and found my mother's wedding veil. I wondered if you might like to use it for your wedding.'

A shudder passed through her. The last thing she wanted was Hugh mentioning her impending wedding.

'Th-thank you,' she stammered, unsure.

He lifted out the sheath of ivory-white, glimmering semi-transparent in the soft light.

'It's beautiful!' She ran the soft fabric through her fingers.

'And look at the beadwork,' Hugh said, showing her a portion. The edge was meticulously finished with fine embroidery, tiny pearl beads giving it weight and a lustrous glimmer. 'It's magnificent, isn't it, with all those tiny pearls. I wonder where it was made.'

But Grace wasn't listening. She was just staring at the embroidery, her mouth ajar. Then she turned to her bag and carefully pulled out her own wedding dress, laying it over a pew, the shade of ivory exactly matching that of the veil. 'Look, it's the same rose embroidery! The veil must have been made to go with this dress.'

'It certainly looks like it.'

Then she laughed. 'But that's it, isn't it! Your mother must have given her dress to my mother.'

He reached out to touch the wedding dress. 'And that would make this my mother's dress. It's beautiful, isn't it.'

'Cressida thinks it was designed by a Parisian couturier, so it makes perfect sense that it was your mother's. She must have heard that the vicar's bride-to-be needed a dress, and she handed over her own. What a generous thing to do – she must have been so lovely!'

'I was too young to know her, but apparently she was quiet and devout. It can't have been easy, being married to my father.' He lifted the bodice, turning the beads to catch the golden light. 'The climbing roses are part of the family crest.'

'Your mother must have looked a vision.' Grace laid the veil beside the dress. They were a perfect match.

'What serendipity, that this dress belonged to both of our mothers.' Gently, Hugh lifted up the veil. 'Why don't you try it on?'

She took a step back, laughing. 'Oh, I shouldn't.'

But an impulsiveness came over her, as she found it often did when she was with Hugh, and she turned to allow him to attach it to the top of her head.

'There you are,' he said, and as she turned back around, he stood looking at her, his hands coming out to spread the soft material around her shoulders. 'It's perfect,' he whispered into the echoing silence.

She stood in front of him, a bride, as she had in her dreams so many times, and she felt something crush inside her as she realized that the man before her would never be her groom. She would be marrying another man, a man she respected but wouldn't ever love.

A sob caught in her throat, and she bit her lip, remembering how grateful she was to Lawrence for marrying her, remembering what she owed him for the care he'd given her father and her after her mother died. Remembering that she had made an unbreakable promise to him.

Hastily, she pulled the veil out of her hair, but the stupid thing caught.

Without a second thought, Hugh stepped forward and helped loosen it. 'I always knew you'd be a beautiful bride. Do you remember the time we played shipwrecks, and we pretended to get married in front of our campfire?' He pulled away, the veil in his hands, his eyes on hers.

Her mouth went dry, and she stood paralyzed, the church so still it was as if the world were holding its breath.

She remembered their pretend wedding as clear as day, as clear as the many times she'd replayed it in her mind.

But it was over a decade ago. And she was to be married to another man in just a few days. She had made that promise now to someone else. Hugh and her past, everything she'd felt, had to be put behind her.

But he only smiled at her. 'Do you remember it too?'

'We did a lot of funny things, didn't we?' she said, wondering why he was bringing this up, and how she could change the subject. Quickly, she began to fold the dress. 'And it was such a long time ago now.'

Carefully, he put the veil back into its package. 'Last week I did something I haven't done since those days. I went swimming in the lake, off that broken-down jetty by the old boathouse.'

As soon as he said those words, her mind went unstoppably to their last swim.

She stopped folding the dress, her eyes fixing on the stone floor.

As if reading her mind, he said, 'Do you remember that last day of summer, just before I left for boarding school, how we raced to the island one last time?' He took a step towards her. 'I always thought it would be us getting married, Grace, all those years ago. That it would be me standing at the altar, turning to watch you as you came through this door.' His voice quiet, he added, 'I thought you always knew how much I was in love with you.'

The air was so still, she felt barely able to breathe. 'I didn't,' she whispered. Her eyes met his for a moment, and there, inside, she could see a different man, unsure, vulnerable.

'Since I've been back in Aldhurst, I sometimes think about that, and I wondered if you were ever in love with me too.'

Panicking inside, she swallowed hard. She couldn't admit to him how much she'd craved him. It would be too much, too hard to bear. She'd be exposed, and more than that, he'd realize how much she was sacrificing, being with Lawrence – that she'd given up on love the day he left.

Her voice wavered as she desperately tried to make light of it. 'We were so young then; we had no idea about real life at all.' Nervously, she turned her attention back to the dress, unable to cope with the tangle of thoughts and memories and feelings inside.

He didn't reply immediately, and then, slowly, he said, 'I know. We've both changed.'

And inside those words, she was sure she heard his disappointment with her, the thought that had plagued her since the evening she'd first met him in the drawing room, that she had grown up to be so different, so devout and hard-working.

Defensively, she said, 'Lawrence is a good man. He'll make a good husband. This is my life now.'

He stepped back, as if she'd cut him away from her. 'I'm sure he will.'

And in that moment, she longed to reach out to pull him back, to touch his face and bring his lips to hers.

But her duty was to Lawrence, her need to rebuild her family, become a vicar's wife, just as her mother had, to serve a greater purpose. She of all people knew the value of integrity and honour.

Frantically, she began to fluster with the dress, folding it back into the bag, repeating Lawrence's guiding words. 'Marriage is an honour, setting a path forward to a stable and productive future.'

He stiffened. 'You make it sound so very rational,' he murmured, and then he heaved a long sigh, glancing to the tall stained-glass window over the altar. 'But I suppose you're right. And I should be thinking the same. The estate will need a lady of the manor. Decisions will have to be made, promises fulfilled.' He turned to her, a stoical smile on his face. 'We both need to forge ahead on our different paths.'

Fraught, she turned away, gathering up the bag with the wedding dress.

Suddenly businesslike, Hugh was glancing at his watch. 'I'm afraid I have to catch my train.' He walked to the door and held it open for her. 'I'm pleased the veil has found its match.'

Outside, the rain had turned into a thin, transparent drizzle.

With a conciliatory smile, he said, 'It was nice to bump into you, Grace.'

'Yes, it was,' she replied, and as they parted ways, both dashing away from each other through the ethereal drizzle, she called out, 'Cheerio!'

And he turned and called back, 'Good-bye, Grace!'

And behind those words she sensed him pulling away from her, that dreadful realization that this would soon be over. He would return to his London life, and she would marry Lawrence. This fragile relationship, more than just a friendship, would soon trail away and be lost for ever.

VIOLET

Of course it was raining. The car had broken down in a sodden leafy country lane, and here Violet was, soaked to the skin and smeared with engine oil, her head and shoulders underneath the car.

'Are you sure you don't want me to have a look at it, Fred?' Lieutenant McCauley's relaxed American tones addressed her from the side of the car, where he stood smoking a cigarette, chuckling at her tenacity.

'I already told you,' she snapped back, 'I came first in mechanics, so do you mind leaving me to do my job?'

'I understand a thing or two about motors, you know?'

'I don't care. This is my car, and I'm responsible for mending it.'

But the man simply couldn't help himself, and before she knew it, she felt the rustle and shove of another body shuffling up beside her under the car.

'What are we looking at here?' he said, as if he knew better than her.

With a sniff of derision, she explained, 'Here is the exhaust,' clanging a long thick pipe with the spanner, 'and here is the base of the engine.' Another clang. 'The wheelbase on the nearside back might be where the leak's coming from. My feeling is that it's brake fluid.'

'Very good, Private Westcott. But since when does a "feeling" substantiate a correct diagnosis?'

His face was right beside hers, too close for comfort, but she was loath to be the one to wriggle away from him, so instead she said with dignity, 'It would be gentlemanly of you to allow a little more space between us, Lieutenant McCauley.'

'Ah, but I'm not a gentleman, or so you say.' Again, that irritating chuckle.

'When I said that, I only meant that you didn't fit into the mould of the British gentleman, and now I can see that I was utterly correct.'

'And I'm positively proud of my heathenness.' He seemed to snuggle towards her. 'Just call me Heathcliff.'

She couldn't help letting out a laugh. 'More like Toad of Toad Hall.'

'Look, we just passed a village with a very quaint-looking pub, the Funny Peculiar or something equally as strange. Why don't we walk back, use the telephone there to call a proper mechanic, and enjoy the wait with a few drinks?' He gave her his charming smile, and for a brief moment, she felt tempted – a roaring fire, her uniform unsticking from her legs . . .

'No,' she said firmly. '*I'm* a proper mechanic, and I will fix this rotten problem if it kills me.' She looked ruthlessly back at the wheel attachment. 'And no self-respecting pub would ever call itself "Funny Peculiar".' Then she added in an almost wistful tone, 'I think it was called the Dog and Partridge.'

'Same thing, isn't it? All these weird names for bars. Isn't it easier to call them all "Funny Peculiar"? That's what I do. It's simpler that way.'

'For your simple brain.'

She shimmied out from under the car and bent over the engine.

Again, his head came down beside hers. 'I don't mean to be disrespectful to your top-student status, but there aren't many types of engine trouble that can be fixed without new parts and a fully stocked professional garage. Your toolkit here might be expansive and dependable, but—'

He was cut short by the sudden rumble of the engine as she activated the starter wires.

'What were you saying?' she said smugly.

He eyed her, and then the engine. 'Well, I'll be.'

They both stood up as she wiped her oily hands on a rag.

'I was right all along,' she concluded with a victorious smirk.

'Well done, Fred.' Lieutenant McCauley patted her on the shoulder, but she shrugged his hand off.

'You're welcome, Mr Toad.'

He grinned. 'I rather like that. But why don't you call me Landon?'

She raised an eyebrow. 'Is that your first name?'

'And I know that yours is Violet.' He took a small step towards her. 'I think we're ready to move into using first names.'

'Well, I think not.' With an on-off smile, she got back into the driver's seat, and he broke rank by climbing into the passenger seat beside her.

'Sir, I believe your position entitles you to take the back seat,' she said pointedly, looking ahead into the wet and windy fields. A crowd of sheep were huddled in a corner of the neighbouring pasture, quietly keeping themselves as warm as they could.

'I thought it would be cosier up here in the front with you.'

She turned her face, and he was smiling at her, a twinkle in his eyes, and she had to confess that beneath the rather unimpressive exterior, the man certainly had charm.

'Oh, all right,' she muttered, putting the car into gear.

They were on the last leg of a long journey, driving to Portsmouth on the south coast for meetings. A large American navy base had been established there alongside the Royal Navy, and their schedule included an overnight stay.

'I wonder where they'll let you sleep tonight, Fred. I'll be in the officers' quarters,' he preened in a mock taunt. 'They'll probably shove you in a dormitory packed with American navy girls, I'd say.'

The thought of going back into a dormitory filled her with dread, let alone one packed with Americans. Not that she had anything against them per se, it was more that she didn't want to be thrown in at the deep end. She'd have to be incredibly careful that they didn't see her voluminous ATS underwear. She'd be a laughing stock.

'I'll survive,' she said snootily, keeping her eyes on the road.

'I'd rather be in a dormitory with just me and you, Fred,' he mused. 'We could have a pillow fight.'

'And I would win,' she couldn't help saying.

Even though she didn't look, she knew that he was grinning. Aware that she was beginning to enjoy his banter, she quickly chastised herself.

Sally had mentioned that McCauley was a known womanizer, devilishly charming and generous to a tee, but a womanizer all the same. British women had endured food rations and no new stockings for three years, as well as the absence of their own men, so no wonder all the Americans had to do was swoop into Britain with their fresh chivalry and a pair of stockings and the women were falling all over them.

Well, it wasn't going to happen to *this* woman, that was for certain.

'Tell me, Lieutenant McCauley. Don't you have a girl back in Connecticut? I can't imagine she'd be pleased about your dreadful attempts at flirting with me.'

'First of all, my flirting isn't dreadful, it's poetic, and second, it's only a bit of fun to while away the journey. Why do you ask?'

An embarrassing blush came to her face.

Why had she asked? It was nothing to her, after all?

And now he knew that he was getting to her.

'I wanted to know who you've been tormenting back in America, but I see now that sadly it's only me.' She smiled wistfully. 'Although I'm sure you annoy all the other girls back at the base too, don't you?'

'But I save all my favourite lines for you,' he said sarcastically, aggravatingly unspecific. 'Which is better than you do for me.' A mock hurt came to his voice. 'Here I am, as charming as can be, and all you're interested in are British lords and dull dukes.'

Biting her lip to stop herself smiling, she replied, 'At least I have a goal, not some kind of flirt-with-every-girl-in-town tactic. I'm sure some poor gullible British girl will end up with more than a broken heart.'

He laughed. 'That could be you if you play your cards right. You're British, and a woman, aren't you?'

'But I'm not gullible.' She smirked in spite of herself as he laughed, delighted with her feistiness.

The navy base was unmissable. The vast area adjacent to the docks was still mostly under construction but included a group of older buildings that formed the core of offices and activities. A series of large field tents stretched across a former pasture, and men everywhere bustled to and fro. Pulling up beside the main building, she turned to Lieutenant McCauley.

'This is where you get out, I believe,' she said smartly.

'Thank you, Fred. I hope our paths will cross later, but if not, rest assured that I'll be dreaming of you.'

'I'm sure I'll have a perfect evening, regardless,' she replied.

He gave her a parting smile and disappeared into the building.

'Parking is to the right and through to the back,' a guard told her. She put the car into gear, and with a large sigh, went to find out what the US Navy proposed to do with her for the evening.

The women's quarters were to the side of the main base, a small warehouse that had been requisitioned. Although an influx was expected, there were currently only six young naval women posted there, most of whom had only just arrived themselves. The large dormitory contained a line of comfortable beds – the Americans clearly had more resources and luxuries than the British Army.

A large redhead called Dorie had been sent to collect Violet from the reception office, bombarding into the room with a smile and a salute.

'Don't you worry,' Dorie said, showing her to the women's quarters. 'You'll be just fine. We're a friendly gang.'

And friendly they most certainly were. While Dorie flustered about plumping pillows and finding the best blankets for her, the others gathered around, all asking questions at the same time.

'What are the guys like over here?'

'Aren't you starved with all the food rations?'

'Were you ever in a bomb raid?'

And finally, 'How can you survive without new clothes?'

Of course, it was this last one Violet seized upon, a topic close to her own heart.

'Well, you'd never know it from looking at me now, but I

used to dress up for balls and dinners, wearing beautiful gowns, the latest fashions from Paris, and shoes – so many beautiful shoes! It's nearly impossible to get high heels these days. All they have in the shops are flat lace-ups, or at best two-inch, because we all have to walk so much with all the war work and fuel rations.' She sighed. 'They introduced clothes rations last year, so we have to be very careful before we buy anything. It began as sixty-six coupons, but this year it's only forty, worst luck.'

'You must have been devastated!' a petite brunette called Nancy said with feeling.

'I was! They announced it on a Sunday morning so that no one could nip out and buy things before it took effect. I'd had my eye on a lovely suit and wish to this day I'd bought it before the rations came in.'

'But how did they give out clothing coupons without anyone finding out?'

'It was very sneaky. Everyone's new food ration book had a spare page of margarine coupons in the back, and we were told that these were to be used for clothes. Heaven only knows how they kept it secret.' Violet looked at Nancy's horrified face. 'Don't you have clothes rations in America?'

'No, but our clothes now have to use less fabric, which is a bore. We can't have ruffles or pleats or turnups, and the skirts are a little shorter in the hemline.' She gave a little laugh. 'I don't know how you survive.'

'I know!' Violet said, but instead of feeling her usual sense of horror, she suddenly laughed. 'But you get used to it after a while. It's incredible how resourceful you can be, adjusting old clothes and so forth. I'm part of a Sewing Circle, and we meet every week to "Make Do and Mend", which is a government slogan to get everyone to do up old clothes.'

'But what do you wear to parties?' Nancy looked horrified at the prospect.

Violet pondered for a moment. 'Times have changed with the war. Fashion for fashion's sake isn't à la mode anymore. It isn't what we look like that's important, it's what we do. Quite often I'll wear my uniform when I go to a dance. Everybody has more respect for a woman in the forces, and anyone selfishly pampering herself with makeup and new clothes has become a bit of an outsider.' She shrugged. 'When I'm wearing my uniform, people stop to thank me for the part I'm playing and more men ask me to dance, proud to be seen with a military girl.'

'But what about big events, like weddings?' Nancy asked. 'How do you get a white dress?'

'You don't,' Violet said, thinking of poor Grace. 'Your best chance of a white wedding is to find someone who has an old one that you can alter or borrow, though most people just wear their uniforms.' Nancy looked aghast, and Violet quickly added, 'Otherwise you can wear your best dress and spruce it up with a nice hat and some jewellery. Homemade jewellery is all the rage now that it's hard to get. You can personalize it according to the regiment of your husband-to-be, like a rose for the Lancaster regiment or a tiny drum kit on a brooch. Most jewellery is made from bits and bobs, although I heard of someone who made earrings from the Perspex of a downed German plane.'

'How creative!' Nancy seemed to shudder at the notion. 'They'd never take our white bridal gowns away back home. It would be too bad for morale.'

Dorie shrugged. 'But I did hear that you can't have a train anymore, and that you had to limit the amount of material, no full skirts and puffed sleeves. At least we have nylon now, and we don't have to rely on imported silk.'

Violet had coerced McCauley to keep up a ready supply of nylon stockings right from the start, awed by their strength and versatility. 'I still can't believe nylon is made in a laboratory from chemicals. It feels like a proper material.'

'They use it to make parachutes and everything,' Nancy said. 'I've even seen it made into a wedding dress, and it shines like silk.'

'What about you, Violet?' Dorie asked, dimples showing in her cheeks as she smiled. 'Have you got a fiancé? Will you be borrowing anyone's wedding dress any time soon?'

Violet made a long sigh. 'Well, the Duke of Davenport is a possibility, but it's early days.' She put on an optimistic smile. 'Although truth be told, he's a little dull.'

Dorie looked baffled, her head to one side. 'Does he have to be a duke? That narrows the field, doesn't it?'

'My father told me never to settle for anything less than a title. He said that I have the breeding, the looks, and the suitable lack of education to satisfy even a prince.' She made a little laugh. 'Though truly, I'm starting to wonder if the whole idea is a bit outdated.'

'You don't seem very uneducated to me.' Dorie laughed.

But before she could reply, Nancy cut in. 'It would be so romantic to marry a duke, though, wouldn't it? She would be a duchess!'

Violet lowered her eyes to the floor, gave a little laugh, and then said, 'Well, at least I'd be living in a stately home – that might compensate for him being such a bore!'

Awestruck, they instantly demanded to hear all about Emershall Castle, and by the end, she decided that she could even put up with Davenport in exchange for such a majestic pile.

Couldn't she?

'But don't you want to marry someone you love?' Nancy said with a gleam in her eye. 'I work with a naval officer in one of those crisp, white uniforms, and the way he looks at me, I could just melt.'

'I want someone kind and fun,' Dorie said with enthusiasm. 'Someone who loves animals, just like me, and wants lots of children.'

Soon everyone was talking about the man they wanted to marry, and Violet realized that there was one thing they all wanted above all else: love.

The evening was one she would remember. The food in the canteen was incredible – she had beef, would you believe it! – and the bed was positively sumptuous. But most of all, the company was fun and enlightening. Dorie expounded on every question Violet had about America, from the breathtaking countryside and the sunshine to the big houses and roads.

'You'll have to come and visit, after the war, that is.' She looked a little wistful, thinking about her home. 'We live on a farm in Vermont, and it's just beautiful out there – you won't see such colours in the autumn anywhere else in the whole wide world.'

They talked until the lights went out, and Violet fell into a sound sleep, dreaming of places she had never been, different lives she could have lived. How much easier life would have been if she didn't have to follow the path her father had laid out for her.

In the morning, as Violet drove McCauley back to their base, her mind was still on the conversation from the previous night. Was she mistaken to marry for status rather than love? After all, the rest of her life was an awfully long time to be stuck with someone as dull as Davenport.

'A penny for your thoughts, Fred?' He was sitting in the front again, trying to nudge her into their familiar chatter. 'Did the American girls keep you up all night?'

She laughed. 'Isn't it funny how different the world can look if you see it through someone else's eyes?'

He laughed. 'Did someone hold a mirror up to you, princess, and make you see that you're now a soldier?'

'Don't be so glib! In any case, it's obvious that I'm not a princess anymore.' She laughed, gesturing to her uniform, her hair.

'So, what prompted this introspection, then?'

'It's just that they were so free, so ready and willing to live the life that was right for them, regardless of anyone else.' She paused for a moment as a flock of sheep blocked a hill pass, a sheepdog careening around them to herd them through a gap in the old stone wall into a field. 'Sometimes I wonder what I'd do if I'd been born into a different life, what would make me truly happy.'

'Now, Fred, you know that only *I* could make you happy.'

'Don't be cheeky.' She slapped his arm playfully. 'But seriously, what would make you happy?'

After a moment's thought, he said, 'If I'm honest, Fred, I would say that deep down I want quite simple things. All my father does is work, and I don't want that, and my mother's a socialite, and I don't want that. I love my job in my father's engineering company. It's good to create things, to meet the people who actually benefit from something that you design and build. We designed a bridge last year, a massive project, and it was great to see the communities around it doing so well. It made the young people stay and the businesses grow. You can see just by driving through how they're thriving now, busy and energetic.'

'That sounds a wonderful achievement.'

'And I know you think I'm just a bit of a joker, but I suppose I want to share my life with someone.'

'And what would this lucky girl be like?' she couldn't help asking.

He thought for a while, and then said, 'Probably someone like my middle sister, Carol. She's good fun and knows what makes me tick.'

'You might not know this, Lieutenant, but you're not allowed to marry your sister.'

'I said someone *like* her, not actually her.' He glanced at Violet with a comical grimace. 'I want to be able to relax, to be myself. We can be together doing anything and everything, and we simply know how the other's going to react or what they're going to say. Instead of judging or thinking the other is stupid or mad or pathetic, we find their idiosyncrasies funny or clever or unique. We enjoy each other, just being ourselves.' He paused, pleased with this notion. 'Yes, that's it, isn't it? That's what everyone's looking for, someone who wants to be enjoyed and loved for who they are.'

She raised an eyebrow. 'And where will you find such a wife?'

'Oh, I don't know,' he said with a lilt in his voice. 'You never know where you might find the right one.' He grinned, giving her a sideways look. 'They might be someone sitting right beside you every day, and you'll never know unless you try.'

Violet rolled her eyes, shaking her head. 'You're incorrigible!'

And he softly replied, 'I know, I know. You only have eyes for dukes.'

'That's right,' she said with a smile. 'No room for toads.'

'Don't you need to kiss a few of them, though, to find your prince?' He puckered up his lips comically, and she pulled away, her steering veering very slightly.

'Oh, stop it! I have absolutely no intention of kissing toads or any other amphibian, only the man I'm going to marry.'

'You'll have to be very sure of him then,' he said. 'I imagine that it'll take quite a few tours of his grand estate to win your heart.'

A small brightness came to her eyes as she thought of the opulent Emershall Castle, but then dimmed as she remembered the man who inhabited it. But in spite of this, she said, 'It's every girl's dream to live in a palace.'

He cast a glance at her, adding, 'Just make sure your palace doesn't turn into a prison, duchess.'

GRACE

The late-afternoon sunshine spilled lazily over Aldhurst Manor as Grace hurried to the great front door, trying to ignore the prickle of apprehension. The last thing she wanted to do was try on the wedding dress, and she could only pray that she didn't bump into Hugh. She hadn't seen him since the rainy morning in the church, and regardless of how many times she'd been through their conversation, she knew that the week of her wedding was not the time to dredge up their past.

The butler let her in, and she made her own way up to the spare bedroom, which now looked more like a proper studio. A larger table was covered with design papers, and the chestnut brown coat Cressida was working on for the IncSoc Utility Design Contest hung on a tall, headless dummy, complete with chalk tailor markings.

'I have to confess I'll be sad when we've finished your dress,' Cressida said as she showed her inside. 'It's been such a long time since I worked on something as complex. For the last decade, I've been delegating so much to my staff that I'd quite forgotten the joy of creating something myself.'

'I'm glad you liked it.' Grace smiled.

'And I've been thinking.' She paused, as if still mulling it around in her mind. 'Since it looks like I'll be here for another few months, I'd like to set up a proper design studio here in Aldhurst Manor.'

'How marvellous! I always thought you should.'

'Well, actually, I was going to ask if *you* would like to help me?'

Grace felt her heart miss a beat. 'What do you mean?'

'I would like you to become my assistant, my dear. Your handwork is impeccable, your eye for colour and form is superb, and your design work is coming along nicely. If I am to take on work, I need an efficient, personable assistant here in Aldhurst, and you, my dear, very much fit the bill.'

For a moment, her wedding anxieties were pushed to the side, a shiver of disbelief mixed with excitement stealing through her. 'Are you sure?'

'Absolutely! I asked Mrs Bisgood if you can be spared from the village shop, and she was delighted for you. While I'm in the manor, you can work with me here, and then you can come to London when I set up there. I can teach you about design as we go along, as my apprentice.' She took a satisfied breath and said, 'Grace, dear. You have to look more thrilled at the prospect or I'll begin to wonder if I should look elsewhere.'

And Grace realized she had been standing with her mouth open, hardly able to move. Quickly, she sprung over to her, beaming with joy. 'What can I say? Thank you! And learning to be a designer too? It just seems too wonderful to be true.' But then, her face fell. 'Lawrence won't like it at all, though. He thinks fashion is trivial, that I should be doing something more useful to the church with my time.'

'Do you always have to abide by what he says? In any case, he'll be in the army until the war ends, and who knows how long that might take. You could be a junior designer by then.'

But her sense of loyalty had brought Grace thudding back to

earth. 'Lawrence is right, though. My duty is to the parish. It isn't right for me to do something that doesn't help others.' She slumped down on a chair, her shoulders slouching inward, her head forward and down. 'I have never enjoyed anything as much as working here with you, Cressida. And if it's true, that I do have an instinct for design, I would love to learn more. I just don't know if Lawrence would ever accept it.'

'You need to have faith in yourself, Grace. I see terrific potential in you.' She began tidying away some magazines and design papers on the table, and Grace felt a jolt of desperate disappointment. This was an incredible opportunity offered only once in a lifetime.

And she was turning it down.

As if reading her thoughts, Cressida said, 'You can still do your parish duties after work and at the weekend. The only thing holding you back is the idea that perhaps it won't seem so very holy to some people, Lawrence and the bishop and so forth. But you need to stand up for yourself, Grace. You're not the one who's a vicar, are you? Can't you have a vocation too?'

Her head drooped. 'Being a vicar's wife *is* a vocation, and Lawrence wants to be a deacon too, a position that expects even more from a wife. I wouldn't want to ruin his chances by taking on a profession that is so far removed from the traditional schoolteacher or nurse.'

'But this is your life too, Grace.' Cressida sat down beside her, and then she asked the question that Grace had been trying to shut out. 'Are you sure that's what you want, Grace, to be a vicar's wife?'

A knot twisted inside Grace. 'Being in service to others is who I am, and that's part of why he loves me. It's what brought us together. And I know that if I took this job I would disappoint him because it would be just for me. He can be so very righteous about these things.'

There was a moment when both women looked at each other, with only the sound of the clock ticking the minutes by as Grace's last days of freedom dripped inexorably away, escaping through the cracks of everyday life like sand through cupped hands.

It was Cressida who spoke first. 'Don't fret, Grace. You don't need to decide straight away.' She slowly nodded. 'I'm sure you can help me in some way or another, whether you take the job or not.'

'Oh, Cressida. I don't want to be ungrateful, and of course I want to help you. I just have a sense of dread that Lawrence would never let it rest. He never seems to forget my little vanities and moments of indulgence.' She made an embarrassed little laugh.

'Grace, dear, why don't you write him a letter when you get home, explain why you want to do it. Then you can see how he responds before making a decision.'

She nodded. 'That's a good idea. It'll give him time to think it over before he sees me. I can't bear it when he's disappointed.'

Getting up, Cressida said, 'Why don't you try on the dress for now. I'll pop into the other room while you change.'

As soon as she was gone, Grace heaved a sigh, pulling the wedding dress from her bag.

Gently, she lay it down on the table and opened the fastenings, as her new husband would do on their wedding night, no doubt.

Panic welled up inside her, but she swallowed hard. *Come on, Grace! This is what you've always wanted.*

With an air of forced practicality, she put on the gown, feeling the smooth coldness of the material around her skin.

As if to calm herself, her gaze drifted to the open window, the edge of the creamy-white curtain fluttering in the breeze, a gull soaring through the sky above the lake.

Outside, late spring was at its very finest, the scent of freshly cut grass seeping inside, reminding her of her childhood, the freedom, the escape.

A movement on the path through the lawns made her turn to see Hugh, home early from work in his Westminster suit. He was walking to the lake's edge, where he stopped, picking up a stone and skimming it across the still, dark water. She watched as it bounced four times and chuckled to herself. They would have done seven or eight at least when they were young. He was quite out of practice.

But then, just as she was about to turn back into the room, he sat on a rock and began to untie his shoes, briskly turning up his trousers all the way to the knee, then peeling off his jacket and tie, tossing them onto the rock beside him. Without hesitation, he began to wade into the water then stopped, standing in the shallows, his hand shielding his eyes from the sun.

She wasn't sure why it surprised her – it's what they'd done all the time when they were young. But it was unlike the Hugh of today to be so carefree, so boyish.

Slowly, he unfastened the collar and cuffs of his shirt and began to roll up his sleeves, bending down to scoop the cool water onto his face and neck, and she noticed how his body moved in the same way as it did when he was a boy, except that now he was more muscular, stronger.

Entranced by his form, she watched, carelessly wondering if he would take his shirt off completely, but then he suddenly turned to look back at the shore, then up at the manor.

His eyes seemed to meet hers through the open window, and quick as a flash, she pulled back, her heart pounding with humiliation – had he seen her watching him?

Trying to calm her breath, she busied herself tidying the table, organizing the design papers.

Perhaps he hadn't been looking at her. In any case, he knew

that she was sometimes there with Cressida. Why was she worrying so much?

'Now, all we need to do is a few final adjustments.' Cressida returned, a box of pins in her hand.

Grace swallowed, her eyes going impulsively back to the window.

But Hugh had gone.

With a flourish, Cressida came over, exclaiming, 'You look truly magnificent! I'm not an expert on wedding gowns, but honestly, you really do make the most enchanting bride.'

'Bride.' A shot of panic seemed to flash through her. 'I can't believe this is truly happening.'

'Why wouldn't it, dear?' Cressida said, rearranging the neckline, carefully avoiding her eyes until she added, 'Unless you're not in love with him.'

A shudder went through her. 'Why would you say that?'

'All I know is that you don't appear terribly eager. Look at Lottie, who is so utterly smitten that it reminds me of being young and in love myself.' She smiled, and then made a dramatic sigh. 'But you go positively pale at the mention of it.'

Grace looked crossly at her reflection. 'Oh, Cressida. I simply don't know anymore. Sometimes I wonder if I should be more than a vicar's wife, but what would Lawrence say – what would everyone think?'

'Listen to yourself, Grace! You only seem concerned with how other people see you. You have to decide what *you* want. It's *your* life. You get to choose how you live it.' She began rearranging the skirts. 'Sometimes I feel that your mother's death set you on a path, and you bravely took it, but then you simply stayed on it, so used to it that you forgot to think of the other paths you could have taken. You've done all you can do to be loved and needed by the whole community, with all your parish visits and helping others. But the one person you seem to have failed is yourself. Decide what Grace wants for a change.'

'But what can I do? I can't stop the wedding now!' Panic rose inside her. 'I can't bear it when people are disappointed with me.'

'Of course you can stop the wedding, my dear. It's never good form to let other people down, but it's far more important not to let yourself down. You only have one life, Grace, and it's short. You can't afford to throw it away on something that isn't right.'

'But I'm not sure what I want, and even if I do, how can I tell if it will ever come to anything?'

'Well, that's a risk you have to take.' Cressida's eyes flickered to the window. 'What is it you think you might want? Hugh, by any chance?'

The words slid out into the room – into the world – and a feeling of terror grew inside Grace that the idea was out there, exposed.

Slowly, she felt herself crumple, and she sank into a chair, her face in her hands. 'Is it that obvious?'

Cressida sat beside her. 'Not to everyone, but I have been spending a little time with the pair of you. It's clear that there was once a strong bond between you, and now it seems that you're growing back together. It's quite endearing, actually. When you're around him, you become more relaxed. There's a lovely humour that comes out – in him too. Perhaps it's always been there, but you've wallpapered over it by trying to be the best parish worker Kent has ever known.'

A laugh spilled out of Grace. 'I think that's what shocked Hugh the most when he first saw me. I used to be so different as a child, and now, well, I'm not really sure who I am. Sometimes I feel as if I'm no one at all.'

'You're Grace, pure and simple. Why everyone has this notion that you have to be one type of person or another is beyond
me. We're all a blend of different ingredients, and I think there's
a great deal more to you than Lawrence sees – or wants to see.'

'But what am I going to do? I feel so much when I see Hugh
– the more time we spend together, the more it's like old times.'
She stopped, barely able to speak about it.

'Were you in love with him when you were young?'

A shiver came over Grace with the truth of it. How she'd
dreamed about him every night, of them running away together,
hiding in the woods, making love under the stars. 'We were children then, it's hard to say. But I did always think he'd be part of
my life. It felt so natural.'

'Did you ever do anything about it?'

A deep blush raced to her face. She'd barely allowed herself
to acknowledge it, let alone tell anyone else. 'Only once, just
before he left for boarding school. It was the end of the perfect
summer. We were swimming in the lake, and well, we began to
kiss. It seemed so right, so instinctive.' She paused, remembering
the magic of that moment. 'So extraordinarily wonderful.'

'And did you ever talk about it?'

She shook her head. 'He left, and then my mother died. I had
to leave school to work and help Dad. When he came home, he
seemed to have better things to do than see me.' She shrugged.
'His father often planned for him to stay in London or visit relatives when he was off school or college. After a while, it was
clear I wasn't going to see him again.'

'Well, you certainly see him now. He makes quite an effort to
be available when you make your parish visits, I've noticed.'
Cressida gazed out of the window. 'I imagine my brother Eustace wanted to keep him away from you. He arranged for Hugh
to marry the Fortescue girl – there's money in that family and
Eustace needed it for the manor.' She gestured to the tired-looking

curtains. 'I don't know what Hugh will do, Grace. But I do know that every path meanders back to the past. Inside, there's always a different part of us existing in another time and place.' She frowned, as if remembering something herself, and then with a sigh, she looked back at the dress. 'For now, though, you need to make your own decisions, and the most pressing one is whether you want to marry Lawrence.'

Grace got up and went to the mirror, looking at herself in the beautiful dress. 'But it's only days away. I can't cancel it now, not when everyone's put so much effort into it. How could I let everyone down? It would be the only topic of conversation in the village for weeks.' She groaned. 'And what about poor Lawrence? He'll be so disappointed!'

There was a pause, and then Cressida said carefully, 'I'm sure Lawrence will get over it. Some of the things you tell me about him make me wonder if he is more keen to have a parish helper than a wife.'

A breeze came in through the window, stirring the curtains and making the dress sleeves flutter. 'Lottie suspects that too. She says there's no passion in him – you know how she adores that kind of thing.' But Grace's face fell as she remembered how he was with Hugh. 'When Lawrence saw Hugh and me in the village hall last week, I was so frightened that he'd be jealous or possessive. But he didn't react at all. He began talking about his work. It was as if he was indifferent, so intent on his own mission that I hardly mattered.'

'He didn't say anything?' Cressida frowned in disbelief. 'Not that I hold jealous rages in high esteem, but I would have thought he'd realize how beautiful you are, how another man might be keen.'

A blush came over Grace's face, unsure how to take the compliment. 'He mentioned my hair being different when we were back at the vicarage, but only in that it was a little frivolous, taking my time away from my duties.' She grimaced. 'I used to think that it was endearingly correct and modest of him, but I'm starting to wonder if he simply isn't interested in me in that way.'

'He is excited about your honeymoon, though, isn't he?'

'We're staying a night in a hotel beside the Canterbury Cathedral Museum. He thought we'd both enjoy it.' Grace gave a muted laugh, but then her face fell. 'But if I'm honest, I was rather glad of it. I have a good idea what happens during honeymoons, and I-I'm not sure I'd like to do that with him.' She blushed.

Cressida most certainly didn't. 'Oh, dear Grace! If you're dreading it, that's not a good sign.' She took Grace's hands and peeled her away from the mirror. 'After Jack was killed, I decided that I would never love anyone else enough to marry, and I have been very happy with that decision. I have been much more content on my own than with someone I didn't truly adore. Times are changing, things are getting better for women, we have more freedom, more say in the home and our work, and we can even petition for divorce now too – although that's still very frowned upon. But we have yet to have that same freedom within marriage. Once you're married, you'll always come second to him. He will be the man you have to love and obey, the vicar under whom you serve, and the head of your household. Don't walk into this thinking that any marriage is a blessing. To many women, it's a drudge, and to others, it's a snake pit. I'm not saying that's what will happen to you, but this doesn't seem to be what you want, and that's never a good start.'

Fiddling with the gauze above the bodice, creasing and recreasing the soft white fabric into place, Grace let this sink in.

'I don't think I can marry him.' The quiet words came out of her as if from a different woman. Her voice wasn't scared nor upset. It was plain, understanding, as if she was finally accepting something she had always known, deep inside. 'He wants me for all the wrong reasons, but worse, I agreed to marry him for all the wrong reasons too. I wanted a family, and now I can see that Lawrence would never be the father I want for my children. My own father is emotional and intelligent and creative, while Lawrence seems only to be intent on being a good vicar – or deacon, or bishop even. My life with him would be nothing like my mother's was with Dad, and it was foolish for me to even think it could be.'

For a moment, Grace looked at the floor, despondent, but then suddenly she shrugged. 'At least now I feel I can take up your very kind offer and learn how to design properly.' But then her face fell. 'Except that I'll be conscripted now that I'm not getting married.'

Cressida put her hand up. 'Don't you remember? Clothes manufacturing is a reserved occupation, so you can fulfil your conscription right here in Aldhurst Manor.'

A strange new breath of air came into Grace's lungs, as if it were the first she'd had for a very long time. 'Thank you, Cressida. I'll work as hard as I can.' A muted laugh came out of her. 'I could become the next Cressida Westcott.'

'You could be the first Grace Carlisle,' Cressida corrected her. 'It will be fabulous to have you on board. We'll make a great team.'

Slowly, Grace slipped out of the gown and hung it up, but instead of feeling sadness at her dream of marrying coming to nothing, she could only feel a sense of liberation, her spirit desperate to run free. 'Thank you for all your help with the dress, Cressida. I'm sorry that it won't be worn, that it was all for nothing.'

'Stop talking such nonsense, child. It's rekindled a keen interest in me. In any case, I believe that Lottie still needs a white dress. And perhaps after Lottie, someone else might want to borrow it. Wasn't it your idea for the Sewing Circle to let needy brides borrow it as necessary? That would be marvellous for the war effort, don't you think?'

Thus it was that as Grace set off for home that evening, she decided it was time to take charge of her life.

She had to stop listening to other people.

She had to follow her instincts.

And she had to make her own decisions.

Without even thinking, she knew exactly what it was that she wanted.

As soon as she got home, she went up to her bedroom and pulled out a single sheet of writing paper.

Dear Lawrence,

I don't know how to start this letter, how to begin to explain what it is that I'm going through. It's the war, really. It puts you in different situations, makes you see yourself in new, unconsidered ways – and sometimes it is as if life is peeled back to show who you really are deep inside.

When I first accepted your proposal, I felt such immense gratitude that you were willing to stand by me, love me through thick and thin. But since then, I have come to realize that I no longer need anyone to stand beside me. I can stand on my own. I know now that I don't have to be married to have my voice heard. I am already a person in my own right.

I'm sure you have gathered by now where this letter is heading. It has no bearing on you or the love and kindness you have to offer a woman in matrimony, only that the woman will not be me. I admire and respect you for your work, for the kind and godly man that you are, and I know now that what I felt was a dutiful love for you as a good man of the church and not the romantic type of love between a man and a woman. Our marriage would have been one of duty, not one of happiness, and as much as I regret having to upset you, I would not have been able to live like that.

With apologies for any upset I have caused,
Grace

CRESSIDA

The following Sewing Circle evening, Cressida and Grace walked down to the village hall, Cressida hoping the supportive group would rally around Grace. Sewing evenings were always good for the soul, sharing news both good and bad, discussing new projects, and listening to Mrs Todd's vastly inaccurate summary of a Hollywood film she'd seen.

But it was the friendship that mattered the most, the sense that they were part of a group, that if one of them was in trouble, they would drop everything without delay.

It was an unspoken rule: All members helped one another out.

Less than a week since she'd cancelled her wedding, Grace swung between relief and self-rebuke. Thankfully, she'd plunged into her new role as design assistant at the manor, but this evening, Grace carried a bag containing her mother's white dress, a reminder of the wedding that was no longer to take place.

'Did you receive a reply from Lawrence yet, dear?'

'A letter came this morning, and he didn't appear all that upset.' She heaved a sigh. 'In fact, he only seemed glad that I discovered my inkling for clothes design *before* we were married. Then he wished me well in my new career.'

'Well, that was a little cold of him. But then again, he never did seem to be a man of passions, did he?'

'No, I don't think he was. But evidently, he saw something good in our engagement, as he said that the experience had made him see that a good marriage could be helpful in his mission, and that the bishop might view the right sort of wife as a real boon to a deacon.' A sad little chuckle came out of her. 'And then he asked if I knew anyone who had a lot of experience in parish work.'

'Didn't I say that he wanted a parish worker, not a wife?' But after Grace's laughter had quieted down, Cressida added gently, 'But it must be upsetting. You deserve to be appreciated for who you are, Grace, not for what you can do for a man's career.'

'Yes,' Grace said. 'It's rather demoralizing, but to be honest, I'm not sure I loved him as much as I loved the idea of being able to have a family of my own.'

'I'm sure you'll find another groom soon enough, one who likes you for you.'

'Well, actually, I have decided I need to take a leaf out of Lottie's book, work out what *I* want instead of accepting the first man who offers.'

Cautiously, Cressida asked, 'What about Hugh?'

'I don't know,' Grace began hesitantly. 'I was hoping to see him, tell him, but he seems to have vanished.'

'Didn't you know? He left for London the morning after you were at the manor, saying he wouldn't be back until Lottie and Flynn's wedding next week. I wondered if he was trying to avoid your wedding. If he feels anything for you at all, it wouldn't have been pleasant to see you marrying someone else.'

Cressida was secretly keeping her fingers crossed that Lottie's wedding would prove the ideal backdrop for romance between Grace and Hugh. In her mind, they both brought out the best in each other. Grace made Hugh kinder and more relaxed, while Hugh spurred the fun in Grace. She lit up when he was there, a spirit inside her reawakened, and it was the same for him too.

The Sewing Circle was already buzzing as they stepped into the hall. Today they were patching children's garments for a clothing exchange.

In her uniform, Violet was pulling some boy's shorts from one of the boxes. 'Some of these donations are positively threadbare.'

'It's unpatriotic to throw away clothes,' Martha said crisply, focusing hard on the shirt she was desperately trying to bring back from the dead. 'Anything utterly irretrievable can go into the spare fabric box. We can use them to cover holes or to make patchwork clothes.'

'No wonder different-coloured pockets are all the rage. *Vogue* is telling us to spruce up our wardrobes with a brightly coloured pocket here or a little rabbit fur around a collar, now that so many people are breeding them for food.' Violet looked closely at two girl's dresses. 'Maybe I could take the top of this one and stitch it to the bottom of this one.'

'Mrs Hanley's been asking for a clothing exchange for weeks,' Mrs Kettlewell said. 'It's the only place where you can swap the children's clothes for bigger ones as they grow. With the government's new rule that even second-hand clothes need clothing coupons, clothes exchanges are the only way for her. Even though children's clothes use far fewer coupons because they grow so fast, she still has to supplement them with her own coupons.'

Martha sniffed moodily. 'It's the same in our household, except we have to donate all of our clothing coupons to save for Lottie's ridiculous trousseau.'

Ignoring Martha's whining, Mrs Bisgood turned to Lottie. 'Have you decided on the outfit for your wedding yet?'

Lottie shook her head. 'I'll have to wear the royal blue gown I got before the war. At least no one expects anything special these days, and it's a lovely fit.'

Cressida gave Grace a nudge, and she stood up. 'I have a much better idea, Lottie.' She brought out her bag. 'I'm keeping my promise and sharing my wedding dress with anyone who'd like it, and I'd love you to be the first.'

With a cry of delight, Lottie bounded forward.

Carefully, Grace took out the dress and draped it ceremoniously over Lottie's arms, the girl hugging her with excitement. 'Thank you, Grace.'

'No, it's you I need to thank,' Grace replied, looking at the dear group, 'all of you. Without you I would never have been able to bring this beautiful gown back to life.'

Lottie could barely take her eyes off the dress, and Cressida watched her with delight, remembering the exhilaration of being in love. Romance and courtship had left her world a long time ago, along with the young men at the Somme, and she was suddenly filled with a kind of longing for what she'd missed, a nostalgia for that feeling of connection.

Grace looked around at the others. 'And remember that I offered it to everyone who helped. We can refit it for anyone who needs it.'

'What about you, Mrs Todd?' Lottie urged with a wink. 'I've seen the way you look at Mr Farlow. Do you think he might pop the question?'

Everyone stifled a laugh as Mrs Todd sat po-faced, her eyes

on her knitting, saying only, 'I'll keep my own counsel on that matter.'

'This is such a lovely thing for you to do, Grace,' Mrs Bisgood said. 'And you know, I'm quite sure I have my old dress somewhere too. We could modernize it, lend it to anyone who needs one. It'll be lovely to give it a second life.'

'That's a wonderful idea,' Cressida said. 'Why don't you bring it in and we can see what we can do with it.'

'Wedding gowns are a much-prized commodity these days,' Lottie said. 'The girls at the parachute factory are always desperate for wedding dresses, and one of the Land Girls at Easons Farm is getting married soon too. They'd all be happy to borrow a dress.'

Violet piped up, 'A friend of mine in the ATS is planning to marry in her beastly uniform. I'm sure she'd be delighted to borrow a proper wedding dress, if she can. Servicewomen get only fourteen clothing coupons a year, so no one has enough for a smart dress. It's impossible.'

Mrs Kettlewell said, 'Since quite a few people seem to be in need of a dress, perhaps we can ask if anyone else in the village has a wedding dress to donate. I might even still have my old one somewhere at home.'

'That's the spirit.' Cressida looked around the room. 'We could form an exchange of sorts, lend dresses to any bride who needs one, completely free and without the need for any clothes coupons at all. What better way to help our fellow women keep up their spirits?'

'We can call it the Wedding Dress Exchange,' Violet said, and she whipped a notebook out of her pocket. 'I'll make some posters that we can put up in the neighbouring villages. Let's see, what shall we say?' A moment later, she held up a sheet of paper.

The Aldhurst Wedding Dress Exchange

Would you like to borrow a wedding dress so that you can have a white wedding?

Do you have an old wedding dress that can be remodelled or mended for other women to use?

Please telephone the Aldhurst Sewing Circle at Aldhurst 467 or pop over to one of our meetings on a Tuesday evening in the village hall.

'I put down the Aldhurst Manor telephone number for now, since Cressida or Grace will be there to answer.' She glanced over at them. 'I hope that's all right?'

'Absolutely,' Cressida said. 'I can ask my clients for their wedding dresses too. That should add some fine ones to our stock.' She looked over the excited group, thrilled with her new idea. Muriel would think she was insane, of course, starting a community charity for wedding dresses – an item she'd never worn herself. But there was a spirit of hope in it, a sense of sharing, of belonging.

Mrs Todd, who had set her knitting aside to darn a woollen cardigan, added, 'You can have mine too. It's a bit old-fashioned, but if you think you'll be able to do something with it, I'm happy to donate it.'

'That's lovely, thank you.' Cressida made a note.

'You'll have to get rid of the dreadful bustle at the back,' Mrs Todd added. 'It stops you from being able to sit down properly.' She huffed. 'The things we had to go through!'

'At least undergarments were available in those days,' Mrs Kettlewell said. 'Corsets are so hard to get with the war. My girls swear that they look just as good without, but I have no idea how I'd fit into my clothes. If I stopped wearing my corset, my back would simply give up on me.'

Martha laughed. 'You're so old-fashioned, Mum. The idea is that you stay slim and fit so that you don't need to wear one. A friend of mine's a Land Girl, and she says you can't do farm work wearing a corset, so none of them bother. It's far more comfortable.'

'I've stopped wearing one too,' Lottie said, getting up and swirling around to show off her trim, corsetless waist.

'Food rationing and war work have made us all much slimmer,' Cressida said. 'I see it every day with my clients. They all need a new tuck here or something taken in there.'

Mrs Todd was looking curiously at Lottie as she twirled around. 'But what on earth do you wear underneath?'

She grinned, glanced over her shoulder to make sure there wasn't anyone at the door, then picked up her skirt to reveal a shimmering pair of white silk shorts, flaring out from a fitted waist and finishing almost indecently close to the bottom of her behind. 'It's a pair of camiknickers!' she exclaimed. 'We got one of the faulty panels at the parachute factory and made half a dozen. Aren't they dashing? Some of the girls have cut up a net curtain to use instead of lace for a trimming.'

She gave another twirl.

'How do they stay up?' Mrs Todd asked.

It was a good question. Elastic couldn't be found for love or money, all available rubber going to make tires for planes and tanks. A rather inelastic replica was on the market, but it didn't have the capabilities or its usual longevity.

And women's underwear had been the chief victim.

'There's a button at the waistband, thank goodness. None of that elastic that gives up halfway through the evening,' Lottie said. 'I was at a dance last week, and as I was chatting to my handsome fiancé, I felt my drawers sliding down my thighs. It seemed a bit indelicate to try to grip hold of them through my dress – by this time they were around my knees – so I simply put on the air of someone who was in complete control of the situation, and let them wriggle down to my feet so that I could demurely step out of them. Then casual as you please, I bent down, picked them up, and tucked them into my handbag.' She let out a laugh, the younger members joining in.

Mrs Bisgood looked horrified. 'What on earth did Lord Flynn have to say?'

She set a hand saucily on her hip. 'He seemed to think it was all very alluring.'

'Camiknickers are all the rage,' Violet interjected. 'I heard that Patricia Mountbatten was given a silk map of Northern Italy by her beau – evidently the stuff of espionage – and she had her dressmaker run up a full set of underwear from it, camiknickers and all.'

Meanwhile, Mrs Todd was still inspecting the undergarment in question. 'But how do you hold your stockings up?' she asked. 'Corsets have clips attached at the bottom, but those modern monstrosities have nothing.'

Lottie grinned, turning around to show off her brown legs. 'I ran out of stockings in 1940. Then I got a bottle of the new Liquid Stockings, but it doesn't last awfully long and it's quite pricey, so I've been using gravy browning. It works well, provided you brush it on evenly and have someone pencil a straight line up the back of your leg.' She turned and grinned. 'You just have to watch out in case there are any dogs around. One whiff of the gravy, and they're after you.'

Laughter went around, Mrs Todd asking, 'But what about the top part? How do you, well, shape your bosom?'

With another glance over her shoulder, she undid the buttons of her blouse, opening it to show them a white brassiere.

'Goodness, is that sturdy enough?' Mrs Bisgood muttered. 'It looks so small.'

'It holds them up quite well, don't you think?' Lottie looked down to admire it.

'Does it use metal underwires?' Cressida asked. 'A lot of them don't because of the metal shortages, but I think you need them.'

'Yes,' Lottie agreed. 'The woman in the shop told me I needed the wire ones, and they were a bit more difficult to get.'

'Well, I think it looks rather ungainly,' Mrs Bisgood muttered disparagingly.

And this sentiment was echoed by Mrs Todd, who folded her arms, concluding, 'It'll never catch on.'

The rest of the evening flew by, and as the women began to put away their work, Cressida's eyes drifted to the window, as they often did these days.

Sometimes she would see Ben, especially now that the evenings were lighter. He'd be striding from the vicarage to the church or to visit a parishioner. He was looking more upright these days, more present, engaging with parishioners, taking care of the church without Grace's help. He'd come out of his shell – and out of his books – and Cressida wondered if she had been part of the reason for that change.

They had become good friends and often spent an evening together, her popping over for dinner, talking about the old days – and the new ones too. Sometimes they'd look over photographs, and other times they'd sit in the cosy living room listening to the radio. One night a waltz came on, one that they remembered from the Chartham Hunt Balls of old, and with a gentlemanly bow, he asked her to dance, and together they waltzed haphazardly around the small living room in the darting warmth of the fire.

As the Sewing Circle ladies began to leave, she watched him

come out of the vicarage, the last vestiges of the golden evening sunshine throwing long shadows across the grass.

Outside the hall, Ben greeted the women as they left, each of them pausing to talk and give Morris a pat, and he waited until they had left before he turned to Cressida.

'I'm glad to see you.' A gleam came to his dark eyes as he led the way to the path. 'Would you care to come for a walk with me? I have some good news for you.'

'Of course,' she replied. 'What is it?'

'Since there's no word about Morris's owners, the vet thinks it's best for me to keep him.'

'That's wonderful!'

'I thought so too. Well, he and I share a love of birdwatching – albeit with slightly different aims in mind – so I thought we'd do well together. He's already taught me so much: to live life to the fullest, to have fun, and to not be afraid to express your enthusiasm.' He grinned.

'What a great partnership it'll be!' Cressida said, thinking it was precisely what Ben needed. She bent down to give Morris an extra rub as the dog gazed up at them with excited devotion, and as she took in the dewy spring evening, the sound of the sewing ladies laughing as they walked home, and the companionship of the sturdy, gentle man beside her, she realized that she was happier in that moment than she had been in a very long time.

VIOLET

Long hours were part and parcel of Violet's job, and it was almost dark as she walked home to the manor through the village a few nights later. Her mind was busy, dwelling on a few German planes seen over Kent that afternoon. There was talk of them being reconnaissance planes, trying to pinpoint military bases ripe for a full bombing mission – bases like Darley Grange. It was unnerving, and although they were told to get on as usual, everyone was wary, watching the skies, wondering if they were next.

'Hello, Violet,' a voice called from behind her. 'Isn't it a little late for you?' It was Grace, hurrying to catch up, laden with two large bags, one in each hand.

'That's army life for you.' Violet eyed the bags. 'It looks as if you have long hours too.'

'We're finishing the dress for Lottie's wedding, and I'm working on a gown for Lady Marley too. I know it's a bit late, but it's such fun to be doing proper design work. You should see Lady Marley's gown!'

For her sake and everyone else's, Violet was exceptionally relieved that Grace hadn't married that old, earnest cleric of hers. He was dull, and he made her dull too. It had only been a week since she'd called it off, but already there was more life in the girl, an energy about her, and Violet liked her all the more for it.

As they left the village and made their way down the narrow lane, night was falling fast around them, the sky a dark blue against the black hilly horizon. Violet felt herself speed up, the shadows eerie and looming.

But just as she did, Grace stopped in her tracks, her eyes open wide. 'Did you hear that?'

'No.' Violet wondered what had got into the girl.

Grace mouthed to her, 'It's a barn owl.'

They stood in silence, and Violet was just about to say that it had flown away, when it came, a low, clear hoot, echoing through the lane.

'I don't think I've ever heard one before,' Violet whispered, surprised by the wistfulness of the call.

But Grace had her finger to her lips. Putting her bags down, she climbed up the bank on the side of the lane to peer through the bushes to the field beyond.

Then something made her stop dead in her tracks.

'What is it?' Although she was in no mood for it, Violet clambered up the bank beside her.

That's when she saw it.

Dangling from a branch of a tree on the other side of the meadow was something long, moving gently as it shone in the dying dusk.

It took Violet only a moment to work out what it was. 'It's a parachute,' she murmured.

Grace added with panic, 'Which means someone had to come down with it, a Nazi or a dangerous spy.' Unconsciously, she pulled on Violet's arm, dragging her to hide behind the bushes. 'We should get someone.'

'No, come on.' Violet tugged her down the row of bushes

between the fields to the tree. 'We can't let all that lovely silk go to waste!'

When they were adjacent to it, Grace looked around anxiously. 'We should get the Home Guard. Archie Kettlewell will know what to do.'

But Violet's hand was on her arm. 'Shh! We don't know whether it's one of ours or not, or even if the person using it is still here.' Her eyes met Grace's with a glint of determination. 'Let's see if we can get the parachute first.'

'You can't be serious!' Grace gasped. 'A Nazi might be in the woods at the far end, just waiting for us to go over so that he can shoot us!'

'Oh, come on, Grace! Just look at that beautiful silk! Think of what we could do with it!'

'It's illegal,' Grace started. 'We're not allowed to keep parachute silk for personal use.'

'It wouldn't be for personal use – we'd be able to make wedding dresses out of it, for the exchange. We'd be doing the community a disservice by letting it go.' Violet let out an exasperated huff. 'In any case, no one follows that rule. At least we'll be creating something to help morale. What better use could there be for it?' She stood, hands on hips. 'In fact, I think we deserve it, for everything we're going through with war work and all these bombs.'

'But we'll be caught,' Grace panicked.

'If you can honestly tell me that you haven't heard of someone keeping a found parachute, then I'll let you fetch the Home Guard.' Waiting for a response that she knew wouldn't come, Violet reaffixed her hat, ready to head over the top of the bank into the field. 'Are you coming or not?'

With a huff of acceptance, Grace whispered, 'Are you trained to deal with situations like this? It could be dangerous.'

'Of course I am,' Violet lied. 'Now, buck up, Grace.'

Slowly, they weaved through the bushes and then made a dash to the base of the tree, no sign of any loitering Nazis.

Sensing Grace's reluctance to step into the open to survey the parachute and work out how to get it down from the tree, Violet mustered herself and strode over to inspect the harness.

'It doesn't have any writing on it,' she said. 'There's no way of telling whose it is.'

'Surely, he wouldn't have left it dangling if it was ours.' Grace peered out from a nearby bush. 'How are we going to get it down?'

Violet sized up the tree. 'I'll just climb up.' She began scrambling onto the first lower branch.

Grace looked around nervously. 'You will hurry, won't you?'

'Of course I will.'

After a few minutes of Violet not getting awfully far, Grace made a loud huff. 'Honestly, Violet, you never were one for the outdoors, were you?' And in a matter of a minute, Grace had clambered halfway up the tree and tightrope-walked along a length of branch to the parachute.

'It's stuck on a twig. I'll give it a shake to let it loose.'

As she shook, she grabbed hold of a nearby branch, causing Violet to say, 'Grace, you really are quite the climber, aren't you? Who'd have known you had such a skill!'

'Thank your brother,' she laughed. 'He was the one who taught me.'

After several shakes, the parachute began to break free.

'Come on, Grace. Give it a bit of oomph!'

'If you think there's a better way to do it, you can climb up here and jolly well do it yourself!' Grace said, laughing. 'Besides, I don't want to tear it,' she said, realizing the worth of their bounty at last. 'You have no idea how soft this material is.'

In the end, she had to get up onto the next branch in order to undo the cloth from a clench of tightly meshed stems, and the parachute fluttered to the ground, ghostly white in the near darkness.

Briskly, Violet began to unstrap it from the harness. 'All right, now you can go and fetch Archie.'

Grace jumped down from the lowest branch. 'But what am I going to tell him? That we found a parachute harness but no parachute?'

Violet shrugged, looking around for something else the airman might have dropped or left behind. 'We'll have to hope he doesn't ask too many questions. We've both known him since we were children, after all. Besides, he's always been keen on me – he's not going to get me in trouble.'

Rolling her eyes, Grace began to run back across the field.

It felt like an eternity before Violet heard the others coming fast through the field. But as soon as Mrs Bisgood shouted, 'Bravo, Violet! You're the heroes of the hour!' she began to feel quite pleased with herself.

The large, comforting form of Archie striding towards her was only tarnished by the worry that he'd ask too many questions. In haste, she realized that she needed to hide the parachute before anyone else spotted it, so she stashed it quickly behind a large bush.

Then she spotted something. In Grace's hand was one of the bags she'd had in the lane. Had she found the presence of mind to bring it with her? Thank goodness she was getting into the spirit of things at last!

With a sideways nod, Grace indicated the bag, which was now empty – she'd evidently moved its contents to the other bag – and she opened it, ready for Violet to covertly roll the parachute inside.

Meanwhile, half the village had gathered to watch Archie and two other members of the Home Guard inspect the harness and search the area for any other clues to the airman's identity or whereabouts.

'I don't suppose you noticed a parachute, did you?' he asked Grace, looking evenly into her eyes.

Violet's pulse quickened. It would be too awful to get this far and then have Grace, the perfect vicar's daughter, be unable to lie.

But Grace replied, 'It's a bit too dark to see anything clearly, don't you think?' Violet let out her breath, impressed with her new partner in crime.

But Archie wasn't finished. 'How did you manage to see the harness in the dark? And what were you doing out here in the field so late in the evening anyway?'

'Oh,' she said, innocent as can be. 'We heard the hoot of a barn owl from the lane and came to investigate.'

For a moment, his eyes went from one to the other. 'I see. And did you find this barn owl?'

She only shrugged her shoulders. 'As I say, it's a little too dark to see anything, isn't it?'

Archie asked a few more questions about the parachute, but no one seemed to know where it had gone. In the end, he had to assume that the airman had taken it with him – although as Mrs Bisgood gave her a large, dramatic wink, Violet had no doubt that Archie wouldn't be at all surprised when a few new silk dresses turned up in their wedding dress exchange.

Little by little the crowd began to disperse, the chill of the night coming in, and the notion of a comfy bed awaiting them.

After everyone had gone, Violet and Grace resumed their journey to the manor. Only this time, Violet was carrying one of Grace's bags for her, and the sound of the pair laughing carried jubilantly through the trees.

VIOLET

Lottie and Flynn's wedding day was sunny and bright, the old church in Aldhurst packed to the rafters with friends, family, and almost the entire village. As she sat in a crowded pew waiting for the ceremony to begin, Violet craned her neck, trying to spot the other members of the Sewing Circle.

'I'll never be able to see through the crowd,' she muttered to Cressida beside her.

The Kettlewells were a large local family, and as far as Violet could see, they had evidently bred like rabbits over the centuries to provide a fine throng of support for Lottie, one of their best, marrying a lord. With many of the men away, the crowd contained mainly women, many with children, and the trills of the organ music were harmonized by shrieks and calls of various youngsters, including one incredibly young Kettlewell letting loose with a full-throttle bellow.

Shafts of sunshine were tinted blue and gold by the stained-glass windows, and the scent of a dozen vases of fresh spring flowers spruced the air with all the excitement and elegance of a good, traditional wedding. It was such a joy to step inside, far away from the militarized world outside.

For war standards, the event was busy, people coming from Canterbury and even London to celebrate Lord Flynn's wedding. As the occasion offered a chance to meet a well-to-do future spouse, Violet had decided against her frumpy uniform. Instead, she wore a springlike primrose-yellow day dress from before the war, setting it off with a matching wide-brimmed hat and a pair of high-heeled shoes. Even Cressida had been impressed with her look.

Yet, no matter how much Violet tried to feel happy for Lottie, she couldn't help feeling a dose of self-pity. It wasn't that it should be her marrying Lord Flynn; no, it was more than that.

'I can't bear this war,' she muttered to Cressida. 'It's making marriage all wrong.'

'Please try to make sense, Violet,' Cressida said, looking straight ahead. 'I'm not sure you can simply say that people marrying is "wrong". Perhaps the drive to marry from the same class – which has only ever been a way to maintain a certain semblance of elitism – has diminished.' She paused in thought. 'Everyone's working alongside people from all spheres with the war. They're bound to meet more varied love interests than usual.'

'But they don't have to *marry* them.'

'I don't see why not, provided they love each other – isn't that the main thing?'

'Marriage never had anything to do with love in the past. My parents never did anything as base as *love* each other. *Love* is going to be the downfall of society at this rate.'

'I know you don't like hearing it, but your father was a traditionalist, Violet. Your poor mother was expected to obey, not love and cherish. Would you really like to have a husband who treated you as an employee or a servant?'

Violet frowned. 'But he always told me that marriage was

about keeping the Westcott bloodline pure. He spoke of my mother as if she were greatly treasured.'

'She was treasured for what she could *do* – continue the West-cott bloodline.' Cressida reached out and gently took Violet's hand. 'She wasn't treasured for who she *was*.'

'You've got it wrong. He was so utterly heartbroken after she died that he never remarried.'

Cressida looked fondly into Violet's eyes, patting her hand to dampen the reality. 'I suspect that he didn't remarry because it was easier for him to enjoy his lady friends and his London clubs without the nuisance of a spouse. He'd already had a wife to provide legitimate offspring, and that accomplished, why should he need another?' She gave her a sorry smile. 'I know it's prob-ably not what you'd like to hear, my dear. But I find it's always better to know the truth.'

Violet felt a tumult of thoughts and memories cascade through her, everything slightly rearranged with this new infor-mation. How long had she spent looking at her father's memory through the eyes of a child, with such naïveté that she hadn't realized that there was more to him than the indulging father she'd known?

'He can't have been as bad as all that, can he?'

'He was a product of his time. That was how he had been brought up.' Cressida let out a large sigh. 'I was there, Violet. I saw it happen. I sometimes wonder if that was why he loathed me so much, because I made my own rules – I had escaped.' Her eyes pierced Violet's. 'You can do that too, you know.'

'He never mentioned you, you know. He couldn't bear to hear your name spoken in the manor. It was as if you had failed him, failed the family.' She felt Cressida flinch and regretted that she'd said it. 'I'm sorry, I should have said that in a better way.'

But Cressida cut her off. 'It's all right, I shouldn't be shocked by it. Eustace always rewrote the past to suit himself, and he was never one to admit he might be wrong.' She looked at her hands. 'It's funny, but I've spent my whole life trying to make up for that – trying to reclaim my name in the family he pushed me out of – but now I see that I'd never have been able to change his mind, no matter how successful or wealthy I became. Ironically, I think it was my success and wealth that made him reject me.'

'That was only because he was proud, of the family name, of Hugh and me too.'

Cressida raised an eyebrow. 'Provided you followed his instructions. Look at how determined you've been to marry a lord, no matter what.' She turned to look at her. 'Violet, your father isn't alive anymore. You can do as you choose now, marry for love if you want. Your choice of spouse will not bring the family down, no matter what your father used to say.'

Violet thought this through. 'Well, what about you? Shouldn't you find love too?'

'My work is my life, and I've found that there aren't many men who would understand that. I would never marry someone just to be married.' Cressida gave her a final, conclusive smile and looked back to the altar. 'But don't think I'm against marriage. I can't wait to see Lottie in that glorious dress. And now that we know that it was also your mother's dress, perhaps you'd like to wear it too. She looked beautiful, your mother.'

'My mother.' Violet's voice withered with sudden emotion. 'What was she like?'

'Well, Angelica was always very pretty – not unlike you, my dear, although she was smaller, more fragile. She was a child, only seventeen or so, and your father was ten years older. I felt so sorry for her – for all the women like her. Her wedding was all pomp and ceremony, everything you'd want from a grand wedding, except love. She was walking into a gilded cage, like a beautiful, delicate bird, trapped.'

'I always assumed she was happy. She'd married a lord and

lived in a magnificent manor house. But perhaps she wasn't, underneath it all.' Violet sighed, and she couldn't help thinking of Lord Ombersley, how close she'd come to marrying him, and yet, what had she known about him? What did he know about her?

The organ piped out the repeated first notes of the Wedding March, heralding the beginning of a new marriage, a new era, and Violet watched as Lottie came down the aisle, elegant in the beautiful long white gown, beaming with joy and happiness.

Through a tumult of emotions, Violet couldn't help admitting that this, a marriage of complete and total love, was better than any 'good match'.

And as she watched Flynn's eyes on Lottie's, she knew that this was the greatest goal in life: to love and be loved in return.

The service was comfortingly traditional, the war outside forgotten for an hour while the familiar vows echoed through the church. When it came to an end and a delighted Lottie and Flynn had walked arm in arm down the aisle, Violet and Cressida followed the stream of people heading slowly to the door.

It wasn't until they were almost outside that Violet spotted Hugh, seated a few rows up from the back. As Violet and Cressida passed him, he nodded a curt greeting, and that's when Violet saw her.

'Oh heavens, he's brought Astrid with him,' she whispered to Cressida.

'Goodness!' Cressida followed Violet's gaze to the elegant woman beside Hugh.

'I hope this doesn't mean anything portentous. Having Astrid in the family is the last thing we need. I was hoping he'd be brave enough to wriggle out of it, now that our father's not around to enforce it.'

'Why? What's she like?'

'A little chilly to say the least. She hasn't been keen to be friends, nor has she spent much time in the village. She seems to think she's above it all.'

Hugh led Astrid out of the church, and it didn't take long to see that she'd put extra effort into her appearance. Her pale auburn hair was perfectly crafted into a series of rolls coming down to the base of her neck, as described in this month's society magazines. Her makeup expertly showed off her face, which was refined rather than traditionally beautiful, with a straight nose and well-defined cheekbones. At her collar bone sat a translucent row of pearls, and even from where Violet was standing, she could smell her expensive perfume.

'That's Chanel No. 5!' she exclaimed embitteredly. 'She must have stockpiled it before the Nazis took Paris.'

'And what about that dress?' Cressida was eyeing the voluminous sapphire designer gown, worn decorously with white gloves and hat. 'It has enough material to make two – if not three! – good dresses! And those gloves? No one wears white anymore with the shortage of laundry soap. How can she keep them so clean?' But evidently Cressida's mind was on more than the gloves. 'With all that money, I wonder why she's so intent on marrying Hugh.'

'The main draw for the Fortescues is the family name and the ancestral home. Aldhurst Manor has belonged to the Westcott family for generations, Latin motto, crest, and all – things that are hard to come by, even with money. And there's a lot at stake for Hugh too. The Fortescues are wealthy and powerful, not a family to be shrugged off lightly, and Hugh is his father's son, after all. If he's been told he has to marry Astrid, that's what he'll do.'

Before Cressida could reply, Hugh approached them, Astrid on his arm wearing the charming smile of one who has found herself in a race in which she appears to be well and truly in the lead.

'Cressida, I'd like you to meet Astrid Fortescue,' he said. 'She kindly agreed to escort me to Lord Flynn's wedding.'

'It's a pleasure to meet you,' Astrid said with more reserve than pleasure.

'Hello, Astrid, lovely to see you again,' Violet said without enthusiasm. 'What a lavish dress. I wonder how you managed to get it with all the shortages and rationing?'

Adopting a superior smile, Astrid said, 'Mama had Norman make it up for me out of one of her old ones, so it's austerity with a twist. Turned out rather well, don't you think?'

'Do you mean Norman Hartnell? Designer to the queen?' Violet stammered, wondering precisely how well connected the woman could be.

'I wondered if it was one of Norman's creations,' Cressida said, admiring the lines.

'It was a special favour.' Astrid swirled it from side to side, enjoying their admiration. 'Hugh tells me you're in the ATS now, Violet. How brave of you to wear that dreadful uniform – why would anyone need so many pockets?' She nodded at Violet's boyish short hair. 'And as for the rule that the hair should never touch the collar, that's simply too dismal. I don't know how any civilized woman can cope.'

'I think Violet looks splendid,' Hugh said evenly, either missing or choosing to ignore Astrid's little put-down. 'And her hair is far more practical now that it's short.' He gave Violet a sideways glance. 'You look like a nymph, albeit a slightly cheeky one.'

Hugh grinned, as did Cressida.

Astrid did not.

Politely changing the subject, Cressida said, 'Violet and I were talking about the roses on your mother's wedding gown, Hugh. It looks so lovely on Lottie.'

Astrid looked baffled, so Hugh explained. 'We found my mother's wedding dress, and it was adorned with climbing roses, which are also on our family crest. It's quite a story. My mother had given the dress to the vicar's wife to wear, and it was her daughter, Grace, who found it.'

Astrid's face grimaced in disdain. 'Why would your mother give her wedding dress to a vicar's wife, of all things? And why would you let the villagers pass it among themselves?'

'Why ever not?' Hugh turned to face her. 'It's rather generous of Grace, as it was of my mother, in the spirit of noblesse oblige, don't you think?'

'Well, I most certainly wouldn't wear a wedding dress borrowed from someone else,' Astrid said with a sniff. 'Nor would I want anyone else to wear mine.'

'You wouldn't wear even a Westcott family dress?' Hugh's tone was placating, as if marriage had not only been discussed but was very much in the offing.

And to Violet's surprise, Astrid merely laughed. 'Absolutely not. Besides, Mama's already asked Norman to make mine.'

An awkward silence hung in the air, until Cressida turned the subject back to the wedding gown. 'It was a shame that Grace didn't get to wear her mother's dress. It meant so much to her.'

'She didn't wear it?' Hugh asked, a frown coming over his face.

'Didn't you hear?' Violet said. 'She broke off the engagement.'

Hugh's breath seemed to falter. 'When?'

'A few weeks ago, probably just after you left. She wrote Lawrence a letter, and supposedly he's being very good about it, but it must be terrifically awkward.'

Astrid looked appalled. 'How very brazen of her to break off an engagement!'

Scowling, Hugh glanced around the crowd, probably trying to find Grace. 'But she was so very set on the marriage. I can't understand why . . .' His voice trailed off, unsure.

'For some reason, she seemed to change her mind,' Cressida explained. 'When it came down to it, she realized that they weren't at all right for each other.'

Astrid tutted loudly. 'How undignified!'

But Violet and Cressida were both watching Hugh, who was rubbing the back of his neck, a muscle tensing in his jaw.

Oblivious, Astrid asked, 'Where's the reception, Hugh? We should stir ourselves if we plan to leave early.'

Hugh's eyes met Violet's as if trying to steady himself for the ordeal ahead, and she suddenly saw how very vulnerable he was, how he needed her as much as she needed him – after all, they were the closest family each of them had. Violet gave him a deft nod, a reassuring smile. Whatever was going through his mind, he had to get through the day.

Dutifully, he lifted Astrid's hand. 'The reception is in Darley Grange. Shall we take the car?' As they departed, his eyes met Violet's with a frozen dread.

Cressida turned to Violet. 'Isn't it rather hasty of Astrid to speak of marriage?'

'From what I gather, the Fortescues have been putting pressure on Hugh to propose. She's been spending more time with him when he's in London, especially since he inherited the estate. If you ask me, he's been dragging his feet, trying to dot every *i* and cross every *t* before taking the plunge. It's more like a cross-nation political treaty than a marriage.'

'Perhaps now he'll call it off,' Cressida whispered. 'He seemed rather shaken by the news that Grace is now single. It wouldn't surprise me if he tries to get out of it, although heaven knows how he'll do that with his reputation intact.'

Violet heaved a long sigh. 'I only hope he does. If that woman becomes lady of the manor, we'll all be in for it. I'll jolly well have to move in with you when you go back to London.' And then she added, 'If you don't mind, that is?'

Cressida laughed. 'I'd be delighted to have you.'

The approach of Grace curtailed their conversation. Beautiful in the same dusky pink dress she wore at the Darley Grange reception, she looked fraught, treading as silently and as carefully as a young gazelle.

In a slightly hushed voice, Cressida said to her, 'I expect you saw; Hugh has brought a young woman from London to accompany him today, Astrid Fortescue.'

She nodded. 'I did see. I know they're promised to each other, but I didn't realize he'd bring her here.'

Together they watched Hugh and Astrid stop to greet a few people they knew, as if they were already a happy couple. Then, with a dreadful sense of misgiving, Violet watched Astrid pull aside a society friend, who appeared to be congratulating her. Hugh, meanwhile, looked as if he couldn't wait for the event to be over. As Astrid returned to his side, he gave her a perfunctory smile as she took his hand in a very public display of ownership.

A photographer began to organize the bride and groom in front of the church for a few pictures, and then it was time for Lottie to throw the bouquet, making a great squeal as she leaped high in the air, tossing the tightly packed pink and yellow bunch high up into the bright blue sky.

Watching from the back, Violet was shaken abruptly by Martha bumping into her while she vied for the bouquet that came tumbling down towards them. And as Martha tripped and fell to the ground, Violet stumbled forward, the bouquet landing squarely in her hands.

'Oh, how ridiculous!' she laughed, embarrassed, helping Martha up and putting the bouquet into her hands. 'Let's say that you caught it, shall we? If it's left up to me to be the next bride, no one else will be married for years.'

But Martha shoved it back at her furiously. 'Don't be silly. It doesn't work like that.'

The reception was to be held in Darley Grange, and as the procession of guests began to walk from the church, Violet turned in surprise when a familiar American voice came from behind her.

'You're looking mighty dashing today, Fred.' Lieutenant McCauley was in his dress uniform. Pressed and gleaming to perfection, he looked quite dashing himself. She realized that she ignored the broken nose and large angular chin these days; had she become used to them, or were they part of his charm?

'I have exciting news for you.' She turned to beam at him as they fell into a walk. 'They think I might be officer material,' she announced proudly. 'I have to go for a five-day assessment and hopefully I'll get into the training course.'

'Bravo! But I hope you realize that even if they make you an officer, you'll always be Fred to me.' He grinned, amused with her exuberance. 'Just as a matter of interest, how did they reach the opinion that you would make a fine officer?'

She made a little skip. 'I have what's known as a "mind for mechanics and engineering", according to my instructors. And apparently, I was recommended by my supervisor. Word is they have high hopes for me. Can you believe it?'

'Oh, I can, I can. I have always had faith in you, Fred. You know that.'

'After officer training, they'll decide what to do with me. The only thing I'm not excited about is that I won't be able to live in Aldhurst anymore.' She paused in thought, but then brightened.

'But I was lucky to get away with it for as long as I did. It truly was a great run, and I owe my dreadful instructor a very big kiss.'

'I thought you only kissed dukes.'

She nudged him. 'Oh, I don't mean that kind of a kiss, silly. He'll get a peck on the cheek and be happy with it.'

The countryside looked glorious in the sunshine, and she was so lost in thought about her new adventure that she hardly realized how unusually quiet Landon was until he said, 'You will make sure my new driver is well-behaved, won't you, Fred? I've become accustomed to the very best service, and you wouldn't want to hear that your high standards have been destroyed by an unthinking replacement.'

She eyed him teasingly. 'Will you miss me, Landon?'

'I've gotten used to our daily chats,' he said, suddenly looking like the boy he must have been, a little hurt at the prospect of his playmate's departure. 'Won't you miss me too?'

'Of course I will. But it's just so exceedingly exciting. And in any case, we'll still be friends, won't we? I can come over to say hello when I'm in Aldhurst, or we can meet up in London. One of my friends has a man she meets in the Ritz for a glass of Champagne every month, and she swears by it, says that it keeps her sane through all the mayhem.'

As her laugh petered away, she realized that he wasn't joining in.

'Oh, don't be so miserable, Mr Toad,' she said. 'I shan't forget you. How could I when you're the only man who's ever been immune to my charms?' She grinned.

There was a pause, and then he said, 'Why on earth do you say that I'm immune to your charms, Fred?'

'Because you are!' she declared, hardly giving it thought. 'You call me Fred, for heaven's sake, and even once said that being with me was like hanging around with the lads. And do you recall that you told me I looked like an adolescent boy?'

He laughed. 'I do have a way with words, don't I?'

'You see, I was never able to be friends with men before because they were always falling in love with me. You must see how tiresome that is in a friend.'

'Naturally,' he replied evenly.

They carried on walking for a few minutes, and then she broke the silence. 'It was a beautiful wedding, wasn't it?'

'It was. They have a lot of chemistry.'

She made a tutting sound. 'Oh, the mythical chemistry! A friend of mine is always talking about it. Apparently, she has chemistry with the stable manager at her father's estate, but I'm not sure what good that'll do for her. She'll never be able to marry him.'

'Why not?'

'What would they live on? She isn't the type of woman to live in a woodshed, you know.' She laughed at the notion. 'It wouldn't do at all. Besides, her family would never speak to her again if she married one of their employees.'

'I'm sure the couple will find a way, if they love each other enough.'

Her laughter dropped. It hadn't crossed her mind that her friend might have wanted to act upon this chemistry, that she might even love the man. 'Her father would be incensed. I don't believe she would even countenance such a notion.'

'Sometimes you just can't help yourself, no matter how much a match doesn't make sense.'

'Have you ever felt like that?' she asked. 'That you can't help yourself?'

He made a little chuckle. 'I did once, but I didn't want to bother the woman concerned. Something told me that she wouldn't be interested.'

'Did the chemistry only go one way?'

'I don't believe so. I think it went both ways. But the woman was hell-bent on marrying to better herself, and I was not perceived as useful in that department.' Again, the weary chuckle.

'But surely, you're quite a catch, Lieutenant?'

'You would have thought so.'

And that's when it struck her.

She looked at him, and their eyes met for a brief, unnerving moment.

But then he nudged her, laughing. 'I had you thinking there for a minute, didn't I?'

And she slapped him playfully on the arm. 'Oh, you prankster! You're worse than a schoolboy with your jokes.'

And taking her arm in his, he led her through the gates of Darley Grange.

As the main house was packed with military operations, the wedding reception was being held in a large marquis tent in the gardens. Soon it began to fill with people and the buzz of chatter rose, waiters whisking around with drinks and guests mingling, everyone putting the war behind them for a day.

Violet became aware of a group gathering on one side of the room, and before she knew it, Landon had pulled her along to see what was happening.

The crowd seemed to hush as Violet cut through to the front, and she was surprised to see her own brother there in the centre with Astrid Fortescue, who was simpering in an improbably modest manner. And as Hugh gazed down at Astrid's hand, Violet's head began to shake.

'No, no,' she whispered to Landon.

Amid congratulating friends, Astrid had removed her left glove to reveal a large, gleaming diamond ring.

Fanning herself in mock modesty, Astrid looked delightedly

around at the crowd as young ladies cooed around it, some breaking into applause and even cheers.

Hastily, Violet looked through the throng for Grace. *She must be here somewhere.*

And then she spotted her, standing at the back, her face as pale as a ghost as she staggered backwards out of the crowd, stumbling to the door.

CRESSIDA

As she and Grace headed into the village for the Sewing Circle the following Tuesday evening, Cressida couldn't help a huff of annoyance. Hugh's proposal to Astrid couldn't have come at a worse time.

'What induced him to override his own feelings is beyond me,' she moaned.

'I'm sure he did what he thought was best,' Grace replied monotonously. The poor girl had been trying to hide her hurt, but Cressida saw through it. Grace had only agreed to come back to work at the manor after she knew that Hugh and Astrid had safely returned to London.

Meanwhile, Cressida felt an enormous thud of guilt. Why had she encouraged Grace to give up Lawrence? Maybe Grace would have been happier becoming a vicar's wife. Perhaps Cressida had let her feelings about her own life cloud her judgment as to what Grace wanted for herself. She couldn't help but feel terribly disappointed in Hugh, though perhaps the very idea of him breaking his betrothal was simply too modern. And was it too farfetched to believe that a lord of the manor – particularly *this* lord of the manor, her brother's son in every way – would ever consider marriage to a vicar's daughter?

'Hugh only did it because he and Astrid were promised to each other, you know that, don't you, Grace?' she said. 'The Fortescues are a powerful family. They wouldn't take well to their beloved daughter being jilted. Hugh would be viewed as a scoundrel by society. He might even lose his position in the War Office.'

'I remember him saying, the last time we met, that he had obligations to fulfil. That must be what he was talking about. I suppose I just hoped that when I called things off with Lawrence maybe there could be a future for us. But it was so silly of me to fool myself into thinking that. Idiotic, in fact.'

Cressida put an arm around her. 'If it's any consolation, he didn't know that your wedding had been called off, and he looked awfully unnerved by the news. I've seen the way he looks at you, Grace, and it must have upset him to think of your marrying Lawrence.'

'But why would he propose to Astrid?'

'Once he believed that you would soon be married to someone else, I imagine he felt compelled to sort out his own future.'

Grace opened her mouth to say something, but then it faded into nothing.

Cressida didn't press her, simply leading the way to the village hall.

The Sewing Circle was as lively as ever, and although Cressida knew it would be good for Grace to see the group, she hadn't expected to see Lottie, just returned from her forty-eight-hour honeymoon, radiating bliss.

'From the look on your face, the honeymoon must have been a great success!' Mrs Bisgood let out a delighted laugh.

'Two days of magic,' Lottie said, gasping dreamily. 'Long, sandy beaches, our lovely little guesthouse, and even though there was a bit of rain, we didn't care. We snuggled up in bed instead.' She giggled. 'It was just a shame it was only two nights.'

'At least you can live together here in Aldhurst,' Violet said. 'Most of my friends found themselves on different sides of the world within a week of their wedding.' She reached for the large bag beside her, catching Grace's eye. 'And that reminds me. We have a little something to share with you all.'

With a swish, Violet drew the parachute from her bag like an angelic magician. On and on it went, and the women all surged forward to see.

'It's as soft as goose down,' Mrs Kettlewell said with a gasp, feeling it between her fingertips.

'Imagine it next to your skin. Heavenly!' Lottie exclaimed.

And as they stretched it out across the table, discussing whether they could get three or four dresses from it, Violet was pulled closer into their tight little circle, like a lone wolf who had finally proven her worth to the pack.

On the other side, however, Grace stood apart.

'Cheer up, dear.' Mrs Bisgood took her arm and gently urged her forward.

'I'm all right,' Grace said, although her fraught tone indicated that she clearly wasn't.

But Mrs Bisgood insisted. 'Come and join us. What you need is something to take your mind off it, a bit of fun.'

Spinning around to her, Lottie piped up, 'What about a good night out? It'll cheer up those flagging spirits and put you back in the game.' She bounded over and gave Grace an enthusiastic squeeze. 'Some of my friends in the factory are going to a big charity dance in Canterbury on Saturday night. Why don't we all go along? There's a rumour the place is going to be packed with American GIs.'

Martha squealed, 'Oh, how topping!' and then looked hopefully at her mother, 'May I?'

'Only if Grace goes.' Mrs Kettlewell sighed. 'I know I can trust her to keep an eye on you.'

Martha grabbed Grace's hand pleadingly. 'Oh, do say you'll go, Grace. I'll help with the sewing for eternity if you do!'

It was rare to see Martha as eager, so half-vexed, half-amused, Grace murmured, 'Oh, all right then.'

A cheer went up, followed by an animated discussion about what each was going to wear, although Grace seemed immune to the excitement, disappearing into the back room to make a cup of tea for Mrs Todd. Her enthusiasm for everything had dissipated. Even the Wedding Dress Exchange and the parachute silk had been left to the others, her drive having vanished into thin air.

'Grace,' Cressida prompted her when she returned with the tea, 'didn't we decide to ask everyone about the designs for the IncSoc Utility Contest?'

'Oh, yes, of course,' Grace muttered, taking out a sheet of paper and addressing the others. 'Cressida and I are determined to get our four picked for the fashion show, and so we want to know what elements of design you like best. Do you like shirtwaist dresses, for example, or do you prefer more of a feminine frock?'

Martha piped up, 'I say the shirtwaist is better. It has a kind of military look too, showing that we're doing our bit. No one wants pretty frocks these days. They make you look as if you're too busy looking pretty to do war work.'

'Very good.' Grace went on to the next question. 'What about belts and pockets?'

'I loathe pockets over the breast,' Mrs Bisgood said with feeling. 'They're too small and everything falls out when you bend over.'

Lottie added, 'And belts are good for giving you a bit of shape with difficult fittings, so I'd stick with them, if I were you.'

'Our last question: What about patterned fabrics? Floral, stripes, or two-tone?'

'Stripes are dreadful,' Mrs Kettlewell said. 'They're so awkward to cut out and sew. Floral is too traditional and feminine, but polka dots are good. I like those two-tone looks the best, sharp and chic at the same time.'

'How are your designs going?' Mrs Bisgood asked.

'Grace is in charge,' Cressida said, urging Grace to regain some of her old enthusiasm. 'We're hoping to have at least one of our designs selected for the big fashion show. It'll be the event of the decade.' Inside, Cressida felt an excitement she hadn't felt for years. The challenge of working on the wartime designs and having such a special team spirit, all of London's top designers pulling together, fuelled her with excitement. But there was a new drive to get it right, a new energy for creativity and finesse.

They had a few sketches to share, and everyone crowded around to see, pointing out the ones they liked the best.

'Can we incorporate some of these designs into the wedding dresses?' Mrs Bisgood asked. 'They're awfully chic.'

'Of course we can!' Cressida said. 'And we have more ideas up our sleeves too.'

The rest of the meeting was focused on the Wedding Dress Exchange, with Cressida proclaiming that her clients were delighted to add their old ones to the collection. It had been good to talk to her customers again, discussing not just business but something more special, an act of wartime generosity at its best.

'Not only has Lady Marley's chauffeur dropped over her own exquisite bridal gown, but two more of my regular clients have also donated to the cause.'

'What tremendous wartime spirit!' Mrs Bisgood came to look over Cressida's shoulder at the list in her hand.

'It's wonderful to have such backing for our little idea,' Cressida said. 'Everyone can relate to the romance of a white wedding.'

'There's a kind of magic, isn't there?' Lottie said, finding a coat hanger and carefully holding up her own wedding gown. 'It's about being able to give someone a fairy-tale day.'

Violet added in a dreamy tone, 'It's about being able to step out of the war. Just for a special moment, you get to take off a boxy, ill-fitting uniform, and instead look mesmerizing in a silky white gown.'

'How many dresses do we have so far?' Mrs Bisgood asked.

Cressida looked down her list. 'We have eight now, including the ones we're making from the parachute that Violet and Grace found. We've managed to get Mrs Bisgood's dress up and running – thank you – and I'm expecting another few from some other clients.'

'We found Mum's,' Martha said without enthusiasm. 'It's rather shapeless. We think it'll need quite a bit of work.'

Mrs Todd's voice rang above the others. 'And I brought my wedding dress along, just in case we can add it to the pool.' She pulled a bag from under her chair. 'It might be a bit old-fashioned, but it may as well be used rather than gathering moths in my attic, even if it's only to patch up another dress.'

Cressida gently held it up. It was a very Victorian affair, complete with puffed leg-of-mutton sleeves, and the dreaded bustle at the back. There was lacing up the back to pull the figure into a painful hourglass shape.

'The waist is so small!' Lottie remarked with wonderment, eyeing Mrs Todd's girth.

'I was slim as a whippet before I started having children,' Mrs Todd replied with a chuckle.

'But it's a beautiful piece of silk,' Cressida said. 'All it needs is a few alterations to bring it up-to-date.'

Mrs Bisgood bustled up to add, 'We're going to need as many wedding gowns as we can get. Now that the word is out, there's more demand than we have dresses.'

'A few of my ATS friends want to be next in line as well,' Violet said. 'I've already promised one for two weeks' time.'

'Tell your friend we'll have one ready,' Cressida said.

'But Mrs Bisgood's right,' Grace said. 'We have more demand than supply. My father keeps getting calls from neighbouring parishes with brides desperate to borrow one. I have a list of ten for the next few months already. It seems that Lottie's wedding was the best possible advertisement.'

Lottie gave a mock bow, but the others looked at one another, suddenly unsure.

'Is this too much for us?' Mrs Kettlewell whispered.

'Not at all!' Cressida said. 'But if we're going to do this, we need more dresses, and we need ones with less work, or we simply won't have the stock to meet the demand.'

'But how?' Martha said. 'We've already pooled our own and plagued everyone we know, and it's not often a parachute comes down around here.'

A glint came to Cressida's eyes. 'Perhaps we could place an advertisement in *The Lady* magazine, asking for wedding dresses for the Wedding Dress Exchange. We can write an advert similar to the one we posted here in the village, but with a nationwide appeal. I'm sure it will attract lots of interest, and hopefully some lovely new dresses too.'

They looked at her uncertainly.

'That's a lovely plan.' Mrs Kettlewell glanced around anxiously. 'But are you sure we're ready for it? We all have jobs, we're all busy. Do we have time for more dresses?'

'We'll find the time, and if they're ready to wear, it won't be any bother at all. If there are ways to get some more, then we should use them,' Cressida said. 'In any case, it will be good for morale, don't you think? Our own special contribution to the war effort.'

'And if we organize everything properly and divide out the

tasks, it won't be so hard.' Violet was making notes again. 'Perhaps we could see if any of the Land Girls can sew. Maybe the school can help too or the Make Do and Mend classes you teach in Chartham, Grace?'

Together, they began to discuss how it would work, dividing up tasks.

And it was this that filled Cressida's mind as she headed out into the night back through the village to the manor, the insects buzzing in the warm night sky, and the hill on the horizon keeping watch over the little place and all its inhabitants.

VIOLET

Before the war played havoc with Violet's social life, one of her favourite rituals was getting ready for a party. She'd set 'Cheek to Cheek' onto her gramophone player and dance around her dressing room as she decided what to wear, perhaps with a cocktail in one hand to put her in the perfect mood for a scintillating evening.

And it was with this in mind that Violet invited Grace over to the manor before the Canterbury dance. It was a cunning idea, even if she did say so herself; not only would it boost Grace's spirits, but it would also ensure that she wore something fabulous. After all, she wasn't going to be cheered up if no one asked her to dance because she was in one of her old, recycled skirts.

'The mood she's in, I wouldn't put it past her to sit in a corner, shrinking into the wallpaper so that no one notices her,' she told Cressida.

'I do hope she agrees to wear something that brings out the best in her,' Cressida fretted. 'I have a feeling she's ready to cast off those dull old clothes she's been wearing. It's as if they've been a costume or façade used to convince herself and the world who she was. I hope she's ready to step beyond that now and allow herself to be the person she really is inside.' Her eyes gleamed with hope. 'You need to get her to relax and enjoy her-self. Find some nice young men for her to meet.'

Violet grinned. 'As a matter of fact, I already have that in hand. I invited Lieutenant McCauley.'

The look on his face had been one of bemusement. 'Let me get this right. You want me to meet you and your friends at a dance so that I can flirt with someone called Grace?'

They had been on their way back from a meeting in London. 'Yes, that's right. Since you're so eager to chat up every girl you meet, I thought it would be just up your street. She's incredibly good-looking, actually, but a bit shy, that's all. Just your type,' she added for good measure.

'How do you know my type, Fred?'

'I would have thought a beautiful young woman wouldn't fall too far out of your range. Unless you prefer the unattractive kind?'

He chuckled. 'Perhaps I prefer to find my own girl.'

'Perhaps you could do both. Do your good friend a favour first, and then you can find your own girl if it doesn't work out. How does that sound?'

'Are you calling yourself my good friend, Fred? I have to say, it's rather a step up since we first met.'

'I've come to see you for the harmless buffoon that you are, Lieutenant McCauley.'

'I thought I'd convinced you to call me Landon these days.'

She smirked. 'You'll come then?'

'All right, I'll do your dirty work, minx. But just remember, a favour should always be paid back in full.' He glanced at her, a grin on his face, and she laughed, wondering what he might have in store for her. He could even make his silly threats sound jolly, and a pinprick of frustration made her realize that she would miss him more than she'd admit.

As she swept around her boudoir to the rousing beat of 'Chattanooga Choo Choo,' she felt quietly triumphant at having set it all up. She'd never pegged herself as the kind of girl who was happy to see another woman being showered with male attention, but then again, she'd never had many good friends. Of course, it was unlikely it would come to anything, but hopefully it would give Grace a boost, send her onto the dance floor knowing that eyes were on her. With the thrill of it all, Violet decided to forgo her uniform tonight, instead selecting a turquoise-blue strappy dress from before the war, sliding on a luminescent brooch, bright white to be visible in the blackout; they'd become all the rage since the dimmed car headlights had taken a ghastly toll on the population.

Later than promised, Grace finally arrived, looking less than enthusiastic about the night ahead.

'Come on.' Violet marched her over to the dressing table. 'We don't have much time. Hugh said he can drive us over at eight o'clock. Archie Kettlewell's taking the others, with strict instructions to make sure they're home early.'

'Hugh is driving us there?' she stammered, turning back to the door. 'Perhaps this was a bad idea. I don't think I'll go after all.'

'Oh, do stop being silly, Grace.' She sat her down at her dressing table and began scrambling through the mayhem for her lipstick. 'I don't know what's going on between you and Hugh, but he's getting married, and you have to show him that nothing's stopping you from living your life either.'

'I suppose so,' she murmured listlessly.

'Let's make you look so ravishing that Hugh will feel absolutely wretched about it, and then you can jolly well find someone even better at this dance. There'll be lots of young men there. Some American officers from Darley Grange are coming too.'

Violet prided herself on her stylish makeup and clothing

choices, and it was with relish that she set Grace's hair into a lovely Victory Roll, adding a touch of lipstick to put a bit of colour back into her.

'We're not like the Germans, you know,' she said. 'Their women are told to be plain and drab, to devote themselves to having babies and winning the war. Here in Britain, they've decided that it's far more jolly for everyone if we look good, which is much more the ticket. It just proves how civilized we are, don't you think?'

Finally, Grace was forced to try on three different dresses, Violet eventually selecting a lovely indigo-coloured one. It was halter necked, exposing more skin than Grace was probably used to, but she barely seemed to notice. Following her curves down to her knees, the dress fitted her remarkably well, and Violet couldn't help feeling slightly peeved that it looked better on Grace than it did on her.

Hugh was waiting for them at the bottom of the grand staircase, donned in a dress suit and tapping his foot impatiently. He had a formal dinner in Canterbury, and Violet was under strict instructions not to keep him waiting.

But as Grace came into view, his eyes lingered over her.

'Hello, Hugh.' A sudden energy came to her voice, and she held her head up, a new inscrutability to her.

'Hello, Grace.' Quickly, he turned his focus onto Violet, looking her up and down with annoyance. 'Isn't it a little cool outside for that kind of dress? Perhaps I should change my plans and escort the pair of you myself. I wouldn't want you to get into any trouble.' A muscle began to pulsate in his jaw as he looked back to Grace, her bare shoulders, the deep neckline.

Violet smirked. 'I'll take that as a compliment, but honestly, Hugh, we don't need a chaperone. Lieutenant McCauley is meeting us there, and Archie Kettlewell will be there too. We'll be in good hands.'

The drive into Canterbury was a quiet one, broken only by Hugh suggesting that he should pick them up early.

'The Nazis are still dropping bombs, you know. And it isn't just London.' His voice had become waspish. 'Exeter was pounded last week.'

'Oh, come on, Hugh. Don't be such a wet blanket. We deserve to have a bit of fun.'

He gave her a hostile, sideways glare. 'I happen to know that some rather improper behaviour goes on at some of these dances.'

'Well yes, Hugh, the improperness would be the bit of fun to which I am referring,' Violet said pointedly. 'Besides, where's the harm? Everyone is enjoying themselves these days.'

Thankfully, the car was now weaving through the Canterbury streets, Hugh ignoring Violet's statement and pulling up outside the great Westgate Hall. Grace quickly got out of the car, followed by Violet, who added to Hugh, 'We'll see you at midnight.'

In moments, they were picked up in the current of people flowing through the main doors and into the capacious hall. A large band was already pumping out jazz tunes at full pelt as people swirled around a crowded dance floor. Tables on the side were populated by couples interspersed with groups of young women awaiting the promised GIs.

They scanned the place for Lottie and the others, but it looked as though they had yet to arrive.

An American voice came from behind Violet. 'I was wondering when you'd get here.'

'Lieutenant McCauley.'

'Landon, remember.' He grinned, looking well groomed in his uniform.

She beamed a conspiratorial smile at him, her eyes indicating Grace beside her. 'How marvellous of you to come.'

But Landon was looking at Violet's dress. 'How could I resist the opportunity to see you all spruced up, Fred. You turn out rather well, I see.'

'Let me introduce you to my friend. Grace, this is Landon. He's the American I drive around.'

'Pleased to meet you.' Grace gave him a perfunctory smile.

'Can I get you a drink?' he asked.

'All right,' she murmured, and then, as if a thought struck her, she said, 'I'd like a cocktail, please.'

With a theatrical little bow, his eyes shooting over to Violet's, he went off, returning shortly with a tray of glasses. 'I have Pink Gins for us all.' He passed them around and raised his glass. 'Cheers!'

Grace took a sip, spluttered a cough, and quelled it with a jolly great gulp. 'It has rather an odd taste, doesn't it?'

'Don't worry,' Landon said jokily. 'The next one will be far better.'

'Will it?' she said, and without another word, she downed the rest of it in one. 'In that case, would you be so kind as to get me another?'

His eyes met Violet's, and then he vanished back to the bar.

A thought crossed Violet's mind. 'You don't usually drink cocktails, do you, Grace?'

'No!' She wagged her finger at Violet, more animated than usual. 'I'm a vicar's daughter, remember? I hardly drink any alcohol at all. But we're here to have fun, aren't we?'

Landon returned with another Pink Gin, which she quickly downed, and then before Violet had time to say anything, Grace grabbed Landon's hand. 'Come on then, let's dance!'

It was 'The Boogie Woogie Bugle Boy,' and Grace, in shocking contrast to her usual placid self, was the life and soul of the dance floor. A space seemed to open up around them as she cavorted left and right, backwards and forwards.

After two songs, Landon persuaded Grace that it was time

for a rest, and together they made their way back to a stunned Violet.

Grace shook out her hair and declared, 'This is much more fun than I thought.'

Just as Violet was about to ask if she'd like a glass of water, a good-looking marine asked Grace to dance, and she tucked her arm through his and virtually dragged him onto the dance floor.

'She's quite something,' Landon said with his lilting smile. 'I'm not quite sure why you described her as shy.'

Violet frowned. 'Well, tonight she's not acting as she normally does.' She raised an eyebrow. 'It's a long story, but I think this new side of Grace might have something to do with my brother.' She sighed. 'Only now he's gone and got engaged. Cressida and I are not at all happy about his choice of fiancée either.'

'Cressida is a recent addition to your home, weren't you telling me?'

'That's right. She's my aunt. I didn't meet her until recently because my father didn't see eye to eye with her. She and Hugh are the only family I have left.'

He grinned at her. 'You can have some of mine if you'd like. There's a whole lot of McCauleys, and they're all slightly outlandish.' He pulled his head up with mock haughtiness. 'Except for me, that is. I'm the only sensible one among them.'

'And the biggest liar too! Tell me about them. What are your siblings like?'

He brought out his hand and began counting off his fingers. 'My eldest sister is a hedonist who loves animals. She lived in Africa for a few years, and now only wears safari clothes. My youngest sister is trying to save half the refugees in Europe; I think she has around a dozen Polish women living in her house. My brother has a desk job in the Air Force, but he usually works with my father. And finally, my middle sister, well, she's just a dear who can't decide who she wants to marry.'

'I'm said to be very talented at matchmaking,' Violet said, preening. 'What are her options?'

But as he began, Violet's eyes went quickly to check on Grace, who was now in the middle of the dance floor in the arms of the handsome marine, kissing him for all she was worth.

Landon's gaze had followed hers. 'I assume that means I'm officially let off the hook then?'

'Oh goodness!' Violet exclaimed.

'And you said she was a vicar's daughter?' Landon said, laughing gently.

Violet shook her head. 'Frankly, I'm not sure she'd even kissed her ex-fiancé.'

'Well, she's learning how to do that pretty quickly. Was it the cocktails? I hope you're not going to blame me for buying them—'

'No, no, it was my fault for not stopping her. Although how was I to know she was going to gulp that second one down too? Those Pink Gins can be quite powerful.'

'And you think she's downing them so fast because of your brother?'

She watched, crinkling her eyes in thought. 'It's the whole episode, I'd say, breaking off her marriage and then watching as Hugh announces he's marrying someone else. She's simply giving herself a dose of what everyone else is doing: living for the day. I honestly can't blame her for it.'

Landon laughed. 'I don't see you living for the day, Fred.'

'Oh, I have standards,' she said with mock primness. 'Please recall that I'm to marry a duke and must therefore keep my reputation spotless.'

'Well, I don't see any dukes around here.' He picked up her hand. 'So why don't you slum it on the dance floor with me? I promise not to blemish your reputation.'

He gallantly led her between the swaying couples. A slow

dance was playing – 'Smoke Gets in Your Eyes' – and he took one of her hands in his, placing his other on her waist.

It felt a little awkward to dance so slowly, so closely with Landon; after all, they were sparring partners, always quipping at each other every day. So she avoided his eyes, looking around to find her friends in the throng. Lottie and Flynn were in the middle of the dance floor, devotion in their eyes, while Martha danced about a foot away from a GI, Archie avidly watching from the side.

Other couples around them were locked in passionate embraces, and Violet eyed them with distaste. 'This isn't my usual type of place at all.'

'I'm sure it's not. A lady like you demands a royal venue, no less. We poor heathens must be grateful for your presence.'

She laughed. 'I told you before, you're more of a Toad of Toad Hall than a heathen, Landon McCauley.'

He pulled her in closer. 'But never a duke.'

It had been a while since Violet had danced cheek to cheek with a man, and the feeling of his arms around her was warm and comforting. As the music played on, she became lulled into the moment, almost forgetting about Grace, who was probably still kissing the marine on the dance floor, for heaven's sake, and honestly, what was that strange ringing sound in the background? She wished it would quieten down and leave her to enjoy this one, solitary dance. Closing her eyes, she felt herself ease into his swaying movements, that heavenly sensation of dancing, as if they were alone on the dance floor.

But why wouldn't that ringing go away?

And then, as it suddenly became louder and the crowd began to break apart, it all became clear. 'It's the air raid sirens,' she said with a groan. 'We have to find a shelter.'

One by one, the members of the band stopped playing, leaving only the increasing noise of the crowd and the wailing drone of the air raid siren, now louder as the doors were opened, the lights dimmed because of the blackout rules.

In the bustle, they were pushed together. His arms went automatically around her to protect her from the jostling crowd, and for a few moments, they stayed like that.

Then she spotted Grace and pulled away. 'We have to get Grace. I can't let her wander off with the state she's in.' Violet grabbed Landon's hand and led him through the crowd after her. Out the double doors and onto the street they went, swept along by the crowd, which mingled haphazardly outside, most people following a stream heading for a public shelter in the centre of the city.

'Grace, Grace!' Violet called, but she was nowhere to be seen.

'She's probably gone with the others to a shelter,' Landon said. 'We need to get going too, before the planes come over.'

And they ran down the middle of the dark street, their footsteps echoing as they followed a crowd heading into a side street. Together they hurried to the large concrete entrance of a shelter and joined the people going underground.

This was one of the purpose-built shelters, cheaply put up at the beginning of the war, completely different from the underground stations Violet had used if there'd been an air raid in London. A narrow doorway led to concrete steps that went underneath a row of shops, and after a sharp turn at the bottom of the stairs, they entered a long, low concrete room without windows. A few lanterns hung from hooks on the ceiling, giving off a dim, shadowy light.

'They knocked all the shop cellars into one big room,' an ARP woman said at the door, and then, seeing the dismay on Violet's face, she pointed to a cupboard door on the other side. 'That's an escape hatch in case the main entrance is blocked. It's little more than a chimney, but they can winch us out if necessary.' She gestured to the already-full floor space. 'Quickly now, find a spot and sit down, before it's all taken.'

She had a point. There were already at least forty people squashed inside, a sea of faces and a cacophony of chatter. The place was empty of furniture and rugs, so it echoed miserably, and Violet exchanged a grimace with Landon before they found a corner and lowered themselves uneasily onto the bare, cold floor.

'I haven't been in a shelter like this before.' Landon tried to keep his tone cheery. 'It's kind of tight, isn't it?'

Violet could see that he too was feeling apprehensive. Remembering the instructions on the wireless – stay calm and cheerful – she put on a smile. 'It's only for a while. In any case, that dance was getting a little hot, wasn't it?'

Heat was not a problem in the shelter. Quite the opposite, and with only a shawl over her evening dress, Violet felt her arms shiver. Within moments, Landon took off his officer's jacket and put it around her. It was heavy and warm on her shoulders.

An off-duty soldier watched them from the other side of the narrow space. 'You Yanks, who do you think you are, coming over here, stealing our women.' Violet guessed that he had been at the pub.

Another woman from nearby argued back at him, 'We should be grateful the Americans are here, helping us win.'

Her friend added with a jeer, 'Don't be a spoilsport just because you can't get any.'

The soldier fumed, turning his face to the door, but his gaze flickered back menacingly to Landon and Violet.

'How horrid,' she whispered. 'Please don't pay attention. He's drunk and jealous. This war's been going on for years now, and then you dashing Americans come over with such a fresh, vibrant spirit, naturally the British girls are going to be keen.'

'What about you?' Landon's face was close to hers, looking

down, close enough for her to smell the scent of his aftershave, the tang of musk beneath. 'Would you be tempted by an American, even though you won't find a duke among us?'

She raised an eyebrow. 'Only if he gave me the very finest silk stockings.'

The warden had closed the shelter, taking in a few desperate stragglers even though they were already over capacity, and the newcomers had to sit crushed together on the stairs.

Having watched the door for Grace, Violet felt a surge of worry. 'I hope Grace found a shelter, preferably a better one than this.'

'Where do you usually go, when the sirens begin?' he asked.

'In the manor, we simply go down to the cellars. There are some old mattresses and blankets down there. We sometimes play cards with the servants to pass the time, and I have to say that our butler is something of a dark horse when it comes to rummy.' She giggled. 'What about you? There must be cellars in Darley Grange too?'

'I haven't been in an air raid yet,' he said. 'It's quite a unique experience, isn't it?'

She sighed. 'It becomes mundane terribly quickly, I'm afraid.'

The sound of the sirens wound down. 'What does that mean?' Landon asked.

'It means the planes are coming. The shelter wardens have to get underground, unless they're fire-watching.'

'Isn't that dangerous?'

She shrugged. 'I suppose it is. You really have no idea what we've been going through over here, have you?' She laughed with bitterness. 'Heroics and death have become commonplace events. We're desperately trying to hold on to our country, doing the best that we can.'

It wasn't how she'd felt at the beginning, when there had been so many false alarms that no one took the sirens seriously. She recalled being in Selfridges looking at hats when the sirens went off; she'd been so incredibly vexed to be told to go to the shelter. How ridiculous she'd thought the ARP wardens, with all their rules and bossiness. Didn't they know who she was? But then the Blitz began, and pictures of the destruction in London covered every newspaper. After that, she'd stopped going there so often, preferring the safety of home.

But now that she was part of it – part of the army – she couldn't help but feel disgusted at her previous self, the spoiled, heartless society girl whose only desire was to marry a lord. She was appalled at how short-sighted, how selfish she'd been when everyone else was putting body and soul on the line.

'I'm glad we came to help you out,' Landon said. 'It felt a little strange to sit on the other side of the ocean watching the newsreels. At least now we're in it together.'

The sound of aircraft came from outside, becoming louder, droning in and out, and the chatter inside the small place began to dampen into a muffled murmur.

'That doesn't sound too bad,' the warden said. 'Only a few planes. Should be out of here soon enough.'

The waning engines became louder and then began to dim. People began to gather their belongings, preparing for the all-clear, which was the same siren played only once.

But no siren came.

'Can everyone please sit back down,' the warden called out, leading to annoyed huffs. 'Seems like there might be another wave.'

The chattering grew. The drunk soldier was starting to say that he was going to head out regardless, while a mother with two young boys complained that someone needed to use the toilet 'urgently.' The warden told her, 'Use your gas mask box' – evidently now an acceptable secondary use for the wretched things.

Then it began.

Starting as a hovering noise in the background, the intensity grew, a hum becoming a drone, and as the volume rose, the chattering stopped, everyone seized with terror.

This wasn't just a few aircraft.

This was a colossal tide of bombers.

And Violet realized that Hugh had been right earlier. The Nazis hadn't given up bombing them. Tonight, it was Canterbury's turn.

The sound grew so tremendous that the walls and floor of the concrete box they were inside began to vibrate under the pressure.

'There must be hundreds of them,' Violet murmured.

She realized they were sheltering right in the very centre of the city, just south of the great cathedral, which must be their main target.

And then the bombs began.

First one then another thud sounded through the vault, the earth around them shuddering. A child started to whimper as her mother muttered the Lord's Prayer.

Then came a colossal cascade of explosions, as if a basketful of bombs had been emptied out from the sky, pounding the streets and pavements, the crunch of buildings collapsing. The lanterns began to swing and monstrous shadows cascaded up and down the walls and ceilings like ghouls coming to seal their doom.

The child began to cry and was quickly shushed by her mother. The crowd collectively seemed to hold its breath, trying not to scream, trying to control the impulse to run.

Violet felt an arm around her trembling shoulders and turned to see Landon looking over at her, pulling her in close. 'We'll be all right,' he whispered in his calm, melodic voice. 'We'll be all right.'

As their eyes met, another explosion rang loudly, along with a colossal jerk of the ground, and she buried her face into his shoulder, turning her body into his so that he could pull her in tightly against his chest.

Then, with an almighty bang, the air seemed to be sucked out of her lungs, out of the concrete box itself, and a great jolt sent a deep crack splitting through the concrete ceiling.

'It's coming down on us!' a middle-aged woman yelled, unable to keep it in any longer. 'We're going to be crushed!'

A young woman beside her urged, 'We've got to stay calm. If one of us lets go, then we'll all start to panic, and where will we be then?' Her head automatically ducked as another round of explosions came.

'We need to get out,' the older woman yelled. 'This shelter's not strong enough. We'll all be buried alive.' She got up and began fighting her way to the door.

'Sit down,' the warden ordered her. 'You're better off in here than out there.'

'I don't care,' she screamed. 'Let me out!'

The warden rolled her eyes. 'All right then,' she snapped, weaving through the people on the stairs to budge open the door.

A whoosh of cold night air came in, dense with smoke, the smell of chemical explosives thick and acrid. The woman's mutterings could be heard until she was outside, and then she was gone, the door banged shut.

The thud of bombs was almost omnipresent, with the occasional earsplitting explosion sending shudders through the ground. The crack in the ceiling was pulling apart, and everyone watched it in panic.

'Maybe we should have left too,' Violet murmured.

'We take our chances either way,' Landon whispered back, his mouth close to her face, and he moved his head and gently kissed her cheek. 'If it's our turn, then it's meant to be.'

She turned her face to his cheek and kissed it too, the feeling of his skin soft and lightly stubbled under her lips. 'At least we're in this together.'

And just as another burst of bombs struck, he turned his face to hers, their eyes on each other's with fear. And almost without thought, they both inched forward so that their lips touched, at first gentle and soft, and then increasing with pressure, as if the only release from the tension and fear was through this one act of sharing.

Whatever came, they wouldn't be alone.

The sound of the bombs seemed to fade into the background as Violet felt the urgent smoothness of his lips, his hands, warm and firm, holding her body closely against his.

With a deafening crack, the whole place shook, and the remaining lantern went out. They were plunged into blackness.

Someone started to sing 'When the Lights Go on Again,' a few others joining in, a shuddering choir pretending to be calm.

The darkness only intensified their kissing, and a desperate, grasping insistence had overtaken them, their mouths on each other's, tugging each other close, her body instinctively pulling into his.

And suddenly she understood why people yearned for love during this war – why they went to such lengths to find it. Why marriage was so fast, people frantic for someone to cling on to, to call their own. Why women were tossing their virginity into the wind, peeling off their clothes to make love while they were still alive – it transcended everything bad that could ever happen. It stripped the Nazis of their power. It was more meaningful than any bomb could ever be.

Gradually, the mayhem and explosions subsided, and then the all-clear sounded through the airless space. People began to gather their belongings, switching on their lights and torches as they made their way to the stairs.

The pair drew apart from each other, suddenly shy. Violet pulled away, flustering with her clothes and hair, glancing around her to make sure people weren't watching.

But they weren't. Everyone else seemed to be a few steps ahead of them, crowding around the entrance to get out, the cold, noxious air from the outside seeping in, giving them a fore-taste of the devastation outside.

Wordlessly, Landon got up and offered her his hand to help her to her feet. She took it and clambered up, but then, instead of letting it go, he held on to it, warm and safe.

As they waited for the others to leave ahead of them, Violet glanced sideways at him, and saw a different look in his eyes, one she had never seen before. It was a look of gentleness, of fear.

Outside, the street was chaotic, voices from wardens and clean-up crews calling to each other, civilians joining in as they tried to find missing neighbours, picking over the debris to sal-vage their lost possessions before the looters got there.

The air was thick with fumes and soot. It was hard to breathe, and after Violet and Landon offered their services to the local warden and were told to 'go on home,' they began to walk to the road to Aldhurst.

'I wonder where Grace got to?' Violet looked down the chaotic street.

'I'm sure she found somewhere safe to wait out the bombs.'

'She'll find a way home – the early morning buses will be run-ning in a few hours.' Violet looked at him. 'Or she can hitch a lift. There's bound to be cars heading back that way, other people stuck in the raid. We should do that too.' She took off his jacket and handed it to him. 'You'd better wear this. There's an unspoken rule here that you have to give anyone in military uniform a ride if you have room for them.'

He let her hand go so that he could put on the jacket, and in its place, she felt the air, cold and hard.

What did the kiss mean to him? she thought.

But more to the point, what did it mean to her? She could hardly bear to think about it, how extraordinary it had felt inside.

As if sensing her need for warmth, he put his arm around her shoulders, pulling her in towards him.

Now that they were out of the city centre, the smoke had cleared, the dark blue skies milky with a smoky fog.

The sound of a car approaching from behind made them turn, and a black saloon slowed down and pulled to a stop beside them.

'Need a lift?' A middle-aged Home Guard officer looked up at them out of his window. 'I'm going to Broughton.'

'Could you drop us at Aldhurst?' Violet asked.

'Hop in the back. It'll be a squash, I'm afraid.'

The back door swung open to reveal a skinny youth in Home Guard uniform surrounded by first-aid kits and stirrup pumps. A larger man sat in the passenger seat, and he turned around to them as they picked up the boxes and bags to get in, replacing them on their laps.

'Canterbury's a bit of a mess back there but thank goodness the cathedral's still standing. We can't let the Nazis take our history from us.'

'We were in a shelter,' Landon said. 'But it sounded as if they had a good try at it.'

'They did! But we had a great team of wardens and fire-watchers up there. Each time the Jerries threw down an incendiary, one of them picked it up and lobbed it down onto the grass. And every time there were fires, they were passed sandbags to put them out before they got a chance to spread. Britain's bravest, they are.'

The conversation went on, the men proud and exhausted by

the group effort. 'We hopped into the car and drove over as soon as we saw the planes going over. All hands on deck.'

'I had a feeling it was going to be Canterbury's turn tonight,' another added, and they began to discuss the Nazis' new raids, intentionally bombing Britain's historical cities and sites.

'They're calling them the Baedeker Raids, after the guide-book,' the man said. 'Picking off our cathedrals and castles as if they're nothing.'

Meanwhile, beneath the bags and boxes on their laps, Landon reached out his hand and found Violet's, and slowly their eyes met, holding each other's gaze until the driver stopped in front of Aldhurst Manor. Reluctantly, she slid her hand out of his, and with a final hesitant smile, she headed into the house.

GRACE

As she stumbled back from the crowd of wardens and fire crews celebrating the survival of Canterbury Cathedral, Grace felt alive with an exhilaration that gripped her like never before. After fleeing the dance hall, she'd shunned the crowds heading for shelters, racing headlong to the historical edifice the Nazis were desperate to destroy.

'I'm a trained ARP warden,' she'd told the marine, unable to lose him since leaving the dance hall. 'I have to help save the cathedral!'

For the next few hours, she'd joined the ladder chains, handing sandbags up to the roof to put out incendiary fires as planes soared around them, pounding the city with bombs. And now, after hours of chaos, the planes had finally retreated and the fires on the cathedral roof put out.

The night air was dense with smoke and explosives, and her hair was matted and wet from the fire hoses, her dress and face smeared with dirt.

'Let's go back to my hotel.' The marine's arm went around her shoulders. Incredibly, she'd persuaded him to help with the bucket line, and he was now eager for some kind of compensation for his troubles.

Without thinking, she reached her fingertips up and touched his lips, as if remembering the feeling of them on hers – how strange it had been to kiss! It wasn't perfect – her mind flew to her first kiss with Hugh and quickly shot back to the wrenching reality that he was marrying someone else. If she couldn't kiss Hugh, then she was jolly well going to find someone else.

At first, she allowed the marine to guide her through the lane, hurrying her to his hotel, but she felt unsettled, glaring at the fires still raging through the crowded little lanes of the city, the shouts of wardens and fire-watchers reporting danger, calling for help. She'd had no idea how much of the city had been bombed.

Pulled away by the shouts for help, she knew that if there was more she could do, more fires to be put out, more people in danger, she had to help where she could. In an instant, she pulled away from the marine, darting through the streets back into the ravaged city centre.

A huge blast of an explosion from a house beside her only made her race faster towards the growing light of the fires in the centre of the city, the fog of smoke and debris getting thicker and heavier like a cloud of death.

A mother and a handful of children, one in a pram, ran away from a burning building. She was crying, screaming at them to keep up with her. 'Come on – run!' Seeing Grace, she called out to her. 'You need to help. There are some children on their own in number eight. Their dad's not with them.'

'Which way?' A middle-aged man in striped pyjamas and a dressing gown was beside her, perhaps another off-duty warden like her.

The woman pointed, and Grace ran, the man in striped pyjamas behind her.

Fire was raging through a terrace of homes, spreading from roof to roof, billowing out of windows, pushing through doors. Every few minutes, explosions shook the buildings as the fire

struck something volatile, new flares of fire surging fast and furious.

Number eight was in the middle of the road, the middle of
the mayhem. The roof was already alight, and as they sprinted
to the door, an explosion sounded, a tower of flames breaking
through the roof, sending roof tiles and slates raining down
on them.

'Are you in there?' She pounded on the door, desperately trying to open it.

Young voices came from the other side – so young they could
be five or even less – and her heart curled. If they didn't get out,
the flames would engulf them in minutes.

'We'll have to beat the door down.' She caught the arm of the
man in pyjamas, and together they thrust their shoulders into
the door.

Once, twice, a quick breath. They looked at each other, des-
pair on their faces.

'Again,' she urged. 'We have to go in harder.'

Then with one almighty heave, they pushed their way through,
the door collapsing in front of them, where three terrified children huddled in horror. The eldest boy – who must have been six
at the most – was holding a bundle that looked frighteningly like
a baby in blankets. Behind them, blue-gold flames licked the
bannisters and staircase menacingly.

Instinct set in as Grace scooped the bundle away from him,
and taking the hand of the smallest boy, she began to run out of
the burning house, the man in pyjamas following with the older
two.

The yawning creaks gave way to a shuddering crack, the
whole building about to come down around them. The timber
was cracking, the brickwork shaking under the renewed pressure. A new rush of smoke and gas seemed to choke her.

Panicking, Grace picked the little boy up to get him quickly outside. She couldn't breathe. The baby had begun to scream, and the boy felt limp in her arms.

Then, with a violent whoosh, a massive explosion came from behind, throwing her up in the air and down onto the street, the colossal roar of the building exploding behind her.

Debris rained down over her back as she tried to cushion the baby and the boy beneath her, bearing her weight on her elbows, which now bit down hard into the jagged fragments on the road. Suddenly there was another explosion, and she felt more debris coming down, as if a showering colossal weight piled over them – a wall perhaps, or maybe the whole building.

They were trapped, unable to move or breathe or think.

Slowly, everything settled. The piercing ring in her ears shut out any other noise, and she opened her eyes to find that they were in darkness. The air was stagnant with soot and smoke, and it hurt when she coughed.

And as the noise and the pounding and the explosions faded into the distance, she realized that whatever they were buried beneath was dense and heavy.

Just as she felt for the two youngsters beneath her, the baby began a croaky cry – not the usual cry of a baby wanting to be fed, but the guttural, panting cry of a small being desperate for air, desperate to stay alive.

She moved her arm, but the rubble didn't budge. It took a great heave of her shoulder to pull back to check on the little boy.

He was unconscious, still and silent, but she could hear his raspy breath. At least that was one small mercy.

There seemed little else for which to be thankful.

'Help!' she cried, wondering how far down they were – if there was anyone up there at all.

Stories about people buried alive in rubble had abounded in the Blitz; some poor souls were down there for days before the diggers could get to them.

But not everyone ended up being rescued in time.

There was a story of a woman feeding her child by biting her finger until it bled, letting him lap up her blood, and it wavered in and out of her mind.

Would it come to that for her?

She pulled the baby in close, trying to sooth its whimpering cries, praying they'd get out soon.

Time slowed as she lay in the darkness, pointed debris gripping her body, digging into her skin through the thin fabric of the dress. Her ankle throbbed with pain.

Then the little boy began to come to, moaning and then screaming in pain or panic, unable to see where they were or anything around him.

'You're with me, it's all right,' she said in the kindest, most reassuring voice she could.

'Who are you? I want Dad. Where's Dad?'

'My name's Grace. I'm an air raid warden. I was helping you and the baby get out, but it seems like we've been knocked over.' She tried to keep her voice casual – it wasn't a drama at all, merely an inconvenience. 'Someone will get us out soon.'

'Dad, Dad!' He began wailing, then sobbing as he dashed his limbs against the sharp debris. 'I can't move. I can't move!'

'We're a bit packed in with all the rubble,' she said. 'But it'll be fine soon. Why don't we play a game where we both call for help as loudly as we can together? On the count of three. One, two, three.' Together, they shouted as forcefully as they could, an elongated, full-throttle 'Help!'

But there was no reply, nothing. Only the silent blackness.

As the boy embarked on a new bout of tears, she tried to placate him. 'You really are jolly good at calling for help. Shall we do it again? One, two, three, help!'

After a dozen more times, an exhausted silence fell upon him.

The baby had gone quiet too, and in a small, abject voice, the boy asked, 'Are we going to die?'

Tears forged down her cheeks. 'No,' she said defiantly. 'We won't die here.'

He said quietly, 'I don't want to die.'

'Nor do I. Somehow it feels like my life's only just begun.'

'But you're old.'

She sighed. 'Sometimes you find that life takes you down a route you shouldn't have taken, and then, if you're lucky, something comes along and you realize there's a better course for you. That happened to me.'

But the little boy wasn't listening. 'I don't want to die.' He began to wail again, and taking a deep breath, Grace bellowed as loudly as she could, 'Help! Help!'

Scuffling from above was followed by the muffled sound of something – could it be people talking?

'Come on, let's shout again. One, two, three, help!' they both shouted together.

And then, to her utter and absolute relief, there was another muffle, this time definitely a voice.

'We're down here!' she yelled. 'Help!' There was more movement from above – were they digging through the debris?

And then came a man's voice, clearer this time. 'Don't worry. We'll have you out in no time.'

'There's three of us down here,' she called out. 'I'm a warden, and I have a baby and a little boy. I'm not sure if the baby's all right. Please hurry!'

Within a few minutes, she felt the rubble around her shift. 'They must be close,' she said to the boy.

The last few minutes were agonizingly slow, the men having to use their hands so that the buried victims weren't struck by the shovels.

Then she saw something, a glimmer of light. She turned her head, blinking into a beaming light that was pointing straight at her.

'There you are!' a man's voice called, warm and comforting, like her father rescuing a lost chick.

The boy stopped squawking and gazed up blankly. 'Dad?' And a pair of hands reached down and picked him up. 'I'm sure he's not far away,' the voice said. 'Is that your baby brother or sister?'

Another pair of hands took the baby from Grace.

'I think she's still alive,' Grace said, grabbing hold of a proffered hand and allowing herself to be pulled to her feet. 'I think she might have been hurt, or her lungs might be damaged.'

The man cradled the baby in his arm, and Grace realized it was the man in striped pyjamas, now without the dressing gown. 'She's fine. It's probably just shock. There's an ambulance here, so we'll take them both to the first-aid centre for a checkup. What about you, miss?'

'Oh, I'm all right,' she said as jauntily as she could, moving her ankle around.

The boy was now on his feet beside her, and he slipped his hand into hers. Together, they followed the others to the junction, where an old black motorcar was acting as a makeshift ambulance, already half full. 'They'll take you to a first-aid centre, where your father will be able to find you,' Grace said, passing his hand over to a young ambulance driver, who briskly showed him where to sit then took the baby, giving her a quick check.

Grace leaned forward. 'I know you don't have space to take me with you, but would you let me know if they're all right, if their father finds them? I'm at the vicarage in Aldhurst.'

'I'm afraid we're a bit too busy to telephone people, but rest assured we'll do the best that we can,' she said warmly, and

Grace was suddenly indescribably grateful for her smile, a bolstering assurance in the chaos. Every day, the newspapers and radio impressed upon civilians the need to stay cheerful, and it usually struck her as a rather futile and transparent gesture. But now, in the thick of the mayhem, she realized that even a weak smile was far more than that: It was a kindness.

After giving the boy a peck on the cheek, she waved as the ambulance drew away, and then turned to look back at the collapsed building.

'We're lucky to have got everyone out.' The chief warden stood beside her. 'You're not from around here, are you?'

'I'm a warden in Aldhurst. I was here for the dance.' She looked down at her dress – Violet's dress – now torn and dirty. 'I wanted to help.'

'Well, thanks to you, those children were saved. Bravo, miss.'

'I wondered where you'd gone.' A voice came from behind her, and there, also looking the worse for wear, was the marine. 'Quite an adventurer, aren't you?'

'It looks like you've been helping too.'

He shrugged. 'Any chance of a kiss as a reward?'

And before she knew it, he leaned his head forward and touched his lips to hers, and whether from exhaustion or relief or simply the exhilaration of being alive, she kissed him back for all she was worth. He responded in kind, matching her passion, her ferocity. It was fuelled with a longing she never knew she had, an insatiable need to have a connection with another human being.

A truckload of heavy lifters had come in to begin the clearances, and in the distance, she heard a familiar voice.

'Grace?'

She pulled away from the marine, confused.

It was Hugh.

Hurriedly, she stepped back. 'What are you doing here?'

Hugh was still wearing his suit from his formal dinner, but like everyone surrounding them, he must have got caught up in the chaos as there was dirt smeared on his temples and his tie was gone, his hair dishevelled.

'I was helping, and then looking for you.' He was striding towards her, his voice distant. 'I thought you might be in trouble after I called the manor and Violet said that she'd lost you in the raid.'

'I'm perfectly fine, thank you,' she muttered.

He stopped beside her, taking in her dress, her hair, the marine. 'I wanted to make sure you got home. But now I see you already have someone to take care of you.'

The marine put a possessive arm around her shoulder. 'We were helping out too, weren't we, Grace?'

Uncertain how she wanted to handle the situation, Grace shrugged his arm away.

Hugh eyed them. 'Well, if you would care to take up my offer, I have the car a few roads away. Perhaps you should bid your friend good-bye.'

The chief warden came over. 'Thank you again, miss – what did you say your name is?'

'Grace, Grace Carlisle. I'll be off now, although I'm sure you'll be busy for the rest of the night.'

'You're probably right. The more we can do now, the better. But you should get some sleep after what you've been through. You deserve a medal for bravery!'

'I only did what any other warden would.' She turned to leave, giving the marine a quick smile. 'Cheerio then.'

Catching hold of her hand, the marine pulled her back. 'When will I see you?'

But she only shrugged. 'Oh, I'm sure I'll be at another dance soon,' she said, hurrying away.

There was silence between them as she followed Hugh to his

car. He gave her his jacket to wear, and she was too cold to decline it. Quietly, almost dejectedly, he opened the passenger door for her, and then he got into the driver's seat. Slowly, the car meandered through the lanes, twice having to reverse as the road was blocked by bomb damage. Smoke lingered in the hazy darkness, the first quiet fingers of dawn colouring the edge of the sky with a light blue glow.

It wasn't until they were out of the city, driving through the countryside that he spoke.

'I knew you shouldn't have gone out tonight. I knew Canterbury would be next on the Germans' list.'

'It was good I was there to help. I was halfway up a ladder in the sandbag chain going to the cathedral roof. We managed to put out hundreds of incendiaries – hundreds of them!'

'Was that why the chief was thanking you?'

'No, that was later. I was trying to get some children out of a burning building when it collapsed. We were buried by an explosion for quite a while.'

He glanced across at her, shocked. 'Are you all right?'

'Yes, and they are too, thank heavens. A bit shaken, but alive at least.'

He was quiet for a moment, and then he said, 'Well done. Not everyone would have done that.'

'What about you?' she asked. 'You look worse for wear too.'

'I knew the car would be useful for driving the injured to hospital or the first-aid post.'

'That was good thinking. There weren't enough ambulances.'

But he didn't seem to be listening. 'Who was that man?'

There was a pause. 'Someone I met at the dance. I'm actually not sure I caught his name.' She felt him look at her sharply. And then before she could stop herself, she blurted out, 'Why should I pretend it was otherwise? He was just another man trying to "rescue" me, not unlike yourself, apparently. But I don't need rescuing. I'm perfectly capable of taking care of myself.'

'How else would you get home if I wasn't driving you?'

'The buses will start soon,' she snapped back, adding, 'I hope you're not going to get all preachy with me, Hugh. I may not know that marine, or see him again, but at least it felt real – *I* felt real.'

He opened his mouth to speak, but she decided that she didn't want to hear what he had to say, so she cut in impatiently, 'And what's more, I don't know why you're acting so judgmental about him. You're engaged, Hugh. In a month or two, you'll have a wife, someone who will share your life, have your children, make you happy. You're living your life, so just let me live mine.'

'Look, Grace, I didn't realize—'

'Why did you say all those things to me when you made me try on the veil in the church?' There, she had said it. 'You were so very familiar, telling me how you'd felt about me when we were younger. How was I supposed to feel? And then you ran off to London for a few weeks without a word, only to come back engaged to Astrid. What were you trying to accomplish?'

He looked at the road ahead. 'You must forgive me. I don't know what came over me. I was just being honest about how I'd felt about you all those years ago. I suppose I was hoping that – oh, never mind.'

'Tell me, what could you possibly have been hoping for, Hugh?'

Hurt and frustrated, he retorted, 'I didn't know that you'd broken it off with Lawrence when I proposed to Astrid. It certainly didn't sound as if you had that in mind when we were in the church. You seemed more convinced of Lawrence than ever. I made the best decision at the time, and now' – he paused – 'now, I have a duty to follow through on my promise. I have been courting Astrid for a number of years. Her father was urging for the betrothal to become official. I did what any decent man would do in my situation. In any case, what else is there between us, Grace? We've only just become friends again, but we live different lives. We're different people.'

A frustrated silence fell over them, then she eyed him, exasperated. 'Why don't you set yourself free from her? Find freedom again, just as we did when we were young. I have, and it's extraordinary how right it feels.'

He made a small laugh. 'You've been drinking, haven't you? And yes, I'm sure it's wonderful to be free, but I'm simply not that person anymore. I have responsibilities now. I have an estate to run, a war to win, and a woman to whom I have made promises.'

'Don't you have responsibilities to yourself too?' she said, but then she laughed. 'Or is that truly what you want?' she uttered incredulously. 'Although I doubt there'll be any swimming in the lake with Astrid.'

He kept his eyes on the road ahead. 'She's never lived in the countryside, but I'm sure she'll get used to it.' Then he sighed. 'Grace, I thought we could be friends. Can we? I don't want to fight like this.'

This wasn't an easy question to answer. On one hand, why should she be friends with someone who'd vanished when she needed him most after her mother died and had now let her down for a second time?

On the other hand, she worked in his manor house, his aunt was her much-loved employer, his sister was a friend. She loathed unpleasantness, and she wouldn't be able to avoid him in the future. Should she simply put it all behind her?

After all, wasn't that what her chaotic Canterbury night had been about? Getting drunk at a dance hall, kissing the marine, running into a collapsing building and risking her life at the drop of a hat? Wasn't the future to do with becoming a stronger person?

With this thought, she opened her mouth to reply, but when she did, a different answer came out. 'No.'

'I'm sorry?'

'I said no, Hugh. I don't want to be your friend. I'm fed up with being that person, the one who does everything for everyone else, who only does what she's expected to do.'

'But I thought that's what you wanted, for us to be friends?'

Something inside her seemed to snap. 'I thought we could, but now I can see that it's impossible. All those years ago, I was in love with you, Hugh, and part of me just can't forget that.' She took a deep breath. 'And I think part of you can't forget that you were in love with me too, which is why you wanted to escort us tonight, why you came to find me – why you wanted to get me away from that marine.'

'But I—' he began, but she interrupted him.

'Can't you see? You've been promised to a woman for many years, a woman who will do your family name proud – something that obviously means a great deal to you and your father. You need to marry her and be happy,' she retorted, and then her voice faltered as she added more quietly, 'and I need to find someone who loves me regardless of class or money or any other ridiculous tenet. I'm sorry that you've decided to stay trapped in your cage, Hugh, but you can't drag me into it. I have found my freedom, and nothing will induce me to be caught up in a situation where I have to pretend to be someone I'm not.'

Through the ensuing silence, she didn't look at his face. She knew it would be inscrutable. He was the kind of man who prided himself in making sure his private feelings were not on display. Outbursts of emotion were uncouth, embarrassing.

At the outskirts of the village, he asked in a stiff, polite way if she would like him to drop her home, 'or is there somewhere else you would like to go?'

'The vicarage will be fine, thank you,' she replied crisply.

The car swept up the short drive, coming to a halt outside. He neither switched off the engine nor turned in her direction.

As she got out, she said curtly, 'Goodnight. Thank you.'

And he, in response, muttered, 'My pleasure,' before he turned the car and left.

She stood at the door, watching his car vanish into the lane in the eerie new light of dawn, and as her bravado from the night faded with the daylight, she couldn't help but feel her heart breaking, like it had so many years before.

Would he ever speak to her again? And did she even want him to?

CRESSIDA

Cressida's design room had spread into the adjoining bedroom, now filled with fabric and paper patterns. With the new work from Canterbury and the Utility Contest deadline just around the corner, she was busier than ever, and she bustled around Grace, who was modelling a shirtwaist dress for the contest.

The young woman looked exasperated. The events in Canterbury had greatly disturbed and exhausted her, but she still insisted on coming to work, plunging herself into her designs.

'I think it needs something to make it stand out,' Cressida muttered. 'Perhaps we could use a different coloured fabric for the button placket running the length of the dress. Or is that becoming too common?'

But Grace was in her own world, her eyes in the middle distance.

Cressida sighed, pulling up her shoulder to stop her slouching. 'I know that things have been strained between you and Hugh since Canterbury. What happened?'

After a long pause, Grace shrugged. 'We argued. He was unhappy that I was kissing someone else, and I told him that he had no rights over me whatsoever. He's marrying Astrid, and I have to get used to that.'

'You must be horribly upset, my dear.'

'I'm furious,' she said. 'He made me feel something for him, helped with parish work, brought me his mother's veil. And the way he looked at me, I could have sworn it meant something to him too.'

'He's probably been reliving something of what he felt as a youth, just like you.'

'Only *I* meant it, while for him it was just a nostalgic trip into the past, a childhood fantasy that he toyed with before attending to his familial duties.'

'I'm not sure what it meant for him, my dear. I only know that he's hardly been back to the manor since.' She sighed. 'Things are going to be difficult once Astrid moves here. I've instructed my estate agent to find a property for me as soon as they can.' She stood back, appraising her work. 'Perfect. Now, could you pop on the evening gown for us to look at next, please?'

The evening dress was mesmerizing, even on Grace's disgruntled form. It was a bias-cut gown in such beautiful rayon that it shone like silk. The design had elegant lines, skimming the skin to use less fabric. Cressida had let Grace take the lead in designing it, and she had chosen a pale sage-green colour, which was overlaid with a darker green leaf pattern. It gave the impression of a willow or a fern, blowing in the wind.

Cressida stood, hands on her hips, watching in awe. 'You look absolutely stunning, Grace.' She walked around, smoothing the material as she went. 'You've learned a lot from making those wedding dresses from the parachute silk you found. Gowns are a particular skill, and a very useful one at that.' She paused in thought. 'Oh, and did you hear that Archie Kettlewell arrested the Nazi who'd abandoned the parachute? He was caught stealing food from a local farm. An angry farmer held him up with his twelve-bore and marched him down to the Home Guard's office.'

'I was relieved when I heard it,' Grace replied. 'It always felt a little uncomfortable that he could still be out there. But it feels rather good that we're sticking it to the Nazis, using their supplies to better our lives with three beautiful new wedding gowns.' She glanced down at the pale green dress. 'When do we have to send in the IncSoc designs?'

'We need to send in photographs by the end of the week. I've asked Violet to take them for us. Then they'll select the final garments they'd like to see, and then the best will be selected for the fashion show. The idea is to display the designs to the Board of Trade, but it'll be far more than that. All the press and fashion magazines will be there, and hopefully it'll be in every newspaper and magazine in the country.' Cressida smiled. 'It'll be the event of the war.'

'I hope they select one of our designs for their final thirty-two.'

'I hope they'll *all* be picked,' Cressida said. 'Never forget to aim high, Grace. Now, stand still, my dear, and I'll make the final adjustments.'

A hand on Grace's hip, Cressida moved her around slightly to work on the other side. 'How did the argument with Hugh end?'

'I told him that I didn't want to be his friend, so I imagine he's decided to be all polite and dignified about it, keeping out of Aldhurst.'

'He's probably doing it for the right reasons – or what he thinks they are. I'm not sure he'd ever go against his father's wishes. It's hard to forget something that's been drilled into you all your life. It takes a great deal of bravery to defy the label people try to give you, forge ahead on a different path, become something new.'

Grace looked pensively at her reflection. 'If I put my all into it, perhaps I could become a great couturier like you one day, become something new.'

'Just take care, my dear. Since coming home, I've come to realize that there's a whole part of me that I seem to have neglected in my eagerness to become a great couturier and prove Eustace wrong. You have to face your fears and make peace with them, or you'll never stop running from them.'

And through the mirror their eyes met. 'I think both you and I, Grace, have to think about what we want from our future. You're in charge of your life, Grace. If there's something that you truly want, you need to go out and do whatever you can to get it. Don't let age-old habits and fear get in your way. You only have to answer to yourself. But whatever you do, don't bury yourself completely in work. Life is too short to spend it alone.'

VIOLET

The US Military Office in Darley Grange was bustling. In Violet's section alone, ten newly trained American Women's Army Cadets, or WACs as they were called, had arrived, replacing the British ATS girls. Violet hadn't been replaced yet, but it was bound to happen soon. In any case, her officer assessment was in just a few weeks, and hopefully after that she would be leaving for training.

But through her excitement was a thread of worry; what was going to happen to her and Landon when she left, if there was even anything between them at all?

She was just Fred to him, after all.

And he wasn't a lord – for heaven's sake, he wasn't even part of the British class system. Although for some reason, that seemed smaller in her mind these days, like her white evening gloves, discarded and forgotten in the midst of the war.

The morning after the Canterbury bombing, Violet had resolutely been on time for work. Exhausted after only two hours' sleep and anxious about how things would be with Landon, she arrived only to find that he had been taken to London by the British colonel to attend an impromptu meeting. What was more, he was to stay in the city for a few nights.

She had three long days to go through what had happened, what it meant to her wavering in and out as she considered what it could have meant to him. Inside the concrete shelter, it had seemed so fearful and claustrophobic, the noise of the bombs, the enclosed space; it was difficult to breathe, difficult to keep calm. Had it simply been fear driving them? Previous kisses with other boys hadn't felt anything like that. In fact, she'd always thought of kissing as a bit wet and pointless. Why did everyone make such a fuss about it?

Well, now she knew.

But what could ever happen next?

Didn't he brag about having a team of girls back in Connecticut? And even if there wasn't anyone special, after the war he would simply go back home, and she would be left here, on her own.

The wait until his return to Aldhurst was interminable. Every time someone arrived at the office, she sat up with a start, trying not to look over, only to discover that it wasn't him.

It wasn't until the third afternoon, as she sat studying at her desk, that she heard his voice at the reception desk.

'Miss me, Sally?' his jovial tone meandered in through the open door.

At once her heart started pounding, and she busied herself reading the engineering specifications for an army truck, part of her preparation for officer assessment. Yet her ears were trained on him.

Why was he so familiar with Sally?

Was there some reason why Sally should miss him?

Perhaps it wasn't only Violet. Perhaps he kissed lots of girls.

Maybe what had happened between them meant nothing to him at all.

Sally laughed and they continued to talk while she gave him his letters and messages from the past few days. His tone was light and odiously flirtatious.

How could she have been so wrong about him, about every-thing that had happened between them?

After Sally, he went to the switchboard to pick up his mes-sages. Violet couldn't hear the conversation clearly, but a lot of laughter was involved – mostly female laughter.

And after that, just as she was refocusing on exhausts, he went in to see the chief's secretary, evidently to make sure she was happy to see him back too.

By the time he eventually stepped into the general drivers' room at the end of the corridor, she couldn't have been more annoyed at the sight of him.

'And how is my driver?' He came towards her desk, his tone normal, almost a little flat compared to the jovial banter with the others. The thought crossed her mind that he might be playing down anything that happened between them to avoid trouble. Liaisons between military staff were an absolute no-no. They would both be seriously reprimanded if anything un-toward came to light.

But still, she couldn't bear for him to walk in and expect her to respond like all the other girls.

'Your driver is busy studying,' she replied evenly, not look-ing up.

'I would have thought you might be more pleased to see me, Fred?' It was asked as a question, a little hurt, but mockingly so, perhaps to throw off anyone listening.

'I thought that we had evolved from you calling me Fred,' she said evenly, shuffling some papers around her desk.

'All right then, Private Westcott.' He said it in a joking man-ner, but she could sense a slight wariness in his voice. 'I hope you will be available in thirty minutes to drive me to Canter-bury?'

'It will be my pleasure.' Her ironic tone matched his, but she kept her eyes lowered.

The thirty-minute wait was fraught. One part of her thought she should remain studiously quiet and distant on the journey to Canterbury. The kissing incident would be quite forgotten, a mere result of the heat of the moment. If he mentioned it, perhaps she would give a light laugh, how silly it had been. Yes, that would send the right message.

Another part of her yearned for the truth. If she meant nothing, then she could smother her hurt and protect her pride. She would get used to it, eventually.

By the time she went to wait at the car, she had yet to decide how to react, but as he walked out of the door to meet her, she felt a new kind of sensation, one she had rarely experienced: shyness.

'It's really great to see you, Violet,' he said softly as she opened the passenger door for him.

'Likewise,' she said rather too brusquely in her nervous fluster.

As the car made its way down the drive, the silence was excruciating.

'Just to confirm, we are going to the Guildhall in Canterbury?' she asked formally.

'Yes, that's right.'

Once they were on the road, she couldn't help wishing that she could act more normally. It wasn't in her nature to be uncertain or abrupt.

In fact, the mood was so awkward that she found it impossible to simply let it continue.

Which is why, as they drove over the crest of the Downs, she pulled the car over and switched off the engine.

The view over the countryside was breathtaking. A patchwork of fields and woodland covered the rolling hills, and in the distance was the sea, the narrow breadth of water all that separated them from Nazi-occupied Europe. The day was a cloudy one, and as they watched, a fine rain began to fall, slow drops of water building softly on the windscreen.

'Your countryside is stunning,' he said gently.

She didn't reply straight away, unable to think properly.

What she hadn't factored into this was how much she wanted to reach over and touch him, to hold him.

How can I let him make me feel like this? she thought, annoyed with herself, with the situation.

'Look, Violet,' he said, reaching out for her hand, but she pulled it away.

'This is all a mistake,' she said, reaching for the ignition. 'We should never have let ourselves get carried away. It should never have happened.'

'Please don't say that.' His voice was soft yet urgent. 'Not when I haven't been able to think of anything else since.'

She looked over to meet his eyes, only to see them on hers, a mirror of her own feelings, her own anxieties.

'B-but we can't. We can't!' She said it as if trying to convince them both, wiping a ridiculous tear from her eye. 'I'm supposed to be a lady, and you're not allowed to fraternize with foreigners. We shouldn't have even started it! We were perfectly happy being friends, Fred and Mr Toad, jaunting around together and putting the world to rights.'

He gave a small smile. 'And now?' He turned his face back to the countryside, the rain building pace, collecting in streams down the windscreen in front of them.

She glanced over and watched his profile, the large, broken nose and the wide jaw, but in the place of any other feeling was a tremendous wave of passion. And she knew, without a shadow of a doubt, that what she felt for him was love. No wonder people made such a fuss about it.

Suddenly feeling hot, heady, she turned and opened the window, and a gush of cool air, damp with rain, spilled into the car.

He turned, and in that instant, she saw the tenderness in his eyes too. He opened his mouth and began, 'I—'

She cut him off, knowing what he was going to say. 'Please, don't say it.' Her voice was a whisper, desperately appealing to him. 'We shouldn't. We can't.'

But he sat looking deeply into her eyes, into her heart, and she felt as if nothing else mattered but this moment; the pitter-patter of the rain as they sat in the warm, dry car, the contours of the rounded hills, the sea, dark and forbidding, and the strange entwining intimacy that wound invisibly around them.

And gently, he leaned towards her, and as his hand touched the side of her face, she felt the blood rush through her body. He brought his face to hers and slowly their lips touched. Before she knew what was happening, she was lost – both of them were. Their careful, delicate kisses gradually became more ardent, more passionate, their bodies pulling closer, entwining with each other's.

There they remained until a stream of sunshine broke through the rainclouds, shafts of light glimmering through the droplets on the windscreen, pulling them back into reality.

'We have to go,' she said hurriedly, biting her lip. 'You're late. We'll both be in trouble.'

He smiled gently. 'I don't care. We can say the car broke down.'

She switched on the engine then turned to him, suddenly impatient. 'But what are we going to do? There's a war going on. Either of us can be moved to another part of the world at any time, not to mention that we both come from different countries – from different continents.'

'All we can do is live for this moment,' he whispered, his fingers sweeping her neck. 'Why think about tomorrow when we need to live in the now?'

Frustrated, she pulled away from him and shifted the car into gear, driving down from the top of the great hills, the sunshine sparkling on the wet fields and pastures, giving the world a heavenly splendour, as if it were coming to life for the very first time.

As the car swept into the broken city, Violet knew that his eyes were on her. His meeting was in the city centre, and as she pulled the car up, the British colonel, who had just stepped out of a car himself, came over to wait for Landon to join him, banishing any further conversation between them.

After getting out of the car, Landon turned back so that the colonel couldn't see his face, and he looked at Violet with such gentle passion that her heart almost burst.

'When would you like me to pick you up, Lieutenant McCauley?' she asked, knowing the colonel could hear them.

He gave her a rueful smile. 'Three o'clock,' he replied, but then, just before he turned to leave, his eyes met hers and he mouthed the words, 'I love you.'

And as if it were the most natural thing she had ever done, she mouthed back, 'I love you too.'

CRESSIDA

A multitude of different shades of white, ivory, and cream covered every surface of the village hall. Tonight, the Sewing Circle was taking stock of their pool of wedding dresses, and while Lottie straightened the gowns, singing 'It Had to Be You,' Mrs Todd joined in, swaying her hips as Violet took a photograph. She was hoping to sell it to a local newspaper to garner more dress donations.

'What happened here?' Laughing delightedly at the sight, Mrs Bisgood stood at the door. 'It's as if we've had an explosion of white.'

'More like a deluge of wedding dresses!' Cressida laughed. 'Lady Marley spread the word in Canterbury, and a delivery of five came this afternoon. Our most requested gowns, however, are the three we got out of the parachute silk. They're proving especially popular with the army girls.'

Lottie paused her singing to say, 'It's just as well we're getting more in. A nurse in Chartham wants to borrow one, and then there's a few more girls from Canterbury.'

'What we need is a proper ledger-style book and a calendar, or we'll never be able to keep all this in order,' Violet said, taking notes. 'I've written to the ATS to ask if they could help organize some of the dresses for the brides in the forces, which would really help us, especially after Cressida leaves.'

The chatter fell silent as the women absorbed this news.

Lottie turned to Cressida. 'You're leaving us?'

Cressida sighed uneasily. 'It's true, I'm afraid. I shall be returning to London in a few weeks' time. I'm sorry to be leaving you in the lurch with all this work to do. I will miss this Sewing Circle dearly. You were all so welcoming to me when I arrived, and I can't imagine how I'd have entertained myself without you.' She laughed, but inside it felt more of a wrench than she was prepared to admit. Her life had grown a lot smaller since she'd been in Aldhurst, and yet somehow it felt so much bigger. These women weren't supportive of her because she was a famous designer; they liked her because of who she was as a person, and through her time here, she'd got to know that person once more. Hidden behind her world of work and business was a caring, emotional woman, not someone who was always strong and tough and resilient, but someone more balanced, a mixture of strength and vulnerability. And instead of her vulnerability making her fearful, it made her more free. She now knew that she wasn't all on her own, that life was about more than hard work and trying to control everything around you. It was about trust and faith. It was about friendship.

'I told Hugh that she should stay,' Violet said, hands on hips. 'But he insists there's nothing he can do. According to Astrid, superfluous house guests will get in the way of her renovations.' Under her breath, she added, 'Wretched Astrid! And Hugh too! Honestly, you should have heard the way he went on about how I needed to do my duty for the war when I got my conscription letter, and yet here he is, letting Astrid dictate who lives in the manor and who doesn't. You would have thought that taking care of his own flesh and blood would be part of doing *his* duty, but apparently not.'

Although he rarely came back to Aldhurst these days, Hugh had surprised them the previous evening, requesting a conversation with Cressida about her future. Clearly embarrassed at having to spell it out, he told her about Astrid's plans and how extraneous family members had to leave. Since she was the only family other than Violet, it was clear this message was meant for her. Astrid was taking full ownership of Aldhurst Manor, and Hugh was evidently unable to stand up for his aunt before his future bride and the Fortescues.

Cressida had telephoned her estate agent the very next morning and told them to accept the best they could get for her immediately, as she couldn't wait any longer. The last thing she wanted was to once again be stuck in a house where she was neither wanted nor respected. Without hesitation, she invited Grace to go with her, but although the girl was keen, she wanted to stay with her father in Aldhurst, promising to come up to London for extra training as necessary until she felt ready to move. Cressida understood; moving to the city, especially with the bombs, was a big decision, and she realized all too clearly how much she'd miss the little village.

'Don't worry, Cressida,' Mrs Bisgood said briskly. 'We'll make sure the Wedding Dress Exchange keeps running like clockwork.'

'It's wonderful to be able to leave it in such capable hands. I have no doubt you'll make it into an enormous success.'

'You will come back to visit us, won't you?' Lottie asked, putting an arm around Mrs Todd's shoulder.

'Of course! It's not far away, and Grace says that there's always room for me to stay at the vicarage. In any case, Grace is helping me with the IncSoc Utility designs, and then she will need my help setting up the shop, my beloved country outpost.'

By now, everyone had heard the news. Cressida and Grace were taking over the clothes shop beside the pub. It had stood empty since the beginning of the war, a victim of clothes rations and shortages, and would soon be home to Cressida's Aldhurst design studio.

'When are you opening?' Martha asked excitedly.

'Fingers crossed, it'll be ready in a week or two. It needs a coat of paint and some furniture. Both are proving difficult to find with the shortages.'

'And Grace will run it without you?' Mrs Todd plonked herself down on a chair.

Grace stepped forward. 'Yes, I'm running it on my own.' And as she spoke, she pulled her shoulders back, her chin up, wearing her new stylish skirt suit with aplomb, and Cressida couldn't help feeling proud of her, taking on the task.

'And I'm managing a new corset repair stand inside,' Mrs Kettlewell said. 'It's proved to be a very lucrative trade now that you can't buy a new corset for love or money.'

Mrs Bisgood chortled. 'Well, you can count me in as your first customer.'

Brimming with excitement, Cressida said, 'We can spread the word about the shop at the IncSoc Utility Fashion Show next week – we managed to get two of our designs into the show, Grace's dress and the skirt suit. All the big fashion names and journalists will be there. Grace has been putting her all into the designs, and it'll be a great way to get them talking about what she'll be doing here after I've left.'

'I'm wearing the skirt suit,' Violet said proudly. 'They're encouraging designers to use normal people as models since that's what the show is about: making top designs for everyday women.'

'And Grace will be wearing her lovely sage-green evening gown.' Cressida smiled to herself. This could be Grace's big opportunity, the moment she'd realize that she was worthy of any great stage.

But Grace only said, 'It will be such a spectacle – our chance to do something truly useful for the war effort.'

Cressida put her hands to her head. 'I almost forgot! I have something else to tell you. When we put the advert in *The Lady* magazine, we included a few of the photographs Violet took of the dresses. Well, now *Vogue* is sending down a journalist to write an article. They're calling us The Wedding Dress Sewing Circle!'

Through the cheers and jubilation, Cressida hid a knowing smile. The journalist in question was her dear friend Muriel Holden-Smythe, the friend to whom she'd sworn that she'd never survive outside London – how very long ago that lunch now seemed! Evidently, Muriel was sufficiently intrigued to propose the article, wondering what Cressida had been up to for all these months. Cressida blanched a little as she thought of how Muriel would tease her for her little country life, but she couldn't help feeling proud of the Sewing Circle, of creating such an extraordinary project as the Wedding Dress Exchange.

After the meeting, Ben met her outside the village hall with Morris by his side. They were on ARP duty together again, and Cressida was looking forward to seeing him, with all the news to discuss. They'd been spending a lot of evenings together, what with Morris's daily walks invariably ending with Cressida popping back to the vicarage for a cup of tea or a relaxed supper. There was so much to catch up on, so many stories to tell, so many feelings to share, and now so little time left to share it all.

But tonight, as they began their blackout tour down the Canterbury Road, Ben had something else he wanted to discuss.

'I wanted to ask you about Grace. I'm worried about her. She hasn't been herself since the business with Lawrence. I've tried talking to her, but she tells me she's all right, that she'll be absolutely fine. I know you two have become close, but now that you're leaving for London, I hope she won't withdraw back into her shell.'

Cressida smiled gently, happy to see that Ben was taking care of Grace instead of the other way around. 'Ever since the Canterbury bombs, she's buried herself in work. She asked me if she could work extra hours to "earn" fabric to make her own new clothes and has already made herself some very professional-looking dresses and skirt suits. Last week, I found Grace's old brown skirt and fawn cardigan in the second-hand box, which I could only view in a positive light. I'm very proud of her, but I worry too. She talks about moving to London eventually, and the change might perk her up. She's found a goal, something to work towards, but she's restless and perturbed.'

They walked in silence for a while, and then Ben said, 'Do you think it has to do with Hugh?'

'I don't think it's entirely unrelated.' She sighed. 'It won't be easy for Grace to watch him get married. My heart goes out to the poor girl.'

She stopped for a moment, taking in the beauty of the sunset, which had evolved into a solitary line of intense red, above which a star began to peer out of the deep blue sky.

'Why are you going back to London, Cressida?' Ben's voice was soft and distant, as if he hadn't wanted to say it at all. It had just come out, a thought voiced unintentionally.

'I have to get back to my business, my career. London is the heart of the industry. It's where I thrive.'

'But you thrive here too,' he said. 'Perhaps better. And you can always get to your luncheons and meetings by train.'

She continued walking, looking at the ground ahead of her. 'It's not as simple as that. I need to immerse myself in it, live it.' She gave him a sideways look and smiled. 'In any case, Astrid doesn't want a fashion house presiding on her estate. And even if she did, I'm not sure I'd want to share it with her.'

Ben made a light chuckle. 'That bad, is she?'

'She's frightfully snobbish, and demanding and petulant too.

Hugh has patience and politeness, so he might be able to get along with her, but I doubt I could for very long.'

'You know that you could always stay in the village, rent a house or stay with us in the vicarage? I know it's not the manor, but you know that you will always be welcome.' His voice was gentle, pressing her to accept. 'We would love to have you.'

She felt a blush coming over her, as if she were suddenly a young woman again, and then she loathed herself for it, pulling herself together.

They'd grown so very close over the months, closer than she had been with anyone for many, many years, and now she was going to have to get used to life without him. 'No, it's time to go,' she said crisply. 'It's been a fun little interlude, but it was always temporary. My old life beckons.'

Had she just called her time in Aldhurst 'a fun little interlude'? She saw a flash of hurt in his face, but it was quickly quelled, and she felt annoyed with herself for speaking in such a facile way. She suddenly felt brittle, as if the part of her that had become solid and unshakable was slowly bending. 'I didn't mean that to sound the way it did.'

But he only smiled. 'That's understandable. Just remember that we will always be here.'

And when his dark eyes pierced into her, she felt something dislodge beneath her rib cage, as if her insides were being re-arranged into a more unsettled place.

They fell into an uneasy silence as they walked. Without thinking, she found herself noticing each curve in the lane, each tree and bush, the sound of the brook travelling down to the river. It was as if she were already preparing for her departure, etching each morsel of the countryside into her mind. It surprised her, this mental note-taking, the reality that she'd truly miss the place.

And it also surprised her that some of what she'd told Ben

wasn't completely true. Her London life was not calling her back, as she thought it would all those months ago. When she'd first arrived into what she imagined was a sleepy, dull little village, she could barely have predicted how it would take hold of her: the beauty of the landscape, the simple, straightforward way of life, and the quirky, enduring spirit of the community. While she appreciated the anonymity a big city could afford, she had also come to appreciate the verve and warmth of village life.

But as she looked at Ben striding beside her, Morris at his feet, she asked herself if there could be something else she was going to miss. Increasingly, her mind drifted to him whenever it wasn't otherwise occupied, wondering what he was doing, wondering if he too was thinking of her. She was almost embarrassed by the way her mind undressed him, admiring his form, his long limbs, the way he moved, agile and athletic. What was happening to her? Where was the Cressida from London, unable or unaware or just plain unwilling to engage with that sort of nonsense?

And although she knew he liked her too, how could she be sure it was in the right way? The prospect of her liking him more than he did her – of making an embarrassment of herself – was paralyzing. It had been such a long time since she'd embarked on something like this. She'd had a few affairs in Paris and the early days in London, but they had been short-lived and superficial, nothing like the sense of togetherness she felt now. It was so overwhelming that she was rattled, afraid it would pull her under if she let herself go.

And it suddenly struck her that there was another path in life she might have taken, one of love and passion and togetherness. Had she met someone like Ben, had she stepped away from her design work, had she opened her heart to it, her life would have been immeasurably different: warmer, lighter, happier. As they finished their checks, Ben went to take Morris home for the night, leaving her to go ahead to the ARP office. And with a brisk shake, she quickened her pace. What was she thinking, to consider putting so much on the line, letting go of the control she'd worked so hard to achieve?

No, I've never wanted that life for myself; I'm just feeling unsettled, she thought, her step hurrying as she let herself into the building and went up the narrow stairs to the little office. *Everything will fall into place once I'm back in London, back in my design house, back in the swing of it.*

VIOLET

It was the evening before Violet's officer evaluation, and she'd rushed about, getting everything ready for the last hurdle between her and officer training: five days of tests and interviews in Army HQ. She'd hoped to spend her final evening with Landon, but frustratingly, she had to drop him off for a meeting in London.

'I'll see you when you're back. It won't be long,' he said, a sorry smile on his lips.

They sat in the car outside the grey ministry building saying their last good-bye for five days, and disappointment surged through her.

'Wretched war!' she muttered. 'How rotten it all is!'

'Come on now.' He took her into his arms, and she felt that buzzing lightheadedness, that sense of togetherness that sent her into a heady tailspin of desire mixed with fear lest it be tugged away from her. 'The war might be wretched, but it's also the reason I met you.'

'Stop being reasonable!' she ordered, pulling him towards her for another kiss.

But it was over too soon. Another car had pulled up, the British colonel clambering out and, seeing Landon, he strode over to greet him.

'I didn't know you were coming today, McCauley.' He held the door open for Landon to get out, and Landon had no choice but to comply, giving her a sorry smile as he turned to leave.

'I was a last-minute addition,' he said to the colonel.

With nothing but a hasty good-bye, Landon shut the car door, and together the two walked briskly to the grand front door. Only as he was about to pass through did he turn, a smile on his face so wide and warm that it melted Violet's heart.

How can this ever last? she thought as she started the engine. *Have I been a fool to get drawn into it?*

In the elation of being together – the sheer wonder at this sensation of love, of being with someone who made her feel so alive and right and free – she had forgotten to think about the future.

It no longer mattered that he wasn't a lord, or even part of the upper class. It no longer mattered that he teased her and had a broken nose. In fact, she loved him all the more for it.

No, what mattered was that his home was on another continent. Not only could the war itself pull them apart, their different armies sending them to different parts of the country – different parts of the world even – but when this war was over, he would go back to Connecticut and she, well, she would stay in Aldhurst, sadder, sorrier, and lonelier.

Perhaps that was why he was so quick with his good-bye today, she thought. Maybe he was thinking the same thing, that this separation would be the first of many, each one taking them further apart, until that long final parting for ever.

Until recently, people hadn't dwelled a lot on the end of the war. It always seemed so distant in the future, if it ended in Britain's favour at all. But since the Americans had joined, things were looking up, and although it might take a few years, the Nazis were already showing signs of flagging. The Russians were causing dramatic losses on the Eastern Front, and weaknesses were beginning to show in the Nazi war machine.

Where before she barely thought about what would happen after the war was over, now it jabbed at her heart like the point of a knife.

Is he letting me down gently before we get in too deep?

Shaking the horrid thought from her mind, she got back to business, which in this case was a couple of errands in London before returning to Aldhurst. The first was to deliver a case of wedding dresses to the Women's Military Centre, where they had agreed to oversee the Wedding Dress Exchange for brides in the forces. It was against the rules to use military vehicles for civilian purposes, but the centre wasn't far from Westminster, and small errands that didn't get in the way of day-to-day business were overlooked. The alternative was using precious fuel for a separate delivery, after all.

After that, her orders were to collect a package from the notorious Rainbow Corner American Red Cross Centre near Piccadilly, and as she parked the car, she felt a shiver of excitement to see the place everyone talked about.

Even before she approached, she could hear the noise. The revelry was cacophonous, the jazz music just about audible behind the throng of chatter and cheers. People were coming from all directions, and she had to wait for a kind GI to let her in before she could get through the door.

The ground floor comprised a capacious dining hall; men and women in all kinds of uniforms – British, Dutch, French, but predominantly American – filled the chairs, the waiters and waitresses bustling between the tables. The sound of voices and laughter was immense, plates piled high with food, beer glasses spilling over. She'd heard about the basement too. 'Dunker's

Den' was a vast space for dancing and bands, infamous for wild parties.

'I've been told to collect a parcel from the officers' room,' she said to a waitress.

'It's on the second floor.' Her accent was American, and as she bustled away, Violet wondered how she felt to be over here, enduring the London bombs, putting her life on the line so many miles away from home.

The upper floors were teeming with activity. The building provided rooms for GIs on leave, a barber, a shop selling American cigarettes, nylon stockings, and sweets, and a collection point for packages from the United States, where a young woman handed over a cardboard package.

'It's for Lieutenant McCauley,' she said, eyeing Violet uncertainly. 'Make sure he gets it.'

'Of course he will,' she snapped. 'I know how to do my job.'

Someone had come up behind her, and as she turned, he said, 'It might be easier to just give it to me personally.'

'Landon!' She staggered back with surprise. 'I thought you were in a meeting.'

Carefully, he took the package from her and pulled her towards him. 'I wanted to surprise you.' He kissed her, then grabbed her hand. 'Come with me.'

She opened her mouth to speak, but he put a finger on her lips. 'Just come. You'll see.'

Down the corridor, double doors opened up into a large, elegant dining space. Officers and commanders were seated at tables along with women either in formal evening dress or uniforms of their own. In a corner, a pianist played Gershwin's *Rhapsody in Blue*, the lilting melodies reminiscent of Hollywood movies.

'The higher ranks eat here, if you would like to join me?' He put out an arm for her to take, and she couldn't help but smile as a waiter showed them to a table for two.

'But what about your meeting?'

'I only had to be there for the beginning. I figured that I could hotfoot it over here in the time it took you to make your delivery to the Women's Military Centre and back.' He grinned. 'Aren't you excited to see me, Fred?'

After a playful shove, she threw her arms around him. 'You mischievous rogue! You should have told me! I'm not even dressed for it.' She looked down at her uniform.

'You will always be the most beautiful woman in any room, Violet.' He reached his arm around her and pulled her in close.

The waiter's cough reminded them where they were, and they took their seats at a small table beside a window.

'What a wonderful place. I never knew it would be so elegant.'

'Just wait until you see the menu,' he said as the waiter handed one to her. 'They have real steak here.'

As she sat, the menu open in front of her, a sensation of happiness flooded through her. Just an hour ago, she was thrown into doubt as to his love for her, and here he was, grinning broadly from the opposite side of a lovely little table in a sumptuous, sophisticated restaurant.

'Thank you for bringing me here,' she said. 'I can't think of a better way to spend my last night before the assessment.'

He reached across the table to hold her hand. 'And I am so lucky to be here with you, not only because you are the most beautiful woman in the room, but also because you are my very best friend. You make me laugh, you make me feel great about being me, and you make me know for sure that we – me and you – need to be together.'

'That's precisely what I was thinking.' She grinned back. 'Well, not the part about you being the most beautiful woman in the room, Landon, obviously, especially with your broken nose, but . . .'

She slowed to a stop as she saw what he held in his hand.

Out of a small, black velvet pouch, a gleaming gold ring spilled into his palm. He picked it up, turning it to admire the glimmer of a large, pure white diamond. 'This is for you,' he said softly, and for once he wasn't smiling, nor was he laughing or joking. He was completely serious. 'Violet Westcott, Fred, will you marry me?'

Everything inside her seemed to come together, gathering inside her heart, which seemed to burst brimful with joy and the raw energy of being alive. Speechless, she slowly found herself nodding, and then in a voice broken by tears, she said, 'Yes, Landon McCauley. Yes!'

And as he slid the ring onto her finger, the room seemed to hush, and then, as the fellow company realized what was happening, a round of applause went up, some cheers and even a whistle as Landon blushed, shuffling his chair closer to hers.

'But, what about all of your girls back home?' she asked.

'There were a few girls I had been keen on.' He grinned. 'But then I realized that the only reason I liked them was because they were the kind of girl I *should* be marrying, not because I genuinely liked who they were. It all became apparent when I found that I was in love with a completely different woman, one who had become my best friend.' He picked up her hand and kissed her palm. 'I don't think I could ever feel this way about anyone else, Violet. You and I, we fit together so perfectly. Some old, eternal part of us both recognized something in the other, don't you think?'

She nuzzled into his neck, which was warm and soft. 'I don't remember when I first knew we were meant for each other.' She let out a small laugh. 'Maybe it was from the first time you called me Fred. I can't believe something so perfect could ever happen to me, that I could be married to a man who I love, and who loves me.'

'You don't mind that I'm not a duke?'

'I don't care if you're a tinker, a tailor, a soldier – well, all that matters is that you are you, perfect for the person who is me.'

Violet leaned her head against his shoulder, and he pulled her in tight. Had she followed her father's wishes, she would have missed all of this – missed the most important, most fulfilling thing in the world.

'But where will we live, here or Connecticut?' she asked gingerly. 'I'm all in favour of adventures, but I've never been to America.'

He kissed her cheek. 'You'll love it there, but I only want to be where you are, so take your time and think about what you want. We have the rest of the war to decide.'

'Wherever we are, the only thing that matters is that we're together.'

The dinner was spent gazing into each other's eyes and making plans for the wedding, which they decided should be soon in case one of them was posted abroad. Only at the end of the meal did he remember the package.

'Oh, yes.' He bent over to untie it, tugging back the brown paper to reveal a flash of white tissue paper. Then, in a single, long sweep, he pulled the contents out, holding it up in the air for her to see.

'A wedding veil,' Violet gasped. She reached out to the gleaming fabric, intricate lace covering the sides and train. 'It's beautiful! Is it' – she hesitated – 'is it for me?'

He grinned. 'I told my parents that I was going to propose to you, and my mother insisted on sending you her own veil, since she won't be able to come to the wedding herself.'

'How thoughtful of her – and generous too.' She gave him a sideways look. 'You must have been quite certain that I was going to say yes for her to go to all this trouble.'

'Was I wrong to take the chance? To hope?'

'Not at all.' She laughed. 'Especially now that I've got a lovely veil out of it.' But her eyes filled with tears as she looked over the finely crafted lace. 'And I have my mother's dress too.' She pulled out a handkerchief. 'It'll be a lovely way to have them both present in some way. I don't think my mother's was a happy marriage.' She put out her hand to Landon's. 'But I think she'd be very pleased that mine will be rooted in love instead of duty.'

'Our only duty now is to each other, Fred.'

A smile came over her face, and she felt a warmth spreading through her that she knew would carry on for the rest of her life.

As he carefully folded the veil back into its packaging, he found a folded letter and handed it to her. 'This is for you.'

It was from Landon's mother.

My dear Violet,

How I wish I were there in person to give you a proper McCauley congratulations, not to mention meet you! In the meantime, a letter with a package will have to send greetings and love in my place.

I can't wait to meet you in person and get to know you better. Landon tells me that both of your parents are no longer with us, and I want you to know that you need never feel alone now that you are part of the McCauleys. We are a big family, and you may not think that we are as proper as your upright British ways, but rest assured, we have generous hearts, so please do not stand on ceremony with us. At home, we are always first a family, and you are now very much part of that.

With this letter comes my own wedding veil. I expect it might be a little out of date now, and it might not fit your outfit properly either, so please feel free to change it as you like. It is my gift to you. I only hope that you think of me over here as you put it on, wishing you luck, love, and happiness. *The veil will be my envoy, there in the place of me to make sure everything is as it should be, and that the bride looks as perfect, as magical, as ever.*

With all my love,
Genevieve McCauley

GRACE

Beneath the sparkling chandeliers in the grand London hotel, the reception at the IncSoc Utility Fashion Show was abuzz with all the glamour and drama of the fashion world. The IncSoc couturiers were hosting the extravaganza to showcase their Utility designs to the Board of Trade, and everyone knew that this was set to change the way people dressed for the rest of the war, if not the decade.

Immaculate men in impeccable lounge suits ordered their assistants and minions around. Elegant women greeted each other with elaborate cheek kisses, shrieking to be heard above the cacophony of voices. Some wore the expensive haute couture of ladies, while others displayed the avant-garde creations of the more innovative fashion houses.

Shoulders back and hair pristinely curled, Grace stood beside Violet, trying her utmost to stay calm. Her work with Cressida had given her a new assurance, and if she reminded herself enough, perhaps she would start to relax.

The few women in uniform were mostly upper-class girls from the Royal Navy, and some of them trotted over to greet Violet, who was prim in her ATS khaki. 'Darling! We're modelling too! Isn't it fabulous that they're including military girls in the parade? But tell me, what happened to your hair? I can't decide whether it's an aberration or devilishly daring.'

'Devilishly daring, of course.' Violet had been in great spirits since her engagement, and when the officer appraisal had concluded that she was 'precisely what we're looking for in our candidates', she had been on cloud nine. She was living a life so completely different from the one she'd imagined for herself, but she couldn't be happier.

Reading a list of attendees, Cressida told Grace, 'All the top journalists from the women's magazines are here, as well as a lot of the newspapers. I must say, it's caused an incredible stir. Some designers have hired professional models, but it's nice to see military girls and war workers modelling some of the clothes. It gives the event a flavour of the utility "Clothes for All" identity.' She gave Grace a smile. 'And you and Violet get to show off your marvellous skills.'

Grace tried to master her nerves. Ever since she'd broken things off with Lawrence, she'd felt a need to tear off the shy, modest mantle of the old Grace and take on the world, find the brave, independent spirit she'd had as a girl. But as she stood in the sophisticated crowd, Cressida greeting the famous couturiers whose names she recognized from magazines and newspapers, she felt increasingly out of her depth.

I'm completely fine, she told herself. *I'm not just a meek parish wife for Lawrence, and I'm not a lower-class girl beneath Hugh's notice. I'm a model and a designer, and my future will be what I make of it.*

'Cressida!' A voice beside them made her turn to see a very glamorous middle-aged woman wearing a dramatic amber and black diagonally striped dress. She pranced over, kissing Cressida's cheeks in the Parisian style. 'I knew you'd make it!'

Cressida beamed back, introducing her to Grace. 'This is

Muriel Holden-Smythe; she's the journalist at *Vogue* who's to interview us.'

'How lovely to meet you,' Grace said, trying to overcome her shyness. 'Your dress, well, it's fabulous.'

'Thank you – and you must call me Muriel. The dress is rather clever, isn't it? It's one by Elspeth Champcommunal – she's the director at Worth.' She glanced around, looking for someone, and then surprised Grace by saying, 'Ah, that's Elspeth over there. Come on, I'll introduce you. She'll be fascinated to meet Cressida's new protégée!'

Wearing a decadent black beret on one side of her head, the illustrious head of the House of Worth was a slim, middle-class woman. Inside her long face was a pair of shrewd, unamused eyes, flickering this way and that as various men and women clamoured around her.

As Muriel and Grace wove through the crowd towards her, Elspeth's eyes brightened. 'Muriel! Come to see the spectacle, have you? Top design brought to the high street shops of every city and town.' She grinned wickedly, pleased with herself. Everyone knew that she was one of the biggest names behind the IncSoc Utility Clothes line.

'I can't wait to see what comes down that runway! Elspeth, this is Grace. She's Cressida Westcott's new assistant. Grace designed one of the gowns in the show today.'

Elspeth looked her up and down, appraising her without embarrassment or restraint. 'I hope you plan to model it yourself,' she said. 'I imagine you're very useful to Cressida.' She glanced around for Cressida impatiently. 'Where is she?'

But her search was cut short by the approach of a man who looked awfully familiar, though Grace couldn't quite place him.

'Cecil!' Elspeth cried. 'I hoped you'd be here.'

It was Cecil Beaton, of course. And who better to capture this moment on camera? The Ministry of Information had employed the famous photographer to depict the war experience, and his pictures had become iconic.

Seeing the intimidation on Grace's face, Muriel patted her arm. 'Don't worry, no one bites. Just keep your head up, and you'll be perfect.'

'I'll try.' Grace smiled weakly, trying to feel buoyed by Muriel's assurances.

That is, until she found herself in a packed dressing room with only twenty minutes before the start of the show.

To say that the long, narrow room was complete chaos would be an understatement. Dozens of women in varying states of undress were vying for a few mirrors, scrambling to put on makeup, borrow stockings, and do each other's hair.

Wedged between an upper-class Royal Navy girl and a seasoned model, Grace had been nudged by enough elbows to make her shrink back against the wall.

'At least it's easy to roll on your stockings when you're being propped up by a squash of bodies,' the navy girl said, making light of it.

'Yes,' Grace replied nervously. Everyone else appeared to know what they were doing – some of them seemed happy to be there, delighted even.

A bossy woman with a clipboard came in and clapped her hands. 'You should all know your order by now. If not, the list is at the side of the stage. Those ready, please make your way into the corridor, and no talking once you're there, please. You'll be heard from the auditorium.'

A trail of models, all looking immaculate, traipsed out of the room, including Violet, who looked stunning in the navy-blue skirt suit, a bright cerise topcoat over her shoulders, ready to be swept off at the end of the runway. As she passed, their eyes met. 'Good luck,' Violet mouthed with an excited little smile.

'You too.' Grace tried to smile back, but it seemed to waver, so she quickly took out her compact to dab the gathering perspiration from her forehead.

At least she knew she was dressed beautifully, wearing the evening gown she had designed, the sheath-like dress that draped elegantly over her frame. 'The dress is perfect for you,' Cressida had said. 'You look like a wilderness spirit in those green shades.'

For a fraction of a moment, Grace had seen the young girl she had been in her mind's eye, adventurous and brave, running through the forest as if the world belonged to her. If only she could grasp that spirit again.

In the corridor, the women had to find their places in the long queue, and Grace quickly slid in front of a tall, blonde professional model wearing a full royal-blue ballgown. There was a perfection to her coiffured hair and makeup, a precision that made her seem almost unhuman.

She gave Grace an unwelcoming sneer, obviously less than pleased to share the stage with amateurs. 'In which corner of the countryside did they find you?'

'Not far away, in Kent, actually.' Grace tried to keep her voice steady, but the woman's dismissive smirk was getting the better of her. 'I'm Cressida Westcott's assistant.'

The model made a derisive laugh. 'Oh, are they getting assistants to model now? How plucky of you!' The word 'plucky' was delivered with a punchy irony.

Suddenly riled, Grace retorted, 'Perhaps more plucky than you think!' But it came out artless and childish.

Before the blonde model could muster a waspish reply, the bossy woman with the clipboard was back, telling them all to shush. 'We're about to begin.'

At once, the line of young women fell silent, their fidgeting stopped, and they leaned forward to hear as the man on the stage made a short speech about Utility Clothes and introduced the IncSoc designers.

'This afternoon, we will see thirty-two different outfits, each of which uses minimal amounts of quality utility fabric while providing well-designed, good-quality clothes at affordable prices.'

The crowd applauded, sitting forward in expectation.

'And now, let's see the clothes that will help Britain win the war.'

The queue of models seemed to stand perfectly still as the first in line, a delicate brunette in a turquoise-blue day dress, donned a refined smile and set off for the stage.

A ripple of applause came from the audience, along with the muffle of chatter. Cressida had told Grace that the Board of Trade ministers in the audience were the ones to impress. It was up to them to decide whether to manufacture each garment in bulk for the public.

Alongside them were the mainstream clothes manufacturers, annoyed that they were being sidelined by the lofty couturiers in what they felt was their area of expertise. 'Mayfair Utility', they called it huffily.

Then there was the jostle of journalists. From beside the stage, Grace could see the flashes of cameras, and couldn't help but think about how those photographs – perhaps even one of herself – would appear in magazines and newspapers across the country in the morning.

The fashion designers themselves sat together, watching eagerly, debating how to configure their next offerings.

Everyone had something at stake.

And as for Grace, she felt she had *everything* at stake. Not only was Cressida's reputation resting on her shoulders, but she was here in her own design too – this moment could determine whether she had a career in fashion or if it had all been a dream, and she'd go back to her little village, nothing to show for her bravery.

Another ripple of applause sounded as the first woman returned, giving the next in line a relieved smile as they passed each other – one off, the next one on.

Violet was fifth in line, and Grace held her breath as she watched her walk evenly and majestically out towards the stage. She wondered what it would feel like, being out there. Would she be able to see Cressida in the crowd? Was Violet, like her, petrified of falling?

Amid more clapping, Violet reappeared backstage. She had taken off the cerise topcoat, revealing the beautiful lines of the jacket, her fingers tucked into the small pocket slotted into the seam. A beaming smile on her face expressed a jubilation at being part of it, at her old world and her new world coming together in such a glamorous spectacle.

As she passed Grace, she put her hand up and crossed her fingers. 'You'll be the belle of the ball,' she whispered.

The queue continued to dwindle, and the closer Grace got to the front, the more the panic rattled her insides.

When the Royal Navy girl in front of her strode through the wings and onto the catwalk, she began praying under her breath.

'I only hope you don't fall over,' the blonde model joked from behind her. 'It's the true mark of an amateur, so humiliating.'

But before Grace had the chance to reply, the bossy woman gave Grace's shoulder a little shove. 'Off you go.'

And with that, Grace walked out onto the stage.

'Grace is wearing a pale sage-green evening gown in a silk-imitation rayon. Sleeveless and with a deep V-shaped back, its sheer fabric allows it to sweep gracefully over her hips, giving her a lovely sleek silhouette.'

She stopped at the base of the runway, as she'd been told to do, holding a pose, her shoulders upright. Then slowly, she began to walk down the catwalk.

And as she went, the sensation of having all attention on her was almost overwhelming. All she could do was focus on walking to the end, where she stopped, as instructed.

A curl of her hair had come loose and was brushing her shoulder, and slowly, she lifted a trembling hand and felt it between her fingers.

And that's when she saw him. At the back, beside a group of men in suits, was Hugh.

He looked straight at her, and as their eyes met, her concentration wavered.

What was she doing? She had to stay focused. Yet she couldn't tear her eyes away from him.

He had gone quite pale as he watched, and she saw him swallow hard.

And as her eyes met his, she knew only one thing: that she would never get over this man.

Suddenly, a blinding flash of light glared into her eyes.

Startled, she took a hasty step back, and there in front of her was Cecil Beaton, the great photographer, his boxlike camera in his hands, his eyes on her.

She struggled to remember what to do, even though she knew it was simple.

Move, turn, walk.

Hesitantly, she turned her head, then her body, and walked back to the door without so much as glancing at the audience again.

In a daze, Grace retreated to the dressing room, where she found a seat and sank down onto it.

Within minutes, Violet was beside her. 'You were simply wonderful!' After taking in her friend's appearance, she added, 'I say, are you all right, Grace?'

'I'm fine, but with all those faces watching me, I must have looked terrified.' Then she added more softly, 'And Hugh was there to see it too.'

'You didn't look scared at all! You looked utterly breathtaking.' Violet beamed. 'I'm sure they all thought you were astounding.'

Cressida bustled in excitedly. 'You're the talk of the show, Grace. It's bound to be one of the best of Beaton's photographs. I bet it'll be the one that'll appear in all the newspapers in the morning. Can you believe it?'

'But when he took that shot, I wasn't even concentrating. How could it have possibly turned out well?' She laughed in spite of herself.

'But that was the beauty of it. You looked like a normal, everyday young woman – albeit an incredibly beautiful one – enthralled by wearing such a glamorous dress, which she can now afford to do because of the utility range. Can't you see, Grace? It's the precise image they've been looking for, and you're one of the designers too. It couldn't be more perfect! Muriel and the other journalists are going to have a field day with it.'

As the show finished and the crowd poured back into the reception area, the volume of chatter louder than before, Cressida, Violet, and Grace made their entrance. Instantly, a clamour of journalists surrounded Grace, begging for her story, vying for details about the dress, how a country vicar's daughter had become the talk of the IncSoc Utility Fashion Show.

And while she tried to answer their questions, part of her began to relax. Maybe this *was* the world in which she belonged.

'We need a few details about who you are.' One of them asked, 'What's your name? How did you become involved?'

'I'm Grace Carlisle, and I became part of the fashion world when' – her eyes danced over to Cressida, urging her on from the side – 'when Cressida Westcott helped me with my wedding dress.' And silently through the jostle and bustle, she whispered to her across the crowd, 'Thank you.'

VIOLET

The morning after the IncSoc Fashion Show, the manor was all abustle. Cressida had been up early, as had Violet, and they were seated at the table on the terrace by the time Grace arrived, the morning's newspapers scattered over the table. The sunshine glimmered over them, the scent of honeysuckle drifting in and out with the soft summer breeze.

'I knew it would be a success.' Cressida was sipping coffee as she perused one of the broadsheets. 'That's why I had the papers delivered specially from London today.'

Violet was busy reading, proud of herself; not only had she modelled impeccably, but she also didn't mind that Grace was the indisputable star of the show. She was even happy for her friend, especially after the debacle with Hugh. 'Come and look, Grace,' she called over as the slim young woman stood at the door. 'You're on the front page.'

Grace gazed down, biting her lip in confusion. There, on the cover of almost every newspaper, was Cecil Beaton's photograph of her.

'It must be disconcerting to see your image in the dailies,' Cressida said, watching Grace's hand trail up to her neck, absent-mindedly imitating her picture. 'Such a beautiful pose.

You look like you've seen a ghost, but in the most glamorous way possible.'

'I agree,' Violet said. 'But what are you gazing at so intently in the audience?' She gave Cressida a flicker of a wink as Grace blushed. They both knew it was Hugh. Violet had seen him at the back too. There could be only one reason for him deciding to attend, and that was to see Grace.

'Oh, look at this!' Cressida exclaimed before Grace could reply. 'There's a mention of the Wedding Dress Exchange and the forthcoming interview with *Vogue* next week. They say that we have twenty-one dresses now, which is already wrong. We drummed up another four at the fashion show yesterday, and several other people promised to send them on. And can you imagine, one of the designers even donated her own dress. Isn't it marvellous how generous people can be! This extra publicity is ideal for getting the word out. We're bound to have more contributions after everyone reads about it in the papers.'

'It's a good thing too, as we're getting more requests,' Violet said. 'Half of the ATS seems to be getting married this summer, and they're all requesting a wedding dress from us.'

'Make sure you keep Grace's wedding dress for yourself, Violet, now we know that it was your dear mother's wedding dress too,' Cressida said, adding to Grace, 'I'm sure you'll find the right man soon, especially now that you have your photograph on all the front pages. I bet there isn't a man in Britain who wouldn't fall at your feet.'

The conversation turned to the future: Violet's training and promotion, and after the war, her planned move to Connecticut.

'It's terribly picturesque over there, apparently. We'll buy a house with some land so that we can get some horses. I told him that I want to carry on with my photography – I haven't had as much time since I joined the ATS – and we won't be far from New York, so perhaps I'll be the next Cecil Beaton only the other way around, capturing America for the British magazines. Part of me is heartbroken to be leaving, of course, but the other half of me can't wait. It's simply too exciting to be starting afresh in a mesmerizing new place.'

They were interrupted by the butler, who came to remind Violet and Cressida about the formal luncheon that day. 'Mr Westcott is bringing Miss Astrid down from London. He is to give her a tour of the manor so that she can begin her redecorating plans.' There was a waver of trepidation in his voice, even the butler not savouring the prospect.

As he retreated back into the house, the three women looked at each other. Astrid would turn the place upside down, as well as the people inside it.

'Why does he have to marry her?' Violet said with a huff. 'I know that they've been promised to each other since they were children, but honestly, I wish Hugh would give up his archaic notions. Look how amazing life can be when you don't have to marry a lord or duke or a Fortescue!'

Cressida sighed. 'He'll figure out how to get out from under his father's shadow eventually, dear, but I won't be at Aldhurst when he does. My estate agent found a place for me to rent in Notting Hill. It doesn't sound perfect, but I'm sure it will do for now. My new London design house will be bigger and better, though. It's in the heart of the fashion world in Bond Street.' She looked at Grace. 'When you come for training, my dear, you must come and stay, bring me a little Aldhurst cheer.'

'Thank you,' Grace replied politely, but the girl had gone as white as a sheet, her eyes flickering over to the door, anxious that Hugh would walk through it at any moment, Astrid on his arm.

He'd mostly been staying in London since the Canterbury bombing, explaining to Violet and Cressida that it was useful to be close to Astrid as their wedding drew near. The event was to be held north of the city, close to her family home in Hampstead.

For the sake of the war, they were limiting invitations, but the Fortescues were sending their daughter off in great style for the times, with a small fortune spent on a great banquet in one of the most exclusive hotels in London. While it was the kind of wedding Violet might have dreamed about before she joined the ATS, she now felt the ostentatiousness was in rather poor taste. Frugal was the fashion these days.

Yet for all his excuses, Violet couldn't help wondering if Hugh was actually staying away from Aldhurst because of Grace. She hadn't mentioned it, but she'd been watching him while Grace was on the runway, and as she stood nervously at the end, as beautiful as the wild deer Violet had once photographed on the far side of the lake, the look on her brother's face reminded Violet of how Landon looked at her sometimes, his eyes lost with emotion. His gaze of love had been mirrored in Grace's eyes too, and now the image was captured for the world to see on the front cover of every newspaper in the country. Violet knew what it was to be in love, and she couldn't help wondering how he felt every time he passed a newsstand, seeing Grace, knowing that the look in her eyes was meant for him – knowing that he would never be able to have her.

But Violet knew better than to mention that. Instead she remarked, 'Frankly, I can't believe Hugh allowed Astrid to toss you out, Cressida. It feels like he's disappearing behind her, following her rules and doing everything she asks. I can't imagine that it's going to lead to a happy marriage.'

'She's an upper-class, educated, wealthy woman, and you understand how much that means to Hugh – how much it meant to your father.' Cressida sighed. 'He's trying to do the respectable thing. I can't tell you the number of times your father lectured me about "my duty to the Westcott name". You and Hugh had many more years of hearing that than I did, and as the heir, Hugh would have had it far worse. Breaking that code of conduct would feel like a betrayal of your ancestors, not to mention a very public scandal now that they're officially engaged.'

'But hasn't the war put paid to all that nonsense?' Violet tidied the pile of folded newspapers on the table. 'Who cares about tradition when you're stuck in a bomb shelter with four hundred pounds of cordite coming down around you?'

Suddenly, Grace stood up, her hands busy re-pinning her hair. 'I'm going to do something,' she announced. 'I'm going to follow my heart, just like you, Violet. Can I borrow some makeup?'

'Of course,' Violet said. 'You can use my bedroom. But what are you thinking?'

'I'm going to talk to Hugh. I'm going to have a proper conversation with him. It might not be what I want to hear, but at least I'll be able to say I tried. Cressida told me to go after what I want, and I know exactly what that is. I'm not going to simply stand back and watch this small sliver of a chance slip away from me.'

'That's the spirit, Grace,' Violet said. 'Why don't I offer Astrid a nice long tour of the manor, leaving Hugh free for you?'

'Oh, that's a good idea, Violet, if you can?' Grace gave a weary smile before whisking herself away to get ready.

It wasn't long before Hugh and Astrid arrived amidst much fanfare. The butler was in full stateliness with the maids ready behind him to take coats and so forth. Astrid looked every ounce the society lady she was, wearing a blue silk tea dress, despite how difficult silk was to come by these days. There was a presence about her, a radiance and perfection, her hair coiled up beneath her blue pillbox hat with utter precision. Violet might have looked up to her when she was younger, but now, with Astrid's lack of warmth and her disdain for anyone less fortunate than herself, Violet could hardly bear to make conversation with the woman.

The staff lined up to meet the future lady of the manor, and Astrid smiled benevolently as they curtsied before her in an old-fashioned show of respect. Moving on, she gave the same condescending smile to Cressida and Violet, as if they too were members of the household.

Solemnly, the butler led the way into the dining room, and they all took their seats.

Once settled, it was Astrid who began the conversation by asking Cressida, 'I gather the IncSoc Utility Show went well?'

Grateful for an easy conversation topic to smooth over the awkwardness around the table, Cressida expounded on the show and how the designs were destined to make a big impact on the war and on people's lives all over the country. Both the navy-blue suit and Grace's sage-green dress had been chosen for mass production.

'Indeed,' Astrid said. 'But it's a shame that those who usually patronize the top couturiers have to share their exclusive designs with the hoi polloi. It takes a lot of the enjoyment out of fashion for me, I must say.'

'We think it's a wonderful way to do our bit for the war. Since I've been back in Aldhurst, I've come to realize that we all have a responsibility to help. I think London high society has a tendency to insulate itself from the war, taking suites in the good hotels, dining out to avoid the food rations, and assuming others will pick up the war work. Sharing good clothes designs is an easy way to show a willingness to help.'

But Astrid merely shrugged. 'Honestly, there wouldn't be such a fuss if everyone had simply been better prepared. People talk about how hard it is with clothes rationing, but they really should have stocked up before the war, like we did. I suppose a lot of people didn't have the forethought, but that feels rather like it's their own fault.'

'Sadly, a lot of people didn't have enough money to buy extra clothes,' Cressida said, incredulous at this woman's obliviousness. 'Not to mention the fact that the surge in demand caused by people stocking up led to a doubling of prices. It was far outside the range of most people's budgets.'

But the starter was being brought in, and Astrid wasn't listening as she inspected a hard-looking leek and potato tartlet. 'I'll have to meet with the cook later too, darling. This looks inedible.'

Hugh's face remained inscrutable, as it had throughout the conversation.

All was silent except for the unavoidable scraping of knives on the crockery as everyone tried to cut through the rubbery tarts.

'I've been thinking, Hugh,' Violet began, 'that I could give Astrid a tour of the house after lunch. It would give us a chance to get to know each other, and I know far more about the place than you do.'

Astrid smiled benevolently. 'What a lovely idea! From what I've seen, the manor needs a lot of work. Hugh tells me your father didn't care for redecorating.'

'He liked the place to remain as it was,' Violet said. 'The décor was part of the heritage, he believed, and it was our duty to preserve history. Isn't that right, Hugh?' Her eyes didn't need to meet Hugh's for her point to be made. 'Tradition and duty come first.'

'And so they should,' Astrid said. 'Duty is the backbone of civilized life.'

'It depends on how much that duty restricts you from living life to the full,' Violet said pointedly. 'Finding happiness and love.'

'But where there is duty, a good life will surely follow.' Astrid gave Violet a conclusive smile and reapplied herself to the tartlet.

Everyone glanced at each other uneasily, except for Astrid, who having politely given up on the starter, was looking at the dining room décor with disparagement. 'I believe this place has never been so much in need of a new mistress.' She turned to the others. 'It looks as if I came in the nick of time.'

GRACE

From the window of Violet's bedroom, Grace watched as Hugh walked down the path into the wood, heading for the far side of the lake. The lunch must be over, and Violet would have begun her tour with Astrid.

Now was Grace's only chance.

With a deep breath, and not entirely sure what she intended to say, she dashed down the stairs and out onto the terrace, hurrying down to the path and weaving through the wood that surrounded the lake. She had an idea of where he might be heading – the old, rundown boathouse – but she didn't know why. Perhaps he was worried that Astrid would tear it down along with the rest of the past, or maybe he wanted her to do so, destroy every particle that could link him to Grace.

Suddenly, the trees opened up and there it was. A heady jolt went through her, a series of memories of her and Hugh playing, talking, lying side by side on the broken-down jetty watching the stars. She hadn't seen the boathouse for years, but it looked exactly the same. Large enough for the long rowing boats from the last century, it now stood old and empty, a yawning wooden shack opening out onto the lake, the jetty protruding over the still water.

Hugh was standing at the very end, looking over the lake, his form so still, it was as if he were part of the scenery himself.

Either he heard the rustle of her coming or sensed that she was there, because he turned to see her, the look on his face impenetrable. She could feel her heart racing, aware of everything around her.

Without a word, she came up beside him, and together they looked over the lake. The breeze from earlier had dropped, and the water was so still you could see the clouds reflected in its surface. Farther away beside the island, a heron took off from the shallows, its wingtips breaking the surface with every downward beat, leaving a trail in the water that slowly dissipated.

'It's beautiful here,' he murmured.

'Magical,' she whispered back. 'Sometimes it's hard to believe we used to dive off the jetty here and swim to the island. It all seems so long ago now.'

There was silence for a moment, and then he said, 'It *was* magical, wasn't it?' He turned, and then suddenly his face broke into a sad smile. 'Those are some of my fondest memories.' He had a stone in his hand, and he skimmed it across the water, making five skips before it sank. 'All those swimming races – I let you win, by the way!' he joked warmly.

'You're only saying that!' she replied. 'But those were the days, weren't they? It's a shame they came to an end.'

'You know, I was devastated when my father sent me away to school. I missed all of this – I missed you.' He took a deep breath, digging his hands into his pockets. 'But life isn't meant to be all fun and games.'

She swallowed, a wave of sadness and nostalgia flooding through her.

'Do you remember when we built a boat from that old water

tank?' he said. 'I wonder if it's still there, at the bottom of the lake?'

A laugh caught in her throat. 'Even now I can remember exactly where you went down, right over there.' She pointed to a place halfway to the island, about forty yards from them.

'You'll have to show me where it was sometime.' He laughed gently. 'I sometimes swim out here. Perhaps I can find it.'

She shook her head, laughing openly like she would have as a girl, and suddenly a new energy seemed to course through her, and without a moment's thought, she turned to him. 'Why don't we see if we can find it now?'

'Well, I'm not sure it's even still down there,' he said, unsure. 'Besides, I'm in a suit.'

But she was already slipping off her shoes.

'Come on, let's go and see, shall we?'

And he watched in amazement as Grace began hastily unbuttoning her blouse, revealing a white slip and camisole beneath. 'Let's pretend we didn't grow up, just this one last time. Let's pretend we're still fifteen, with our whole lives ahead of us. Let's find that sunken boat.'

'But, well, it's not terribly proper, is it?' He began to laugh, his head shaking as he slowly began to unbutton his own shirt, unsure what to do. Nervously, he glanced back towards the manor, which was hidden by the woodland surrounding this end of the lake.

'Let's do something for ourselves, just as we used to, forget about the others for a few moments. Where's your spirit, Hugh?' She knew she was risking everything, that she could be humiliated beyond belief if he didn't join her, but she couldn't stop. 'All I want is one final jaunt into the past before I face a very adult future. You have to come with me, Hugh. Won't you?' She looked up at him beseechingly.

'All right,' he said uncertainly, taking off his shirt, his chest beneath firmer, broader than it had been when she'd last seen it.

Without waiting for him, she slid off her skirt, grateful for the camiknickers Lottie had given her, and dived in.

The sharp cold of the water sent a shock through her body. But then, as her arms and legs stretched out as she began to swim underwater, she felt alive and free – she'd finally found that wild exhilaration she'd been chasing since the end of her engagement.

When she came up for air, he was still on the jetty. He'd taken off his trousers, beneath which were a pair of men's undershorts, and taking in his muscular thighs, she quickly averted her gaze, ducking to find the lost vessel.

Under the water, she opened her eyes, peering into the strangely familiar opaque water around her. How much time they had spent diving in the lake! She felt as if she still knew every cranny and curve beneath its surface.

Through the haze of the water, she saw the figure of Hugh diving in after her, coming towards her. As he reached her, they both came back up for air, treading water. There was a smile on his face, an open, unaffected smile that made her smile back, as if all that existed was them, in the lake, the sun in the sky beaming down on them as it had so many years ago.

'Did you find it?' His dark hair was wet, and he pushed it back.

'It's somewhere close to here.'

Down again she went, taking off through the water, spotting the tank ten yards away. Without turning, she knew that Hugh was following her, having seen it too. And she wondered if he was looking at her in the same way that she did him, her body flexing and moving through the water, her white silk slip and camiknickers swirling around her body. She could hardly believe she'd been so daring as to strip down in front of him, and yet it felt so natural, so right. She wanted to live life without holding back, without any regrets, and she was starting that today.

The tank was smaller than she remembered and coated with a thick layer of green. Weeds grew from its interior without restraint. Hugh swam around to the other side of it, and together they looked around it, finding a hole that she remembered on the side.

They came up for air, laughing and smiling like children. 'Shall we bring it up?' he said.

'No, let's leave it there,' she laughed. 'Some mistakes need to stay in the past.' But she regretted her words as soon as she'd said them. She wanted to hold on to what they had so desperately, but it felt so temporary, so makeshift, like the tank itself, destined to drown.

His mind was evidently on the same thing. 'Since we're here, we may as well get into the spirit of it and race to the island.' His eyes gleamed, heady and reckless. 'First one wins.'

Off they went. Grace threaded her arms through the water with a rhythm and speed she'd forgotten she had.

But she couldn't keep up with Hugh, who was already standing waist-high in the shallows grinning as she waded to reach him. As she came close, he took her hand and pulled her towards him, as if to help her out of the water, but then he stopped, his laughter dropping as his eyes went from her eyes to her mouth, to her underwear, now clinging to her body.

He's going to kiss me, she thought, suddenly desperate for him to do so.

But then he stopped.

'I've never forgotten that kiss, Grace,' he said.

She was standing right in front of him, his lips inches from hers.

'If I start kissing you now, I'm scared that I'll never stop,' she said.

He swallowed. 'I don't know how I'm ever going to get over you, Grace.'

And without thinking, she reached her hand up behind his neck and pulled his mouth towards hers. The wet softness of him, the taste so familiar, so heavenly and brutal at the same time. She felt his hands, warm and tender, on her back, which arched towards him, the sensation of his body against her own overwhelming.

Together they stood in the shallows entwined; she neither knew for how long, nor did she care. It was as it always should have been. Him and her, in their own place, together. It was where they belonged, like two parts converging to make a whole, two lost and wild spirits meeting at last.

Then suddenly, reality came crashing back.

A scream from the lakeside made them pull apart rapidly.

There, on the jetty beside their discarded clothes, was Astrid, raging with fury. 'Hugh!'

Next to her was Violet, her eyes wide in shocked delight, particularly in the face of Astrid's fury.

Grace, mortified to be caught out not only with Hugh but also in her underclothes, slid down under the water while Hugh swam back across the lake. By the time Grace resurfaced, he'd reached the jetty, and she watched him hastily pull on his trousers and then his shirt.

'What's going on?' Astrid was demanding.

'It's nothing, Astrid.' Hugh was striding up to her. 'We would always swim in the lake as children, so we thought we'd swim together one last time.'

'And the kiss? Did you do that as children too?'

'Well yes, actually, but we were just caught up in the nostalgia of the moment, darling. There was nothing else to it.'

How could he say it was nothing?

Something inside Grace broke. He had returned to the formal, stiff Hugh, telling Astrid that what to Grace had been a monumental reawakening had meant absolutely nothing to him.

Astrid's stance softened ever so slightly, her arms unfolding. 'Well, I'm not at all sure about this,' she blustered, looking around to give Grace a venomous stare. 'I think we should leave now, Hugh. We can discuss this on the way back to London.'

With that, she strode briskly back towards the house, followed by Hugh, still trying to appeal to her. A few paces behind them trailed Violet, glancing anxiously back to Grace as she swam slowly to the jetty.

By the time Grace had reached the shore, they were out of sight. Dripping, she pulled herself out of the water and slowly began to dress, glad of the privacy to pull herself back together. She had never felt so hurt. Hugh had told Astrid he'd just been caught up in the moment, as if it had been nothing more at all. Grace had put herself on the line so wholly and utterly, only for him to drop her as soon as his promised bride entered the picture.

How much more clear could it be?

And as she began to walk slowly back to land, the heron soared back across the water, its wings as wide as a kite's, retaking its place in the mirrorlike shallows, as it watched, always watched.

CRESSIDA

The photographer arranged the Sewing Circle ladies in two rows. Sitting at the front were Martha, Mrs Todd, Cressida, and Mrs Bisgood, with Grace, Violet, and Mrs Kettlewell standing behind them. Lottie went on the end beside her mother, wearing the brightest cherry-red lipstick that Cressida had ever seen.

The journalist from *Vogue* magazine, Muriel Holden-Smythe, arranged the original wedding dress across their laps at the front, grinning at Cressida. 'I hope you're ready for the deluge of interest you'll get once this article comes out.'

'Let's hope we will! But are you sure I should be in the middle?' she asked Muriel. 'This isn't about big names. It's about everyone getting involved and our little Sewing Circle, how together we can make a difference in this war.'

'I like that idea,' Muriel said, taking note. 'But I do think that having a famous face will attract the attention of our readers, shining an even brighter light on all of you. And if I can also get it to attract the attention of my editor, we might even get a mention on the cover. Ever since Audrey Withers became editor, we're doing more articles about the war, what it means to women in the services, in the underground shelters, in everyday life, like the Wedding Dress Sewing Circle. In this day and age, women want opinions too, and where better to get them than a forward-thinking fashion magazine. After all, doesn't fashion reflect the era?'

With spirit, Martha said, 'Absolutely! It's about time women's magazines gave women more oomph!'

And Mrs Todd added, 'I think we always had opinions, we just had to keep them to ourselves – well, sometimes we did.'

Martha and Lottie made a small cheer, and Mrs Todd re-affixed her hat in case she wasn't looking her very best.

Cressida smiled at the little group, surprised by how much she was going to miss them when she left for London. If she were honest, all she felt was an inkling of exhaustion at the thought of living in a silent flat by herself, of having to oversee staff. And then there was the pain she felt at having to leave Ben too. She pushed the thought away, unsure what to do with it.

The photographer whisked around checking the light and angle. She was a modish woman in her late thirties with a boyish haircut. Before the shoot, Violet had cornered her to discuss her photography. She was determined to make a go of creating and selling her own photographs, and Cressida remembered picking up Violet's box Brownie when she'd first arrived in Aldhurst, how much the army had changed her.

Once the pictures were over, Muriel beckoned them to a table. 'Now, why don't you all sit down, and then I can begin my questions. First of all, how did it all come about?'

Cressida explained how she was inspired by Grace wanting to share her dress with those who helped to mend it. 'The entire process has been in the spirit of Make Do and Mend – refashioning an old dress into something modern instead of buying it new, and then getting more wear out of it by letting other people borrow it.'

'And then other women began to donate their dresses?' Muriel prompted.

'That's right. It's wonderful how generous people can be! But even with all of our new donations, we're still in desperate need of more. With as many weddings as there are, our supply can't quite keep up with the demand.'

'And while many women are happy to donate their dresses for free,' Mrs Bisgood added, 'sometimes they're desperate for a bit of money, or they're sad to part with something that symbolizes their union with their beloved husband, especially if he's away from home. We'd love to come up with a way to thank them for their donations, perhaps by starting a fund to help where necessary.'

Smart in her uniform, Violet sat forward. 'And the women who borrow the dresses are unbelievably grateful. You should see their faces when they're handed a lovely white dress. My friends at the ATS are lining up to use a dress. Who wants to be married in clumpy shoes, woollen stockings, and a boxy khaki jacket?' Violet motioned to her own. 'And because we've had so much demand, the Women's Military Centre has even offered to help run an arm of the scheme specifically for brides in the forces.'

Muriel turned to Mrs Kettlewell. 'And why do you think it is so important for a bride to wear a white wedding dress?'

'A woman wants to feel her best self on her wedding day. She wants to look her most beautiful, knowing that all eyes will be on her, and that the photograph of her and her husband will always be there, setting the scene for the rest of her married life. It is a momentous occasion, the beginning of the rest of a woman's life, and we all want to mark the moment.'

'And it's all part of the tradition too,' Mrs Bisgood added. 'All the regalia – the veil, the bouquet, the shoes, and most of all the long white dress – everything has to be in place, carefully and lovingly prepared and organized.'

'It's the theatre of it,' Lottie piped up. 'Every girl dreams of having a white wedding, all eyes on her looking as beautiful as ever.'

'Frankly, I think it shows the Nazis that no matter what they do to us, they'll never break our spirit. We'll always find a way to carry on doing things our own way,' Mrs Todd said with great gusto.

The journalist was busy writing. 'That will make a marvellous quote. I heard that German women aren't even allowed to keep their old wedding dresses, they have to donate the material to the forces. Old wedding veils are to be used as mosquito nets by the troops in the tropics. The clothing situation is so dire in Germany that you can't get shoes or even clogs for love or money, and their clothing coupons have undergone so much inflation that they're virtually worthless.' She made some notes. 'Now, my next question is: How do you deal with all the different styles and conditions of the dresses?'

Everyone looked at Grace.

'We rework them to make them into something today's bride would be proud to wear. Sometimes we have to be quite inventive, depending on the age and condition of the dress.'

The journalist looked over at Grace, sitting very upright in a deep ochre fitted dress. 'All of you ladies are heroes to the women you help, but you, Grace, are something of a hero in another respect too. Didn't you help save some children from a collapsing building in Canterbury?'

Grace shrugged, uncertain as to why Muriel was shifting the focus on to her. 'Anyone else would have done the same.'

'But weren't you buried alive, along with two of them?'

'A lot of people helped that night, it wasn't only me.' A frown came over her face, as if remembering the horrors they all simply took in their stride. 'This war has changed a lot of things.

It's stirred up how we see life and death – how we value the importance of our own individual lives in a world where people are dying daily in an effort to save our community, our entire way of life.' She paused, her eyes on the floor. 'We need to think about everyone, if necessary put our own lives on the line to do what each of us can do for the whole.'

'I agree wholeheartedly,' Muriel said, writing hastily.

Grace continued, 'The war has taught us that we have to stand up and take action, to take risks. Life without bravery is life without freedom. It's why there are so many weddings – couples want to take advantage of every day they have together. We all have our moment to stand up and do what we can, from saving lives to sharing a wedding dress.'

Cressida watched as Muriel's eyes sparkled. The article was going to be a popular one. Everyone wanted heartwarming stories of community spirit, people joining forces to overcome the difficulties of war, and this one also provided a way they could get involved too. A few lines at the end would invite readers to offer their own wedding dresses to the project.

With a smile, Muriel said, 'So essentially, uniforms and rations are fair enough, but just one small pleasure, one day in which a woman can feel special, is like a dream come true.'

'That's right.' Grace's voice wavered, her eyes becoming distant and glassy with tears. 'For every woman, there's that one perfect man, the one that makes being alive a true joy, whatever you have to face in this horrific war.'

Silence fell over them. There was no need to unravel the sense of emptiness and betrayal in the poor young woman. It was there for all to see.

There was no better way to conclude the interview, and as Muriel got her belongings together, everyone clamoured around to thank her before Cressida walked her to the station.

'It'll be good to have you back in London, Cressida,' Muriel said as they passed down the lane beside the church. 'But I must say, I'm impressed with the way you've been able to liven up this little backwater in your time here.'

Cressida smiled. 'I think perhaps it's the backwater that has enlivened me. But yes, we must make an appointment for lunch. It'll give me something to look forward to once I'm back in the throng.' She began to describe her new building in Bond Street. Thankfully, it was already decorated, so she only needed to organize some furniture. Her staff had been alerted, fabric had been ordered, sewing machines delivered. 'The new Cressida Westcott Fashion House will be up and running in no time.'

Muriel eyed her. 'Do I detect a little misgiving? Aren't you thrilled to return?'

But Cressida only laughed. 'Of course I am, Muriel. I simply can't wait.' If she said it enough, perhaps she'd start to believe it.

The station was as quiet as usual, but soon the sound of an engine came from the distance, and the train slowed as it came into the station.

'Good luck with your move, darling,' Muriel said, kissing her cheek. 'And have your assistant call mine to arrange lunch as soon as you can.'

Amid prolific waving, the train pulled away, and Cressida strolled back to the village deep in thought.

These days, it was almost habitual for her to pop into the church to see if Ben was in the vestry. But today, she didn't need to look. He was walking towards her, his eyes glistening in the late-afternoon sunshine and Morris trotting beside him.

'I was hoping I would see you,' he said as they met beside the village green. 'Would you care for a walk with me? There was something in particular that I wanted to talk about.'

They fell into step, heading behind the church to the track meandering through the meadow down to the stream.

The late afternoon sun filled the narrow path that ran between brambles and trees, and insects buzzed lazily around the undergrowth, the scent of wildflowers light in the air: chamomile, rosehip, and wild honeysuckle.

But the beauty of her surroundings wasn't forefront in her mind.

He took her arm in his, Morris bounding on ahead of them, and she turned to look at his profile; he had all the beauty of Grace but in a more rugged way, his jaw more prominent and his temples broader. But it was his eyes that were truly striking, large and dark, so intense it was as if a light were shining right into your soul. There was a presence about him, as if he filled every particle of air with his calm, studious gravitas.

'What is it you wanted to discuss?' she asked, pulling him gently closer, enjoying the intimacy that had grown between them.

'Well, first of all, I wanted to ask you about Grace. Things seem to have gone from bad to worse for her, and she mentioned that something happened at the lake on the estate? Were you there? She's kept any details to herself.'

'I wasn't there, but I heard about what happened from Violet. I believe Grace chose to live for the day and took a risk; she told Hugh how she felt about him. And if what I heard is to be believed, they shared a kiss, which Astrid saw. To be honest, I was rather proud of her. It took a great deal of bravery.' Her smile fell. 'But then Hugh vanished up to London with Astrid, trying to pass it off as nothing – a sorry conclusion if ever there was one. I have no doubt that it was hard for Grace to hear, but perhaps it's better for her to know where she stands. At least now she can try to accept it.'

'Oh dear! I knew it couldn't be anything good.' He gazed down the track to the stream. 'So the wedding is still on between Hugh and Astrid?'

'I believe so. There was a great deal of shouting when they returned to the manor, but she's a determined girl, set on marrying him, and I can't see that changing. I'd imagine she'll simply keep tabs on him, just to be on the safe side. Astrid Fortescue likes to get her own way, and she's even bringing her own servants down here to ensure that she gets it.'

'Any sign of Hugh visiting the manor without her?'

'No one's heard from him since he and Astrid went back to London that afternoon. I remember her shouting that she couldn't trust him in Aldhurst on his own, so I can't imagine he'll be back before Violet's wedding next weekend. Astrid doesn't seem particularly keen on the village, so goodness knows what it's going to be like when she comes to live here.'

Ben shook his head. 'Especially after Hugh made such progress, getting to know the community, the people who rely on the estate. I never thought of him as one to be bowled over like that.'

'She has him pinned into a corner with her father's clout and his name at stake, and she knows it. She's not the type to let an advantage fall by the wayside.'

They continued in silence for a while, then Cressida said, 'With all this going on, I wish I wasn't leaving so soon.'

He stopped, the evening sunshine flickering through the trees, pinpricks of golden light wavering as a breeze caught the leaves.

'That's another thing I wanted to talk to you about.' Ben turned to her. 'Cressida, I wish you didn't have to leave at all. This war and the last one, it's made me realize how short life is, how it can all come to an end so quickly, so suddenly. It made me decide on something I've been thinking of doing, and knowing my daughter was brave enough to do it has made me see how much of a coward I would be if I didn't do likewise.' He paused slightly. 'I decided I should tell you how I feel before you leave.'

Her breath caught in her throat, part of her desperate to hear him, part frantically trying to ignore the feelings that had been building in herself.

He picked up her hands in his. 'The first time I met you, at the Chartham Hunt Ball when we were eighteen, you were wearing a rose-coloured gown that made you shine with laughter and joy. You had that clever wit and that determined sparkle in your eyes, as if you knew exactly who you were and what you wanted. You were intoxicating. Jack was head over heels in love with you, and I could see why.'

Slowly, she said, 'You were always so quiet, subdued.'

'I always held part of myself back. You two were so happy together, and I found a bride of my own, my dear Elizabeth.' He smiled gently. 'When she died, I didn't think I would ever feel that way again.'

'It must have been so very hard.'

He lifted her hand to his lips and kissed it. 'Which makes it strange to get to know you again now, so many years later. So much has happened. We've both lived whole lives without each other. And now the regard I had for you all those years ago has turned to something far deeper. I love you, Cressida, and I think I always will.'

Her heart seemed to lift and expand, and before she knew it, he took a step towards her and very slowly bent his head down and kissed her. His lips were soft, careful, delicately touching hers as if any sudden movement might frighten her away. Slowly, he pulled her closer, the feeling of his body against hers warm and firm, and she felt an unbearable emptiness inside, desperate to be filled, desperate to be loved.

Suddenly, an alarm bell sounded in her head, and she pulled

away. 'But I'm leaving Aldhurst next week, Ben. Why tell me this now? Why are you making this harder?'

'I want you to stay in Aldhurst, Cressida.' He pressed her hand. 'I know you love it here. It's written all over you: your smile, your easy banter with the ladies, the way you respond to everyone who stops to greet you. It's because you're part of this place now.' Then he smiled gently. 'And because I think you care about me too.'

Her life had never felt so fragile, as if it could disintegrate: her work, her control, her never-ending sadness for Jack. With any unleashing of her emotions, she was undermining the very foundation of her world. How could she let herself be so vulnerable? How could she depend on another person, a relationship that would threaten to sideline her career, her future, herself?

She felt tears spring to her eyes. 'Of course I love you, Ben. Of course I do. I didn't think I'd come to Aldhurst and fall in love with a man I knew decades ago, but it happened. My heart misses a beat every time I catch a glimpse of you through the village hall window.' She took a deep breath. 'I love you, Ben Carlisle, so very deeply, but I can't give up everything I've ever worked for to stay here. It would mean giving up part of myself, and I can't do that. You have to understand.'

He watched her as if in a dream, and then he smiled, his eyes dropping to the ground as he began a gentle, bittersweet laugh. 'I knew there was a risk you'd say that.'

Taking a hasty step towards him, part of her heart breaking at what she was doing, she said, 'I'm so sorry. I just can't. It's not who I am.'

'Being with someone doesn't mean you have to give up your life, Cressida. It means you can share it with them. I know you've done everything on your own up until now, but I've seen the way that leaning on Grace and on the Sewing Circle has lightened your load. You can lean on me, and I can help lighten your whole life.' His eyes glimmered with the enticement of a new beginning.

She swallowed hard. 'That's a lovely idea, Ben, but London is my world, and you can't lean on anyone there; that's how you lose everything you've built. You can only rely on yourself, and that's how I live. It's the only way I know.'

'But accepting help doesn't mean you're weak, Cressida. It means you're human. And after all you've said about Grace's bravery for taking a risk, why won't *you* take that chance yourself? How much risk is there really, if you open yourself up to having a full life that involves another person as well as a career?' He added gently, 'I'm not asking you to sacrifice anything. I want you to keep designing, to keep doing what makes you happy, to keep building your business if that's what you want.'

A minuscule crack was wedged open inside her heart, and panicking, she pulled away, stumbling back from him. 'I can't, Ben. I'm sorry, but I can't.' Then seeing the hurt in his face, she quickly said, 'But just because we can't be together, that doesn't mean we can't be friends.'

But he too had moved back. 'I'm not sure that's a good idea.' His eyes looked up at her, dark and intense. 'I'm in love with you, Cressida. I want a real, loving relationship with you.' His eyes glanced back to the path. 'And I'm not sure I'm tough enough to simply be friends whenever you happen to be in the village.'

'It's not like that,' she said. 'We could still mean everything to each other, just as friends. It's been like a little piece of heaven being down here with you, an escape from the real world.'

'That's just it, Cressida. This *is* my real world, and you coming into it isn't an escape. I don't want a friendship that would only be a reminder of something I can never have.'

With that, he turned back onto the path, sliding his hands into his pockets and continuing down to the stream, the splashing water indicating that Morris was already there.

'Ben?' she called after him, desperate not to let him just slip away.

And he slowly turned. 'I know that my job as a cleric is to help where I can, to bend to the wishes of others, but I'm also a flesh-and-blood man, Cressida. If you don't want me, you have to let me go.'

Life seemed to hang in the balance, where a gesture or a word could change the course of the future for ever, and Cressida stood paralyzed by her own need for certainty. She couldn't risk herself or her identity, and unable to stop him, she knew she had no choice.

She watched as he turned and continued away from her down to the stream, waiting for him to pause, to look back. But he didn't, and soon the path curved into the wood by the water, and he vanished out of sight.

And she was on her own, the breeze cool on her face as dusk drew near.

Slowly, she began to walk home, taking a different route through the meadows that ran alongside the lane to the manor. Wildflowers proliferated, the bright red poppies standing out, reminding her of the last war, the last man she had loved, deceased these past decades. Had she let Jack's death define her entire life? Slow tears formed at the corners of her eyes and were hastily wiped away. How could she have hurt Ben so unthinkingly? She should have made him realize at the start that she could never give him everything. She should have stopped him from falling in love with her.

She should have stopped herself from falling in love with him too.

And suddenly, all she wanted was to go back to London. It was a place where everything and everyone made sense, where no one could be hurt, where the rules of her life were logical and strict. And speeding up, she strode home to begin packing her things.

All this pain would soon be a thing of the past.

VIOLET

It was the morning of Violet's wedding, and Aldhurst Manor was a whirl of trotting up and down the stairs, the telephone ringing with friends shrieking congratulations, and bathroom doors opening and closing with increasing frenzy. Someone had put the gramophone on, and 'In the Mood' echoed jauntily through the great hall and up into Violet's bedroom.

Violet had been up since dawn, desperate to not miss a single minute of her wedding day. Her short hair had been coaxed into a style she liked to describe as 'Greek Goddess,' and her makeup was subtle yet chic.

In charge of ironing the wedding dress, Cressida was taking the place of the mother of the bride, wearing an elegant duck-egg-blue dress to be set off with a dashing wide-brimmed hat.

Joining them in Violet's bedroom, Grace arrived, looking poised in the sage-green dress she'd worn in the fashion show. It was now de rigueur for maids of honour and bridesmaids to wear their own best dresses in order to save coupons, and Violet had urged her to look her very best. She knew that Grace had given up on the idea that she and Hugh would ever be together, but Violet hadn't. She'd much rather have Grace for a sister-in-law than Astrid, and she'd keep trying to get the two of them together right up until Astrid had the wedding ring on her finger.

'It's a glorious day outside, Violet. The sun has come out for you.' Grace smiled, but as she pulled herself away from the window and draped herself onto a beige chaise longue, her fingers toyed nervously with a curl that had slipped its pins, falling onto her shoulder. 'I don't suppose Hugh's here yet, is he?' she said, lowering her voice. 'I'm going to try my best to avoid him. Astrid won't be pleased that I'm here, and I don't want there to be a scene on your big day. Besides, I'm hoping that if I keep on pretending that nothing happened, maybe it will eventually start to feel that way too, and then I can forget about the whole thing.' She tried to smile weakly, as though she was fine, but Violet knew she wasn't. Hugh hadn't been in touch, which she didn't think was entirely proper of him. There had been no apologies, no explanations, just silence.

Looking at her through the mirror on her dressing table, Violet said, 'He left a message for me last night to say that he would meet me at the church door, which is cutting it a bit fine, in my opinion. That's all I've heard of him since he vanished to London with Astrid. He'd better not be late as he's the one escorting me up the aisle.' She put on some lipstick and then thought better and wiped it off. 'I'm sure Astrid will be absolutely glued to his side all day; I wouldn't be surprised if she even tries to walk up the aisle with us.'

But Grace didn't comment, and Cressida was too busy with the wedding dress. 'This truly is the most beautiful gown. Is it time to put it on?'

'I think it must be.' Violet stood in her white silk underwear as Cressida pulled it carefully down over her head and shoulders, Grace straightening the bodice.

Delicately, Violet turned to one side, watching her image

reflected in the mirror, the skirt falling in cascades to the floor. 'I wonder if I look at all like her, like my mother.'

'You're a far happier bride, that's for certain.' Cressida tweaked the fabric around the shoulders. 'I'm so proud of you for choosing the life you want instead of the one your father wanted for you.' She met her eyes and nodded. 'You, my dear, will be the happiest bride I've ever seen.'

Grace stood beside her, gazing at the dress. 'It looks so dazzling on you, Violet. Isn't it strange how the same dress can look so different on each of us?'

Realizing that it must be difficult for Grace to see her in it, Violet reached out and took Grace's hand in hers. 'It's wonderful that it's as much my dress as it is yours, and I'm forever grateful to you for letting me wear it.'

Carefully, Cressida brought over Landon's mother's veil and fixed it into Violet's hair.

Together the three women stood back.

Grace sighed. 'I never thought I would say this, but you have met your perfect match with Landon.'

'It's a shame he'll be taking you away from us at the end of the war,' Cressida said. 'I feel that we've only just got to know each other, the real heart of the Westcott family.'

Putting an arm around her, Violet pulled her close. 'I wish I'd known you years ago, Cressida. My life would have been a lot different if you had been in it. One thing is for certain, you'd have given me far better advice than my father ever did.'

'It all turned out for the best in the end, though, didn't it?'

And as Violet looked at all of them together, she thought of how just six months ago, she never would have imagined that these two women would be the ones by her side on her wedding day. Cressida had been keen to get back to London, Grace had been drab and meek, and Violet herself had been rather too much like Astrid, spoiled and snobbish. So much had changed, and she was truly relieved that it had.

'Sometimes we just need someone with a fresh perspective to hold up a mirror and show us who we really are – who we could become, if we put our minds to it,' Cressida said.

The old village church was bathed in sunlight as the bride and her two companions made their way through the graveyard.

Outside the church doors, Hugh stood immaculate in a morning suit, speaking to Ben, and Cressida went inside to join the guests settling for the ceremony. Violet felt Grace stiffen beside her as they approached.

'You look sensational, Violet.' He bent his head to kiss her gently on the cheek, and she sensed his breath falter as his gaze shifted momentarily to Grace, then away again.

The organ music began, the first notes of 'The Wedding March' ringing out into the peaceful air. Hugh took Violet's arm and led her to the open doors. 'Shall we?'

And there, in front of the altar, turning to smile at her, was Landon. He had never looked so handsome, so beaming with warmth and love. A tumult of utter joy spread through Violet as their eyes met. Here he was, her best friend, her favourite person in the world, and her true love, all rolled together into one.

She felt her heart soar. Now that she felt such a love, it was almost impossible to think that she would have made do with a duke just for the sake of a title. How idiotic she'd been! Love, surely, is the finest goal of any life worth living.

In the congregation, a sea of faces turned towards her. There were the Sewing Circle ladies, joyfully smiling, Martha and Mrs Bisgood giving her a thumbs-up, Mrs Kettlewell wiping away a tear. Her eyes met Mrs Todd's, the old woman giving her an almost imperceptible wink, as if to say, 'you've done us proud.'

There, ahead of her now in the front row, was the familiar

and steadfast figure of Cressida, her new family, who'd arrived precisely when she needed her the most.

And as she walked slowly up the aisle wearing the dress her mother wore all those years ago, Landon watched her from the altar, his lopsided smile making her heart dissolve into an ocean of love. How exciting their life was going to be, how warm and fun and chaotic, but most of all, how very tender.

GRACE

Grace trembled with emotion as she walked behind Violet and Hugh to the altar. It was all she'd ever dreamed about. There she was at the altar, with the man she loved standing not a foot away from her side. But this wasn't her wedding, and he wasn't her groom.

Try as she might, she had thought of little else than the kiss since the impromptu swim. It was imprinted on her memory, the softness, the intensity, the passion. But the joy of the memory fractured as quickly as it arrived, dissolving into nothing.

In its place was an emptiness, as if *she* were nothing.

There had been a moment, as he greeted Violet outside the church, that he'd looked at Grace, and she felt that intensity, that connection with him. But then it was gone, his gaze averted, his smile polite as he took Violet's arm. She had to stop trying to read into his every look and action, stop hoping against hope. He had made his choice, and he hadn't chosen her.

As the congregation settled for the ceremony to begin, Grace took her place in the front row, realizing with a shudder that Hugh was stepping back to take the place beside her. Her pulse pounded, and she glared straight ahead, desperately trying to stay calm.

'We are gathered here today . . .'

Lost in her tumult of emotions, she hardly listened to the introductory address and was startled when her father called for the lesson, belatedly remembering that she was to read it.

As serenely as she could, Grace walked to the lectern, looking over the faces of well-wishers.

Hesitantly, she began. 'The reading comes from 1 Corinthians 13. "Love is patient; love is kind."' She paused, glancing up, sensing Hugh's eyes upon her. '"Love is not envious or boastful or arrogant or rude. It does not insist on its own way; it is not irritable or resentful; it does not rejoice in wrongdoing but rejoices in the truth."'

Her mouth was dry, and she stopped for a moment, trying to swallow. Looking up, as if drawn to him, her eyes went straight to his.

And as their gaze met, she lost track of where she was. All she could think was that he was there, watching her.

Her eyes connected with his, unable to look away, and she felt her voice faltering as she spoke the final lines of the reading, '"Love bears all things, believes all things, hopes all things, endures all things. Love never ends."'

A murmur rippled through the congregation. Suddenly close to tears, Grace lowered her gaze and walked down from the lectern.

Back at her place in the pew, she felt the presence of him beside her, yet she resolutely looked ahead, trying to calm herself.

But then, softly at first, she felt his hand beside hers.

She stopped breathing for a few moments, wondering if she'd dreamed it. But without turning, she sensed his fingers slowly intertwining hers, the warmth of his touch radiating up through her hand, her arm, and into her veins.

His hand gently curved around hers, sliding it into his, the pressure both soft and firm under his grasp.

And there it remained for the rest of the ceremony, disconcertingly warm, until it was time to process behind the bride and groom down the aisle to the door.

Outside the church, eight men from Landon's unit formed an arch of swords and the bride and groom delightedly dashed through, followed by Grace and the rest of the wedding party. A crowd gathered as the congregation began to pour out, like a riptide pulling Grace and Hugh in different directions. Grace found herself beside Violet, shaking hands and greeting the guests, while Hugh was on the other side of Landon, and she was conscious of him there, knowing that he could hear every word she said, as she could hear him.

Everyone watched as the photographs were taken, people chatting in the sunshine, little girls in pastel frocks chasing around the green. Other guests had already begun to make their way to the manor for the reception, but Grace stood back, preferring to wait until everyone had gone. She watched for Hugh in the crowd, hoping to talk to him, the feeling of his hand on hers still etched into her skin. But he too seemed to have vanished.

'Would you care to walk with me to the reception?' Her father came up behind her. He had removed his ceremonial clergyman's robes and was now looking dark and pensive in a suit and tie. A few evenings ago, he'd outlined the contretemps that had occurred between him and Cressida, and she felt dreadful for him. She knew how utterly dismal it could be to offer someone your heart only to have it rejected.

She smiled, giving him her arm. 'You and I, we will always have each other.'

Inside the manor, the noise of the exuberant crowd echoed through the galleried entrance hall. The great ballroom had been opened up for the event, and a long table ran the length of the room, covered in crisp white tablecloths, the cutlery and crystal glasses gleaming for the wedding banquet.

Grace was seated with the best man on one side and Lord Flynn on the other, keeping her entertained until the best man rang a spoon against his wine glass to capture everyone's attention for the speeches.

'Ladies and gentlemen, today we are celebrating the wedding of Violet and Landon. It is traditional for the first speech to be from the father of the bride, but in his absence, today we have the bride's older brother, Mr Hugh Westcott.'

There was a round of applause, and Grace watched as Hugh stood up, straightening his tailcoat behind him.

'I had a speech prepared about marriage, the binding of two families, and the sanctity of tradition.' He paused, smiling as he looked around the room. 'But I shan't bore you with things you will have heard a dozen times before, or at least you will have done if you'd spent any time with my father.' A muffled laughter went around the room. 'Instead, today I want to talk about love.'

There was a wave of murmurs, and then silence.

'Love,' he began, 'is a word used to mean so many things, how a child loves a mother, how a dog loves an owner, how a husband loves his wife. But sometimes there is a deeper kind of love,' his voice slowed, 'a love between friends, a love that lives inside us like a never-ending flame that burns so brightly that, regardless of what happens in our lives, it will never be extinguished.

'My dear sister, Violet, has found this love with Landon. As friends and colleagues, they spent days together while she drove him to his meetings, talking about their lives, their dreams, joking and laughing, slowly realizing that they were falling in love. There is something special about finding love through friendship, that gradual knowledge that what you need has been there all along, that this is what love truly is, that you know this one person so totally and utterly, as they know you.'

There was a pause as he collected his thoughts, the audience quiet, waiting.

'I know, Violet and Landon, that you will be incredibly happy, and I only wish that you remember that what you have is the most special thing a couple can have: a love that is true and deep and timeless.'

He picked up his glass. 'And now I ask you all to join me in a toast.' And as the diners lifted their glasses, he turned and looked directly at Grace, raising his glass to her alone with the words, 'To true love that will never die.'

His gaze stayed with her as the applause went up around them, a few people looking from him to her, sensing that his speech was, in actuality, also about them.

'Well, I say!' Flynn thumped a hand on her back. 'I didn't see that coming! Never known Hugh to be so heartfelt.'

There are moments in life when you don't understand all that is happening, your blood is pumping too fast, too chaotically. It seems like an extraordinary, incredible dream. As the next speech began and Hugh slowly sat down, his eyes softened as they looked into hers, a gentle smile coming to his face.

The speeches went on for eternity, it seemed, but when they were over, and when the toasts and congratulations had finished, and as the sound of conversation grew and people began to leave the table, she watched as Hugh walked to the great double doors to the terrace and beckoned her to follow.

As she carefully trod onto the terrace, the sunshine beamed bright and warm on her face, the gardens spread out before her, the hills on the horizon beyond.

Hugh was standing at the side, watching her.

Wordlessly, she went to him, and they stood looking at each other, so utterly still it was as if time had stopped moving.

'I love you,' was all he said.

She felt a lump hard in her throat. 'But aren't you supposed to be marrying someone else?'

'No.'

Her words came out slowly, 'I don't think I understand.'

'After our last meeting, I knew that I couldn't go through with it. I love *you*, Grace. I love you so deeply, so perfectly, that whatever the consequences, I knew I couldn't marry Astrid. Just one kiss was enough for me to know that I would regret having to part with you for the rest of my life. No one makes me feel so right and natural and free. I knew that I had to be with you if I wanted even a chance at happiness.'

'But you were promised to her, engaged. What about your father's legacy, your reputation?'

'I've realized that none of it matters. I know that my father would be turning in his grave, but honestly, Grace, I would much rather make you happy than him. I don't want to lose the woman I love, whatever the cost.' He looked out onto the lake. 'I was brought up to be the lord of the manor. My father pounded it into me: duty, always duty. I always thought that to lose that would be to renounce the very soul of me. But after I returned to London with Astrid, I realized that it was the very thing that had already taken my soul away. Anything left of me would have been quickly devoured by Astrid and the Fortescues.'

'Are you sure, Hugh?' She looked at him uncertainly.

He turned to her, their eyes meeting as he reached up and tucked a curl of hair behind her ear, gently stroking her neck with the back of his finger. 'It's already done, Grace, and I have never been more certain of anything.'

'But what about Astrid?'

'She wasn't pleased. I think half of north London might have heard, she screamed so loudly.' He laughed gently. 'Naturally, one of the things she threatened was to have me removed from office, and her father reiterated that particular threat during an extremely uncomfortable lunch I had with him yesterday.' He shrugged. 'But it doesn't worry me. I wasn't in politics to make a name for myself. I was in politics to help people. And now I know something else too.' He pulled her close and looked down into her eyes. 'You've shown me that there are plenty of other ways to help people, and I know that I'll be of much more use to the world with you by my side.'

And slowly, gently, he bent his head down and kissed her.

The rest of the day became a blur of dancing, talking, and finding clandestine kisses in deserted corridors. A thrill burned inside her like a great bonfire, exploding sparks of joy as she realized that it was truly happening: Her hand was in his, her arms around him, as they had been so many years ago. Only now it felt more than that. It was a true, real passion, not a fleeting, clandestine kiss of two youngsters secretly in love.

Violet and Landon were the stars of the day, dancing cheek to cheek, spinning exuberantly, chaotically in love. When it was time for them to leave for their honeymoon, after a few words to the crowd, Violet bit her lip mischievously and threw her bouquet haphazardly askew.

Was it her aim to plant it in Grace's hands? Who can say?

Grace only knew that when Violet turned to look out of the car as it pulled away down the drive, her delighted eyes met Grace's with the widest smile in the world.

VIOLET

The last days of summer always held that lethargic headiness, as if nature longed to laze in the golden hues, the ripening fruits heavy on the boughs, trying to cling on before the inevitable scents of autumn stole in from the woods.

Coming from her temporary new home in Darley Grange, Violet felt suddenly awed by the harvested fields, the prettiness of the peaceful village as her footsteps echoed around the quiet lane. Outside the new design shop, the Sewing Circle ladies had already gathered, brimming with chatter and excitement, and Violet found her pace quickening to greet them.

It was going to be a wrench, dragging herself away from Aldhurst, let alone Landon, when she left for officer training. Their honeymoon had been for only forty-eight hours, but it felt as if so much had changed within that precious time.

She raced up to join her friends outside the new claret-coloured shop awning. The sign had been repainted too, the words *Cressida Westcott* in loopy white script, the artful work of Lottie, who had added an adjustable panel onto a dress to make space for her growing bulge.

'I can't believe pregnant women don't get any extra clothes rations.' She stroked her stomach proudly, even though the bump hardly showed. 'You only get a few extra points at the end so that you can buy some little things for the new baby.'

In the shop window, where there had once been a few battered mannequins, there was now a single, pristine beige tailor's dummy wearing a simple yet stunning peacock-blue gown, tapered elegantly at the waist.

'How utterly splendid,' Mrs Bisgood proclaimed. 'I can't wait to see inside.'

Her wait wasn't long, as soon, grinning, Grace and Cressida unlocked the door. 'Welcome, ladies, to the new Cressida Westcott Design Rooms.'

'Golly!' Martha said as she and the others swarmed inside, looking at the refined fabric armchairs and sofa in the sumptuous main room.

It was a large space, completely transformed after a jolly good clean. The floor was now covered with a luxurious Persian rug borrowed from the manor. Freshly painted walls provided an elegant, expansive look, bright white interspersing beige panels. A rail of gowns stood along the far wall, and a chintz sofa set before a low table from the manor made for a stylish environment in which to spend a morning contemplating a new garment.

The back room had been converted into a dressing and fitting room, a curve of mirrors arranged to show the wearer from every angle.

'And now, the part that will be of most interest to the Sewing Circle,' Cressida announced, leading them to a door at the side that opened into a narrow staircase, 'the sewing room.'

At the top of the stairs, they gasped in delight.

The room was light and airy, one half containing the treadle sewing machines that had been in Cressida's rooms at the manor and rolls of fabric in the corner. On the other side, a long table with chairs awaited meetings, design ideas, and plans for the future.

'The Sewing Circle is very welcome to use this as their meeting room. I know the treadle machines will come in very handy.' Cressida stood proudly aside.

'What a useful work area,' Mrs Bisgood said, while Mrs Todd poked about in various cupboards. 'Is there somewhere to make a pot of tea?'

'And look over there.' Martha ran to a tall rail along the side wall, a tumult of white and cream billowing beneath. 'The wedding dresses. Can we store those here too?'

The clipboard was hanging on the end, and Violet scooped it up. 'We have thirty-four now, would you believe? My mother-in-law is quite marvellous, you know. When I wrote to thank her for sending her veil, I mentioned the Wedding Dress Exchange, and she said she would see if she could get donations from her friends. Landon tells me the Connecticut ladies are always keen to help out where they can, so we should prepare for a deluge. Word is that Eleanor Roosevelt herself wants to get involved!'

'Sometimes it's the small gestures that can mean the very most,' Grace said, linking an arm through Mrs Todd's. 'It's as if we're all holding hands, through the generations and across the ocean, an invisible team of women all supporting one another through this dreadful war.'

Violet looked at the list. 'It's good news all right. We have more orders coming in from all over the country now that word is out.'

'I hope we'll be able to keep up with them all,' Mrs Todd said. 'With Violet going to her officer training, and Cressida off to London, I hope you're not going to vanish too, Grace. You three have been the backbone of the whole operation.'

But Mrs Bisgood put a firm hand on hers. 'We'll be as right as rain. I'm organizing some of the other local women to help, and Grace has asked her Make Do and Mend classes to pitch in. Ever since Queen Elizabeth told the papers she's restoring a hat and the princesses are knitting for the troops, everyone's become far more enthusiastic about helping out. Martha's even managed to rope in the boys at school.'

'And I'll be here from time to time too,' Cressida added. 'London's not far away.'

Martha frowned. 'Cressida, are you sure you want to move to London? Now that Astrid's no longer coming, surely you can stay?'

'As much as I have loved my time here, the London fashion world is anticipating my return. I need to get back to being Cressida Westcott, London couturier.' She concluded this with a sharp smile, the type that would go down better in Bond Street than Aldhurst.

They put on brave faces, nodding despondently and saying they understood, except for Lottie, who was always one to wear her heart on her sleeve. 'But how will we get on without you? You took a little make-do sewing circle and gave us the vision for the Wedding Dress Exchange – you even had us featured in *Vogue*!'

'That wasn't all down to me. None of this would have ever happened without you. And don't worry, I'll be just a phone call away if you need anything.' She beamed at them. 'But I know you'll do absolutely fine without me. The Sewing Circle is as productive as ever, and the Wedding Dress Exchange is working like clockwork, especially since Violet organized the army to look after the military brides. Grace is a talented designer, and Mrs Kettlewell and Lottie have become terrific seamstresses. The rest of you are first-rate at mending clothes, and even you, Mrs Todd, know how to create an outfit from a few scraps or an old curtain.'

Martha laughed. 'Do you know, I went to a friend's house last week, and my dress was exactly the same material as her green floral armchair. It was made from the same pair of curtains. We all had a good laugh about it.'

As she spoke, Violet crept over to the corner, where Lottie and Grace were beckoning her to help with something.

Underneath a box was a chocolate cake. Although it wasn't decorated – icing cakes was now illegal with sugar in such short supply – the words 'Good-bye, Cressida' had been written on a card resting on top.

'I made it last night. It's an eggless sponge, but I found some cocoa powder to spruce it up a bit,' Lottie said to Violet as they carried it out of its hiding place.

'Surprise!' they called, bringing it forward.

'Goodness,' Cressida exclaimed. 'What's all this?'

'We wanted to wish you luck in your new home in London,' Lottie declared. 'And to say thank you for everything you've done for us here in Aldhurst.'

Then Mrs Bisgood stepped forward to give a short speech. 'Cressida, you came into our village and into our hearts, just when we all needed someone to give us new inspiration. From all of us, thank you.'

A cheer went around, and gratefully, Cressida nodded her appreciation. 'If there's one thing I hope I've taught you, it is to act from your heart and to be brave and bold, even if it means living a more unconventional life.'

Everybody laughed as Mrs Todd adjusted her green hat, Martha calling out, 'Although some of us have always been a little more unconventional than others.'

Mrs Bisgood grinned. 'I think this comes from all of us when I say that you will always have a home here in Aldhurst. You began your life in this small village, and hopefully a part of your heart will remain here always.'

Her eyes watering, Cressida clenched her lips into a smile as she looked across the room. 'It's not so much the small village that I'll miss, rather the wonderful group of friends inside it.'

CRESSIDA

Before Cressida was quite ready for it, the morning of her move back to London had arrived. Her makeshift sewing room in Aldhurst Manor had been returned to its former status as a bedroom, only the occasional thread of ivory white or sage green giving away its previous temporary life. She remembered when she'd first come to the manor, how eager she'd been to leave it. Now, the place was more of a home than her Chelsea house had ever been.

Brusquely, however, she bucked herself up. London would be fun, busy, organized. A lunch with Muriel had been arranged, and there were the IncSoc Utility meetings to attend and her new design house to launch. All eyes would be on her, and she was riding a wave of success.

But then there was Ben. How she would miss him, even though the bittersweet tang of their last meeting only reminded her how necessary it was to leave. She had been trying to avoid speaking to him since that awkward conversation, and it was probably just as well. She was missing his company more than she cared to admit, the memory of their kiss so soft, so right.

'Blast the man for being so sensitive!' she fretted.

No, she was better off back in London, the place where she

fitted in and no one asked anything of her. In London, she made sense. She could disappear into her work and try to forget everything.

As Violet and Grace accompanied her down the stairs, Cressida told them about the place her estate agent had found for her.

'It's a lovely flat with two large bedrooms, so you're always welcome to stay. I'm renting this time as I don't want to risk losing another house to the bombs. A van will come to pick up my suitcases and the rest of my design accoutrements later this morning.' She looked down at her handbag. 'It's incredible to think that when I arrived with just this, it contained everything I had in the world.'

'And now you're going back with a lot more.' Grace put an arm around her waist.

Cressida pulled them both close. 'A new family and new friends.'

Slowly, they walked out onto the driveway. Violet had pulled the old Bentley up in front of the house to drive to the station, and she gave Cressida a crisp salute and opened the door for her, taking the small suitcase she was carrying with her on the train. 'Please step in, ma'am.'

'How efficient you've become,' Cressida said, getting into the back with Grace.

As the car made its way down the lane to the village, Cressida looked out of the window into the clear, bright morning. The sun flickered in and out as the trees went by, the view of Aldhurst Hill golden-green before it was blocked from view by the row of cottages marking the beginning of the village, their pretty front gardens dotted with the pinks and reds of September roses.

Around the bend into the heart of the village, the church spire peered over the graveyard and vicarage, as it had since she was a child. Cressida imagined Ben inside, working on his sermon or organizing the meeting with the ARP later in the week.

As she watched the church, the door opened, and then, suddenly, there he was, his tall, broad-shouldered form striding out into the sunshine, and she quelled a yearning to stop the car, to run over to him, unsure of what she would say, what she would do.

Seeing the car, he started, but then a soft smile came over his face, and he raised his arm and waved, all trace of discomfort gone, only love and warmth and acceptance. And as she waved back, it felt as if the sun had come out, just for him, beaming throughout her world – only to go back in as they rounded the corner to the station. Disappointment seeped through her like the cold draft of reality when a warming fire is put out.

The station came into view, and Cressida brought her thoughts back to the present. She needed to pull herself together, remind herself of who she was.

The only problem was that part of her wasn't so sure if she was still the same solitary, tireless woman she used to be. It was as if she were still the same, but now she was something else as well. She was part of the community, a friend, an aunt, and an individual who had needs, emotions, desires.

Violet pulled up outside. 'Right, here we are.' She opened the door, and together the three of them walked through the station to the platform.

The sound of the train came almost immediately, a growing whisper on the tracks below, then a faint thrum of pistons in the distance. Soon enough it came into view, drawing to a halt beside them.

Violet gave Cressida a great hug. 'I'm sorry you're leaving, but I know that from now on we will always have each other, the family we always needed.'

From inside her bag, she brought out a gift, a small book wrapped up in newspaper, proper wrapping paper impossible to find these days. 'Grace and I have this for you. But you have to promise not to open it until you're in your new place.'

Cressida took it, puzzling over what it could be. 'Thank you. It looks like I'll have an interesting evening.'

With tears in her eyes, Grace put her arms around Cressida. 'How can I thank you enough for all that you have done? When I needed a true friend, you were there. You gave me a job, you gave me skills and confidence, and you gave me a home in your heart. In mine you have found one too.'

Cressida wiped a tear of her own. 'If there's one thing I've taught you, I hope it is to stand on your own feet, be brave and bold. And of course, I can't wait to see you when you come up to London for training.'

'We'll all miss you,' Grace said.

Cressida's eyes watered for a moment, then she clenched her lips together and climbed into the train.

The whistle blew, and as the train pulled away, she looked out of the window. There they stood, waving from the platform, Grace's tall, lean elegance in her stylish blue dress beside Violet, upright and standing to attention in her uniform. How dear they both had become to her.

The train built up speed and plunged into a tunnel beneath a road bridge, emerging into a gold and red autumn woodland, the village out of sight, London on the new horizon.

Loneliness seeped into her, like fingers of cold threading their way through her veins, but she quickly shook herself. It was her on her own now, Cressida Westcott, top London couturier, returning to her London design house. She took a deep breath.

She knew what she had to do: get herself back into business, plunge herself into her work, stop dwelling on what might have been.

The countryside gave way to the suburbs, and soon the train was chugging into the city, the buildings worn and devastated by the Blitz. There was a feeling of desperation as the old city's breath staggered and wheezed with soot and exhaustion. Yet it still forged on, an old gentleman who would suffer anything rather than surrender.

Bustling with bodies, Waterloo Station was filled with American GIs yet again, their uniforms crisp, their young, optimistic faces a joy to behold for a population shattered by war. They were waiting for trains down to the south coast, no doubt. There were rumours that an invasion of occupied Europe was being planned, troops amassing for a big push.

The tide was turning in the war, but there was still a long way to go.

Down inside the Underground, remnants of the station's other life as a bomb shelter were visible: a woman selling tea from a big teapot, signposts directing shelterers to makeshift first-aid posts, a boarded area with the word LADYS painted on the outside, and a homeless man with a black-and-white dog. For one horrific moment, Cressida thought of that dreadful night of the bombs, but then, as the dog wagged his tail, she found herself rubbing his ear, setting aside the past. Life was for living, after all.

'You two look like you could do with a good lunch,' she said, giving the man some coins before heading to the platform.

She took the Tube to Notting Hill Gate, and before long, she found herself walking down a street of splendid whitewashed Victorian mansions.

A suited middle-aged leasing agent met her at the door and showed her into her new flat. The place was dull. Apparently, the owners had taken themselves and their best belongings to the safety of the west country at the first whiff of danger. Sparsely furnished, it felt small and drab after living in rambling Aldhurst Manor. However, needs must, she supposed, and she began to settle herself back into this new version of her old life.

But as soon as the agent had gone, a strange desolation crept inside her, like insects crawling beneath her collar. There was a stale, airless smell of mothballs and old polish, and an ugly mahogany clock ticked loudly from the mantlepiece, echoing through the austere chill.

'Typical, the only décor left is some gruesome clock,' she muttered, picking it up, wondering where to put it.

To rid herself of the nudging unease, she briskly set to, walking around and working out where she would put what. The house came furnished, and dark, heavy armchairs and tables sat gloomily in each room, and she planned what she could do to brighten the place up.

At least the bedroom was a good size. A window overlooked a small courtyard where someone had optimistically built an Anderson shelter, its rounded corrugated roof making it look frail and pointless. The street behind must have been bombed much earlier in the war as there was a glaring gap in the row of tall terraces, reminding her all too poignantly of the night she was bombed.

Putting her handbag on the bed, she sat beside it and opened it. Underneath her gloves, there was her gift, and although she hadn't meant to open it until the evening, she found herself in need of any warmth it could bestow. Her fingers fumbled to take out the book-like package, and as she slipped it out of its wrapping, she gasped.

It was an autograph book, a keepsake filled with signatures and memories.

Her pulse fluttered as she quickly opened the first page.

This is to remember your time with us, Cressida, and all the fun we had together.
   With love, Violet and Grace

And there, as she turned the page, was a photograph. They were all there, the Sewing Circle in the village hall, smiling, Lottie and Martha waving, crouched on the floor at the front. It was taken by Violet at one of her very first meetings, and Mrs Bisgood was there at the back, her arms wide as if she were embracing the whole group. Beside her was Mrs Todd, her knitting tucked under her arm.

'Before she learned how to sew,' Cressida murmured.

Grace was wearing that old brown skirt and the fawn cardigan held together with a safety pin.

'Thank goodness those dreadful clothes have gone.' Cressida laughed.

At the end of the group, having pressed the self-timer and dashed over to join them, was Violet, her long blonde curls trailing down over her shoulders. How different she had looked back then! There was a pretty, vacuous look about her that was long gone. The army had given her the confidence and the bravery to be the clever, resourceful woman she was inside.

And there, among them all, was Cressida herself, her arm in Mrs Todd's, and she remembered how tightly the old woman always gripped her, as if ensuring that neither of them ever fell. Cressida's prim suit and makeup suggested that she hadn't been in Aldhurst for long. It wasn't that she had let herself go over time, rather that she had embraced the countryside with flatter shoes and more versatile clothes. After all, it was tiresome having to constantly get dust from the road out of her nicer London-style clothes. She'd even adjusted her designs to accommodate wartime chic, more useful clothes for bombs and evacuation into the countryside.

Today, to mark her return to London, she was back in a crisp suit, but it felt tight and constricting around her. The neat pillbox hat seemed overly ornate, and her high heels cumbersome.

She turned the next pages, to find them filled with words and good wishes from the Sewing Circle. Mrs Bisgood recounted the time she taught them how to 'turn' a dress by picking it apart, turning the pieces over, and then re-sewing it all back together. Martha made lengthy notes on how successful the Wedding Dress Exchange had been, noting some possible improvements. Mrs Todd recalled an evening when Lottie had taught everyone to dance the cancan, only it was so bad that Cressida had renamed it the 'can't-can't'.

Then there was another photograph, this one of Violet in her new uniform, standing to attention. Beside her and in her school uniform, Martha stood to attention too, their broad grins giving away their delight at the idea.

The next photo showed the ladies with their second and third wedding dresses, Mrs Todd's and Mrs Kettlewell's. Lottie and Martha were holding them up against themselves and acting like Victorian brides. In the background, Cressida could see the other women chattering as usual, catching up with people's news, sharing some jokes, sometimes even a song or two. Among them was Cressida herself.

Sometimes it's just the simplicity of sitting with others, together in spirit and endeavour, that makes life feel right.

As she turned onto the next page, she caught her breath. There she was with Ben, standing outside the church, and they were talking to each other, laughing. She remembered that day. Violet had come into the village to practise her photography, and they hadn't even known she'd taken the photograph until they heard the click.

'Don't waste the film on us,' she'd called to Violet.

But the girl had only laughed. 'You look as though you've just got married.'

Although they'd quickly mocked the idea as ludicrous, now that Cressida looked at the result, she saw that they did indeed look like a happy couple. A smile radiated out of her – out of them both. And as a strange wrench inside of her took hold, she felt an unsettling pang of dismay.

Was she missing out on something special?

There are times in life when you think about the different paths your life might have taken. Jack's death, her brother's torments, and her obsession with success had forged her into the person she was and the life she had – it had all seemed so inevitable and complete. But what of the other lives she could have lived if fate or chance had simply twisted in a different direction?

And a small voice whispered inside of her, 'What path would you take now?'

Suddenly, it all felt too much, too overwhelming. Quickly, she turned to the next page, the very last one.

There were heartfelt wishes from Violet and Grace, and on the opposite side of the page was the final photograph, one of Violet, Grace, and herself. It had been taken by Martha outside the church after Violet's wedding. They smiled into the camera, their arms around each other, the sun in their eyes, the dress that brought them together gleaming in the sunshine.

As she looked down at the photograph, she felt her heart melt, and before she could stop herself, she took it out of its corner holders and pressed it against her chest, missing her old friends with such a ferocity that she bent her head down in tears.

Some dreadful feeling had taken hold of her, an emotion she had never experienced in her entire life.

She was homesick.

GRACE

It was a single sheet of paper, folded in two and tucked into an envelope marked 'Grace'. Someone must have slipped it through the vicarage letterbox while she'd been working late at the new design shop.

Come and find me.

She smiled to herself. How long had it been since she had received such a note?

Without a moment's hesitation, she tucked the paper into her dress pocket, tugged on her coat, and headed out the door.

Darkness was falling. The nights were coming in faster, cooler than they had been, and autumn was in the air, the scent of yellowing leaves blending with bonfires. She dashed down the lane, her heels resounding through the shadows. Then she broke off through a gap in the old stone wall, trotting up a track between the pastures, vanishing into the wood that led to the side of the lake.

Come and find me.

It had been their special code, for their special place.

As soon as she was in the woods, her pace slowed as she

looked for the ripple of the lake through the lattice of branches, the moonlight striking the water.

Suddenly it was there.

The shape of the boathouse could be seen through the trees, and she dashed towards it, scooting around the outside to the jetty, where she climbed up onto the platform.

And it was as she turned to look inside that she saw the most breathtaking sight she'd ever seen.

From inside the boathouse came a flickering, dim light, the interior and platform bathed in the soft, silken glow of a dozen candles dotted haphazardly around the old, empty space. It gave the place an otherworldly feel as if it were trapped in a different time.

And there, sitting on the edge of the jetty looking over the lake, was Hugh. His eyes went up to meet hers, and a smile spread across his face so full of love that she could weep.

Wordlessly, she went and sat beside him, as she had done so many times, so many years before. It was as if that was their place, their bodies imprinted into that spot, overlooking the water.

As she slid down and took off her shoes, as he had, she said, 'It's magical here.'

She felt the side of his body next to hers.

'It's where it all began,' he said softly.

She sank in closer to him. 'You used our old code. It's been such a long time.'

'I thought it was apt.'

He pulled his hand from his lap and opened it. On his palm was an antique gold ring. 'Before she left, Cressida gave me my grandmother's engagement ring. I would like *you* to be the one to wear it, Grace. It belongs to you.' He looked into her eyes. 'Will you marry me?'

She gazed at him, overcome. 'Yes,' she murmured, and then

again, this time louder, more firmly. 'Yes! I can't think of anything so right, so completely perfect.'

'I love you, Grace, and I've loved you for so long, it's as if
you're a part of me. I can't imagine how foolish I was to even
entertain the notion of being with anyone else. You're the only
one for me, Grace, the one that makes me feel so instinctive and
complete. And now we have each other back, I never want to let
you go.'

And with that, he took her hand and slid the gold ring onto
her finger. It was beautiful, three amethysts in a row, encrusted
with tiny diamonds between them.

He bent his head and kissed her, gently at first but then
increasing in passion and tenderness, an intertwining of their
spirits as the world lay peacefully watching.

'It feels as if I've got to know you all over again,' he whispered
into her hair. 'And you've reminded me that life is about other
people, about our community, that sense of belonging, of love.
And now I know that's all I need.' Gently, he pulled her onto his
lap and put his arms around her, their bodies effortlessly mould-
ing into each other's.

Together they sat for a while, in each other's arms, looking
out into the moonlight, talking about their new life together.

'Do you think we'll have to sell Aldhurst Manor?' She rested
her head on his shoulder. 'Violet said that without the Fortescues' money there might be too many debts to pay, and then
there's the death taxes too. I know it's been hard for large estates
like this to make money these last few years.'

He shook his head. 'Some things are far more precious than
striving to keep a family heritage or marrying to preserve the
Westcott manor. In any case, I've been looking into selling some
of the better arable land to the west, and although I hate to
break up the estate, at least we'll be able to hold on to the house.'
He took her hand in his. 'We'd be happy anywhere, you and I,

but I thought we could try to make a go of it here. I'm not be-
holden to my father's ideals, but I do love the old place. All of
my best memories are here with you.' He kissed her hand. 'And
now that I feel part of it even more than before, I couldn't leave.'

She pulled closer to him. 'Oh, to stay here would be wonderful. I love this village, the parish, the manor.'

He gazed out onto the water. 'For years I hardly thought of it,
I was so intent on living up to the Westcott name in London,
showing my father that I could do it, that I was more of a man
than he thought me. But now, all I see is the beauty of the place,
what I can do as the real, working lord of the manor.'

As they looked out over the lake, thinking it all through, she
gazed around at the boathouse. 'Since this is the place where it
all began,' she said, 'it's a shame we can't hold the wedding reception here, beside the lake.'

'Why can't we?' He grinned. 'We could set up a long table on
the grass beside the boathouse.' He looked over the grassy
meadow beside them. 'All it needs is a little tidying up, some
garlands and lights for decoration.'

She pulled him in close, laughing. 'That is precisely what
we'll have, a lakeside wedding.'

'I'm sure we can organize the tables and a wedding banquet
to be brought outside. It'll be wonderfully different.'

She looked from the lake to him. 'Just like us.' She put a hand
up to his face. 'It's like the end and the beginning, all rolled into
one.'

But just as he was about to kiss her again, she got up, a grin
on her face as she began to unbutton her dress. 'And to mark the
occasion of our engagement, let's do it our own way.' Within a
moment, she slithered out of her dress and dove into the water,
only resurfacing to call out to him, 'I'll race you to the island.'

CRESSIDA

Sometimes life turns out in unexpected ways, and it was this that was on Cressida's mind as she sat at her desk working late one evening. Her new office was a modern, well-organized room on the second floor of her new London design house, and although her revived business was bustling with vitality, she felt oddly out of sorts.

It had been a few weeks since her return, and easing back into London life, if she were honest, had not been as straightforward as she had imagined. Who would have thought that half a year in a village in Kent could change her perspective so much?

It wasn't that she didn't still love designing and running her business; she loved it almost more. She enjoyed the challenge of setting up again, the prestige of her position, and welcoming back her customers. The Duchess of Kent had been in twice already, desperate for new gowns from her favourite couturier.

Yet she missed her friends at the Sewing Circle, and she missed Violet and Hugh, that comfortable closeness of being part of a family. She thought of the village, how the moonlight would be striking the old church spire and the roofs of the cottages and shops as it always had done. She thought of Mrs Todd, singing musical hits to her cat as she knitted in front of a fire, Mrs Bisgood organizing the ARP office, Martha at her desk formulating how she could single-handedly take on Mr Hitler, and dear Lottie, who beneath the swish and swagger was the kindest of them all. Then there was Violet – Cressida had loved watching her blossom into a dynamic young woman – and Grace, the bland, grey duckling who had grown into a beautiful swan.

And she realized what it was that had been missing in her life.

She had found a kinship, a band of friends who, regardless of what happened, would stand strong for one another.

And how she missed them!

It helped that Grace came to London for training, but it was never for long enough. And being with Grace only reminded her of Ben, the relationship that never was. Her thoughts strayed to him more often than she liked. One glance at Ben's photograph threw her mind into a different place, as if the memory of those conversations, the companionship they had, was woven around and through her, softening her, making her more aware and full of life than she ever would have thought.

Impatiently, she got up from her chair and walked into the main studio. Everyone had left for the evening, and the lights were out, the desks empty. She had taken to her old practice of working late. In the past it was because she refused to fail, making it her duty to show that women could get to the top. But now it was because she wanted to escape her lonely flat, and if possible, escape her own misgivings.

She leaned against the door frame. The only light came from her office behind her, dimly casting shadows of the chairs around the long tables, the swatches of fabrics tacked to the wall, the pinks and yellows and ambers muted to greys and beiges in the darkness.

The sound of a knock came from the front door downstairs.

It was probably a late delivery, and they could jolly well come back in the morning.

But the knock continued, tapping out a tune, two knocks then a third.

A curious smile crept over her face, and she swiftly trotted down the stairs to the door.

There, through the glass in the window, her eyes met a very familiar and heartwarming sight.

'Ben.'

She opened the door, and there they stood, a smile growing on her face as she watched it doing the same on his.

'Cressida.'

After a few moments of them looking at each other almost incredulously, she stood aside and beckoned him to come in.

'Grace told me I would find you here,' he said.

She laughed, a gentle breath of relief at seeing him, at being able to be herself. 'Did she say that I'd returned to my old ways, working late?'

'Something like that. I thought I would come and give you some company.'

She led him into the customers' reception room and gestured for him to take a seat on the sofa. As usual, he was wearing his vicar's collar and dark trousers, today with a sand-coloured casual jacket, as comfortable as an old friend.

'I would offer you a cup of tea, but I think we're out of milk.'

'I didn't come for tea.' He looked very intently at her, still with the smile.

'I could have a look to see if we have some sherry. We usually keep some for Lady Worthing. It lubricates the fittings, shall we say.'

'No, thank you. I didn't come for sherry either. I came to see you, and do you have any idea how good it feels to do just that?'

She let out a small laugh. 'It feels rather good to see you too.'

'Now, could you please come and sit down, because I have something to tell you.'

Dutifully, she perched on the other side of the sofa, turning to face him.

'I know what you think of my philosophers, Cressida, but there was one, Bertrand Russell, who said, "To fear love is to fear life, and those who fear life are already three parts dead."'

He smiled, reaching a hand out to hers and taking it so softly, so smoothly, that she felt a breathlessness catch in her throat.

'I realized that I will have enough time to be dead,' he continued. 'For now, I want to be alive, properly alive.'

Gently, he took his hand away and slid it into the inside pocket of his suit, bringing out a small, black box, now open to reveal a plain silver ring.

She let out a gasp.

Regardless of its simplicity, it was the most utterly beautiful thing she had ever seen.

'Will you marry me, Cressida?' There was a coy smile on his lips, as if tempting her to say yes.

A laugh of incredulity broke from her. 'Well, I don't know. I'm not sure what's changed since we last spoke.' Her voice was gentle, and she bit her lip in confusion.

'I would move here for you, Cressida. I'm sure the diocese can find someone to fill my role, and they're in need of more clerics in London. Now that Grace is marrying Hugh, she'll be moving to the manor, so we'll always have a place to stay in the village when we want to see them.' He chuckled. 'Wherever you are is where my home will be. My life, as you know, is not an affluent one, so I can't offer you riches or luxury. But what I can offer you, money cannot buy: riveting conversation, a disobedient dog, and absolute, unconditional love.'

She laughed. 'Well, I have missed Morris, I suppose.'

'And me?' His eyes glimmered enticingly.

She waded through the deluge of emotions that flooded her mind. The idea that marriage wasn't for her had been packed into her no-nonsense framework for so many years that the notion of actually marrying someone seemed simply ludicrous, incongruous with who she was.

But she wasn't the same woman whose Chelsea house had been bombed six months ago.

As she looked at the man in front of her, the soft smile on his gentle, handsome face, she was aware of a very different feeling mingling among the rest, one of tenderness.

As if reading through her small laugh and her reticent smile, he said, 'I know you might need time to think about it, but I thought I would leave this ring with you, for you, as honestly there isn't anything in the world I would like more. I will wait until eternity for your reply, and although the wait will be hard and long and lonely, at least I know the question is there.'

He took her hand in his and wove his fingers between hers. 'I'm in love with you, Cressida.' He took a deep breath. 'And I can't bear the idea of our last conversation being the end of our story. I've missed you so incredibly these last few weeks. I want you back in my life, and hopefully you want me in yours, to start afresh, together.'

She took a deep, unsteady breath. 'I want to thank you for your very kind, considered offer, but—' she broke off, unable to find the words. 'You know me, Ben. I have my business to consider.' She made a small laugh. 'My life is not conventional, that's why I haven't had a man in it for so long.'

'You forget, I'm not a conventional kind of man.' His voice was quiet and silken. 'And we wouldn't be a conventional kind of couple. I'm willing to fit around you.' He smiled, taking her hands in his. 'We would simply be ourselves, two individuals living life together, enjoying each other's company, loving each other.' He pressed her hands gently. 'After all, what else matters?'

She thought about pulling her hands away, but his touch felt so warm, so right.

'I don't want you to change or give up your business – I want you to succeed. I don't need you to be a vicar's wife or a cook or a maid. I need you to be you, Cressida, witty and intelligent and strong.' His eyes looked into hers imploringly. 'Will you marry me?'

And before she knew it, the word had come out. 'Yes.'

The air around them seemed to pause.

What had she said? Her brain spun with censorship and panic before an explosion of elation burst within her.

'Yes, I will.' Her reticent smile became a beaming laugh of joy. 'I will marry you, Ben Carlisle. I will.' Deep inside her, the last thread of resistance snapped, and she realized that to surrender to happiness wasn't the downfall she had told herself, if indeed it was a downfall. It was better – far more joyful and thrilling and real – than she could ever imagine.

Laughing with her, Ben put his arms around her, pulling her in close to feel his warmth. 'We shall be the happiest pair that ever lived.'

And with that, she turned her face to his, and with a tremendous wave of love and tenderness, they kissed.

GRACE

Ironed, mended, and gleaming in readiness, the wedding dress lay on the bed in the small vicarage bedroom.

'Now, let's try to get this gown on without creasing it,' Cressida said as she gently pulled the lengths of satin down over Grace's waist and hips to the floor. 'Breathtaking,' she murmured as she stood back to look in the mirror. 'Absolutely breathtaking.'

But Grace's thoughts were elsewhere. 'The first time I looked at myself in the dress, I only saw my mother. But now, I just see myself, exactly the way that I should be.' She sighed. 'Thank goodness you came along and helped me to see what I had been missing all along.'

'Do you know,' Cressida said, 'I knew that you two were meant for each other the first time you came to the manor. Do you remember, you were holding the wedding dress when he came into the drawing room?'

Grace laughed. 'I thought him a pompous oaf, and he thought I was as meek as a church mouse. I seem to recall that neither of us was particularly kind.'

'Maybe that was why I felt it. You would both have been far more polite if you hadn't meant so much to each other.'

'How true that is! I can't imagine being so brutally honest with anyone else.'

Cressida led her out. 'Come on. The Sewing Circle ladies are down in the kitchen, desperate to see you.'

When Grace appeared at the kitchen door, they rushed over to see.

Lottie called out, 'Goodness, you look gorgeous, Grace!'

But it was Mrs Bisgood who gathered her up in a hug. 'What a beautiful wedding gown. It's perfect – absolutely perfect.'

Martha stepped forward, touching the soft white fabric. 'I was wondering if I might borrow the dress, Grace, for when I get married.'

'Isn't marriage a little premature, young lady?' her mother said.

Martha arched an eyebrow. 'It's always good to have a plan.'

But Grace was already saying, 'Of course you can borrow it. Everyone can!' She put her arms around the women. 'You have all helped me so much.'

'Twirl around, Grace! Let's see our good work,' Mrs Todd said, and Grace turned, the dress cascading around her as if she were an elegant swan opening its wings to take flight.

With final hugs and laughter, the Sewing Circle wished her luck and peeled away to take their places in the church. Time was moving on, and the wedding would be ready to begin.

Only Violet and Cressida remained, the latter picking up the veil and gently lifting it up and over Grace's head, an age-old ritual repeated once again.

Each of them picked up a bouquet, an artistic collection of pink and red roses from the manor, entwined to match the embroidery on the dress and veil, an acknowledgment of the Westcott bride who, so many generations before, had loved climbing roses so much that they covered the whole estate.

Together, the three women made their way out of the vicarage and through the graveyard, and Grace paused for a moment by her mother's grave, taking a red rose from her bouquet and placing it on the ground. 'I know you're with me in spirit,' she whispered, but instead of sadness, she only felt a shared joy, knowing that her mother would be smiling down at her, happy that she had found a life and a love that was true to the wild and free spirit that Grace was inside.

Outside the church, Ben stepped forward to kiss her cheek. 'You look enchanting.'

Grace watched as her father's eyes went to Cressida's. The pair of them were planning a small wedding within the next month. Never one to let convention stand in her way, Cressida had already moved into the vicarage, saying, 'I don't care that we're not yet married, we're living together, and that's that.' The village was so elated for them that no one mentioned this irregular living situation to the bishop. Cressida's staff in London had looked aghast at her move back to Aldhurst, but she told them, 'I intend to expand, so don't rest on your laurels thinking that Cressida Westcott is going out of business.'

Grace's arm in his own, Ben turned to her. 'Are you ready, my dear child?'

And with a keen enthusiasm, she nodded as the organ music began.

The church was packed, but the only face that mattered to her was that of the man waiting for her at the altar.

Hugh stood watching, his eyes meeting hers with unstoppable love. He wore a well-cut morning suit; a single dusky pink rose on his lapel, a rose for her.

Grace felt her heart explode. Every moment of their lives together came flooding back to her, riding wild horses on the hills, building dams for the beavers in the river, kissing on the island long ago, and now every spare moment they had together.

As she began her procession up the aisle, her footsteps measured on the ancient stone slabs of the floor, it felt as if the world had slowed. On either side, the whole village had come for her, for both of them. The parishioners, the bereaved and needy she visited, the people she had helped, they were there to cheer her on. She barely remembered all the people she'd comforted over the years, but here they were, here to thank her, to support her as she had supported them.

On the front row beside Cressida sat the Sewing Circle, all grinning broadly at her. Mrs Todd sported a large pink hat, and beside her Lottie was as glamorous as ever, her favourite blue dress taken out even more to accommodate the new baby growing inside.

As she reached the front, Grace looked at Hugh, their gazes meeting and her lips automatically parting into a wide smile. Never had she been so happy.

As it was her father leading, the service was a little more personal than usual, the wedding vows said with special gravitas and even a little humour too: The short sermon was about the special duties of a good son-in-law to the father of his bride.

Grace had chosen her favourite hymns, and a team of children from the Sunday School came to the front to sing a tuneful rendition of 'All Things Bright and Beautiful,' a very small girl in the front not singing a single word, just looking out into the audience with unabashed pride.

Then came the part where Hugh placed a ring, the symbol of their union, on her finger. And as he held her hand in his, their eyes met, and with a soft smile he whispered, 'Until death do us part.'

Outside the church, a great crowd gathered to congratulate the bride and groom, a long line of well-wishers waiting to shake their hands, to admire the wedding dress that had already seen so many of their loved ones happily wedded.

At the very end was her band of ladies, shuffling to hold themselves back until she opened her arms to hug them, all of them coming together in a great circle, together in heart.

The photographer arranged the couple for a few pictures in front of the arched door, and she imagined a photograph framed, standing on the mantel in the great drawing room for years to come. How their children – even their grandchildren – would look at it, marvelling at how young they looked, how happy, and probably old-fashioned too, she mused with a laugh, wondering what the world would look like fifty, sixty, or even seventy years into the future.

Then she imagined all those other mantelpieces holding a photograph of that very dress, each with a different, elated bride, and with a great burst of energy, she tossed the bouquet high into the air, to the roar of shouts and cheers from the crowd as everyone gathered to catch it.

'I've got it this time.' Martha stole in with utter determination, bustling through, positioning herself directly where it was supposed to land –

But the bouquet seemed to spin at the last minute, straight into Cressida's hands. Not quite knowing what to do with it, she offered it to Martha, but the girl only said with a huff, 'Not again!'

By the time Grace and Hugh set off for the boathouse, everyone had already gone ahead. It was only the two of them, walking hand in hand through the countryside they loved. As they followed the green and blue painted arrows on tree trunks and gateposts through the pastures and woods to the lake, the sound of merriment grew. Suddenly, they rounded a corner, and there, on the edge of the trees, was the boathouse, garlanded with bunting and flowers, and the lake serene, glistening in the sunlight.

The party was already in full swing, the sound of the band spilling American jazz into the surroundings, and Lottie singing 'All of Me' with great exuberance. The guests danced on the makeshift stage, Martha tugging a bewildered American officer up to dance with her. Others stood by the lakeside, children buzzing around like bees, in and out of the guests, skimming stones over the water, and taking off their shoes to wade in the shallows.

On the grass beside the boathouse, a long table with crisp white tablecloths had been set up, resplendent with silver cutlery gleaming in the sunshine. The wedding banquet was to be served outside, but first, they had to greet their guests.

As the happy couple arrived, the well-wishers gathered to welcome them, calling for a few words before the proceedings began.

Hugh took Grace's hand in his. 'My wife and I' – he grinned lovingly at Grace – 'want this wedding to mark a new era for the manor and for Aldhurst too, an era of support and together-ness. And it is a pleasure for us to begin that here today with the marriage of the parish with the estate, a true allegiance that will forever be at the very heart of our dear, beloved village.'

Great cheers went up, and as she spotted the Sewing Circle in the throng, Grace couldn't help wanting to say a few words of her own, and she waited for everyone to settle down before she started.

'This story began with a wedding dress.' She looked down at her beautiful gown. 'It was in my father's attic, ravaged by moths. But I took it to the Sewing Circle, and we rejuvenated it, made it into something better than any new dress could ever be, a symbol of our unity in this time of war. It became the first gown in the Wedding Dress Exchange, our way to show that we might be losing our homes, our families, and our normal way of life, but there are some traditions that live on in spite of the Nazis – that romance and hope and love can flourish, no matter what our enemies do. It is a reminder that the most important part of us – our hearts – will always be free.'

A roar of approval and applause rippled through the crowd, and then Grace continued, this time a little more sombrely.

'There are times in everyone's life when we need support, we need to be part of something bigger, to feel those threads between us pulling us together. After my mother died, I quickly found out how crucial that is. The Sewing Circle, through our nights of sewing and talking, taught me that our friends provide more than just company. They form an invisible net that is so strong and wide that it can catch any of us if we fall.'

She glanced over to meet Hugh's gaze.

'And here I am, wearing the dress that my mother wore, as well as my husband's mother, my new sister-in-law, and one of my best friends too.' She smiled over at Violet and Lottie. 'We are part of a circle of women, sharing the same dreams, holding hands through the centuries. They are all there, if you look hard enough, if you untangle the threadwork, peeling away the layers of stitching to find the fragments of lives, of hopes, and of love woven throughout.'

AUTHOR'S NOTE

The first time I came across the story of a shared wedding dress was in the memoirs of a young vicar's wife who would let any prospective brides wear her own wedding dress for their big day. The gown was passed from woman to woman, half the village's wedding photographs featuring the same one dress, each time adjusted to fit. It was a magical tale, brimming with the very heart of home-front camaraderie: individuals and groups joining forces to help each other.

After more research, I discovered dozens of individuals and local groups who collected and distributed wedding dresses from Scotland to Cornwall. Then, in the middle of the war years, romance author Barbara Cartland heard that military brides had to get married in uniform and felt this was an abomination. She began her own collection of wedding gowns to loan to military brides, enlisting the forces to help her out. It wasn't until later in the war that Eleanor Roosevelt heard about the shortage of wedding dresses and appealed to American women to donate their dresses to their fellow brides in Britain, leading to the establishment of a large, more organized pool. These last elements were beyond the scope of this novel, but I would like to thank all the women, both in Britain and the United States, who donated their dresses. What a wonderful difference it must have made, and what an incredible mark of unity and support it must have sent.

The wedding dress shortage, as well as the general shortage in clothes, was caused mainly by the loss of imports due to shipping lanes being bombed. In addition, much home-produced fabric was going towards uniforms and military needs. As silk was imported, using it for anything other than parachutes was illegal. In order to address the shortfall in clothes, the British government came up with three strategies: clothes rationing, the Make Do and Mend programme, and the Utility Clothes range.

Similar to food rationing, clothes rationing began in Britain in 1941 and continued until 1949, trying to fairly dole out the short supplies of fabric, pegging prices so that poorer citizens wouldn't have to go without. The National Archives holds a great quantity of leaflets and posters explaining the notoriously complex clothing point system and changes thereto, and I spent long hours going through these, comparing them to information from my interviews and research, and trying to patch together a good idea of how it must have felt to live under such rules.

The Imperial War Museum is home to some lovely posters about the Make Do and Mend programme, and again more detailed leaflets and books about it can be found in the National Archives. From repurposing men's jackets into a skirt or pair of shorts to reducing hems and using the extra fabric to patch up worn clothes, the Make Do and Mend programme involved a great deal of small ideas, instructions, and tips to reuse, recycle, and reduce the amount of fabric and clothes everyone wore.

The novel contains many tips and stories about how people got through clothes rationing during the war. These come from a variety of interviews, books, and archives. One or two have had their dates very slightly changed to fit into the book, such as the tale of Patricia Mountbatten's underwear made from a silk map of Northern Italy, which didn't happen until 1943. Also, to prevent confusion, I used the term 'skirt suit' rather than 'costume', which was used to describe a skirt and matching jacket at the time. Parachute wedding dresses became all the rage after the war, when every airman gave his parachute to his wife-to-be upon arriving home. However, during the war, using downed parachutes for clothes was illegal, and although these 'disappeared' on a regular basis, most of the contraband silk went into black-market underwear and was only sometimes, allegedly, turned into a wedding dress.

The Utility Clothes programme focused clothes manufacture on a smaller range of practical yet stylish clothes so that more could be made with the fabric and manpower available. It began in 1940 and continued until 1952. Many of the original designs for the incredibly popular IncSoc Utility Clothes still exist in the National Archives and the Imperial War Museum, and I have been lucky enough to find a few photographs too. Arguably, the streamlined Utility Clothes with simple lines and the emphasis on endurability and quality have become an enduring hallmark of British fashion.

As you can imagine, many people who lived through the era have stories to tell about the clothes, and it is these stories that form the backbone of this novel. The first story – and one that spurred the idea for the novel – is one that my mother told of herself as a small child having to wear a bathing suit knitted by my grandmother. Of course, it was far too big, and then, to her utter horror, it became even bigger once she was in the water. My grandmother swears she used a proper government-issue pattern, but I have yet to find evidence of such a pattern. It is this concept – that any need can somehow be worked around – that sums up the era to me: We have to keep on swimming, and we'll find a way to do it.

My grandmother Eileen Beckley was a prolific, if not terribly exacting, knitter. She would tell me how it was considered un-patriotic during the war to simply sit – in the living room, on the train, in a bus – without knitting something, either a piece of clothing for you or the family, or woollies and socks for the troops. Even though there was a shortage of wool, you could always unravel an existing garment and use the wool to transform it into something completely new. Sewing came less easily to her, and I can imagine her struggling through a pattern to make a school uniform that wouldn't quite fit my mother properly.

My mother, Joan Cooper, became one of the best amateur tailors I have ever known. She would buy designer patterns so that she could wear Dior, Jean Muir, and Balenciaga to stun everyone at evening events. She knew precisely how to doctor the patterns, making them fit her better or look better, adding embellishments or taking them out, a belt here, a wider shoulder there. I gained most of my knowledge about making and mending clothes from her, and this has been augmented by materials in the National Archives and the Imperial War Museum as well as some excellent books on the subject: *Make Do and Mend* by Jill Norman, *Make Do and Mend* by the Imperial War Museum, and *Fashion in the 1940s* by Jayne Shrimpton. Other books that gave more background on rationing include: *Spuds, Spam and Eating for Victory* by Katherine Knight, *The View from the Corner Shop* by Kathleen Hey, and *The Taste of War* by Lizzie Collingham.

The IncSoc Utility Fashion Show was one of the most iconic fashion events of the Second World War, and I decided to dramatize the life of a top couturier going through the process of designing and entering garments for the event, what it must have felt like to compete for those thirty-two slots. I took my information mostly from a few good books: *Make Do and Mend: A Very Peculiar History* by Jacqueline Morley, and *Fashion on the*

Ration by Julie Summers. Cressida Westcott is, of course, a fictional character, but she is loosely based on the illustrious head designer at Worth, Elspeth Champcommunal, who appears in the IncSoc Fashion Show scene in the novel. There were very few female couturiers in those days, and Elspeth had the drive and character to make a great impact, becoming a forerunner for women designers to come.

Meanwhile, women's journalism was changing too. Under the editor Audrey Withers, *Vogue* magazine changed from focusing purely on fashion and the way women look to become a place where they could learn about the war. Cutting-edge journalists on the front, such as former model Lee Miller, photographed and wrote about the war, the role of women, and the reality of Europe at siege. Instead of considering female readers passive creatures only interested in their appearances, they were expected to have opinions, and *Vogue* was encouraging them make those opinions. The character Muriel Holden-Smythe is a fictional journalist at *Vogue,* helping to depict these changes.

Details about the Air Raid Precautions and the Baedeker Raids in Canterbury come from newspapers of the time and first-hand accounts in books. *Debs at War* by Anne de Courcy details some fascinating interviews with women involved in various wartime services, and gives a sense of how it must have felt to be in the ATS and to volunteer in the ARP in a great bomb raid. *Millions Like Us* by Virginia Nicholson also contains tales of extraordinary courage and endurance.

As with all my novels, I would never have been able to recreate the past without the voices of that era recounting real-life stories: the intriguing, the funny, and the heartbreaking. I continually interview people who lived through the war, and there is nothing quite like hearing their stories firsthand, digging out the details to imagine how it must have felt to have been there. The BBC's archive 'WW2 People's War' is a treasure-trove of personal stories from the war with many fascinating and heart-felt memories. And finally, thanks go, once again, to the women and men who wrote about their daily lives for the Mass Observation project during the war, all of which are now held in the University of Sussex Archives.

ACKNOWLEDGEMENTS

At its very heart, this is a tale about a group of friends, how they support and help each other, how by joining forces and working together they can achieve great things. I am lucky enough to have such a dear group of friends. My beloved writing group, Barb Boehm Miller, Julia Rocchi, Emmy Nicklin, and Christina Keller, meets either virtually or in person every month or two to read and critique each other's work, to share news and information about writing and publishing, and to catch up with our lives. Together, we celebrate the successes and help mourn the losses, but most of all, we are simply there for each other, and I am honoured to dedicate this book to them. Thank you.

My great thanks go to Hilary Rubin Teeman, my outstanding editor at Ballantine. Her guidance and intuition for plot and character are invaluable. Thank you so much for all your help and support. I would also like to thank editorial assistant Caroline Weishuhn, who has been an incredible help with her insight into the novel as it progressed. My special thanks go to Kara Welsh, Jennifer Hershey, and Kim Hovey at Ballantine Bantam Dell, and thanks also go to the wonderful team who made this book a reality: Pamela Alders, Erin Korenko, Ada Yonenaka, Belina Huey, Dana Blanchette, and Ella Laytham. Special thanks go to Morgan Hoit and Christine Johnston for working wonders with marketing and publicity.

My fabulous agent, Alexandra Machinist at ICM, brings immense charm and wisdom to every new book. A huge thank-you, Alexandra! Special gratitude also goes to Karolina Sutton, my wonderful agent at Curtis Brown in London. Thank you for your great help and support. Huge thanks also go to Sophie Baker, my dynamic translation rights agent at Curtis Brown in London, and to my publishers around the world.

I am incredibly fortunate to meet other authors, journalists, and artists and would like to thank the community for its support and warmth. Elaine Cobbe combines great writing wisdom with irrepressible character and charm – thank you so much for your help. Thanks also go to vibrant and witty Vikki Valentine, whose friendship and wonderful sense of storytelling have been a godsend. Massive thanks go to Cathy Kelly, who has become a wonderful friend as well as being an exceptional and inspiring author. For her photography and endless humour, artist Gaynor Darby has been a magnificent help – thank you for your support.

Other people helped along the way. Hearty thanks go to my uncle, David Beckley, who sadly won't be here to support and share news about this new book – you are always on my mind and in my heart. Thanks also go to Cheryl Harnden for her generosity of spirit and wonderful humour – your help and support have been invaluable to me. Laura Brooks and the entire Brooks family deserve massive praise and thanks for all their help. Immense gratitude goes to the invaluable Courtney Brown for her tremendous energy and resourcefulness, as well as her legendary hospitality and unstoppable joie de vivre. My thanks also go to my teachers at Johns Hopkins, especially to Mark Farrington and the master of sentences, Ed Perlman.

Any book about sewing has to include a word about my wonderful mother, Joan Cooper, who taught me to sew on her old hand-crank Singer while she whipped up designer dresses on her new Bernina. Both an inspiration and a great teacher, she helped me make my own wedding dress, and when I wrote about those moments in this novel, Cressida walking around Grace to check the seams of her wedding dress, my mind goes inevitably to my mother, in her guest room, making the final adjustments for my wedding day. Thank you for everything.

Finally, very special thanks go to my sister, Alison Mussett, for the flair and insight she put into editing, reading, and advising on plot and character. Her unflagging support, humour, and spirit are invaluable, as well as being a wonderful sister and great friend. And lastly, massive thanks go to my family, Lily and Bella and my wonderful husband, Pat, without whom this book would never have been written.